Through A Glass Starkly

From birth I had been raised to believe in the Confederacy, in its perfection and its ideals. But, in that context, what *was* my job, anyway? The same as The Monitor Service here? To track down those who posed a threat to the Confederacy's system—or who abused or perverted it—and send them to psychs, or to the Warden Diamond, or, on rare occasions, to their deaths.

True, the Confederacy was a far better system than Ypsir's Medusa, but the people here did in fact mostly believe in that system, including the TMS. In *their* minds they were no different from me. Did that make us different—or the same?

Medusa was a perversion of the Confederacy's system and dreams, but it *was* a distorted mirror image. Why did I feel uncomfortable with the reflection it showed me nonetheless?

MEDUSA:
A Tiger by the Tail

Book Four of
THE FOUR LORDS OF THE DIAMOND

JACK L. CHALKER

A Del Rey Book

BALLANTINE BOOKS • NEW YORK

A Del Rey Book
Published by Ballantine Books

Copyright © 1983 by Jack L. Chalker

All rights reserved under International and Pan-American
Copyright Conventions. Published in the United States by Ballantine Books, a division of Random House, Inc., New York,
and simultaneously in Canada by Random House of Canada
Limited, Toronto.

Library of Congress Catalog Card Number: 82-90893

ISBN 0-345-29372-X

Manufactured in the United States of America

First Edition: April 1983

Cover art by David B. Mattingly

For Walt Liebscher, the elfish Puck of science fiction for over forty years. Those who haven't met him or read him have been missing something unique and wonderful.

Author's Note

This is the fourth and climactic *Four Lords of the Diamond* novel. It was preceeded by *Lilith: A Snake in the Grass, Cerberus: A Wolf in the Fold,* and *Charon: A Dragon at the Gate.* These books should be read first, in order not to spoil the overall effect. If you have not yet read them, don't hesitate to buy this book —but demand the others at the same time. Good booksellers should have them all.

For those who have been following the odyssey of the nameless agent, here is its conclusion, with all loose ends neatly tied.

—Jack L. Chalker

Contents

THE WARDEN DIAMOND

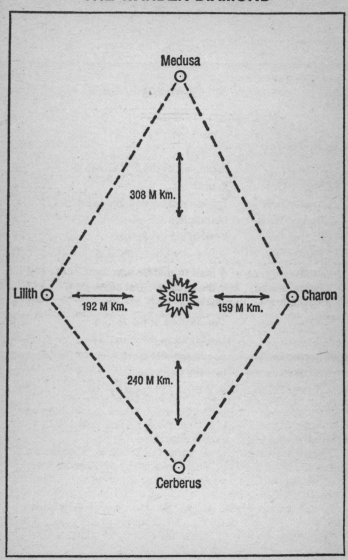

Beginning of the End Game

════════

1

There is nothing quite like the sensation of calling your worst enemy up for a friendly little chat. The face appeared on the little screen, although such communication often dispensed with visuals. In this case, both sides were curious to see what the other looked like.

He looked at the face on that screen and understood immediately why everyone who had seen it feared it. It was the handsome face of a man in middle age, trim, lean, and somewhat military, but the eyes got you right away. They seemed hollowed, like a skull's eyes, yet not empty—they burned with an undefinable *something* that seemed both eerie and impossible.

"Yatek Morah here," said the man with the strange eyes. "Who are you and why do you demand to speak to me?"

The man on the other end gave a slight smile. He was on a huge floating city in space, a picket ship and base camp for those who guarded the four prison worlds of the Warden Diamond, a third of a light-year out and beyond the range of the Warden's own peculiar weapons. "I think you know who I am," he told Morah.

The strange man's brow furrowed a bit in puzzlement, but, suddenly, he nodded and gave a slight smile of his own. "So the puppet master is finally out in the open."

"Look who's talking!"

Morah gave a slight shrug. "So what is it you wish of me?"

"I'm trying to save a minimum of fifty or sixty million

lives—including your own," he told the man with the burning eyes. "Perhaps a great many more than that."

Morah's smile widened. "Are you certain that it is we who are in danger? Or, in fact, that *anyone* is."

"Let's not beat around the bush. I know who you are—at least who and what you *claim* to be. I have been observing your behavior of late, particularly that in the Castle on Charon. You claim to be Chief of Security for our hidden friends here in the Diamond, and I'm willing to accept you at your word—for now. I certainly hope you're telling the truth."

Morah sat back and thought a moment. Finally he said, "It appears you know a great deal indeed. How much *do* you know?"

"I know why your alien friends are there. I know pretty well where they *have* to be. I know the nature and purpose of the Warden Diamond and its interesting little beasties. And I know for a fact that your bosses will fight like hell against any move against the Warden Diamond. Furthermore, I know that *my* bosses will make just such a move when my report is analyzed. What I *don't* know is how strong a resistance your bosses can put up; but they are defending a relatively small position against the resources of an enormous interstellar entity, one which, if you are truly Morah, you know well. In the end, things could become horribly bloody for both sides. Perhaps your bosses could get a number of our worlds and your robots will mess up a hundred more—but we'd get the Diamond. And I mean totally. That means that, no matter what we lose, you and your bosses lose more."

Yatek Morah remained impassive to the logic, but still appeared interested in the overall conversation. "So what do you propose?"

"I think we should talk. By 'we' I mean your bosses and mine. I think we'd better reach some accommodation short of total war."

"Indeed? But if you know so much, my friend, you must also realize that the very existence of this little exercise came about because my bosses, as you call them, in consultation with our people, determined that the Confederacy can *never* reach an accommodation with another spacefaring race. So we'll have our little conference, and both sides will say all the right things, and then we'll sign some sort of treaty or somesuch guaranteeing this or that; but the Confederacy will not honor that any longer than it feels it has to. They will send in their little missionaries, and they will find that they have come across a civilization so alien that they won't be able to understand it or its motives."

"Do you?"

Morah shrugged. "I know and accept them, even if I do not completely understand them. I doubt if any human ever will—nor they us. We are the products of two so totally alien histories that I doubt if even an academic acceptance of one another's motives and attitudes is possible. On an individual basis, perhaps—on a collective basis, never. The Confederacy simply cannot tolerate something that powerful that is also inscrutably different, particularly with a pronounced technological edge. They would attack, and you know it."

He made no reply to that, because he could find no flaw in the argument. Morah was simply presenting human history from its beginnings. Such was the nature of the beast —as he should know, being human himself. So instead he changed the subject slightly. "Is there another way? I am in something of a trap myself, you know. My bosses are demanding a report. My own computer analyzer had to be talked into letting me out the door of my lab to come up here and make a call—and it never would have done so if it thought I was going to call you. When I return, I will have a matter of hours, perhaps a couple of days, to make a report. I will be forced to make it. And then the whole thing will be out of my hands. I am running out of time, and that's why I'm coming to you."

"What do you want of me?"

"Options," he told the strange, powerful man. "Solving your little puzzle was simple. Solving the bigger problem is something beyond me."

Morah seemed deeply impressed. Still, he said, "You realize that I could prevent you from making that report."

"Possibly," he agreed. "But it would do no good. The raw data has already been shifted, and they have a Merton impression of me. They could, with some trouble, go through this entire thing again in a very safe area, and come up with the same report. Besides, I doubt if they would believe I died accidentally—so killing me would tip more of your hand."

"The problems of killing you safely and convincingly are hardly insurmountable, but what you say is true. Doing so would buy very little time. But I'm not certain you *do* have the total picture. It would be a pity to sacrifice the Warden Diamond, but only a local tragedy. You have failed to consider all the implications of what you have learned. And, it is true, things are iffy should that happen. But there is at least a forty-percent chance that such an outcome would not adversely affect my bosses' plans and hopes at all. There is more than a ninety-percent chance that it will not *completely* be a washout from their point of view."

That disturbed him a bit. "How long would they need for a hundred-percent success rate? In other words, how much time are we talking about?"

"To do things right—decades. A century, perhaps. I know what you're thinking. Too long. But the alternative will not be the disaster to my people you counted on, only a major inconvenience."

He nodded glumly. "And if they are—inconvenienced? What sort of price will they exact on the Confederacy?"

"A terrible one. We had hoped from the beginning to avoid any sort of major bloodshed, although, I admit, the prospect of fouling up the Confederacy has great appeal for us. Foul them up, perhaps try and overthrow them from within, yes—but not all-out war. That prospect appeals not at all to the thinking ones among us, and is exciting only to the naive and the totally psychotic." The frown came back a bit. "I wonder, though, just how much of the truth you really *do* know."

He sat back in his chair, unable to keep a little bit of smugness from his expression and tone, and told Morah the basics. The Chief of Security was impressed.

"Your theory has some holes," he told the man on the picket ship, "but I am extremely impressed. You certainly know . . . enough. More than enough. I'm afraid we all vastly underestimated you. Not merely your agents down here in the Diamond, but their boss as well. Particularly their boss."

"Then you, too, have some holes in what *you* know," he came back. "One particularly major one. But I'll give you that one as a gift—you'll find out sooner or later anyway, and it might help you in plotting a course. All of them—all four—are not my agents. All four are quite literally me. The Merton Process, remember."

It had been a complex and elaborate plot by the Confederacy, to counter, in part, an even more complex and enormous plot by their enemy. The Confederacy had been fat and complacent all those centuries, and then, suddenly, it had been confronted with evidence that an alien power of superior technology had discovered them, had fashioned such perfect robots to replace key personnel that absolutely no known method would detect them, and that the Confederacy was, in fact, under some sort of systemized attack. The focus of the attack was the Warden Diamond, four human-habitable worlds used as prison planets for the most brilliant criminal and perverted political minds. The perfect prison, since all four worlds were contaminated by an organism that fed, somehow, off energy available only within the Warden system. The organism invaded the bodies of all who landed there, mutating them and giving them strange powers; but it also imprisoned them, as the organism could not survive far from the Warden system's sun —and neither could anyone it inhabited.

But placing the top criminal minds and political deviants together on four worlds in contact with one another had created the most powerful criminal center ever known, one whose tentacles spread far from the Warden system and continued to run the criminal underworld of a thousand planets remotely, and more efficiently, than ever before. But all these masterminds were trapped, and they hated the Confederacy for that trap.

Into that situation had come the aliens. Technologically superior to the Confederacy, they were numerically inferior and so alien that they could neither take on the Confederacy openly and win nor do so secretly. Then they encountered the Warden Diamond and realized what the four worlds held. A deal was struck. The heads of the four worlds—the most powerful and ruthless criminal minds alive—the Four

Lords of the Diamond were approached with a proposition. Use their own power and the technology of the aliens, together with their knowledge of mankind and the Confederacy, and subvert it. Cause so much trouble, so much disruption, that the Confederacy would be too concerned with its own problems to even think of the Warden Diamond.

Marek Kreegan, Lord of Lilith, himself a former agent for the Confederacy, came up with a detailed plan for replacing key personnel all over the Confederacy with the impossible robots. Through Wagant Laroo's operation on Cerberus, the robots themselves were first primed with the minds of the very people they would replace. The Cerberans could swap minds as a byproduct of the Warden organism and also had Dr. Merton, creator of the mechanical-mind-exchange process being used experimentally by the Confederacy, to make it work right. Aeolia Matuze of Charon ran a world where almost anything could be easily hidden, so it served as the meeting place between aliens and agents—and as Morah's base of operations. Finally, Talant Ypsir, Lord of Medusa, provided the hardware, raw materials, and in-system transportation of alien technology—and, perhaps, even the aliens themselves. Each of the Lords also controlled vast underworld organizations within the Confederacy itself.

Kreegan hoped to avoid a terrible war, but he intended to disrupt and perhaps break up the Confederacy itself, leaving a fragmented bunch of worlds he and his fellow Lords could take over. The aliens had promised that, in return for removing the Confederacy's threat, they would provide a means to escape from the Warden Diamond and its insidious organism.

But when a robot's cover had been blown, and it had demonstrated its superior capabilities, the Confederacy quickly caught on to the plot and came up with one of its own. To send an agent down on the Warden worlds was not enough. The Lords controlled their worlds; besides, any agent down there was trapped, too, and soon would figure out which side best represented his future.

But, using the Merton Process, the mind of their top agent was simultaneously placed in the bodies of four convicted criminals with long histories; each was sent to one of the four Warden worlds. Also implanted within each was the means by which whatever they saw and did would be transmitted to their original agent, in orbit on the picket ship. With the aid of a sophisticated analytical computer, it was hoped he would be able to piece together the puzzle of the Warden Diamond. In the meantime, his own personality should add psychological reinforcement to the command given the agents down below—kill the Four Lords, disrupt their timetable, buy time for the Confederacy.

But as the agent watched, even experienced, each of his counterparts' lives on Lilith, Cerberus, and Charon, he had also watched as his counterparts—himself—threw aside their basic values, their loyalties, the precepts of the Confederacy which he/they had accepted and to which he/they had devoted a lifetime. Now, convinced he'd figured out the plot and being pressured by his computer and his superiors, he was telling Morah this. It was not self-confidence that made him tell the mysterious, still unseen aliens' Security Chief the secret; rather, it was to inspire confidence. Morah knew and had close at hand at least one of "him"— Park Lacoch of Charon. Now Morah would know just who he was really dealing with.

The Security Chief was suitably impressed. "All of them you? Fascinating. In a sense, it's taking Kreegan's robots one step farther. All right—I agree *we* could probably strike a deal. But I suspect if you've lived those lives along with them, you're not quite the man they sent any more— and they know it. I know the first for a fact, for we are having this conversation. I infer the second from your own statements. You do not expect to survive the next encounter in your lab. So that leaves me nowhere, you see. Any deal we might strike is certain to have no validity to your bosses. Still, I am touched by your attempt—and by your devotion. You do not have to go back into that lab, you know."

The agent looked squarely at the screen, into those weird eyes that none could look into in person. "If you know me at all, you know that I do. My title is Assassin, but I am no hired killer. I have a job to do—if I can."

"Just hypothetically—if you *can* survive this last entry

and the report, what would you do? Where would you go? Not back to the Confederacy, surely."

He grinned. "Are you making a hypothetical job offer?"

"Perhaps. I hope you *do* survive. It would be most interesting to talk to you at length."

He laughed. "You have only to talk to Park. Or Cal Tremon. Or Qwin Zhang. Or—hmm . . . I'll be damned. I don't know what name I've got on Medusa. I haven't gotten to that one yet."

Morah was impressed. "You figured out all you have without Medusa? You have an amazing mind."

"I was bred for it." He sighed. "If I survive, we will meet, and soon. If I do not, then the others, different as they now are, will carry on."

"It would be fascinating to have the five of you together. That is something to think about."

"Fascinating, yes," he admitted, "but I'm not sure I'd be the one in the group who'd be the most popular."

"Perhaps. Perhaps. I suspect we would have four equally clever, equally ambitious, but different individuals. Still, I thank you for your warning and your offer. I will convey the details to the proper authorities. I, too, hope that massive war can be avoided—but wiser heads than mine will be needed." He paused. "Good luck, my enemy," he added sincerely, then broke the connection.

He sat there, just staring at the blank console, for several minutes. *You have not considered all the implications . . .*

He was missing something. Morah had been too casual, too sure of himself. One piece, one vital piece, remained. Perhaps it would be found on Medusa. It had to be.

Mirror, mirror . . .

He didn't want to go back into that room. Death waited there, death not only for himself but for millions more at the least.

I'm of two minds about this . . .

Morah's attitude, now—was it bluff and bravado? Would he pull something? Or was he serious in his hard confidence?

Would I lie to you?

Sighing, he rose from his chair and walked back to the lab cubicle attached to the rear of the picket ship.

2

The door to the cubicle he generally called his lab opened for him and then hissed closed with a strange finality. The entire module was attached to the picket ship, but was internally controlled by its own computer. Everything was independent of the ship if need be—power, air, and air-filtration systems, it even had its own food synthesizer. The door was, of necessity, also an airlock; the place was essentially a container with a universal interlock, carried in a space freighter and then eased into its niche in the picket ship by a small tug. Since the module did not have its own propulsion system, it was definitely stuck there until its securing seals were released and it could be backed out by a tug.

The controlling computer recognized only him, and would be resistant to any entry attempt by another—and lethal should the intruder succeed. The trouble was, he knew, the computer had been specially programmed for this mission by the Security Police, and not all that programming was directed toward his safety, survival, and comfort.

"You were not gone very long this time," the computer remarked through speakers in the wall. It sounded surprised.

"There wasn't much to do," he told it, sounding tired. "And even less I *could* do."

"You made a call to one of the space stations in the Warden Diamond," it noted, "on a scrambler circuit. Why? And who did you call?"

"I'm not answerable to you—you're a machine!" he snapped, then got hold of himself a bit. "That is why the two of us, and not you alone, are on this mission."

"Why didn't you use me for the call? It would have been simple."

"And on the record," he noted. "Let us face it, my cold companion, you do not work for me but for Security."

"But so do you," the computer noted. "We both have the same job to do."

He nodded absently. "I agree. And you probably have never comprehended why I'm needed at all. But I'll tell you why, my synthetic friend. They don't trust *you* any more than they trust *me*, for one thing. They fear thinking machines, which is why we never developed the type of organic robot the aliens use. Or, rather, we did once—and lived to regret it."

"They *would* be superior," the computer responded thoughtfully. "But be that as it may, as long as they control my programming and restrict my self-programming, I'm not a threat to them."

"No, but that's not really why I'm here. Left to your own devices—pardon the pun—you would simply carry out the mission literally, with no regard for consequences or politics or psychology. You would deliver information even if doing so meant the loss of billions of lives. I, on the other hand, can subjectively filter those findings and weigh more factors than the bare mission outline. And that's why they trust me more than you—even though they hardly trust me, which is why you are here. We guard and check one another. We're not partners, you know—we are actually antagonists."

"Not so," the computer responded. "You and I both have the same mission from the same source. It is *not* our job to evaluate the information subjectively, only to report the truth. The evaluation will be made by others—many others, better equipped to do so. You are assuming a godlike egocentric personality that is neither warranted nor justified. Now—who did you call?"

"Yatek Morah," he responded.

"Why?"

"I wanted him to know that I knew. I wanted his masters to know that as well. I find war inevitable. However, I also find that his side loses everything, while we lose a great deal but hardly all. It was my decision to face him with that fact and to give the ball to him, as it were. Either he and his masters come up with a solution, or war *is* inevitable."

"This is a questionable tactic, but it is done. How did he take it?"

"That's just the trouble. He took it. It didn't seem to worry him or bother him. That's what I had to know. He *is*, I believe, sincerely interested in avoiding war for his own purposes, but he is not worried about it from the viewpoint of those who employ him. It was the one thing I could not get from the field reports—a direct sense of how the aliens view the war threat."

"It was only a viewing scanner on a single individual," the computer noted. "He could be bluffing. All things considered, how else *could* he react?"

He shook his head slowly from side to side. "No. Call it gut instinct, call it hunch or intuition, or whatever you wish—but also call it, too, experience. Reading the length of pauses, the slight tone of voice, the subtle shifts in the body to bad news and flawless reasoning. There is still something missing in our information. He as much as said it himself."

"That is interesting, however. He confirmed the basics?"

He nodded. "We're right—dead on. That was the other reason for the call. Still, I feel no joy in it—for if we're completely right, then what factor has been overlooked? To have all one's deductions and inferences confirmed is gratifying. But to discover that, being right on the wildest stretches of logic, you have missed a factor that they consider decisive—that is frustrating."

"I believe I understand. This is what made you return, was it not? You fear the Confederacy and me as much as the aliens—perhaps more. Yet you came back. Such conviction, when faced with your brilliant deductions, carries weight. All right. We are missing a factor. What is it?"

"There's no way to know. Morah came out and told me that I'd not carried my deductions to their logical conclusions." He sighed and drummed his fingers against a desk top. "It must have to do with the nature of the aliens. He called them incomprehensible, basically, yet he said he understood what they were doing. That means it is a question not of deed but *motivation*." The fist slammed down hard on the desk. "But we *know* their motivation, dammit! It *has* to be!" Again he struggled to get hold of himself.

"We are still handicapped in one way," the computer noted. "We have not yet met the aliens, not yet seen them. We still know nothing about them other than the inference that they breathe an atmosphere similar to human norm, and are comfortable within normal temperature ranges."

He nodded. "That's the problem. And *that* I'm not likely to get from Medusa, either, unless there's some miracle. A psychotic killer who sees them thinks of them as evil. A psychotic Lord thinks of them as funny-looking but hardly evil, just self-interested. And intellects like Kreegan and Morah see them as a positive force. And that's all we really know, isn't it? After all this . . ."

"No race lasts long enough to reach the stars and do all that this one has done unless it first acts in its own self-interest," the computer noted. "We can probably dismiss the evil concept of the criminal on one of dozens of bases, the most probable being that these aliens are subjectively terrifying to look at, or smell putrid, or something of that sort. It is hardly likely that their evolution, even given some of the same basics as humankind, is anything like that of humans."

He nodded. "I keep thinking of Morah's inhuman eyes. He claims he is not a robot and that he is the same Yatek Morah sentenced to the Diamond more than forty years ago. We need not believe him, and should not, but let's for a moment take his statements at face value. If he *is* who and what he claims to be—then why those eyes?"

"A Warden modification, possibly self-induced for effect. He could do it easily on Charon."

"Perhaps. But, perhaps, too, those eyes mean something more. What does he see with them? And how? A broader spectrum, perhaps? I don't think they are totally for effect. For protection, maybe? I wonder . . ."

"Still, the bottom line remains your report," the computer noted. "I will admit that I, too, am somewhat curious, even though I have the basics."

"Medusa first. Let's complete the set. Maybe my missing piece will be found there. Or, maybe, what I experience will jog my mind to see those missing implications. It can't hurt."

"But Talant Ypsir lives. The mission is incomplete there."

"We are beyond caring about the Lords of the Diamond now, I think, except, perhaps, in some sort of solution if one is possible. I need information. Medusa will have the most direct contacts with the aliens. Let me get the information I need."

"But whether or not it is there, you will still make your report after that?"

He nodded. "I'll make my report." He got up and walked

forward to the central console, then sat down in the large padded chair and adjusted it for maximum comfort. "Are you ready?"

"Yes." The computer lowered the probes, which the agent carefully attached to his forehead. Now he simply lay back and relaxed, hardly feeling the computer-induced injection that cleared his mind and established the proper state for receipt and filtration of this kind of information.

Thanks to an organic module inside the brain of his other self down there on Medusa, every single thing that had happened to that other self was transmitted to the computer as raw data. Now it would be fed into the mind of the original in the chair, filtered—the basics and unimportant matter discarded by his own mind—and that other self would give a basic report both to the agent in the chair and to the computer as if the man were there in that room —which, in a very broad and very odd sense, he was.

The drugs and small neural probes did their job. His own mind and personality receded, replaced by a similar, yet oddly different pattern.

"The agent is commanded to report," the computer ordered, sending the command deep into the agent's mind, a mind no longer quite his own.

Recorders clicked on.

Slowly, the man in the chair cleared his throat. He mumbled, groaned, and made odd, disjointed words and sounds, as his mind received, coded, and classified the incoming data, adjusted it all, and sorted it out.

Finally, the man began to speak.

CHAPTER ONE

Rebirth

═══════════

After Krega's talk and a little preparation to put my own affairs in order—this would be a long one—I checked into the Confederacy Security Clinic. I'd been here many times before, of course—but not knowingly for this purpose. Mostly, this was where they programmed you with whatever information you'd need for a mission and where, too, you were "reintegrated." Naturally, the kind of work I did was often extralegal, a term I prefer to illegal, which implies criminal intent—and much of it was simply too hot to ever be known. To avoid such risks, all agents, of course, had their own experience of sensitive missions wiped from their minds when they were over.

It may seem like a strange life, going about not knowing where you have been or what you've done, but it has its compensations. Because any potential enemy, military or political, knows you've been wiped, you can live a fairly normal, relaxed life outside of a mission structure. There's no purpose in coming after you—you have no knowledge of what you've done, or why, or for whom. In exchange for these blanks, an agent of the Confederacy lives a life of luxury and ease, with an almost unlimited supply of money, and with all the comforts supplied. I bummed around, swam, gambled, ate in the best restaurants, played a little semi-pro ball or cube—I'm pretty good, and the exercise keeps me in shape. I enjoyed every minute of it, and except for my regular requalification training sessions—four- to six-week stints that resemble military basic training only nastier and more sadistic—I felt no guilt over my playboy life. The training sessions, of course, make sure that your body and mind don't stagnate from all that good living.

14

They implant sensors in you that they constantly monitor and decide when you need a good refresher.

I often wondered just how sophisticated those sensors were. Having a whole security staff witness all my debauchery and indiscretions once worried me, but after a while I learned to ignore it.

The life offered in trade is just too nice. Besides, what could I do about it? People on most of the civilized worlds these days had such sensors, although hardly to the degree and sophistication of mine. How else could a population so vast and so spread out possibly be kept orderly, progressive, and peaceful?

But, of course, when a mission came up you couldn't afford to forego all that past experience you'd had. A wipe without storage simply wouldn't have been very practical, since a good agent gets better by not repeating his mistakes. In the Security Clinic they had everything you ever experienced, and the first thing you did was go and get the rest of you put back so you would be whole for whatever mission they'd dreamed up this time.

I was always amazed when I got up from that chair with my past fully restored. Clear as my memory was once again, it was hard to believe that *I*, of all people, had done this or that.

The only difference this time, I knew, was that the process would be taken one step further. Not only would the complete "me" get up from that table, but the same memory pattern would be impressed on other minds, other bodies —as many as needed until a "take" was achieved.

I wondered what they'd be like, those four other versions of myself. Physically different, probably—the offenders on the Warden Diamond weren't usually from the civilized worlds, where people had basically been standardized in the name of equality. No, these people would come from the frontier, from among the traders and miners and free-boosters who operated there, and who were, of course, necessary in an expanding culture since a high degree of individuality, self-reliance, originality, and creativity was required in the dangerous environment in which they lived. A stupid government would have eliminated all such, but a stupid government degenerates into stagnancy or loses its vitality and growth potential by standardization. Utopia was for the masses, of course, but not for everyone or it wouldn't *be* Utopia very long.

That, of course, was the original reason for the Warden Diamond Reserve. Some of these hardy frontier people are so individualistic that they become a threat to the stability of the civilized worlds. The trouble is, anybody able to crack the fabric that holds our society together has, most likely, the smartest, nastiest, most original sort of mind humanity can produce—and, therefore, he is not somebody who should be idly wiped clean. The Diamond, it was felt, would effectively trap those individuals forever, yet allow them continued creative opportunities. Properly monitored, they might still produce something of value for the Confederacy—if only an idea, a thought, a way of looking at something that nobody else could evolve.

Of course, these felons were anxious to please, since the alternative was death. Eventually such creative minds made themselves indispensable to the Confederacy and insured their continued survival. The possibility had been foreseen —but it wasn't altogether unwelcome, either. Like all criminal organizations in the past, this one provided services that people were convinced should be illegal or were immoral or somesuch, but which masses of people wanted anyway.

The damned probe hurt like hell. Usually there was just some tingling, then a sensation much like sleep. You woke up a few minutes later in the chair, once again yourself. This time the tingling became a painful physical force that seemed to enter my skull, bounce around, then seize control of my head. It was as if a huge, giant fist had grabbed my brain and squeezed, then released, then squeezed again, in excruciating pulses. Instead of drifting off to sleep, I passed out.

I woke up and groaned slightly. The throbbing was gone, but the memory was still all too current and all too real. It was several minutes, I think, before I found enough strength to sit up.

The old memories flooded back, and again I was amazed at many of my past exploits. Considering my surrogate selves couldn't be wiped after this mission as could I, I made a mental note that those surrogates would almost certainly have to be killed if they did have my entire memory pattern. Otherwise, a lot of secrets would be loose on the Warden Diamond, many in the hands of people who'd know just what sort of use to make of them.

No sooner had I had that thought than I had the odd feeling of wrongness. I looked around the small room in which I'd awakened and realized immediately the source of that feeling.

This wasn't the Security Clinic, wasn't anyplace I'd ever seen before. A tiny cubicle, about twelve cubic meters total, including the slightly higher than normal ceiling. In it was a small cot on which I'd awakened, a small basin, next to which was a standard food port, and, in the wall, a pull-down toilet. That was it. Nothing else—or was there?

I looked around and easily spotted the obvious. Yes, I couldn't make a move without being visually and probably aurally monitored. The door was almost invisible and there was certainly no way to open it from inside. I knew immediately where I was.

I was in a prison cell.

Far worse than that, I could feel a faint vibration that had no single source. It wasn't irritating; in fact, it was so dim as to be hardly noticeable, but I knew what it was. I was aboard a ship, moving somewhere through space.

I stood up, reeling a bit from a slight bout of dizziness that soon passed, and examined my body. It was smaller, lighter, thinner than I was used to, but it was clearly the body of a male of the civilized worlds. What made it different, or unusual compared to my own, didn't hit me right away, but I finally put my finger on it. It was its unspoiled, unmarked newness, a body not yet in full development— not even much pubic hair. It was the body of someone extremely young. It wasn't *my* body, and I could only stand there, stunned, for I don't know how long.

I'm not me! my mind screamed at me. *I'm one of* them *—one of the surrogates!* I sat back down on the cot, telling myself that it just wasn't possible. I knew who I was, remembered every bit, every detail, of my life and work.

The shock gave way after a while to anger—anger and frustration. I was a copy, an imitation of somebody else entirely, somebody still alive and kicking and perhaps monitoring my every move, my every thought. I hated that other then, hated him with a pathological force that was beyond reason. He would sit there comfortable and safe, watching me work, watching me do it all—and, when it was over, he'd go home for debriefing, return to that easy life, while I . . .

They were going to dump me on a world of the Warden Diamond, trap me like some kind of master criminal, imprison me there for the rest of my life—of this body's life, anyway. And then? When my job was done? I'd said it myself upon awakening, passed my own sentence. The things I knew! I would be monitored at all times, of course. Monitored and killed if I blew any of those secrets—killed anyway at the completion of it, for insurance sake.

My training came into automatic play at that point, overriding the shock and anger. I regained control and considered all that I knew.

Monitor? Sure—more than ever. I recalled Krega saying that there was some sort of organic linkup. Are you enjoying this, you son of a bitch? Are you getting pleasure from vicariously experiencing my reaction?

My training clicked in again, dampening me down. It didn't matter, I told myself. First of all, I knew what he must be thinking—and that was an advantage. *He*, of all people, would know that I would be a damned tough son of a bitch to kill.

It was a shock to discover that you were not who you thought you were but some artificial creation. It was a shock, too, to realize that the old life, the life you remembered even if you, personally, didn't experience it, was gone forever. No more civilized worlds, no more casinos and beautiful women and all the money you could spend. And yet—and yet, as I sat there, I adjusted. That was what they picked men like me for from the start—our ability to adjust and adapt to almost anything.

It was not my body, but I was still me. Memory and thought and personality were an individual, not his body. This was no different from a biological disguise, I told myself, of a particularly sophisticated sort. As to who was really me—it seemed to me that this personality, these memories, were no more that other fellow's than my own. Until I got up from that chair back in the Security Clinic I'd really been somebody else anyway. A lot of me, my

memories and training, had been missing. That old between-
missions me was the artificial me, the created me, I thought.
He, that nonentity playboy that presently did not exist, was
the artificial personality. Me—the real me—was bottled up
and stored in their psychosurgical computers and only allowed to come out when they needed it—and for good
reason. Unlocked, I was as much a danger to the power
structure as to whomever they set me against.

And I was good. The best, Krega had called me. That's
why I was here, now, in this body, in this cell, on this ship.
And I wouldn't be wiped and I wouldn't be killed if I could
help it. That other me, sitting there in the console—somehow I no longer hated him very much, no longer felt anything at all for him. When this was all over he'd be wiped
once more—perhaps even killed himself if my brother
agents and I on the Diamond found out too much. At best
he'd return to being that stagnant milquetoast.

Me, on the other hand . . . Me. I would still be here,
still live on, the *real* me. I would become more complete
than he would.

I was under no illusions, though. Kill me they would, if
they could, if I didn't do their bidding. They'd do it automatically, from robot satellite, and without a qualm. *I*
would. But my vulnerability would last only until I mastered
my new situation and my new and permanent home. I felt
that with a deep sense of certainty—for I knew their
methods and how they thought. I'd have to do their dirty
work for them, and they knew it—but only until I could
get around it. They could be beaten, even on their own
turf. That was why they had people like me in the first
place—to uncover those who expertly covered over their
whole lives and activities, who managed to totally vanish
from their best monitors. To uncover them and get them.
But there'd be no new expert agent sent to get me if *I* beat
them. They'd just be putting somebody else in the same
position.

I realized then, as they had undoubtedly figured, that I
had no choice but to carry out the mission. As long as I
was doing what they wanted I would be safe from them
while still in that vulnerable stage. After—well, we'd see.

The thrill of the challenge took over, as it always did:
the puzzle to be solved; the objectives to be accomplished.

I liked to win, and it was even easier if you felt nothing about the cause—then it was just the challenge of the problem and the opponent and the physical and intellectual effort needed to meet that challenge. Find out about the alien menace. The outcome no longer concerned me either way—I was trapped on a Warden world from now on anyway. If the aliens won the coming confrontation, the Wardens would survive as allies. If they lost—well, it wouldn't make a damned bit of difference, only continue the current situation. Thus, the alien problem was purely an intellectual challenge and that made it perfect.

The other problem created a similar situation. Seek out the Lord of the particular Diamond world and kill him if I could. In a sense doing so would be more difficult, for I'd be operating on totally unfamiliar ground and would, therefore, require time and, perhaps, allies. Another challenge. And, if I got him, it could only increase my own power and position in the long run. If he got me instead, of course, that would solve everybody's problem—but the thought of losing is abhorrent to me. That set the contest in the best terms, from my point of view. Trackdown assassination was the ultimate game, since you won or you died and did not have to live with the thought that you lost.

It suddenly occurred to me that the only real difference that probably existed between me and a Lord of the Diamond was that I was working *for* the law and he—or she —against it. But, no, that wasn't right, either. On his world *he* was the law and I would be working against that. Fine. Dead heat on moral grounds.

The only thing wrong at this point, I reflected, was that they were starting me at a tremendous disadvantage and I disliked having more than necessary. The normal procedure was to program all pertinent information into my brain before they sent me off on a mission—but they hadn't done it this time. Probably, I thought, because they had me on the table once for four separate missions—and the transfer process, to a new body, was hard enough without trying to add anything afterward. Still, knowing this put me in a deep pit. I thought sourly that somebody should have thought of that.

Somebody did, but it was a while before I discovered how. About an hour after I had awakened a little bell clanged near the food port and I walked over to it. Almost instantly a hot tray appeared, along with a thin plastic fork and knife that I recognized as the dissolving type. They'd melt into a sticky puddle in an hour or less, then dry up and become a dry powder shortly after that. Standard for prisoners.

The food was lousy but I hadn't expected better. The vitamin-enriched fruit drink with it, though, was pretty good, and I made the most of it. I kept the thin, clear container, which was *not* the dissolving type, in case I wanted water later. The rest I put back in the port, and it vaporized neatly. All nice and sealed. You couldn't even draw more than a thimble full of water at a time from the tap.

About the only thing they couldn't control was my bodily functions, and a half-hour or so after eating my first meal as what you might call a new man, I just had to go. I tugged on the toilet pull ring on the far wall, the unit came down—and damned if there wasn't a small, paper-thin probe in the recess behind it. And so, I sat down on the john, leaned back against the panel, and got a brief and relief at the same time.

The thing worked by skin contact—don't ask me how. I'm not one of the tech brains. It was not as good as a programming, but it allowed them to talk to me, even send me pictures that only I could see and hear.

"By now I hope you're over the shock of discovering who and what you are," Krega's voice came to me, seemingly forming in my brain. It was a shock to realize that not even my jailers could hear or see a thing.

"We have to brief you this way simply because the transfer process is delicate enough as it is. Oh, don't worry about it—it's permanent. But we prefer to allow as much time as possible for your brain patterns to fit in and adapt without subjecting the brain to further shock and we haven't the time to allow you to 'set in' completely, as it were. This method will have to do, and I profoundly regret it, for I feel that you have a difficult enough assignment as is, perhaps impossible."

I felt the excitement rising within me. The challenge, the challenge . . .

"Your objective world is Medusa, farthest out from the sun of the Diamond colonies," the Commander's voice con-

tinued. "If there is a single place in the universe where
man can live but wouldn't want to, it's Medusa. Old
Warden, who discovered the system, said he named the
place after the mythological creature that turned men to
stone because anybody who'd want to live there had to
have rocks in his head. That's pretty close to the truth.

"The imprint ability of this device is limited," he continued, "but we can send you one basic thing that may—
or may not—be of use to you on Medusa. It is a physical-
political map of the entire planet as complete and up-to-
date as we could make it."

That puzzled me. Why would such a map *not* be of
use? Before I could consider the matter further, and curse
my inability to ask Krega questions, I felt a sharp back
pain, then a short wave of dizziness and nausea. When the
haze cleared, I found that I had the complete map clearly
and indelibly etched in my mind.

There followed a stream of facts about the place. The
planet was roughly 46,000 kilometers both around the
equator—and in polar circumference, allowing for topo-
graphic differences. Like all four Diamond worlds, it was
basically a ball—highly unusual as planets go, even though
everybody, including me, thinks of all major planets as
spherical.

The gravity was roughly 1.2 norm, so I would have to adjust to being a bit slower and heavier than usual. That
would take a slight adjustment in timing, and I made a
note to work on that first thing. Its atmosphere was within
a few hundredths of a percentage point of human standard—far too little difference to be noticeable, since nobody I know ever actually experienced that human standard in real life.

Medusa's axial tilt of roughly 22° gave the world strong
seasonal changes under normal circumstances, but at over
three hundred million kilometers from its F-type sun it was,
at best, a tad chilly. In point of fact, something like seventy
percent of Medusa was so glaciated that it consisted of just
two large polar caps with a sandwich of real planet in
between on both sides of the equator. Its day was a bit
long, but not more than an hour off the standard and hardly a matter of concern. What *was* a concern was that those
wonderful tropic temperatures were something around 10° C

at the equator or at midsummer, and that could drop to–20 at the tropic extremes in midwinter. But the life zone *did* extend for some distance beyond that—up and down to a jagged glacial line at roughly 35° latitude, give or take a few degrees, and in that subtropical zone at midwinter a brisk –80° C. Some climate! I sincerely hoped that they provided free insulated gear from the moment of arrival, particularly since that map in my head said that a number of cities were located in the coldest areas.

Continents were pretty much irrelevant, since the seas were frozen down to the habitable zones all the time and down to almost the tropic lines half the year. There were three distinct habitable land masses that I could see from the map, though, so you might as well say three very wide and very thin continents. Throughout the habitable latitudes there was a lot of mountain that didn't help the climate much, and a huge amount of forest, all of which seemed to be various evergreen types. Nothing familiar, of course, but familiar types in any cold climate.

A rocky, terribly cold, hostile world. Calling it human-habitable was stretching things a bit, no matter the air you breathed. About the only thing of interest was that Medusa, of all places, showed the only evidence of vulcanism on any of the Warden worlds. No volcanoes—but that would be too much, anyway, for any person to stand. But there were large thermal pools, hot springs, and even geysers in the midst of the barren wastes, some in the coldest regions. Obviously there was something hot beneath many parts of the surface.

There *was* animal life, though—mostly mammals, it seemed, of a great many varieties. That figured, really—only mammals could survive that kind of climate. Some were nasty, some harmless, some a little of both, but nothing alive could be taken for granted on such a fierce, harsh place where just staying alive took tremendous effort.

Well, I'd better start loving it, I told myself. Short of suicide, there was no way to avoid calling it home. At least it was a supposedly modern and industrialized world, so there *would* be creature comforts.

"Medusa is ruled with an iron hand by Talant Ypsir, a former member of the Confederacy Council. Ypsir attempted to engineer a coup of sorts more than thirty-five years ago. It was hushed up, and he dropped from sight and disappeared from the news, but the object of his coup was to make fundamental changes in the way the civilized worlds, and even the frontier, were organized and administered. His system was so brutal and so naked a grab for absolute personal power that he eventually shocked even his most ardent adherent's who betrayed him. Unlike Charon's Aeolia Matuze, also once a Council member, Ypsir was never popular or trusted, but he had an absolute genius for bureaucratic organization and was at one time head of the civil service. Be warned that he and his minions run Medusa with the same brutal, methodical system he once hoped to impose on all mankind, and that the cities are models of efficiency, as is the economy, but in every way absolutely under his control. His government controls *only* the organized settlements, however—although that is the bulk of the more than twelve million people estimated to be Medusa's current population. As his industries are fueled from the mines on the moons of Momrath, the gas giant that is the next planet out from Medusa, and there is little in that wilderness except water and wood, he makes no effort to extend his authority to that wild area."

I remembered Matuze well, but I had to admit I'd never heard of this Ypsir. Well, it was long ago and the Council was pretty large. Besides, who the hell ever knows the head of the civil service anyway?

As to who I was, I got my first mental picture of myself from the briefing, and it was a bit of a shock. I'd had a sense of being younger, true—but the body I now wore was little more than fourteen, barely into puberty. It was, however, a civilized-world-norm body, and that was good enough, although it was from Halstansir, a world I didn't know. I could infer a lot, though, simply from the skin, basic build, and facial features. I was now relatively tall and thin, with a burnt-orange complexion, and the boyish face had jet-black hair but no trace of sideburns or beard, almond-shaped black eyes, and fairly thick, flat nose over broad lips. It was a strong, handsome face and body—but very, very young-looking.

So what was a fourteen-year-old boy doing on his way to the Diamond? Well, Tarin Bul of Halstansir was a rather exceptional young lad. The son of a local administrator, he'd been raised in pampered splendor. But Halstansir's Council member, a man named Daca Kra, had apparently used the boy's father as a scapegoat in a minor scandal, exposing him to ridicule and personal ruin. The older Bul just couldn't stand it, and, refusing psych treatment, killed himself instead. Such things happened occasionally, particularly on the upper political levels. What *didn't* happen, even occasionally, was what the boy, who just about worshiped his father, had done then. Taking advantage of the natural sympathy of the first families of Halstansir, Tarin Bul had plotted, planned, and trained to get to a reception for Daca Kra—where he'd assassinated the Councillor, in mid-handshake, by the rather quaint and ugly method of disemboweling the man with a sword used in physical training. The boy was a prepubescent twelve at the time, which caused more problems than the nearly unprecedented assassination.

Of course we picked him up and got him off-planet, where we had him evaluated by psychs, but he'd withdrawn from the world into a better one of his own imagination after carrying out the kill. The psychs could hardly reach him at all, though they spent a lot of time trying. Normally they would have simply done a complete wipe of his mind and built a new personality, but Kra's family used some influence of its own. So now Tarin Bul was out of his shell and on his way to Medusa—but not really. Bul had died as soon as my mind displaced his. *I* was now Tarin Bul, and I wondered how an ex-Councillor would take to a boy who'd killed one of his colleagues.

Still, that would be a ways off as yet. I could see certain real advantages in the body—not the least of which was the fact that I had an extra thirty years or so on my life—but there would also be disadvantages as well. There would be the tendency to treat me as a child—and, because it was my cover, I had to go along to a certain extent. But though children get a bit more license than adults in simple behavioral areas, they are also subject to more rigid social controls. That realization led me onto the path of determining my best and most effective persona. The fact that Bul was a male of the civilized worlds born to a political family meant his IQ and general formative education would be expected to be well above average. The fact that he'd engineered a successful assassination and survived, even being sent to the Warden Diamond, was another plus. I would have no trouble convincing anyone that I was quite a bit older than my years, which eased the problem quite a bit. Being a tough, smart kid would be an easy and useful role to play.

I lay back down on the cot and put myself in a light trance, going over all the briefing information, filing, sorting, thinking everything out. Particularly important were the details, large and small, of Bul's short life and family, since it was in that area I'd be most vulnerable to a trip-up. I also studied his mannerisms, nervous habits, and the like, and tried to get myself into the mind-set of a small but deadly assassin.

By the time I reached Medusa I knew I'd *better* be perfect for my own sake. I had another assassination to add to Tarin Bul's total still to come, and though I hoped they would underestimate me, I did not for one moment underestimate Talant Ypsir.

CHAPTER TWO

Transportation and Exposure

Except for the regular meals I had no way to keep track of time, but it was a fairly long trip. Nobody was wasting any money transporting prisoners by the fastest available routes, that was for sure.

Finally, though, we docked with the base ship a third of a light-year out from the Warden system. I understood the situation not so much by any sensation inside my cloister but from the lack of it—the vibration that had been my constant companion stopped. Still the routine wasn't varied—I assumed they were waiting for a large enough contingent from around the galaxy to make the landing worthwhile. For now, I could only sit and go over my data for the millionth time and, occasionally, reflect on the fact that I probably wasn't very far from my old body—as I'd come to think of it. I wondered if, perhaps, he didn't even come down and take a peek at me from time to time, at least from idle curiosity—me and the three others who probably were here as well.

I also had time to reflect on what I knew of the Warden situation itself, the reason for its perfection as a prison. I had not, of course, swallowed that whole. Though there was no such thing as the perfect prison, this one had to be close. Shortly after I was landed on Medusa and started wading in and breathing its air I would be infected with an oddball submicroscopic organism that would set up housekeeping in every cell of my body. There it would live, feeding off me, even earning its keep by keeping disease organisms, infections, and the like in check. The one thing that stuff had was a will to live and it only lived if you did.

But the organism needed something, some trace ele-

27

ment or somesuch that was only present in the Warden system. Nobody knew what and nobody had been able to do the real work necessary to find out, but whatever it needed—other than you—was found only in the Warden system. Whatever it was wasn't in the air, because they ran shuttles between the worlds of the Diamond and in them you breathed the purified, mechanically produced stuff with no ill effect. Not in the food, either. They'd tried that. It was possible for one of the Warden people to live comfortably on synthetics in a totally isolated lab such as a planetary space station. But get too far away, even with Warden food and Warden air, and the organism died. Since it had modified your cells to make itself at home, and those cells depended on the organism to keep working properly, you died, too—painfully and slowly, in horrible agony. That distance was roughly a quarter of a light-year from the sun, which explained the location of the base ship.

All four worlds were more than climatologically different. The organism acted consistently in what it did to you on each planet. But—possibly because of distance from the sun, which seemed to be the determining factor in its life, the organism did different things to you depending on which world you were first exposed to it. Whatever it did stuck in just that fashion even if you went to a different world of the Diamond.

The organism seemed to be vaguely telepathic, although nobody could explain quite how. It certainly wasn't an intelligent organism, though it behaved predictably. Still, most of the changes seemed to involve the colony in one person affecting the colony in another—or others. The individual provided the conscious control, if he could, and that determined who bossed whom. A pretty simple system, even if nobody had yet been able to explain it. I vaguely understood, though, that Medusans were unique in the Diamond in that the Warden organism colony inside you affected you alone in some way, not others. Well, we would have to see.

As for Medusa itself, all I really knew about it was that it was terribly cold and hostile. I cursed again at not having been fed the proper programming to prepare me fully—it would cost time, possibly a lot, just to learn the ropes.

Almost six days—seventeen meals—after I'd arrived at the base ship there was a lurching and a lot of banging around that forced me to the cot and made me slightly seasick. Still, I wasn't disappointed—it meant that they were making up the consignments and readying for the in-system drop of these cells. I faced what was to come with mixed emotions. On one hand, I desperately wanted to be out of this little box that had provided nothing but endless, terrible boredom for such a long time. The problem was, though, that when I next got out of the box I would just be in a much larger and probably more comfortable box—Medusa itself, no less a cell for being an entire planet. And if my new situation would provide diversion, challenge, excitement, or whatever, lacking in this box, it might also prove, unlike this box, very, very final.

Shortly after the banging started, it stopped again. After a short, expectant pause, I felt a vibration indicating movement. It was much more pronounced than before, telling me that I was either on a much smaller vessel or located nearer the drives.

Still, another five interminable days—fifteen meals— passed before we reached our destination. Long, certainly, but also fast for a sublight carrier, probably a modified and totally automated freighter. Then the vibrations stopped and I knew we were in orbit. Again I had those mixed feelings of trapped doom and exhilaration.

There was a crackling sound and a speaker I'd never even known was there came to life.

"Attention all prisoners!" it commanded; the voice was a metallic parody of a man's baritone. "We have achieved orbit around the planet Medusa in the Warden system." Nothing I didn't know, but the announcement was, I reflected, probably telling the others, however many there were, for the first time. I could understand what they must be going through, although, I was lucky to be going in with my eyes open even if no more voluntarily.

"In a moment," the voice continued, "the doors to your cells will slide open and you will be able to leave. We strongly recommend you do so, since thirty seconds after the doors open they will close again and a vacuum pump will begin sterilization operations within the cells which would be fatal to anyone who remains."

Nice touch, I thought. Not only did that insure against breakouts en route, you moved or you died on their schedule. I couldn't help wonder whether anybody chose death.

"Immediately after you enter the main corridor," the voice continued, "you will stand in place until the cell doors close. Do not attempt to move from in front of your cell door until it closes or automatic guard equipment will vaporize you. There will be no talking in the corridor. Anyone breaking silence or failing to obey orders precisely will be dealt with instantly. You will receive further instructions once the doors close. Ready to depart—*now!*"

The door slid open, and I wasted no time in stepping out. A small white box, complete with marks for feet, indicated where you were to stand. I did as instructed, galling as all this was. There was something to being totally naked and isolated on a ship controlled only by computer that humbled you more than was right. I experienced a sense of total futility.

I could still look around and realized that I'd been right. The place where we stood was basically a long sealed hall along whose sides the little cells had been attached. I looked up and down and counted maybe ten or twelve, no more. The cream of the crop, I thought sourly. A handful of men and women, naked and bedraggled, beaten prisoners now, about to be dropped off and left. I wondered why my companions had been chosen rather than wiped, considering the transportation costs alone. What had the computers and psych boys found in these dejected specimens that dictated that they should live? *They* didn't know, that was for sure. I wondered exactly who did.

The doors snapped shut. I waited expectantly, perhaps to hear the scream of somebody who didn't move fast enough as the air was pumped out, but there was no hint of melodrama. If anybody had taken that way out, it was not evident.

"At my command," the voice barked from speakers along the ceiling, "you will turn right and walk, slowly, in single file, as far forward as you can. There you will find a special shuttle that will bring you to the surface.

You will take seats from front to back, leaving no empty seats between you, and immediately strap yourselves in."

I heard some muttering from a couple of my fellow prisoners. Instantly a brief but very visible spurt of light from a side wall hit with an audible hiss just in front of the offenders' feet. They jumped slightly at this demonstration of power, but all the grumbling and mumbling ceased.

The voice had paused for this interruption, but now took up its instructions with no reference to it. None was needed.

"Right turn—*now!*" it commanded, and we did as instructed. "Walk slowly forward to the shuttle as instructed."

We walked silently, definitely in no hurry. The metal floor of the corridor was damned cold, which made the shuttle preferable to this damned refrigerator. The shuttle itself was surprisingly comfortable and modern, although the seats weren't made for naked bodies. I sat about three rows back and attached the safety straps, then waited for the others to enter. My first impression had been close, I noted. The shuttle itself could seat twenty four, but there were only nine of us—six men and three women.

The hatch closed automatically and I heard the hiss of pressurization. Then, without further fanfare, came a violent lurch and we were free of the transport and on our way down.

The shuttle was much too modern and comfortable for mere prisoner transport, I told myself. This, then, had to be one of the interplanetary ships regularly used for transportation between the worlds of the Warden Diamond.

The overhead speakers crackled, and a much nicer female voice that actually sounded human came on. It was a great improvement.

"Welcome to Medusa." The voice sounded like a cool, urbane tour guide. "As has no doubt been explanied to you, Medusa is your final destination and new home. Although you will be unable to leave the Warden system after debarking on the planet, you will also no longer be prisoners, but, rather, citizens of the Warden Diamond. Confederacy rule ended the moment you entered this shuttle, which is owned in common by the Warden worlds, and is one of a fleet of four shuttlecraft and sixteen freighters. The System Council is a corporate entity recognized by the Confederacy as fully and internally self-governing, and it even has a seat in the Confederacy Congress. Each of the four worlds is under a separate administration, and the government of each planet is unique and independent. No matter who you are or what you have been or done in the past, you are now citizens of Medusa and nothing more —or less. Anything done prior to right now is past history that will neither be remembered, filed, or ever again referred to. Only what you do from this point, as citizens of Medusa, Warden system, will matter."

Yeah, sure buddy. And I also still believe in fairies. If they expected me to believe that the powers-that-be on Medusa didn't know anything about our past and didn't keep good records, they had a very low opinion of my intelligence.

"We will arrive at the spaceport at Gray Basin, Medusa, in approximately five minutes," the shuttle voice told us. "There you will be met by representatives of the government, given protective clothing, and then taken to a sheltered center where all your questions will be answered. Please be prepared for extreme cold; Gray Basin is in the northern hemisphere, which is now in winter season, and conditions are extremely harsh. Do not lose your guides or go out on your own. The climate at this time of year can prove lethal in a very short time to new arrivals. Although technologically quite comfortable, Medusa is somewhat primitive by the standards of the so-called civilized worlds, and the physical requirements of Medusans differ from those of other humans. Therefore, expect to find the interiors of buildings quite cold. A special place just for you has been prepared, and you will be taken there. Our government is a model of efficiency, necessary for this harsh world; please do not disregard its authority. Again, welcome to Medusa."

Although the lid was off, nobody really said much for the rest of the trip—partly because we were still conditioned by our so recent imprisonment; the rest was nerves. Me included. This was it, I told myself. Here we go.

The descent was extremely bumpy once we hit the atmosphere, but whoever was at the controls knew his or her business. Despite the turbulent air, the pilot managed a nice descent, then glided right up to and into the dock.

In less than a minute I could hear the airlock door mechanisms operating, and the indicator went from red to orange to green. There was a pneumatic hiss, then the doors rolled back. For a moment, none of us moved. Finally, those nearest the hatch stood up and walked out the open door. Sighing, I got up and did the same.

The walkway was bitter cold. We were all stark naked, so there was no time to think as we ran for the terminal. A man and a woman waited for us just as we came inside, by which time I was already turning blue. They shouted at us to get over to a table and take protective clothing as quickly as possible and put it on. None of us needed any urging. Although it was pretty tough finding anything in my size, I did the best I could. I saw that the stuff was standard thermal underclothing, then parka, pants, and soft boots all lined with some sort of fur, with matching fur-lined gloves. Getting them on helped, but I was so damned cold I knew it would take some time to thaw out.

"As soon as you're dressed, line up here!" the woman shouted in a commanding, drill-instructor-type voice.

I did as instructed, feeling a bit as if I was back in training. Only when I was standing there did the reality hit me. Here I was, on Medusa—and even as that first blast of frigid air had hit me, my body was being systematically invaded by an alien organism that was to be my permanent jailer.

CHAPTER THREE

Orientation

The couple who had met us looked lean, tough, and mean. They radiated an arrogant sort of cold, businesslike power. Both were dressed in fatigue-green uniforms and wore rubber-soled black shoes, but the uniforms were rather light and did not seem to offer much protection against the cold. In fact, these two were dressed in such a way that you'd swear the ambient temperature in the terminal was not below freezing but rather somewhere in the temperate range. Their uniforms bore sewn insignia of rank—if they followed the usual standard here, the man was a sergeant, the woman a corporal—and an odd-looking, snakelike insignia on their right pockets, but that was it.

We all lined up, turned, and looked at the couple, who stared back at us as if we were some kind of disgusting specimens for a lab dissection. I took an instant dislike to them both.

"I'm Sergeant Gorn," the man said. With his clipped, officious voice he sounded like every sergeant I'd ever heard. "This is Corporal Sugra. We are orientation leaders and medical technicians for your group. I think you are as dressed as we can manage. Don't worry if you have size problems—everyone does. When you become more acclimated to Medusa, you will be issued a full set of tailored clothing. First we must transfer you to the orientation center, so follow me and we will board a bus just outside." With that he started walking and, after a moment's hesitation, we all followed. The corporal brought up the rear.

The bus was of an odd magnetic-drive design, with hard, molded seats, two strings of internal lights, and not much else. There was no operator and, as we quickly discovered, no heat. It was built like a fort, though, so we would be sheltered from the noisy wind and thickly blowing snow if not from the biting cold. As soon as the last of us boarded, the corporal took a card out of one of her pockets and stuck it in a slot in the front panel of the bus. The doors closed with a *whoosh* and we were off rather smoothly and quickly, emerging from the tunnel into Medusa proper.

The spaceport was located some distance from the town. We managed to run out of the blizzard after some ten or fifteen minutes and gained a little visibility of a world that was still totally snow-covered. I could see high mountains off in the distance, grim and foreboding. There was no sign of life out there, though—I had no idea how much snow was there, but it was more than I'd ever seen outside of a polar ice cap.

The bus, however, was an impressive vehicle, smooth and sturdy, that apparently was guided along some sort of under-snow tracking system. The system made sense, for no matter how high the snow piled up the bus would glide just above it.

We slowed, suddenly, but without any jerking, and approached a large building that loomed up out of the sea of white. We stopped, waited, then started up again, stopped again, waited, then glided on, the tracking system now clearly visible ahead.

Sgt. Gorn picked up the microphone. "We are entering the west gate of the city of Gray Basin," he informed us. "Because of the unpleasant weather around here, much of the city is built underground—in fact, under the permafrost. The two stops we made were to clear force fields, without which the gates would be open to wild animals and other unpleasant creatures that do, in fact, roam that landscape you have seen.

We took another turn, then came to a complicated track-switching area. The bus stopped, then cautiously proceeded once again as a series of lights changed on all the tracks; the bus eased onto one of them. We moved along another two or three minutes at a slow but steady speed, then emerged from the tunnel and into the city of Gray Basin proper, which was as modern-looking as the bus. It seemed to go on forever.

"The city is not in a cavern," Gorn informed us, "but

is built in the same manner as are the domed cities on some of the most hostile frontier worlds. In fact, it's something of a domed city upside down, in that we built the city and then roofed it over. Most Medusan cities not on or near the equator are built like this. Gray Basin has a population of seventeen thousand and is the commercial center of the north."

The map in my head showed me pretty much where I was. The eastern continental land mass, it seemed, and at about 38° north latitude. On most worlds this would be a fairly pleasant climate; here, it was tundra.

Despite my warm clothing, the cold was beginning to get to me. I had spent the last several weeks in perfect climate control, and my body was not used to this kind of extreme. Even in the bus, where things should be fairly stable in temperature, it was still damned *cold*.

We wound through streets past neat-looking modular apartment buildings and what must have been office buildings and shops, finally pulling up at a blocky, monolithic four-story building made out of some blackish stone. The doors hissed open.

"Please follow us into the building," Gorn said. Despite the "please," it still sounded like the command it was. "Do not hold back. You will have to climb two flights of stairs. Do not get lost."

We followed the same route-step as before, entering the building and walking down a wide corridor with offices and other corridors branching off to the right and left of us. We then reached a stairway and climbed it, keeping up with Gorn as best we could. I think most of us were a bit surprised to be winded by a mere two-story climb, our sedentary imprisonment notwithstanding. Not only were we all out of condition, but the slightly heavier gravity was telling.

The blast of warm air when we entered the first room on the third floor was as unexpected as it was tremendously welcome. Despite my clothing, I frankly hadn't realized how terribly cold I was until the pain that the heat generated hit me. It took a few minutes before I could really think of anything else and look around.

The first room, the heated one, was fairly large and furnished in a utilitarian manner, with long, hard folding tables and collapsible chairs and not much else. There were no windows, a fact our hosts were quick to explain.

"Just take seats anywhere and get accustomed to the temperature change," Gorn told us. "This room and the three adjoining rooms have been raised to 21° for your initial comfort. These are the only directly heated rooms, so stay within them at all times. We chose this area to heat because, with no windows or other outside vents, it is the most efficient system." He walked over to a nearby door. "If you'll come in here, I'll show you the rest of the place."

We followed—slowly, still not recovered completely from exposure—and found that the second room was a large barrackslike area with eight double bunks, four on each side of the hall. The mattresses appeared to be paper-thin and none too comfortable, but I'd seen worse. The place was well-maintained, although obviously seldom used. Beyond was a third large room, with a large common shower and three open standard toilets, plus four small sinks with mirrors. Again it looked seldom-used, but serviceable.

We followed Sgt. Gorn back to the "lounge" area and took seats. As yet nobody had removed his thermal clothing and I had no inclination to do so myself. I felt as if I would never be warm again.

It was Cpl. Sugra's turn at us. She looked like a lot of women cops I've met in my work—not unattractive, but hard, cold, and worldly; her voice matched. For the first time I could look at her and Gorn and see a bit beyond the manner and the uniforms. Their complexions, which at the spaceport and on the bus were a granitelike gray, now seemed lighter, almost orange. There was a certain toughness to their skin, which, on close inspection, resembled the hides of great animals. Soft they were not.

"I'm Corporal Sugra," she began, reintroducing herself. "Sergeant Gorn and I will be with you over the next week. We will be staying right down the hall from this complex and will be available to answer your questions and give you basic preparation. At various times others from the government will come in to talk about specific areas. Now, we understand you have just come from a bitter experience, and you are now most concerned about what this new world is like and what it both has for you and will do for you."

And *to* me, I thought.

"First of all, is there anyone here who does not know why Medusa and the other worlds of the Warden Diamond are used by the Confederacy for exile?" She paused a moment, then seemed satisfied that we all knew at least the basics.

"The micro-organism that is now within all of your bodies will be making itself at home. Please don't be alarmed. You will find there is no sensation, no feeling at all that anything is different. In fact, you will probably feel increasingly *better* as this process goes on because, despite the best medical care, the human system is riddled with disease and physical problems of one sort or another. Since the Warden organism depends on you for its place to live, it wants that place to be in as good a condition as possible. So it will repair what is wrong, make more efficient that which is inefficient, and will not only cure you of any diseases or infections you might have but prevent any new ones. That's how it pays you back; it's a good deal."

A big, gruff-looking man near me gave a low cough. "Yeah—but what's *our* price?" he grumbled.

"There is no . . . price, as you call it," she responded. "As you may know, it is theorized that the Warden organism was native only to the planet Lilith and was spread by early explorers to the other three worlds, where it mutated to survive. Some people on Lilith have the power to order the Wardens around, inflicting pain and pleasure and in some cases even creating and destroying through willpower alone. On Charon this ability is even more pronounced, with physical and mental power giving those trained in controlling their Wardens almost magical abilities over themselves and others. On Cerberus minds are actually exchanged between the people as a by-product of the Warden organism. In all cases there are more positives than minuses in the by-products. But here on Medusa survival dominates all other things. The organism here is more colonial in nature, sticking to whatever it's in and not bothering with others."

"You can't be saying that there's no effect," a skeptical woman put in.

"No, there *is* an effect, but it is limited to each individual. It is also universal and automatic, so that no willpower or training is required. Everyone can use it equally, making Medusa a far better place. What it did to us, what it *is* doing to you, is totally altering your basic biochemistry. We look human, we act human; but under the microscope we are not human. Here, on Medusa, the Warden colonies survive in us only as long as we ourselves survive. So the colonies mutated humanity here to survive the climate, no matter what. The changes are far more extensive and comprehensive than on the other three planets. Our entire cellular structure is modified, with each Warden colony in each cell in total and complete control, ready to act at a moment's notice, either independently or collectively as required."

"To what end?" I asked, genuinely curious. "What does it do?"

"Instant adaptation to whatever the needs of the organism are," she told us. "We can survive almost any temperature extreme. Our bodies can consume and use almost any substance to provide whatever energy is needed under any conditions. We could go stark naked into that snowy wilderness you saw coming in and we would neither freeze nor starve. Water is our only requirement. We can adapt to extremes of radiation, drink boiling water, even walk barefoot on hot coals. Medusans are in every way superior to humanity, or even to those of the other three worlds. Instant evolution, it's been called. What we need, we have or become. As I say, the system is automatic—no thought or direction is required."

"That's why the bus and buildings were unheated," I thought aloud. "You don't need heat."

She nodded. "Natural insulation is enough to keep everything fairly uniform and comfortable for us. These uniforms mark our station and rank, and provide such handy things as pockets. They in no way provide protection, because we don't need any—and neither will you."

She paused to let that sink in a bit, then looked over at Sgt. Gorn and nodded to him. He took up the briefing.

"For now you will remain in these specially heated and insulated quarters," he told us. "Over the course of a week, the Warden organism will make Medusans out of you physically. Our purpose is to make you Medusans socially and politically as well. We have here a society that is one of man's old dreams. Every single man, woman, and child here is superior in every physical way. To that our current First Minister, Talant Ypsir, has added his considerable skills at political organization and social engineering to create a highly advanced society. On Lilith or Charon you might wind up as primitive migrant workers. Here we are technologically advanced, with all that implies. Your place in our society will be determined by your mind and skills, not by any physical or technological limitations. This world looks harsh, I know, but once it no longer threatens you it becomes a world of wonder and beauty and comfort. You are lucky to be Medusans, considering the alternatives."

I wondered about that.

The barracks-style setup meant we nine would get to know one another pretty well, at least in a superficial sense. Although one couple preferred not to talk at all about their pasts, from the six who would it was clear that this was a very unusual crop. Every single one of the six—seven, including my cover—had killed at least one other human being in a cold and premeditated way. I suspected that all nine of us represented the most violent kinds of criminal minds. No smugglers or embezzlers here—we were the cream of the crop.

As the "kid" in the group, I found the others curiously kind and protective toward me, almost to a one. Those who have never encountered real criminals before might find that a bit hard to believe; but, in fact, most criminals are pretty nice, ordinary people except for one little area. All these people were extraordinary, because in contrast to my—Tarin Bul's—rather direct and sloppy job, they had all killed in extremely clever technological ways.

Just how Talant Ypsir planned to turn such people into model citizens of his new superior society we all discovered the next day. A tall man came in, looking granite-gray in the same way Gorn and Sugra had when we'd first met them. He introduced himself as Solon Kabaye, Gray Basin's Political Commissioner. His uniform was all black but still styled in the military manner. He had gold braid on his sleeves and a golden-colored belt. On his pocket was the obvious government symbol—a stylized woman's head with a hair full of what had to be snakes. His manner was easygoing and conversational, like that of most politicians; I may have been the only one to notice his skin color change from that light gray to the oranger shade of Gorn and Sugra. Here was a graphic indication that something inside him worked very differently from anything we were accustomed to.

"I'm going to be basic and blunt," he told us, "because that's the best way to start. Let's go over a couple of facts right away, shall we? First—you're stuck. There is no escape from Medusa, no place to run. Therefore, you'd best get used to the world as quickly as possible and settle in as best you can. Your future—the rest of your lives—is here, tied to Medusa. The system works, and it works well. It takes into account our planetary assets, our inherent problems and limitations as Warden citizens, and it gives a strong measure of prosperity to the people. The system evolved over the past century, as various ideas were tried and discarded. This one works. You didn't ask to be here— but you put yourselves here by your own actions. We didn't ask for you, either. Frankly, unless you possess some new technological knowledge that could be of use to us, you're not really needed here. So we have to find out just where you fit—then you fit. You either fit, or you take that last step into the deferred oblivion from which coming here saved you. That's the bottom line."

This was tough talk, and very discomforting as well. Still, it was also very professionally timed. We were stuck here, on an alien world, waiting for a something we couldn't see, hear, or feel to take over our bodies. Quite simply, we had no real options. After the first night they had even taken away the thermal wear while we slept, leaving us with nothing but flimsy white hospital-type gowns. Try to run now, boy, out into a frigid wilderness.

"Sounds like the Confederacy," Turnel, the ruddy, gruff resident grouch of our group noted half under his breath. Of course Kabaye heard him and smiled slightly.

"Perhaps it does. The Confederacy is a society that exists because it works. That doesn't make it the *best* society, or the most efficient, or anything else, but it's there because it works for the majority of people."

"Well, we're the minority," noted Edala, a tough, worldly woman prisoner.

"True," Kabaye agreed. "We all are. I was born and raised in the Confederacy, same as you. So was Talant Ypsir, our First Minister. And now we're here, and you're here, and, ironically, folks like the First Minister and myself find ourselves the government rather than opposed to the government. We're faced with the same problems as the Confederacy, and we have additional problems because of Medusa's limitations. Our advantage, though, is that Medusa is the wealthiest of the Warden worlds since we control the raw-materials sources, and, with a Warden organism not trying to get in the way of building stuff, we can best exploit these resources. So, let me tell you the score here and then I'll tell you how you fit in."

The "score," as it were, was that we came from a somewhat totalitarian society that believed in the basic goodness of man to a *very* totalitarian society run by men and women who were convinced that humans would always, given a choice, do the wrong thing. Therefore, a society tightly and rigidly controlled, in which all the rules were known and posted and no violations were tolerated, was Ypsir's new vision. It turned out to be not nearly as new as he thought, but a very old idea indeed.

There were less than thirteen million Medusans, scattered around the so-called temperate zones in small, enclosed cities and towns linked by magne-bus and a freight service using the same tracks. Electric power was generated basically by geothermal wells, and the location and size of the cities were determined by just how much power was available. Medusa controlled the Diamond's freighter fleet, digging raw materials out of the mineral-rich moons of the next nearest neighbor out-system, the great ringed gas giant Momrath. These were unloaded at specific freight terminals strategically located around the planet so that the cities could be most economically served. The reason for cities like Gray Basin was not only their large geothermal sources of power, but also because, being so far north, magne-tracks could be laid over the permanently frozen ocean to the north and thus connect continents. Air travel was available, but it was expensive, subject to frequent nasty weather conditions, and not practical for heavy freight.

Some of the cities were quite large, but most had between fifty and a hundred thousand people. All were self-contained, and all nonequatorial ones were, like Gray Basin, dug in rather than built on the surface; and each one specialized in just a few industries. Gray Basin, for example, specialized in transportation and related industries on the surface. All of the magne-busses, some of the freight containers, and much of the buried guidance track were made here. One town built computers—a surprise to me, since I'd assumed that such things would be strictly prohibited by the Confederacy guardians. A few specialized in food production and distribution, mostly synthetics and food imported from Lilith and Charon. It *was* true, as Sugra had told us, that we could eat almost anything— yet, as Kabaye was quick to point out, the fact that we could eat human flesh did not mean that we preferred it to steak. Being able to eat something was not the same as either liking it or enjoying it.

Clearly Medusa's economy worked closely with that of Cerberus, next in-system. The Cerberans helped design the products Medusa made, and handled just about all the computer software, as well as taking raw materials like basic steel, plastics, and the like we turned out and making things that were of use on their and other worlds but not here. For example, the very concept of a speedboat was ridiculous on Medusa, but on the Cerberan water world speedboats were in great demand.

The factories and industries of Medusa were basically automated, but there was a job for every human. Natives went to state schools from ages four to twelve, then were examined in a number of areas including aptitudes and intelligence potential and placed in the particular training track for which they were most suited. This was a bit more ponderous than the Confederacy's method of breeding you to your job, but it served the same purpose.

Also contrary to Confederacy custom, families were maintained for those early years, although they were often nontraditional and always state-determined. Group marriages and group families were the rule, partly because of the need to bear and raise children and partly in the name of "efficiency," a word of which I was already tiring.

There were forty-four wage steps, or grades possible, although the top four grades were strictly top government personnel and there was only one Grade 44, naturally.

The easiest way to think of the society, I reflected, was as if everybody—every man, woman, and child—were in the military, attached to a mission section. Within that section were most of the grades, with grade reflecting rank and, therefore, power. The state, or your section of it, provided common meal facilities, food, clothing, and shelter, and also made available the amenities that could be bought with the money you made. The pay seemed relatively low until you remembered that all the basics were taken care of and anything you earned could be spent on luxuries.

There were three shifts a day, each running eight hours, with the hours adjusted for the differences from Confederacy norm. The work week was six days, with the seventh off, but different industries took different days off so there was no universal off day. To make sure all worked well and smoothly, there was the Monitor Service.

I suspected it was this Monitor Service idea that got Talant Ypsir his one-way ticket from the Confederacy to the Diamond. Though I doubt if it would work on a thousand worlds spread over a quarter of a galaxy, the system worked fine, it seemed, on Medusa, though none of us liked it, least of all me.

Every single room in every single city and town was monitored. Not just the rooms, but the streets, alleyways, buses, you name it. Just about every single thing anyone said or did was monitored and recorded by a master computer or, really, the huge computer bank that was actually in orbit around the planet. Whoever wrote the computer program should be tortured to death.

Now, obviously, not even the galaxy's greatest computer could really analyze all that data, and this was where Ypsir was diabolically clever. The Monitor Service, a sort of police force that ran this system and was generally just called TMS, programmed the computers to look for certain things—phrases, actions, who except for them knew what?—that would cause a computer to "flag" you. Then a human TMS agent would sit down and with the computer's aid review anything about you he or she wanted, then haul you in to see why you were acting so funny or being so subversive. Nobody knew what the flag codes were, and a certain amount of totally random harassment was maintained by TMS just so the bright guys couldn't figure them out.

The system, as Kabaye pointed out proudly, did, in fact, work. Productivity was extremely high, absenteeism and shirking extremely low. Crime was almost nonexistent, except for the rare crime of passion which the computer couldn't flag in time to stop. But even if you managed to commit it, as soon as the crime was discovered the TMS could call up the whole scene and see exactly what was what.

Violators were tried in secret by TMS courts, extremely quickly it seemed, and given punishment ranging from demotion to being handed over to the psychs—many of whom were Confederacy crooks and sadists sentenced here themselves—for whatever they felt like doing to your mind. The ultimate punishment, for treason, was what was known as Ultimate Demotion—you were shipped off on a very unpleasant one-way trip to the mines of Momrath's moons.

It was an ugly system, and extremely difficult to fight or circumvent unless you knew exactly where the monitor devices were and what would and would not constitute a flag. That made it a near-impossible challenge, particularly for a kid whose background would suggest that he not be allowed too near any world leaders. In a sense, though, I liked it. Not only was this a real challenge, perhaps my supreme challenge; but Medusa was, after all, my type of world—technologically oriented and dependent on that technology. If I *could* find a way, too, the system would actually help. TMS, and, therefore, Talant Ypsir, must be pretty damn confident and secure.

But the more complex the challenge, the more I would have to know, and learn. This would not be easy by any means, and no mistakes would be tolerated by the system. It would take some time, perhaps a very long time, before I could confidently know enough to act.

After Kabaye's visit conversation was muted and sullen, to say the least. There were a number of attempts to figure out where the monitors were in the various rooms, but none of us found one that night.

Still, the third day's lessons proved to be pretty instructive as, one by one, even our most private whispers of the day before were repeated back to us by our hosts. Here was an effective demonstration of how efficient the fixed system really was—it selectively picked up one whisper even when masked by other whispers as well as fairly loud sounds. I was most interested in seeing pictures to check the angle and, therefore, locate the monitors; but we were shown none. We reached a general consensus that we were in one hell of a planetary jail cell, but there was nothing, at least for now, that any of us could do about it.

On the fourth day, we were tested and interviewed. Various officious-looking clerks wearing the same kind of military garb as Gorn and Sugra subjected us individually to a battery of tests that took much of the day. They then conducted general interviews.

At the end of the whole thing, each of us was taken into a small room we hadn't known about for a final interview.

She said her name was Dr. Crouda, and I knew immediately by her whites and her medical insignia that she had to be a psych. That really didn't bother me—not only was I trained and fortified against the general run of psych tricks, but I was in some ways the creation of the best psychs in the Confederacy. What I needed, though, was a good performance that would cement my cover and do me the most good overall.

She motioned me to a chair, sat back behind a small desk, and looked over my files for a moment. "You are Tarin Bul?"

I shuffled with kid fidgets in my seat. "Yes, ma'am."

"And you are fourteen?"

I nodded. "A few months ago. I'm not too sure of the time. It's been a real long time since I could remember anything but prisons and psychs—beg pardon, ma'am."

She nodded and couldn't suppress a slight smile. "I understand perfectly. Did you know that as far as we can tell you are the youngest person ever sent to the Warden Diamond?"

"I sorta guessed that," I answered truthfully.

"Your education and training and your genetic inclinations are toward administrative work, but you're hardly ready at your age. You realize that, don't you?"

Again I could only nod. "I understand." Right now, in the normal course of things, Tarin Bul would still be in school.

She sighed and looked over her reports. Real written files, I noted. How novel. "Now, your tests show a true inclination for math and a strong grasp of computer principles and operations. Have you given any thought to what you'd like to be?"

I thought a moment, choosing the best tack. Finally I settled on the one I thought most in character. "Lord of the Diamond," I told her.

Again the smile. "Well, I understand that. But, realistically, considering your abbreviated education and your likes and dislikes—is there anything you really find yourself drawn to?"

I thought a moment. "Yes, ma'am. Freighter pilot." That wasn't much of a risk, since it was right in character—but, oh how I wished I really *were* a freighter pilot! Money, mobility, status, and a lot more.

"That's not unreasonable," she said, thinking it over, "but you are a long way from the age at which you could even enter pilot training." She paused and threw me the typical psych curve. "Have you ever had any sexual experiences either with girls or with boys?"

I acted shocked. "No, ma'am!"

"What do you think of girls?"

I shrugged. "Oh, they're okay."

She nodded to herself and scribbled something, then asked, "How do you feel about being here? Being sent here, I mean?"

Again I shrugged. "Beats bein' dead, I guess. I haven't seen enough of this world to tell otherwise."

Again the nod and the scribble. "I think we have enough for now—Tarin, isn't it? You may go. Tomorrow someone will be in to talk to you, and then we'll know where you're going."

For now that sounded fair enough. I left.

I hadn't really had any problems with that battery they threw at me earlier. I had seen such tests before and understood exactly how they were weighted and scored. I had skewed my aptitudes upward in certain specific areas, like electronics and mechanics, as well as computers, while keeping the Tarin Bul background as consistent with what would be expected of my breeding and training. I could see and understand their problem with me, though. The fact was, I was too old to fit directly into their fixed planetary training system and too young to go to work properly. The best I could do was present myself as some sort of smart-ass genius and hope for the best.

On the fourth day my skin turned an orange-brown, as did that of four of the others. In a sense the change excited me, since I knew now for the first time that something major really *was* happening inside me; but it gave me a chilling feeling as well.

Gorn and Sugra were obviously pleased by the development, and the morning was spent with the five of us undergoing a few physical tests. The first one was simple and basic. I was dressed only in the flimsy hospital gown, when they took me out into that cold corridor and down to the first level of the building. For a while I thought they were pulling some kind of fast one—I felt a chill when the door opened and we stepped out, but the chill was rapidly replaced with a feeling of growing warmth and comfort, until I felt perfectly normal once again.

I was not normal, though, which I realized just by looking at the backs of my hands. The burnt orange quickly faded out, replaced by a more neutral grayish coloration. And yet, I *felt* normal—felt just fine, thank you, and as human as ever.

The first level was now staffed with a receptionist and a few people moved in and out; but the place was by no means crowded. We were the object of a few stares, but little else.

Satisfied that we felt all right, Gorn led the five of us outside into the street. Again there was that slightly chilling feeling, followed by a comforting warmth, and that was that. I felt warm as toast and perfectly comfortable despite the fact I was barefoot and wearing nothing more than a glorified bedsheet. In a sense, the test was reassuring, since some of the fear of the unknown and uncontrollable vanished with the realization that I really didn't feel unusual or extraordinary or different.

Satisfied with our progress, they led us back to our quarters. When I entered, I felt a really strong blast of heat, which faded as quickly as had the chill, leaving me feeling pretty much as I had in the street outside. Now at least I felt like a Medusan. I still wished they would tell us everything about this Warden transformation—I was quite sure they were withholding a lot of information on the theory that what you didn't know you couldn't use— but there was no way to approach the problem directly. I'd have to wait and learn in the streets, or by accident, dammit.

That afternoon those of us who had "acclimated"—as they called it—were summoned, one by one, into the small office. When my turn came I walked in, expecting another psych, but found instead a man I'd never seen before.

"Tarin Bul? I am Staff Supervisor Trin of the Transport Workers Guild. I'm told you have ambitions to be a pilot."

My emotions soared. "Yes, sir!"

"Well, that's possible. Your literacy level is off the scale, your mathematical level nearly that, and you have a command of computer theory far beyond any expectations. But your education is still not really advanced, and you'll need some more height and a couple of years of age before we can enroll you in pilot's school, if we do. However, you have been assigned to the Guild. Now, don't get your hopes up. You're coming in rather awkwardly—considering your age and experience, or lack of it. You don't quite fit. Nor do your tests really indicate a direction or focus. That means you're in the right Guild for your ambitions, but at the lowest level. We can't put you in school—you're too old for the integrated program and too young for advanced training. Therefore, it has been decided that you will be given a position—we call them slots—at the lowest level of the Guild, as well as administered self-study computer courses in a number of areas to allow you some preparation for the fuutre."

I nodded seriously. The rating wasn't as good as it could have been, but it was more than enough to start.

"The lowest levels require hard, unpleasant, boring work," he warned. "But you will be observed and, if you do well both at work and in your courses, you will be advanced accordingly. Whether you are advanced to pilot or driver training, or to some other area, will depend on your work habits, diligence, your supervisor's ratings, and how well you integrate yourself into our system. Understand?"

"Ah, yes, sir. Um . . . how old do you have to be to enter pilot's school?"

He smiled. "The minimum age is sixteen, the average age eighteen. The program is one year, then there's an additional year of in-service apprentice work before you can be considered for full licensing."

I nodded. Still, while trying to convince the man that I was more than eager to work my way up and please everybody for the next two years, the back of my mind said "two years" in a far different tone. Two years was a long, long time. . . .

CHAPTER FOUR

Workin' on the Railroad

The next day I was given a small card that bore a number and a symbol on the front and had a series of dots of some magnetic material on the back. The symbol was a bolt of lightning flanked by two solid black lines—rails, it seemed. The symbol of the Transportation Guild. True to their word at the initial briefing, I also received a set of tailored uniforms in my size. They were in the satiny red color of the Guild and bore the same symbol on the pocket. A small suitcase contained some basic toiletries, including, I found, a razor, something I wouldn't need for a while. Also included was a pair of red rubber-soled shoes, just to improve footing on the smooth floors and sidewalks of the city.

The card contained my name, new address, Guild, work assignment, and various control numbers. It was even my bankbook. The Central Bank of Gray Basin held an account in my name. Every time I wanted to pay for something I had to stick my card in the appropriate slot and the amount would automatically be deducted from my account. I was impressed. Pretty much like home, although my bank stake was only a hundred units.

The basic currency was the unit—work unit, I assumed —which was broken into a hundred smaller divisions called bits. A pretty standard decimal system. Things must be fairly cheap.

Beyond that I received some insincere "good lucks" from Gorn and Sugra and some far more sincere ones from my eight comrades, now all turned, or acclimated, to the Warden organism. I picked up a bus-route map of the city that told me how to get to where I had to be, and

51

that was it. Clutching my small overnight case, I was out the door and on the streets of the big city.

Once temperature was no longer a problem, the city seemed much like those domed cities I'd been in on several other worlds. Factories and such were easy to spot by their design, but mostly because their exhaust vents went straight up to the illuminated ceiling and on through it. With temperatures fairly well equalized inside and out, there was no problem with frost, although occasional ice crystals floated in the air. Curiously, my breath did not show in the cold. I wondered just what the hell that bug had made us into, since I was pretty sure I was still a warm-blooded mammal.

The buses were pretty easy to find, and in their automated style worked very well. The locals seemed to be guided by single magnetic strips buried within the street paving itself and ran on rubberized tires—synthetic, of course. They had sensors at the clearly marked and color-coded bus stops and would stop if anyone was within the painted stop zones. The door was something of a turnstile, unlocking when you stuck your card in the side slot and passing you through without giving any opportunity for a second person to sneak by—an interesting indication to me that this place wasn't as crime-free and rock honest as had been made out. I suspected a lot of petty crimes were attempted even by ordinarily honest folk. It was just about the only way you had to feel like you were getting back at the system.

The bus was not only comfortable, it had a handy map above the windshield that illuminated where it was on its route and where the transfer points were. With that and my own set of directions I had no trouble crossing town, changing twice and winding up exactly where I was supposed to be. There was something, certainly, to be said for Medusan efficiency.

During the ride I just sat back and studied the city and the people. They looked a rather ordinary lot, all dressed in these identical uniforms, color- and badge-coded as to guild and grade. It took no real detective work to figure out that the militarylike rank and uniforms of Gorn and Sugra were those of the dreaded TMS, who certainly had to socialize only among their own. Whenever a green fatigue uniform was visible, you could see everybody else pretending to ignore it but shying away fast. And TMS people, of course, radiated arrogant disdain for the masses and joy in knowing they were powerful and feared. The cops were certainly the enemy here, and for good reason. I had never seen a system with police force more in control of things. Idly I wondered how you entered TMS—and who were *they* afraid of?

Around the city's core, with its office buildings and cooperative shops and markets and central terminal, the residential and manufacturing areas were arranged in something of a pie-wedge design. The wedges seemed to alternate between heavy industry and residential units, all of which were four-story affairs composed of what looked like identical apartments. I later learned this was not the case, however. Family units had one room per family member over twelve, so some were fairly large suites; and the top grades had pretty swanky suites just for themselves.

My own destination was T-26, a unit that looked much like all the others. I punched the stop button and jumped off as the building number went past the window, which meant I had to backtrack a block. I hesitated only a moment, then walked up and entered the main entrance.

The place was like a dormitory. The ground floor had a lobby with computer screens giving general information, including schedule changes and even sports scores. A pair of double doors led to a common dining hall. Apparently the residents of the building ate here, cafeteria-style, although the food was certainly prepared elsewhere. There wasn't much room for a kitchen.

Doors on either side led to communal stores. There was a small pharmacy, a tailor, a shoe shop, and the like. Apparently they were only open one hour on each side of each shift change. They also couldn't be very large, I told myself, as it wouldn't be efficient to have actual stores in each building unit. Each was staffed by one clerk, who simply took in what you had—shoes to be fixed, for example, or an order for toiletries and such—then sent them to a central store which had the shoes fixed or filled the order. What you wanted was ready when you came back from a shift. Not a bad system. If it wasn't for TMS I might actually be impressed by this place, I told myself.

There was a small elevator cage at each end of the hall, too, I noticed, so I would not have to climb the stairs.

My instructions said I was to report first to T-26, Room 404—which, I assumed, was on the fourth floor—and get settled. I would be contacted there and told where to go and what to do next.

Room 404 was where it should logically have been. Since there was no key, only a card slot, I inserted my card and the door slid open.

It was a small room, about five meters by four, but it had been sensibly laid out by somebody who'd obviously done hotel work. The two beds looked comfortable and standard—after the cell and then those barracks cots they looked wonderful—and there were two reasonably spacious closets, plenty of drawers along the wall opposite the beds, and a CRT terminal that was unfamiliar in design but pretty easy to figure out.

A side door led to a toilet, shower, and basin, which, I saw, we shared with the room next to us. I say "we" simply because when I looked in the closets, then in the drawers, somebody's stuff was already in them. The owner didn't appear to be much bigger than I from the size of the clothes, but I'd have to wait and see.

Although the room monitors were cleverly concealed to blend in with the surroundings, they weren't hard to locate. The one in the bathroom was in the center of the overhead light, and the one in the main room was almost certainly integrated into the centrally located smoke and fire detector. I wondered idly if they had the closets covered. Though the idea seemed pretty ridiculous they probably did. Ypsir and his TMS apparently had that kind of mind.

I checked the computer terminal for messages but there were none apparent. I didn't yet have the codes needed to call up the less routine stuff. Since I had received no instructions beyond coming here and waiting, I put my stuff away in an empty drawer and stowed the overnight bag in one of the closets, then went back to the terminal and gave it a good going-over. It was extremely primitive by my standards, but *did* have the basics, both keyboard and voxcoder for two-way communication. The thing was a combination terminal and telephone, possibly even a picturephone. Considering the obvious technical limitations the Confederacy imposed on the Warden Diamond, this really was a slick piece of home-grown work. After deciding I didn't have the proper tools to disassemble the frame and see what really made the machine tick, I abandoned it for the time being, walked over to the bed, leaned back, and relaxed in the nice, downy softness. I promptly fell asleep.

I was awakened perhaps two hours later by the sound of the door *whooshing* back to admit someone. Deciding that discretion was the better part of valor and all that, I remained motionless, curious to see who it might be. My eyes opened wide and I sat straight up when I saw the newcomer. I really hadn't been prepared for this.

"Oh, hello!" she said, spotting me. "You must be Tarin Bul."

The girl was very young—I couldn't really tell how young—quite small and slightly built, hair cropped as short as my own. I was still sitting up in bed, staring, mouth agape, trying to adjust to the fact that she was a she, when she started removing her uniform.

"Hey!" I cried out, feeling very awkward indeed. I was no prude, but societies have rules and the one I came from wasn't quite *this* casual.

She stopped, a little puzzled. "What's the matter?" And she meant it.

"Um—you're taking off your clothes in front of a perfect stranger."

The idea struck her as funny. "Oh, you're supposed to take yours off, too. The Monitor should have told you. I guess somebody's asleep at the switch today." She finished removing the last of her clothing, which she folded into a small ball, then opened a drawer, from which she removed a plastic bag, stuffing in the clothes. "Below Supervisor grade it's not permitted to wear uniforms in your home dorm. Don't you know *that?*"

I shook my head slowly, trying to decide if I was being put on. My wits returning, I realized that what she was telling me made perfect sense from the TMS viewpoint. You couldn't carry in anything without taking it out of your clothing first, and being totally nude was the ultimate invasion of privacy, somehow. Now, I'd gone nude in mixed company many times, usually on plush resort worlds with seaside villas, and never thought anything of it. But this was a whole different kind of experience, and it took some getting used to.

She held out the bag. "Come on—before the Monitor sees you. Off and in the bag."

I sighed and decided that it wouldn't be in character if I caved in too easily. "But—you're a *girl!*" I was suddenly very cautious, mentally. The mere fact that I *hadn't* been called on such a rule indicated to me that they were observing my behavior and how I acclimated socially. The fact that I was fourteen was some protection, but it wasn't total. I had to assume that any government capable of putting a superhuman robot in the most secret rooms of Military Systems Command could easily know about the Merton Process and deduce the truth given half a chance.

She stood up straight and shook her head at me in wonder. "Are all people Outside so shy and upset by so simple a thing?"

Her question told me two facts straight off, if she was indeed what she seemed. First, she was a native of this world, and, second, I was the first person from "Outside"— that is, outside the Warden Diamond, and maybe even outside of Medusa—she'd ever met. Ordinarily such knowledge would give me some advantage and leeway in slips, but I couldn't assume that whoever was monitoring me was as inexperienced or naive.

I sighed, gave in, and removed my clothes, tossing them into the common bag. She tied the bag off and left it on the floor. "I'm Ching Lu Kor," she introduced herself. "Ah— you *are* Tarin Bul?"

I nodded nervously. "Uh huh."

She looked me over mock-critically. "You're not so bad. I always heard people Outside were all soft and flabby, but you look pretty good."

I shuffled nervously, creating my proper *persona* as I went. "Uh—I haven't had a lot of exercise in a while, but I made do."

She sat down on the corner of the bed opposite mine. "What'd you do to get sent here? Or shouldn't I ask that?"

I shrugged and sat back on my bed. "I executed the murderer of my father," I told her. "Nobody else would."

She frowned and appeared to be a little taken aback by that. Clearly a crime of that magnitude was hard for someone brought up in a totalitarian world like Medusa to fathom. But clearly she understood the implications of the act, even if it seemed impossible to her. She even seemed impressed. A romantic, I decided.

"Are you hungry?" she asked suddenly, getting away from the subject. "I'm starved—I've just come off shift. You're lucky—no work until 1600 tomorrow." She jumped up from the bed. "Come on. We have to drop off the laundry anyway. Then you can tell me all about Outside, and I can tell you all about here."

That seemed a fair trade, but I decided some hesitation was in order. "We go eat—like this?"

She laughed. "You really *are* hung up, aren't you? They'll have a psych on you if you don't relax a little." She turned and waved at the room. "Besides, somebody's *always* looking at you anyway. What's the difference?"

She had a point there. I let her pick up the clothes bag and followed her out the door, then stopped. "Hey—what about the cards?"

Obviously I had said something funny again. "You don't need cards in your own *home*," she responded as she headed for the stairs.

She was certainly right about nudity. Old, young, male, female—everyone walked about and sat and talked with no inhibitions at all. Here and there would be people in uniform, either somebody with rank who wanted everybody else to remember it or those still coming in from work or leaving for it. Apparently there were staggered start times for the shifts within the two-hour active period, probably to ease the mass-transit load.

The cafeteria was about half full, with the usual eating-place bustle and unintelligible mass-conversation buzz. There were no menu choices, I found—you went up, punched a button, got a covered tray, then went to a table and sat down. Water and a selection of three beverages at a self-service area in the center of the cafeteria provided the only option.

The food was unfamiliar but tasted pretty good. I was never very fussy about food and was certainly no gourmet, so I adjusted to this as easily as if I'd eaten the stuff all my life. After the jail mush and blocky slop of the reception center it was a real pleasure to have a recognizable plate with entrée, vegetables, and dessert. The meat seemed a standard synthetic, but the fruit and vegetable appeared fresh. I remembered that Medusa imported a fair amount of food from the warmer worlds category. Keep the masses happy, I thought, even if they *can* eat tree bark.

I was struck by a number of things as I sat there eating, including at least one fact that amazed me. Here were these people in the most totalitarian society I'd ever known or experienced, and they were sitting back, relaxed, talking, looking, and sounding for all the world like any cafeteria crowd anyplace—except, of course, for their bare hides. Far from making me relax more about Medusa, the observation that here was a totalitarian society that *worked* —worked so well that the generations born and raised into it felt completely at ease—made me nervous. I had to admit that Talant Ypsir might be an unpleasant individual, but he was damned smart.

My other observations were on the more practical side. Medusans *looked* about as human as anybody else, particularly a frontier world population. Yet subtle differences that might otherwise go unnoticed were immediately apparent to an Outsider such as myself. The skin textures seemed far more leathery, somehow; the hair was also far stiffer, wiry. Even the eyes seemed somehow different, almost as if shaped by a master sculptor out of marble, without the shine and liquidity of human eyes.

I knew that I, too, now shared these characteristics, yet I felt perfectly normal, not in the least bit changed. My skin had the same look as the skin of those around me, yet it felt normal, soft, and natural to me.

A third observation was that I was the youngest-looking person in the cafeteria, although several very young people were there. Well, nothing to do but get to know my roommate a bit more. She certainly seemed anxious to get to know me.

"How old are you?" she asked. "They told me you were young, but I figured you'd be my age."

My eyebrows rose. "How old *are* you?"

"Sixteen two weeks ago," she told me proudly. "That's when I started work here."

"Well, I'm close to fifteen," I answered her initial question, stretching the truth a bit. There's far less of a gap between fifteen and sixteen than between fourteen and sixteen. I wanted to press a bit further on her comment, though. "Who told you about me? And how come you and me are together here?"

She sighed. "They really didn't tell you *anything*, did they? Okay, three weeks ago I was just graduated and still in Huang Bay—that's way south of here—with my family. I knew I was going to get assigned soon, though, and, sure enough, my orders came through. I was inducted into the Transport Guild and sent here to start work. About a week ago I was called down to the Supervisor's office and told that I was being paired with one Tarin Bul, a young man sent here from Outside, and that the two of us would work as a pair thereafter. They also told me you'd have some ideas and ways I might find strange—and that's certainly true. In fact, all this is still a little strange to me, although it's the same kind of setup I grew up in. My assignment's inside, though, and away from the water."

"Huang Bay's on the equator, then?" I knew where it was exactly thanks to the handy map in my head, but it was a logical question.

She nodded. "Nearly, anyway. It's a lot prettier than here, with all sorts of flowers and trees. Not that this is really bad, though. No animal or insect problems, and the fruit's fresher." She paused a moment. "Still, I kind of miss home and family and all that."

I understood perfectly. Although I'd never been raised in any sort of family atmosphere, or had any close personal attachments, I could well see how someone who had been would be very lonely and homesick in this situation. That she accepted the wrench in her life so unquestioningly, said something important about the society. That wrench also explained why she was glad to see me.

We put our trays in the disposal, dropped the laundry by the small window that now had a uniformed attendant, then went back upstairs. We would see the rest of the place later; now it was time to get to know each other better, and for me to start learning the rules.

Apparently once the door was activated by a card the first time it opened when it recognized you, because the room door slid back and we walked in. First Ching checked the room terminal, then, finding it still blank, sank back down on the bed and looked at me. It was far too soon for me to do anything but sit on the other. I didn't wait for an opening, though.

"You said downstairs that we were paired—does that mean what I think it does?" I asked her.

"Depends on what you think it means. Everybody's paired who hasn't started or joined a family group. From here on in, we do everything together. Eat, sleep, go out, work—even our cards have identical account codes, so we can spend each other's money."

I gave a wan smile. "What if we don't get along?"

"Oh, we will. The State ran us through a lot of checks with their big computers and came up with us. The State doesn't make mistakes."

I certainly hoped that wasn't true; frankly, I knew it wasn't. But what the hell. "That might be true for native-born Medusans, but they can't know as much about me as they do about somebody born and raised here." And how! At least—I hoped not.

She seemed upset. "You mean you don't like me?"

"Now, I didn't say that. I think I could learn to like you a lot, but I don't really know you yet, and you don't know me. And I don't know Medusa at all—which should be obvious."

My seeming honesty calmed her a little. "I guess you're right. But there's so little *to* know about Medusa."

"That's only because you were born and raised here. What you take for granted I don't recognize at all. This pairing, for example—is it always a girl and a boy?"

My question got her giggling a bit again. "That's silly. You put *any* two in a pair and one of 'em's gonna be a girl."

"How's that?" Now I was genuinely confused. There was something here I was missing, and it was tough to find.

She sighed and tried to summon patience without sounding patronizing, but she didn't quite make it. "I still don't see what your problem is. I mean, I was a boy once myself and it was no big thing."

"What!" But with my surprise came the dawn, and with

a lot more gingerly asked half-questions I managed to find the key. The key was the basic Warden precept on Medusa: survival.

Unlike the rest of the Warden Diamond, on Medusa the Warden organism was not all-pervasive. It depended upon the living creatures, plant and animal, of Medusa for its survival. On places like Lilith and Charon the little buggers were in the rocks and trees and everything, but here they concentrated only on animal life forms—and they changed those life forms to insure their own survival. That meant Wardens couldn't reproduce beyond their host's capacity without deforming that host and making the host less likely to survive in general. Thus, there was a premium on making certain that the bisexual humans—and animals, too, it seemed—reproduced as well.

Children were born basically neuter, although physiologically they would be classed as female, I suppose. When puberty hit, between ten and thirteen years of age, they acquired sexual characteristics based on the group with which they lived and with whom they most frequently associated. The vast majority, perhaps seventy-five percent, of the people of Medusa were female since you needed more females than males to assure regular reproduction.

Frankly, I hadn't been out in Medusan society enough for this concept to have sunk in, but, thinking back to the groupings on the buses and even in the cafeteria, it *had* seemed that there were an awful lot of women. . . .

"Let me get this straight," I said at last, trying to sort things out. "If we were to, say, join one of these group families, and it already had its share of men, I might change sex?"

She nodded. "Sure. Happens all the time. Nobody thinks much of it, really."

"Well, *I* do," I told her. "Everywhere else, even in the Diamond, I'm told, if you're born male you stay male and if you're born female you stay female. This system is going to take some getting used to."

The sociological implications were staggering, but beyond that it raised a broader question: if the Warden organism could undertake as major a change as *that* in, apparently, a very short time, what else could it do? The potential was there for making Medusans totally self-deter-

mining malleables—if they could control the Wardens,
rather than being controlled by them. If that were somehow possible, you could literally change your appearance
by willpower, become anybody—or the semblance of any
thing—you wanted. I raised the possibility with her.

"There're always stories about that sort of stuff, like
out with the Wild Ones, but nobody I know has ever seen
it. Not because you *order* it, anyway. Sometimes that kind
of thing just *happens,* but it's nothing anybody can control."

The whole idea excited me. Anything that can just happen can somehow be controlled, particularly on a world
with computers, psychs, and other modern mind- and body-
control techniques. I would bet my life that Ypsir either
had top researchers working on it or else had already
figured out the means to do it. Of course, if that were true
then you couldn't trust anybody's appearance. But I could
understand why the ability would be very sparingly used
and the very idea of it tightly suppressed, even ridiculed. A
total society of malleables would bring this totalitarian state
crashing down easily. I was beginning to see some possibilities here after all. But I couldn't dwell on the subject.
Not now, particularly.

"The Wild Ones? Who are they?"

"Crazy people," she told me. "Savages. They live out
there in the wild, outside the State. They're a pretty primitive, pitiful bunch, very superstitious and spending all their
time just staying alive. I know—I've seen some of 'em."

I frowned, more interested than puzzled, but appearances
were everything in this business. "But where did they come
from? I mean, are they exiles from the State? Castoffs?
Runaways? What?"

She shrugged. "Nobody's sure, but they've been there
since before the State was even founded. Most likely they're
the descendants of early settlers, explorers, or whatever,
who got cut off from civilization."

I didn't really believe that, but I *could* believe they were
people—and the children and grandchildren of people—
who just couldn't abide the State and its increasing control
and had opted out. I had no doubt they were as primitive
as Ching described them—this was a hard, nasty world—
but some would consider that life preferable to this fishbowl

existence. It was handy to know they were there, and help-ful, too, to know that the Medusan State extended only to the cities, towns, and transport networks and left most of the rest of the planet wild and free. I didn't particularly like the idea of grubbing in snow for branches and roots, but knowing this gave me an option—and on Medusa, right then, I badly needed options of any kind, even unappeal-ing ones.

I turned the conversation back to Ching. Best not to dwell on anything of real interest, lest unseen watchers grow suspicious. There would be plenty of time to extract additional information in bits and pieces.

"How come you're here in a basic job?" I asked her. "I *know* why I'm here—I don't quite fit anyplace right now, and won't until I'm older. But you were born here. What kind of job is it you have, anyway?"

She was more comfortable on this subject. "I—we—clean and restock trains and occasionally buses. It's pretty easy work, really."

I was surprised again. "Don't they have robots to do that sort of thing?"

She giggled yet again. "No, silly! Oh sure, they use indus-trial robots a lot, but in complicated passenger places like trains and buses it takes a human to clean up after another human. Besides, the State doesn't believe that just because a machine *can* do a job it is good or healthy for machines to do it."

That sounded like a recitation of holy writ, but it was okay with me. We were both janitors—so what? But she hadn't answered my first question.

"You're a smart girl," I told her, only partly flattering her, "and you speak very well. You have an educated vocabulary. So how come you're down here with us low-graders?"

She sighed and looked a little uncomfortable.

"If you'd rather not tell me, I will understand," I said soothingly.

"No, it's all right. I'm adjusted to it now. And yes, you're right, they say my IQ's way up there—but it's not much good to me. You see, back a long time ago, maybe when I was born or even before, something funny happened in my head. They say it's like a short circuit in an electrical line, only the affected area is so tiny they can't find it and fix it. In most things I'm just as normal as anybody else. But when I look at words, or bunches of letters, they get all mixed up, somehow." She pointed to the computer terminal. "I can do fine on that thing with voxcoder. But I look at the keys and they all just sorta run around in my head. I can understand the voice fine, but I get all mixed up when anything's printed on the screen." She shook her head sadly and sighed once more. "So you're looking at the smartest illiterate on Medusa, I guess."

I could understand her problem—and the State's. In a technological society, it was necessary to know how to read. No matter how you cut it, it was necessary to read the repair manuals, or trace an engineering diagram, or follow procedures for getting out of a burning building. On any of the civilized worlds she might have been treated, although this sort of thing—"dyslexia," it was called—had never been wiped out. Still, it didn't quite make sense to me, considering the holy Wardens.

"How come the Wardens don't fix it?" I asked her. "I thought nobody gets sick or has problems."

She shrugged. "The experts they sent me to say it's because I was born with it. Maybe it was the way I was made up, and the Wardens think that's the way I should be. They finally said that even if they found it and fixed it my Wardens would probably un-fix it, 'cause they think the way it is, is the way it should be. I learned to accept my handicap, but it drove me crazy, mainly 'cause I was smarter than most of them who got good test grades and are now in school working toward good jobs."

I could sympathize with her on several counts. Anybody could sympathize with the frustration of being smart and also restricted, but I realized that this Warden business was kind of tricky on birth defects. It proved to me that only genetically engineered humans were truly moral or practical—not that I needed any proof, since I was the product of genetic engineering myself and so was Tarin Bul.

"So does that mean you're stuck being a waitress or janitor or something else like that?" I asked her. "Doing those jobs machines can't or don't do but which require no reading?"

"Oh, I can do a little better than that, if I prove it," she answered confidently. "After all, if I can *talk* to a computer and the computer can *talk* back I can still use it okay. But, yeah, you're right. Beyond a certain point there are lots of jobs I *could* do but literate persons could do a little faster or more efficiently, so they get the jobs. But that's not what I'm supposed to do anyway, after a while. Why do you think they paired us, anyway?"

I thought a moment. "Because neither of us fit?"

She laughed at that. "No—well, maybe. I hadn't thought of that. But eventually we're supposed to found a family group. I'll be the Base Mother—I'll maintain the house and take care of the kids. And I'll be able to teach 'em when they're young, and nobody's gonna mind if I need a vox to do the budget. It's not so bad. Better than being in a dead-end job, or any of the alternatives, like being a Goodtime Girl or working the mines of the moons of Momrath."

Aha! Another set of pieces fall into place. "Then, in a way, we're married. At our age!"

She gave me a big smile. "I guess you can say that. Sort of. Why? When do people marry Outside?"

"Well, mostly they don't," I told her honestly. "Most people are genetically engineered to do a particular thing and to do it better than anything else. You were raised by specialists and trained for what you're going to do, then you do it. But, yeah, there are *some* marriages." All types, too, but there was no use complicating things for her. "Most people don't bother, though."

She nodded. "They teach us something about Outside, but it's really hard to imagine anyplace else than here. I know a couple of people who've been to Cerberus, and that's strange enough. They switch minds and bodies all the time and live on trees in the water. Crazy."

Body-switching, I thought. My counterpart there must be having a field day. "That sounds pretty weird to me, too," I assured her. "But maybe one day I'll see it. They think when I'm old enough I can become a pilot."

That romanticism lurking inside her peered out of her face again. "A pilot. Wow. Have you ever flown anything before?"

I shook my head from side to side. "No," I lied, "not really. Oh, my father occasionally let me take the controls once we were underway, and I know everything there is to know about flying. But, I mean, I was just twelve when I got arrested."

That brought my past back into focus, and, as I suspected, she was trying not to think in that direction. Still, she asked, "If you were born in a lab or something and raised in a group, how could you have a father?"

That was an intelligent question. I was becoming more and more impressed with her. "Those of us in certain positions, like politics and administration, have to have some kind of family so we can learn how things work and make the personal contacts we need," I explained. "So, when we're five, we're adopted by someone in the position we're intended to be in someday. Sometimes it's just business, but sometimes we grow real close, like me and my father." Acting time, boy—give a good performance. Face turns angry, maybe a hint of bitterness in my voice. "Yeah—like me and my father," I repeated slowly.

She looked suddenly nervous. "I'm sorry. I won't bring it up again unless *you* want to."

I snapped out of my mood. At least the performance was good enough for her. "No, that's all right. He was a great man and I don't want to forget him—ever. But that was long ago and it's over. Here and now is what's important." I paused for dramatic effect, then cleared my throat, sniffled a little, and changed the subject. "What about these Goodtime Girls? What are they?"

She seemed relieved at the opportunity to get out of a sticky situation. I hoped I'd just laid to rest a lot of otherwise inevitable prying about a past I really didn't have, the area most likely to trip me up. "Goodtime Girls is a general title for the entertainer class. It's a dead end, but they're put under psych so they don't think much." She shivered. "I don't want to talk about them. They're necessary, of course, and serve a need of the State, but it's not anything I'd like." She suddenly yawned, tried to repress it, couldn't, then shook her head. "Sorry. It's getting near my bedtime, I guess. I usually like to sleep in the middle of the off-time, so I have time before work to do things. If you want to do it differently we'll have to work something out."

"That's all right," I assured her. "I'll adjust to your schedule for now. You get some sleep—I'll manage. If I can't drift off, maybe I'll just explore the dorm for a while and see whatall is here. I'll need a couple of days to make the shift to this sleep time."

She nodded sleepily and yawned again. "If you *do* go out, don't go beyond the inside of the dorm, though. It's a rule that pairs should do everything together." Again a yawn.

"That's all right. I'll be good," I assured her good-naturedly. "I have a good teacher."

I let her crawl into bed and she was soon fast asleep. I did not go out, at least not then. Instead I just lay there, thinking about all the new material I had to sort through, what I had learned, what I had to work with, and what potentialities might be here for mischief.

Ching was going to be an invaluable asset at the start, that was for sure. She was smart, romantic, and a knowledgeable native guide. But in the long run she would be a problem. You can't overthrow a system or set up the assassination of a Lord of the Diamond when you have for a constant companion someone raised always to believe in and trust in the system. As a romantic, she might easily wind up falling in love with me—which would be okay—but that would also mean that she might just turn me in to TMS for my own good.

There were ways, although they'd take some time and ingenuity. But talk about long-range planning! The only way to separate Ching and myself, obviously, was to get her pregnant and stick her home with the kid. And I was only fourteen and a half years old and still technically a virgin. . . .

CHAPTER FIVE

A Friendly Chat with TMS

My job was, in fact, as easy as Ching had made it out to be. Machines still did the real work—we just guided and directed them and made complete inspections of the passenger cars, buses, and train-crew quarters simply because humans will stick things and drop things and wedge things in places no machine would ever think of looking, let alone cleaning. How many times was I guilty of sticking stuff under a seat or between cushions just because it was convenient? It might be healthy if everyone had to spend a couple of months cleaning trains and buses before being allowed to ride them.

Ching was so happy to have a friend at last and something solid to hang on to that she was far more pleasure than inconvenience. Hoping to get us involved in Guild hobbies and recreational activities, she took full advantage of our off time to show me the city and its services and frills, which were quite a bit more elaborate than I had expected.

Gray Basin was nicely laid out once you understood the initial logic of it, and this, she assured me, was pretty much how all cities on Medusa were laid out, even the ones above ground. Just about everything was prefabricated, which allowed for expansion, change, and growth with a minimum of displacement and trauma. Everything, everywhere, just sort of fit together.

There was theater, well-mounted if heavy on the musical fluff mixed with propaganda and duty to the State, and you could punch up an extensive library of books on your dorm terminal, even order a hard copy for delivery for a small sum. The books were heavy on technical and practical subjects and not much on literature and politics, for obvious reasons—no use contaminating fresh minds.

Far less fettered were art galleries, which contained some of the finest human art and sculpture anywhere—no surprise, because most of them had been stolen from the best museums of the Confederacy and were here more or less on protective loan. A substantial native art group was allowed to do just about anything without State interference as long as the themes weren't political, at least, not political in a way that contradicted the official line. There was music, too, even an entire Medusan symphony orchestra—one of many, I was assured—that fascinated me by performing great compositions from man's far past that I had never heard or heard of, as well as newer and more experimental stuff. I had to admit that, somehow, living people creating music was somehow better, more alive and pleasing, than the expert and flawless computer musicons I had grown used to in the Confederacy. The musicians had their own guild, headed by a woman who, it was said, had come to Medusa voluntarily. An expert musicologist and musician herself, she was an anachronism back in the Confederacy, but she had known Talant Ypsir and had joined him in exile when he offered the carrot of a real, primitive, wide-open musical program that would be planetwide.

As for our own dorm, it had its own basic activities, and we had use of Guild common facilities like gyms and playing fields. A number of sports teams were organized around both intra-guild and inter-guild rivalries, and they certainly were a help both in meeting other people regardless of grade and for keeping in shape. In fact, the only Guild that didn't seem to have teams or outside activities was TMS. I was told that they *had* tried it, once, in a campaign to give them a friendlier, more human face, but it had been a disastrous failure. You just can't relax and have fun with a group whose members could do nasty things to you if you so much as protested a call.

Besides, even TMS didn't find it much of a challenge to win every game they played, no matter how lousy they'd played. So, they kept to themselves, being their normal prying, lousy selves, and everyone tried to ignore them as much as possible.

In truth, working and playing with Ching, I almost *did*

feel fourteen years old once again, and I really enjoyed it
—but not to the point of not concentrating on my main
task, which was to put together a plan that would eventually dispose of Talant Ypsir. I pretty much gave up my
ideas of doing anything beyond that—although that was
surely enough!—because of the restrictive nature of the
society. They could be entertaining aliens and churning out
humanoid superrobots in every third office building in Gray
Basin, and I would neither know it or have any real way
of finding out.

Still, any move against the government of Medusa would
have to be based upon what was, as of now, only a theoret-
ical possibility. The society was locked in too tight, and was
too well run, to do any real damage unless the monitor
system could be negated. To do that, I would somehow
have to learn if this malleability principle was really possible, and, if so, how to take advantage of it myself.

Just how closely we were monitored was brought home
at our every-other-week private sessions with a liaison
between the Guild and TMS. We were generally asked to
explain this or that action or comment we had made, often
out in the open. I quickly understood that this was not
really an inquisition, nor were we accused of sedition or
any sort of wrongdoing—it was merely a reminder that we
were always observed, and, as such, better just start totally
accepting the system and thinking and acting right at all
times.

Close to the end of my third month on Medusa I had
become increasingly aware of changes in both Ching and
myself—physiological changes that were hard to ignore.
When I'd first met her, she'd been thin and spindly and,
while cute, not really what you'd call well endowed. She
was filling out now, and it didn't take long to realize that
this was no late pubescent growth but a direct Warden
action in reaction to my stimulus. She was fast becoming
an extremely sexy woman with all the right equipment.
Clearly the hormonal triggers the Wardens employed to
bring about the physical changes were also having the expected psychological effects.

As for me, I was undergoing the same sort of transformation. I was filling out, becoming hard, lean, and muscular, sprouting body hair, and experiencing substantial sexual

sensations. This helped my overall plan in the sense that I was beginning to look less like a fourteen-year-old kid. It also helped in that playing the role of the sexually repressed kid was driving me nuts anyway. Still, I was kind of nervous. It was within my acting abilities to simulate almost anything, but the role of a fourteen-year-old inexperienced virgin might well be beyond me. Fortunately, it was Ching who finally brought up the subject, and also allayed my real fears on that score.

"Tarin?"

"Uh huh?"

"Do you feel—anything—when you look at me?"

I thought a moment. "You're a pretty girl and a good friend."

"No, I mean—well, *beyond* that. I do when I look at you most times. Real funny feelings, if you know what I mean."

"Maybe," I answered cautiously.

"Uh . . . Tarin? Have you ever . . . made love to a girl before?"

I acted startled at the question. "I was twelve when they arrested me. When did I ever have a chance?" I hesitated a moment. "Have *you?*"

She looked suitably shocked. "Oh, *no!* What do you think I am? A Goodtime Girl?"

I laughed, walked over to her, and patted her soothingly. "Take it easy. So we're both new at it." Or very good liars, I thought. Still, she sounded sincere, which made the job much simpler. In a society where sex is generally available to all, one of the more boring things is watching two people make it through some kind of closed-circuit hookup. Even if TMS got their jollies that way, we'd be such a small and uninteresting lot considering the whole population it would hardly be worth noticing. But if she were experienced, *she* could tell.

And so, finally, tentatively, we made love, and that was a real mental release for me. As for Ching, she was in fact awkward and inexperienced and the whole thing was new to her, but she wound up with a happy and radiant high the likes of which I'd never seen before. In the days that followed the psychological changes in her were incredible. She was happier, far more self-confident, and given to spontaneous and automatic displays of affection, even on the job. This was a bit embarrassing at times; I wasn't used to such displays, let's face it, nor to any kind of attachment. I'd always been a loner and proud of it—you had to be in my kind of business.

But we had sex a lot, which only reinforced everything.

On a different note, I found an electronics hobby club sponsored by the Guild, and actively joined it. It occurred to me that this was the best way I had to see the engineering philosophy behind Medusa's society, and it would give me access to the tools to counter that technological threat when the time finally came.

That time was bothering me, though. Here it was three months along and I was really not ready to begin. I was still outside the establishment, still denied the tools and positions I needed, and even more cemented into the fairly pleasant daily regimen of low-grade Guild work. I had as much information and as much access to tools and technology as I needed to perform my duties, and I would get no more without some really dramatic or radical changes, changes I simply could not initiate.

Interestingly enough, TMS provided me with the kick in the rear I needed. We were returning from work one day, holding hands and talking about nothing much, coming across the street from the bus stop to the dorm, when a small vehicle pulled up across the street and its driver looked over at us. Now, individual vehicles were rare enough to cause attention and apprehension, and there was no mistaking the military green of the woman at the controls or that look of inner power on her face.

We tried to ignore her as best we could, but the TMS agent got out of the car and walked briskly and confidently toward us. When it became obvious that we were the object of her attention, we stopped. Ching gripped my hand so tightly I thought it was going to be pulled off.

"Tarin Bul?" the Monitor asked, although she knew who I was from the time she'd left her headquarters.

I nodded. "Yes?"

"This is a routine check. Ching Lu Kor, you will proceed to the dorm and go through your normal routine. He should be back in a few hours."

"Shouldn't I go with him?" Ching protested. "I mean, we're *paired*. . . ."

Brave girl, I thought, but I said, "No, it's all right, I'm sure this is just routine, Ching. You go on. I'll tell you all about it when I get back."

She let go of my hand, hesitantly, and seemed to appeal to the Monitor with her eyes—but met only a steely blank response. The Monitor turned and walked back to the car and I followed, after kissing Ching lightly and giving her a reassuring pat and squeeze. But she was still standing there, looking frightened and upset, as the Monitor and I climbed into the car and sped smoothly out and away from the Guild sector.

It was the first time I'd been in an independent vehicle since coming to Medusa, and I paid a good deal of attention to how the officer drove the car. It seemed a simple affair, basically electric-powered and limited to city duty, with a small steering wheel and one-knob accelerator and brake. There was also an on-off switch, I noted, but no key or code pad. These TMS folks were pretty confident.

I knew I was supposed to be terrified and all that, but I couldn't bring myself to look or act that way. The fact was, this was the first odd or unusual thing that had happened to me since I'd started work at the Guild and it sure broke the monotony. Besides, maybe the experience would yield some new information. One thing was sure—it was no routine check as the agent had said; I'd seen a lot of folks picked up for those routine checks, and they always took the pair or family as a group and never, never sent a personal car for them.

We went through and beyond downtown, to a small, low, black building on our right. We turned into a back alley on the side of the building, then made a sharp left and actually drove inside, gliding smoothly into a prepared stall in a garage with automatic hookups for recharging, energizing, and cold protection that came out and started work the moment we stopped and the "off" switch was flipped. The cold-weather protection was something I was well aware of; machinery wasn't as tolerant of temperature as we Medusans, and special care had to be taken to make sure they worked correctly in our lovely climate.

"Follow me," the Monitor instructed, and I did, walking with her to a nearby elevator, then into it, and up two floors. The doors slid back to reveal a somewhat familiar scene to me—squad rooms looked like squad rooms the galaxy over.

My monitor, who still hadn't so much as given me a name and who wore only one stripe, checked in with the desk sergeant, then turned to me. "Your card." She held out her hand, and I gave it to her, and she, in turn, gave it to the desk sergeant. Now I was stuck here until they wanted to let me leave.

We walked behind the desk and down a hall that led to a complex of offices, mostly with arcane names on the door. I became a little nervous when we stopped in front of a door marked SUBVERSIVE COUNTERINTELLIGENCE and walked in. That was too close to home. I felt a twinge as I considered that an enemy who could penetrate your deepest military headquarters might just get a leak as to an agent being dropped in their midst.

I followed my Monitor in, closing the door behind me— an old-fashioned one, I noted, with coded lock. The office was large and impressive, a big room with a desk in the center that was larger than could possibly be useful, a comfortable chair behind it, and just about nothing else. People stood before whoever belonged to this office, and probably at attention.

The chair turned and I saw that it held a tall, strong-looking woman, military-type, wearing not stripes but a major's leaf. A big shot indeed. I was both more worried and suitably impressed.

The private approached the desk in good military fashion, came to attention, and saluted. "The citizen Tarin Bul, as ordered!" she snapped.

The major nodded casually and did not bother to return the salute. "That'll be all, private. You may leave us."

"As you wish!" the Monitor returned smartly, then did an about-face and walked past me to the door and was out. I was now alone with a big cheese in TMS circles here in Gray Basin, where, I understood, there was only one general and two colonels. That made this one a Department Chief—Grade 30 or better for sure.

I just stood there, well back from the desk, looking uncomfortable and curious. For a while the major just looked back at me. Finally she said, "Come here."

I approached the desk, which still put some distance between us. Not much on the desk, either, I noted. This was a show office to impress not only folks like me but the lower-downs. The real work of this department was done elsewhere.

Again the stare. Finally she asked, "How do you like Medusa, Bul?"

I shrugged. "Better than a lot of places, I guess. I don't have any complaints, except maybe that the job I've got's a little boring."

She nodded, not at all taken aback by my less than cringing attitude. Here was a pro, I realized from the start —but, well, so was I. Still, my demeanor was not easily overlooked. "You're not nervous at being brought in here like this?"

"Should I be?" I countered. "Your people should know better than anybody that I haven't been a bad boy."

That brought a very slight smile to the corners of her mouth. "That is probably true, but it doesn't necessarily mean anything. Maybe we think your thoughts are impure."

"They are," I assured her, "but they're no threat to Medusa."

She seemed a little taken aback by my statement, but didn't let it get to her. Clearly she was used to dealing with a different sort of personality than mine. Well, who knew? But either I acted in character or correctly from her point of view—and I'd been on the other side of a desk like that too many times not to know exactly what that point of view was—or I triggered a greater suspicion. I was a new boy on the planet, no matter what, and I could not be expected to react like the natives.

She sat there a moment, looking me over thoughtfully. "You're a bright boy. I almost think that you are not what you seem."

That was uncomfortably close. She knew her business. "I haven't been around long enough to fake much," I retorted. "But I've gone through more cop interrogations and psych sessions than most old people have."

She sighed. "Fourteen going on forty . . . Your situation is—unique, I admit. I know that politics played a part in your coming to us, but I suspect it was also the uniqueness of your situation. They didn't know what to do with you."

She paused, then asked, "What *are* we going to do with you?"

"Is there any reason for not letting me continue to live my life?" I returned, a little surprised at this attitude. "Or isn't it permitted to ask why I was brought here?"

"Ordinarily, no. And you weren't brought here for anything you've done, Tarin Bul. In fact, you've been something of a model citizen. But sitting here, talking to you personally, I get this *feeling* about you. There is just something about you that smells . . . dangerous. Why do you smell dangerous, Tarin Bul?"

I shrugged and looked as innocent as can be. "I don't know what you are talking about, Major. I *did* execute a man, but that was simple justice. Others that came in with me would willingly kill for no real reason."

She shook her head negatively. "No, that's not it. Something about you is . . . odd. I suspect that this is what was smelled by the Confederacy and their psychs as well. That is the reason they sent you to the Diamond, although, somehow, I feel we would all be better off if you weren't Medusan." She sighed again. "That is in the simple way of a warning, Bul. I'm going to be watching you extra carefully."

"I assumed I was being watched extra carefully anyway, considering I'm a newcomer."

She did not respond to that for a moment, but finally got to the point. "Have you been . . . contacted by anyone we should know about?"

The question was surprising. "Don't *you* know?"

"Can the bullshit, Bul!" she snapped. "Answer the question!"

"I wasn't being funny," I assured her. "You've got to admit that's a pretty weird question for Medusa, though."

Her anger subsided as she realized that, of course, I was right. She had already admitted by her very question that this system wasn't nearly as infallible as they claimed, nor as all-inclusive. It was a potentially damaging admission, and one I valued highly. "Just answer yes or no," she said at last.

"No," I responded honestly. "At least, not by anybody outside my normal life and job. What *is* this about, Major?"

"Some of the others who came here with you have been

contacted by subversives," she said in another, even more startling admission. "None of them are now in Gray Basin except you, but it's my job to find out if these enemies of the people have spread to us. Logically, they would contact you if they were."

"I've heard nothing about them or this," I answered truthfully. I didn't add that I could see the all-powerful TMS's terrible embarrassment at anything like this. Subversives meant those opposed to Ypsir, TMS, and the system—natural enough, but in a society this regimented and monitored, allegedly perfect in its enforcement procedures, even a minor flaw would be a matter of great concern. Clearly somebody had found that flaw. On at least a verbal level somebody was operating against the Medusan government and had somehow circumvented their fancy computers, monitors, flags, and recorders. That meant more than a real genius at electronics—that meant an inside job. It meant that the leader of this thing had to be either a highly placed government official or somebody fairly high up in TMS.

"They call themselves simply the Opposition," she told me. "We don't think there are many of them, but the smaller and more cell-like their organization the more difficult it is to destroy. Since you have not been contacted, we must assume that they are not yet in Gray Basin." She paused a moment for effect. As I said, a real pro. "How would you and your pair-mate like a promotion, Bul?"

Surprise followed surprise, and I could hardly repress my excitement. At last some room to move. I could almost guess what was coming next. "You know we would," I told her. "And what's the price?"

Again that faint smile. "The price could be very high indeed, Bul. Two of those who came in with you are dead now. One joined them but was not very clever. The other refused them—and was executed by them, we believe. A third joined, slipped, and tried to bluff things out with us. She was given to our psychs. She had a very strong mind and will and fought to the bitter end. Still, we got some information from her, but at the cost of her own mind. She's now a Goodtime Girl for her city government. She smiles a lot and does whatever she's told—she would jump off a building or behead herself if asked—but she doesn't exactly *think* any more."

I'm afraid the sudden hoarseness in my voice wasn't at all feigned. Frankly, I could stand death. It was a part of the risk my profession always ran, and one that all of us accepted. I also had no real fear of routine psych probes or even physical torture. I was trained and prepped by the best for that. But I have to admit that a total assault on my mind, enough to break it, *was* possible. So although they would still get no information from such an effort, they could, in fact, destroy me mentally. It was always a possibility, one that revolted me.

"Do you want to become a Goodtime Girl, Bul?" she asked, sensing my discomfort.

"No. Of course not," I told her, my voice weak.

"Well, here is what we are going to do. Two of those people were in the city of Rochande, more than sixteen hundred kilometers southwest of here. It so happens we run three trains between Gray Basin and Rochande, two of which are freights. It is the passenger-freight combination train that interests us, since we have some information that at least one contact was made on that train. We intend to assign you to that train, on a regular basis, as a normal promotion. Since the trip, with preparation and cleanup, takes a full shift, you will have two residences, one here and one there, and work different directions on alternate days. We believe that, sooner or later, either on the train or at Rochande, you will be contacted."

It figured. Bait. But the actual routine sounded like fun, and it would give me the first opening in my own little campaign. "And when—if—I'm contacted?"

"You will join. You will go along with what they ask. We don't want you to just report a contact. We want you to join the organization, perhaps for some time. We want to know who these people—this cell—are. We want their leader, because she will be the only one with enough information to take us further."

I nodded as several questions immediately leaped to mind. "Ah, Major, I may not be very old but I was trained for organization and administration. I know how these political things work. First of all, I will *never* know their real names, most likely, and only one of them will know mine, unless we run across each other by accident in the street or on the job."

"But you'll know what they look like and you're a bright boy. You'll be able to figure out a lot of information about many of them. Somebody will make a slip about her family, or somebody else will betray knowledge that will indicate her Guild, at least. Eventually we'll have pictures from your description to match with our computers, and we'll come up with a fair number of them. Don't worry—we understand the limits of this work better than you do."

"All right, I'll accept that. But the one that *they* killed worries me. That means they have some way to check sincerity. One of 'em's probably either a psych or a technician for a psych lab. That's going to be hard to fake."

She gave that smile again. "You *are* a bright boy. Your objection can be very easily disposed of. The equipment has to be basic and portable. They can't possibly do a full job on you. The solution is very simple, then—you tell them all about this meeting and you tell them about me."

"Huh?"

"You tell them you're playing along with us, but you really sympathize with them. That will be the truth—don't bother to deny it. The ambivalence will be enough to confuse their devices, our psychs assure me. You're still new enough and fresh enough to cause no problem on that score."

I frowned and looked nervous at the suggestion, although she was perfectly correct and it was exactly what I was planning to do anyway. "How sure are you about that?"

"Very," she assured me. "Believe me, we have the best here. And it worked before. The third one, the one whose mind is gone, was one of ours. Unfortunately for her, she went too far over to their side and tried to double-cross us. In that case, what happened to her will happen to you, Bul. Remember that."

I shivered. "I'll remember," I assured her. "But—sooner or later they'll rig some way to make a final test, and that'll be with the full gear. I'll have to go through that before I'll really know who they are."

She nodded. "We anticipate that, although we have no direct knowledge. There is some evidence that this operation is Confederacy-backed, by person or persons unknown elsewhere in the Diamond who are, if not in the Confederacy's employ, at least working against us. When that kind of test comes, you will be ready. The one who went before you passed it, we think—with the help of our own people. If you get into trouble on that, we will give you a basic psych overlay that will fool them. We're certain it will, since it will simply build on those anti-State parts of your own nature and background. We will make a rebel out of you, and then we will unmake it."

I could hardly tell her that I could make any psych probe read exactly what I wanted, probably including their best. "All right—I understand so far. But if this works so well, why did they kill one of us?"

"She wasn't working for us, directly. We mishandled the situation and have learned from our mistake. We made no mistakes the second time—except that she got to the point where she decided to play *us* for suckers. You're our third, Bul. We have all the prep techniques down pat now, and we've covered our trail on the last two very well. Nobody, and I mean nobody, except you and me knows about this arrangement right now. At the proper time, two others in TMS, one a top psych, will be informed—and that will be all. There is no recording in this office, no record at all of what happened here. A very convincing and totally fictional dressing-down for a minor infraction is being substituted."

"Okay. I admit I'm very bored cleaning buses and I would sure like some more credit. Besides I can play a pretty good part. It wasn't easy getting into that reception back on Halstansir, you know, particularly carrying a sword."

She liked that. I wondered if she were native, as her accent suggested, or a convict. Probably I would never know.

"I am glad you approve, Bul—but you realize you have no choice in this matter?"

I nodded. "I've had very few choices in my life."

"Now, we'll get on to the procedures for reporting. You will not report to or trust your terminal or other TMS officers. I will give you a code which can be keyed from any terminal. It is simply a variation on getting your credit and debit statement from the Central Bank—and it *will* give you that. But it will also be a signal to me. Key it, and

I will know, and you will be picked up for a routine inter-
rogation as you were today. Understand?"

I nodded. "One thing, though—what about Ching?"

"While we have been having this talk, Ching was picked
up and taken to the psych used only by my special branch.
Oh, don't look so worried—there will be no change. All
we've done is to reinforce a weakness already obvious in
her. She practically worships you now. From this point,
that will simply dominate. You'll notice no change, nor will
she even be aware that she's been to a psych—as far as
she's concerned, she'll have been waiting for you in your
room all this time. But she will be very uncritical of your
attitudes and inclinations on the social and political front.
She was born and raised here. As a loyal native, she would
have turned you in for your own good, or reported anything odd to us. She won't now. If you say to betray the
government, she will go along with you. If you join the
Opposition, she will go along and accept it. And if you later
betray the Opposition, she will think all the more highly of
you for it. They will have no trouble passing her on that
basis. That is one reason we thought of her as a logical
pair-mate for you. As with most totally frustrated people,
she is an incurable fantasizing romantic."

I didn't like the idea of messing with Ching's mind—she
had enough problems as it was—but it didn't seem too bad,
and it would keep her out of trouble as long as I was all
right. However, she would now be exposed to exactly the
same dangers—and fate—from either side that I faced, and
she was not well prepared for it. I liked her too much not
to worry about what might happen, but I *was* a professional. If it had to be, it had to be—and, if it came down
to her or me, I knew I would have no such romantic no-
tions.

CHAPTER SIX

A Disloyal Opposition

Ching was, as promised, no different on my return than when I'd left her and, also as advertised, she told me that she'd been waiting in the room for me worriedly for the previous few hours. If I hadn't been told differently, I would have sworn she was narrating the correct version of events, rather than just what she was told to remember.

Two days later we were both summoned to the Guild Hall for an audience with a top-grade supervisor. I played the surprised worker that Ching genuinely was. There we were informed that we had shown ourselves more than capable of higher positions. Effective immediately, we were being promoted to In-Service Passenger Attendants, Grade 6, and would shortly be assigned for a week of training and evaluation. Since we'd been Grade 3s (I never did learn what 1s and 2s were—I could hardly imagine anything lower than bus cleaners) this was a substantial jump, although it was, of course, contingent on our successful training and initial job performance evaluations. The job actually only warranted a Grade 5, but the extra bump was given because we would now have two homes many kilometers apart, and would have double toiletries and the like. At our previous level you owned virtually nothing at all— you couldn't afford it—but, while we wouldn't be very well off compared to many others, we would now have a bit left over from basic expenses for luxuries.

We presented our cards, which were run through a computer and popped back to us apparently unchanged, but we knew that the information now reflected increased grade and status. We also had two days until our new shift, an afternoon one, would properly cycle so we could join our crew. We actually had some time to kill and made the most of it. Ching was particularly excited and pleased by the turn of events, and I tried as hard as I could to share in her joy and excitement. Doing so was tough when you knew what was really going on.

Two days later we went down to the main passenger terminal and found Shift Supervisor Morphy, a distinguished-looking woman in early middle age who looked a little like civilized worlders. A native most definitely, I decided, but a child or grandchild of a civilized worlder and a frontier type. These were very common on Medusa.

The job wasn't very glamorous or exciting, despite the fancy titles. Basically we patrolled the cars, wiping passenger's noses, answering their stupid questions, explaining how to get food or drink or how to operate the seat terminals as well as making sure that all the amenities were working properly. In some ways this was worse than cleaning buses. In that job, I mostly stood around and goofed off while seeing that the cleaning machines did their jobs properly, while here I was constantly exposed to the public and observed by shift supervisors as I walked from one end of the train to the other and back. And I had to be *very* neat, and *very* clean, and always smile, smile. . . .

In one way the job was similar to tracking down and confronting criminals. Both were filled with repetition and long, boring stretches, yet both were at the same time interesting and disgusting.

Our train usually had two or three passenger cars and the rest freight. The freight level remained constant but the passenger car number increased or decreased according to demand. In the first week we had one six-car passenger train and another that had only one, but never did we have a run with none.

The training period was really grating at times, with every little thing criticized. I almost belted Morphy more than once. The week seemed to last forever. Finally, though, we were on our own and less closely supervised, and things eased up a bit.

Train crews had distinctive uniforms, nicely tailored and with overly large insignia on them. Since a lot of our own Guild's members used the trains to get to and from where they were needed, there had to be some way to tell the specific train's crew from others in transportation. We looked, in fact, pretty elegant by Medusan standards, but that was par for the course. I remember a fancy resort once, long ago, that used a lot of human attendants just to give the place a more elegant and personal feel, and the best-dressed people in the joint were the doorman and the waiters.

Our new room in Rochande was virtually identical to the one back in Gray Basin, the only difference being that it was on the third, not the fourth, floor and the beds were against the left rather than the right wall. A mirror image, basically, to remind us where we were.

Rochande, however, was quite different from Gray Basin if only because of its geography. It was a food-distribution center for the region, and, therefore, a space-freight port. It was also pretty far south, comparatively speaking, and while the winter still hit it was neither long nor hard, and the city was on the surface rather than dug in and roofed over. There were also huge forests around, and quite a number of exotic plants, which gave the place a whole different feel, even if the city's pie-shaped design and dull, blocky architecture was depressingly familiar.

The trip south, once through the electronic barricades of Gray Basin, was interesting, too. You could see the climate gradually change as you moved south, with occasional breaks in the thinning snow patches, showing hardy grasses at first, then some bushes, and eventually increasingly larger trees. Finally we were more or less out of the hard winter and into a more temperate zone. The world was not nearly as bad as Gray Basin made it seem, though there was not a sign of cultivation or even roads in sight for the entire distance. More than the climate and vegetation changes, that was the true contrast on Medusa, one brought home with every trip. In the cities and towns, and on the sleek, smooth, modern trains, you were in a highly techno- logical, modern society though a regimented one. Outside the cities was a primitive world.

It was a world that said to have genuine threats al- though I'd been able to learn very little about it. Basically, the people were very secure in their modern pockets on this wilderness world and most of them had never been beyond their society's protection. What exactly was out there, other than wild and vicious animals, some of whom could change their shape, was really unknown. I found the stories about shape-changing most interesting and made it a point to re-search those animals as much as I could with the library access on the terminal. Apparently the Medusans didn't even like to study these creatures, at least not publicly. If, in fact, some of those creatures could shape-change—something not even alluded to in the descriptions—I could see why Medusan authorities wouldn't want the opportunity to plant ideas like mine into crooked heads.

The dominant life forms were mammals, however, something I found interesting but logical—reptiles couldn't really have much of a future on a world as cold as this, and in-sects would have too short a developmental season each year to do more than fill an ecological niche. Even the ocean creatures, as far as was known, were air-breathing mammals, since, apparently, the algae and plankton that would support a real fishy evolution was low, and the seas were relatively shallow.

The familiar pattern of animal development was here, though, with one vegetarian species called vettas eating mostly grasses and another called tubros eating mostly leaves and other parts of trees, apparently instinctively trimming but not killing. The big, nasty brutes were the harrar, who mostly ate vettas and tubros. There were sev-eral hundred subspecies of the two vegetarian types, and several varieties of harrar. The rest of the animal kingdom was varied, vast, and mostly invisible, but fitted into the normal balance of nature in totally expected ways. I con-centrated on the dominant life forms, except for the smaller creatures that were poisonous or nasty, because I hoped to find some clues in the big ones to what I was looking for.

As for looks, the vettas had large, flat, toothy bills, big, round eyes, short necks, and legs that were very wide, clawed, and padded, and yet they could move when they had to, at speeds up to forty kilometers per hour for short distances. The tubros had long, thin snouts, necks that bent in all directions and were longer than their bodies, and enormous, clawed limbs that were almost handlike. Their tails somewhat resembled their necks, and they occasionally used these tails as decoys when checking to see if the coast was clear. Apparently the tails came out if bitten. Tubros weren't very fast, but they could climb trees in a flash and could sleep either right side up or upside down, clinging to strong branches or trunks. Vettas had no real defense except their speed; tubros, however, could be nasty when cornered, and could use that tail of theirs like a whip.

The harrar was the hardest to pin down. Mostly it looked like a huge, undulating mass of fur, skin, and taloned feet that were almost birdlike. It generally walked, looking ridiculous, on those legs; but when it caught prey, two small, nasty hands in that fur were strong enough to tear heads off. Somewhere in that lump, was the biggest mouth relative to body size that I'd ever seen, with row upon row of teeth. The harrar interested me the most, since it was, according to the legends, a shape-changer. This critter would need to eat a lot to feed that big body, and it could hardly climb trees or outrun anything going forty kilometers per hour.

The sea creatures seemed to mirror those on land, except that there were more levels with far greater interdependence, starting with the little slugs that ate bacterialike organisms near the surface and also scavenged the bottom, up to water-born counterparts of the vettas and tubros. Despite smooth sides and flippers and fins, these looked very much like their land counterparts—but were omnivores, eating smaller animals as well as surface and bottom water plants. There was also an amphibious version of the harrar, which appeared to be a one-ton or more lump of gray or black with dorsal and tail fins, little beady eyes, a big, big mouth—and little else. This sea carnivore, called makhara, seemed totally unable to cope with swift prey— yet it had to do pretty well to keep that mass of fat happy. How did it do it? How, in fact, could *it* even grab its prey? These questions, too, were not only unanswered in the texts, they were unasked.

There were no tubros north of the twenty-eighth parallel, where the trees became too small or intermittent to support such life. But there were snow vettas able to burrow under meters of snow and ice to get at whatever was down there, and harrar to hunt them. That, too, was interesting. Lots of stuff on the unique life cycle of the snow vetta, nothing but a mention that the harrar were there. That implied that there were no snow harrar, and again brought up an interesting question: how did the dark, bulky, ungainly *harrar* ever catch its quota of snow *vetta,* many of whom spent most of their time burrowing deep beneath the snows?

Ching, to my surprise, became interested in some of my studies. It was amazing to me that someone born and raised on Medusa knew so little about the bulk of the planet. But she was aware of her ignorance—after first confessing that, until I looked into these things, she'd never even thought about them—and eager to fill the gap.

One thing was for sure—they were really scared of those harrar, even in the highest councils of Medusa. You had only to think of the double energy guard around Gray Basin's entrances, and even Rochande had a double perimeter fence of the same lethal energy barrier around it. Of course, such a system, for the protection of the public —sold and accepted as such—also kept the people tightly inside their monitored cities and protected trains. Even those trains were sealed compartments, totally insulated from the outside world, almost as if they were spacecraft sealing off their occupants from some lethal, alien environment.

Man had always triumphed over the most vicious and lethal carnivores on world after world. Yet here it seemed almost as if the legendary harrar were allowed to breed and roam and multiply; and they probably were, not so much from technological as from political motives. Raised in insulated cradle-to-grave technological pockets, most Medusans probably couldn't survive a day without those conveniences they took for granted. This suited the Medusan authorities very well indeed.

Whether the doing of Ypsir or of his predecessor, this was a unique society and something of a work of genius, based on the fact that Lilith and Charon supplied so much food there was no necessity to raise any on Medusa, and technology had maintained the closed culture of Medusa and fed it.

We worked some six weeks with nothing happening, and I was beginning to grow bored and worried and fidgety once more. Neither TMS nor this mysterious Opposition I only half believed in had surfaced, and I was beginning to wrack my brain once more for a different opening.

Ching dismissed my irritation as moodiness, something she was used to by now, but I was determined to do something to get me off dead center and beat the system. Of course, just when I'd given up all hope or belief in the Opposition, I heard from them. And heard is the right word, although they took a leaf from Krega's notebook.

We had a separate crew's toilet on the train, just forward of the first passenger car, and, as usual, I went there to take a piss. Such occasions were one of the very few times I was separated not only from Ching, who had to keep working while I went and vice versa, but also from the supervisors and general passengers. There was, of course, a monitoring device in the john.

"Tarin Bul?" I heard the voice, electronically distorted, and looked up and around, puzzzled. I'd been called by vox on the terminal many times, but the voices had never sounded as inhuman as this.

"Yes?"

"We've been watching you, Tarin Bul."

"Aren't you always?" I cracked, zipping up my pants and going to the washbasin.

"We are not TMS," the voice told me. "We do not like TMS very much. We suspect that, by now, you don't like them much, either."

I shrugged and washed my hands. "I'm damned if I do and damned if I don't on that one," I told the voice sincerely. "If this is a test by TMS and I say I don't like them, I'll get picked up and asked why. If, on the other hand, I say I just love TMS, they'll pick me up for sure and rush me to the nearest psych. So I'll pass on the answer, and unless there's something else I've got to go back to work."

"We are not TMS," the voice told me. "We are in opposition to the TMS and the current government of Medusa. We are powerful enough to feed a false signal, recorded earlier, of you sitting on the toilet to TMS monitors while we use this channel to talk to you."

"Says you," I retorted.

"You're no native, programmed to this life. Why do you not accept what we say?"

"For one thing, if you're that powerful you don't need me. And if you *do* need me, and are that powerful, then you're either phony or pretty incompetent rebels."

"We *don't* need you," the voice responded. "We *want* you. That is a different thing. The more people in more guilds we have, the stronger we become, the better able to manage this world after it is ours. You in particular have two attributes of value to us. You have mobility due to your job, which is invaluable in our society. And, you are not a native of this world, and sooner or later it will drive you crazy."

"Maybe it already has," I said, retaining my skeptical tone. "But let's say, just for the sake of argument, that I believe you're who and what you say. What good does it do me?"

"Listen carefully, for we will say this only once, and time is short. Someone will soon miss you and come in demanding to know why you are not back at work. You have one chance and one chance only to join us. At your next layover at Rochande you have a day off. Go to the matinee show at the Grand Theater that day. Sit in the balcony. Leave to go to the bathroom halfway through the first act. We will contact you."

"And my pair-mate?"

"Not at the first meeting. Later we will arrange for her as well. This communication is ended. Guard your comments."

And, with that, things were, allegedly, back to normal. I left quickly and returned to work. Ching noticed that I seemed cheerier than I had for weeks, but couldn't figure out why.

We always went out for a special meal and a show on our day off and when I suggested the Grand, Ching wasn't the least surprised. As instructed long ago, I keyed in the code on my terminal that told me how much credit we had for our day on the town—and simultaneously let my TMS contact know that things had, finally, started to roll. I had no intention of double-crossing either side until I'd gotten what I wanted from this assignment, and certainly not until I could get away with it.

When you're sitting in the middle of a dark and crowded theater you can instantly make yourself a villain in a number of ways, but the worst is to go to the bathroom in the middle of the show. I finally made it to the aisle through the curses and dirty looks—made worse by the sure and certain knowledge that I'd be back—and proceeded to the upper lobby, where the large rest room was located. As I passed the last row of seats—far more sparsely populated since they were so far from the screen you might as well have dialed the show on your terminal—a hand shot out from a darkened seat, grabbed my arm, and pulled me over with such force I almost lost my balance.

All I could really tell about her was that she was tall, lean, and looked to be a pure civilized worlder. "Listen, Bul," she whispered, "just sit down and make like you're watching the show. Let me do the talking."

"Fair enough," I whispered back, and sat.

"Are you still interested in our organization?"

"I still don't believe in it," I told her, "but I'm here, at least out of curiosity."

"That's enough—for now. Just two blocks north of this theater is a small café, the Gringol. Go there after the show. Order what you like from the menu. Wait for us. We will take care of things from that point on, both with you and with TMS. If you are not there, you will never hear from us again. Now get up and go to the toilet."

I started to open my mouth and respond, then thought better of it, and did as instructed.

Ching and I watched the rest of the show, then wandered outside, where it was still light but would not be for much longer. I suggested a walk to get the kinks out of my leg. In the middle of the second block north of the theater, I spotted the small sign for the Gringol and turned to Ching. "I'm getting hungry. Want to get something?"

"Sure. Why not? Got anyplace in mind? How flush are we?"

"Not very," I told her, and that was the truth, despite the extra cash. "Let's see what this café has." The maneuver was nice and smooth and natural, and she didn't suspect a thing.

The place was small and dimly lit, although, of course, that would not matter to TMS and its ever-present monitors. Still, in a world with cafeteria sameness, the occasional trip to a restaurant or café, with an actual menu from which to select meals, was a real treat. Sometimes, the food in small places like this was even prepared by humans with their own special recipes, mostly Warden exiles or those with recipes passed down from exiles and pioneers.

"Looks expensive," Ching said dubiously. "Are you sure we can afford this?"

"Probably not, but what the hell," I responded, picking a small two-person table in the back and sitting down. The place was almost empty, although a few more people drifted in as we sat. A human waitress arrived from the back and handed us small menus. There weren't *that* many choices, but the few available promised to be "special recipes found nowhere else on Medusa": a Cerberan algae steak, an unusual Charon fruit plate, and other Warden specialties, including some meat dishes, I noted. The menu bragged that nothing used was synthetic. I doubted that, but at least such a declaration meant they'd try hard to make you believe it. The prices were fairly reasonable, so when the waitress suggested a special Lilith wine I looked at Ching, then sprang for it.

Frankly, I was surprised at the suggestion, considering our obvious youth. The wine arrived and was poured from a small wooden flask. I picked mine up, looked at Ching, and smiled. "Ever had alcohol before?"

"No," she admitted, "but I've always been curious about it."

"Well, you'll know why you haven't. Try it." I sipped mine, and she drank hers as if it were a glass of water, then made a curious face. "It tastes—funny."

It was actually a very good wine, considering I had no idea what it was fermented from, that tasted like a high-class white from the civilized worlds. "You don't like it?"

"No—I mean, yes. It's just—different."

The waitress was soon back to take our order, and we gave it and relaxed. It occurred to me that either the wine or something in the food might contain a drug, but that didn't worry me. I expected it.

I looked over at Ching, who was already looking a little glassy-eyed and just smiling and staring at me. She was small and alcohol was new to her and would hit her. She sighed, "I feel real good. Relaxed." She reached for the flask, poured more wine, and drank it fairly quickly. I was still sipping my first glass, of course, feeling fairly human and normal for the first time since I woke up on that prison ship.

Whoever this Opposition was, they were a most civilized underground. While whatever it was, was somewhere in the meal, they let us finish it before our consciousness just sort of faded out without either of us even noticing. Half expecting it, I could have established mental defenses to block the effects—but that would have defeated the whole plan anyway.

I awoke in a smelly tunnel, with several dark forms hovering near me. The place smelled really cruddy, like raw sewage, and it took no brains at all to figure out that I was somewhere down in the drainage system under the city.

Whatever they used was no more than a light hypnotic; I could break it fairly easily, but that wasn't something Tarin Bul was supposed to be able to do, and so I simply rearranged my mind-set while keeping myself under at about the same level as the drug or whatever—but with autohypnosis replacing the substance. If agents could be subdued by such simple chemical means there'd be no use breeding them and training them so extensively.

I could not quite make out the dark shapes, even though they were very close. Either they wore some all-encompassing black hooded garments or they were using some sort of disrupter field.

"He wakes to level one," a woman's voice said.

"It is time, then," another—a gruff man's voice—responded. "Here—let me check." He kneeled down very close to me, and a black, ghostly arm and hand opened one of my eyes, checked my pulse, and did other routine checks. He got back up, seeming satisfied. "It's okay, Sister 657, you want to take him?"

"Tarin Bul—do you hear us?" the woman's voice asked softly.

"Yes," I responded dully.

"You understand that this is your point of no return? That you may tell us now to restore you and nothing more will ever be said nor will you hear from us again? But, if you continue, you are committed to us, and should you compromise or betray the Opposition you will forfeit your life."

"I understand," I told them. "I did not come here to turn away."

They seemed to like that. "Very well," Sister 657 said, "then rise and follow us."

I did as instructed, thankfully noting that I had been on a dry wooden platform and not in that gunk below. We were, in fact, walking on catwalks over the river of sludge, somewhere beneath Rochande in a maze even those who worked in it would need a map to negotiate. Not these folks, though; they knew just where they were going. Despite the twists and turns, I was pretty sure I could get back to where we started, but that knowledge did me no good. I had no assurance that that starting spot was anywhere near the café, since I had no idea how long I'd been out.

Finally we made a turn and walked over a temporary catwalk maybe three meters long. It led to an opening in the tunnel wall beyond which was a dimly lit room full of maintenance equipment. Several more dark shapes were in evidence, perhaps a dozen in all including my captors, which was a good thing. With all the ropes and probes and cables and patch can about, there wouldn't be room in the place for many more.

They sat me down on a crate in front of them, whereupon I relaxed. The stuff they gave me would be out of my system by now anyway, and they'd be the first to realize that.

Sister 657 seemed to be the leader. Nice touch, that, just the camaraderie title and a simple number. The odds were that her number made her very high up indeed—I assumed, correctly as it turned out, that the numbers referred to cell and city and only one to the individual's within the cell.

"Behold a possible brother," Sister 657 intoned. I hoped I wasn't in for a night of silly mumbo-jumbo and secret lodge stuff. "We give him the number 6137. He is awake, alert, and open to questions."

"Brother—why do you want to oppose the government?" a woman in the back asked me.

"It's pretty dull," I responded, which got a few chuckles.

"Brother—why do you wish to join us?" another woman asked.

"*You* recruited *me*," I pointed out. "Right now you're

the only game in town, so, okay, I'll join up. But I really don't know what you stand for, and maybe your ideas on running Medusa are worse than the government's."

Some whispers around, as if I'd said something I shouldn't, but I intended to be blunt. What little I could pick out seemed to concern how cocksure and self-confident I was for one so young.

"He makes a good point," Sister 657 broke in, defusing the whispers. "We have told him nothing of ourselves. Perhaps we should before going any further." She turned to me. "Brother 6137, we don't bother with oaths, hand-shakes, or ceremonies. That's for the superstitious masses. However, I should tell you that, like most groups of this sort, we are more united in our opposition to the current government than we are in what to replace it with. Still, a lot more can be done with this world than this society per-mits, and it can be done effectively without having the government watch you go to the bathroom. We are strong, powerful, and well-positioned; but the means of overthrow has, as yet, eluded us. Right now we concentrate on get-ting recruits, gaining as much technical information on the local level as possible in each place, and establishing our-selves in each major population center on Medusa. It is a start."

I nodded. "But you can just as easily become a powerful debating society," I pointed out. "Look, I was born and bred to politics. Had things gone differently for me, in a few years I'd have been in planetary administration instead of sitting here waiting on passengers. Don't patronize me or think of me as a kid. I leave that to the people I want to underestimate me. For example, I think you should know that TMS knows you're in Rochande and put me out as bait."

There was a lot of shuffling and gasping at that one. Finally the leader asked, "Are you sure you know what you just said?"

I nodded. "Why hide it? You snuffed one of theirs and they got some information from another, and I was the logical bait. So they bumped me to a job that would bring me here. Frankly, I was getting sick and tired waiting for you people."

"He admits to working for TMS!" a woman almost shouted. "Remove him—now!"

"If I were a really effective TMS agent or plant the last thing I would have done would have been to tell you what I just did," I pointed out—falsely, as a matter of fact. The outburst worried me. Amateurs. Damned play-at-revolution amateurs! I had hoped for better.

"And will you tell TMS that you have contacted us, and joined us?" Sister 657 asked.

I nodded. "Sure. And you'll have to cook up something occasionally for me to feed that stonelike major or they'll pick me up and put me under a psych machine. They did that to one of your own—I don't know any names—a few months back, another newcomer like me, breaking her mind. I don't want anything like that happening to me, so if you're as powerful as you say you are I expect protection."

The man—possibly the only male other than myself—rose for the first time. "You make good sense, young man. You are very clever. Perhaps too clever. I almost wonder about you. The Cerberans, it is said, can make robots in any shape or form that cannot be told from humans. Ones that can assume the characteristics of any of the four Warden worlds."

"I'm no robot," I assured him, "but that information interests me." I paused, as if thinking over some weighty matters, then showed by my face and manner that I had made a decision. "In point of fact, I'm going to tell you something that isn't even on my records. Something Medusa, and, I suspect, Halstansir doesn't really know. I was a ringer back home. I didn't come out of the administrative breeding pool nor out of their schools. Do you think a high-class administrator could have managed to get into a reception and chop off a top politician's head with a sword? No, for reasons that are old history and have no business with you or anybody else any more, I came out of the assassin's pool."

There. A nice white lie that allowed me to be a little more of myself while at the same time protected my real identity and purpose. Who knows? My logic was so good maybe the kid *had* been from my old school at that. I'd like to think so. It disturbs me that an amateur could have pulled off that job so neatly.

And they bought it, hook, line, and sinker, just because it *did* make good sense. My first meeting, and already I'd engineered at least a social promotion for myself. As I said, amateurs.

"This explains a lot about you and your manner," Sister 657 said. "If this is so, then you are a far more valued recruit than I—we—had originally hoped for." Interesting slip, that. It implied that I knew her and she knew me, and I didn't know that many older folks on Medusa. She seemed unaware of her slip, though, and continued.

"Our time is run for this matter," she told us. "I propose we administer a small hypnotic and replace him at the café. Later, this week or early next, 6137, you will be called to the company psych for a routine check. There one of our people will add her own little bit to your testing, and we will check out your facts. If you prove out, then you will join our group, leaving for meetings in the same manner, but without the drug, from various small cafés. Objections?"

I shook my head. "Not on the psych stuff, no. But I suggest we continue to use the Gringol, at least for me. It wouldn't make any sense at all to compromise other cafés and similar places, since I am both being watched and obliged to report to TMS. Everybody else can use different spots—but keep me on the café. Eventually they'll put a transmitter on me somewhere, probably one I know about and one I won't, but I assume you have some kind of scanning for that sort of thing. If not, the next time or two, I'll show you how to build one. They'll assume any failure in the gadgets is your doing, anyway."

"Why do I feel *we* just joined *him?*" a woman in the front said grumpily.

I smiled.

They were smooth, I'll say that. Ching had passed out, but with the careful administering of additional doses of the hypnotic—a native plant, since anything else would be quickly negated by the Wardens—she was hardly aware that time passed at all. Nicely susceptible to the hypnotics, as most people are, she accepted a reasonable romantic scenario set in and near the café that, the Opposition assured me, would be supported in TMS records.

I dutifully keyed in the major on the terminal later that night, and, sure enough, the next day, after returning to Gray Basin and getting something to eat, TMS had another "random pickup," this time of both of us, although we were separated, once at headquarters.

The major, whose name, I learned, was Hocrow, was more than interested in my account, which, no doubt, was being checked and verified by countless scanners and sensors. No doubt, indeed—because she not only had a chair for me this time, she insisted I sit in it. Still, I had no worries about them, either—not only could I control just about all my important bodily indicators to make those machines read any way I wanted, I insured things by telling nothing but the truth, leaving out, of course, some of the inconvenient details.

"We have monitors along that whole area under the café, and in every maintenance room," the major grumbled, "and we did a total check when it was obvious you could have gone nowhere else. They showed nothing. How is it possible?"

"One sewer looks exactly like another," I pointed out, "and most of it is totally uninhabited most of the time. It's pretty easy to patch in and substitute an old recording of a sewer doing what sewers do."

She nodded. "And all the monitors are on one cable down there, to save money. I *could* make them all independent, which would compound their troubles no end, but that would be a rather obvious ploy."

"Not to mention the fact that, unless you did it to the whole city, something that would not only be obvious but would cost a fortune and disrupt the place for months, they could just move to a different sewer. But surely you already knew they were in the sewers."

"We did. It is the most logical place, anyway. But any attempt to breach that cable should set up all sorts of flags in Control."

"Well, there are two possibilities there. One is that they have somebody in Control who can be at just the right spot to cover up this sort of thing when needed. The second possibility is that you've simply been outclassed technically.

This system of yours is pretty sophisticated, but it would be easy for a Confederacy tech team to beat and you know that better than I do."

"Are you suggesting that the Confederacy is behind this group?"

"It seems likely—but indirectly. Maybe they supply the smarts from someplace like the picket ship or their own satellites, but the people are home-grown. I don't know—for all their technical wizardry, they seemed to me like kids playing a game, sort of a more dangerous version of trying to beat the automatic doors on the buses and trains. They're *playing* at revolution, at least the ones I saw were."

Hocrow looked at me strangely for a moment. "Is what you told them about actually being a bred assassin true?"

"Yeah, it's true. Big money was paid, too. I was a long-range hidden gun in a power play my father planned. They got the jump on him before he was ready or I was old enough to be a factor, and I admit I was too young—too emotional—then."

"Then you wouldn't avenge your father's death if it happened now?"

"Oh, sure I would—but I wouldn't have been caught."

She mulled that over, just sitting there, looking up at the ceiling for quite some time. Finally she nodded to herself. "That's what was bothering me so much about you before. It fits. It explains a lot." She gave that icy smile again. "It seems you are misplaced. You should be in TMS."

I raised my eyebrows. "I thought I *was*. Otherwise, what are we doing here?"

She sighed. "One thing does bother me. If you have your preliminary training and all that special design, how will we ever know which side you are really on?"

I chuckled. "No matter what, I have limited experience. If you and your entire staff of monitors, psychs, and the like can't be sure of me, then your system's too shaky to have any hope of long-term survival anyway. Either you can do the job or you should give it up."

That was blunt, almost daring talk, but it was also guaranteed to play directly to a solid cop's ego because, frankly, it was true. The fact that I was trained to beat any system didn't mean I couldn't be beat. It only meant they had to be up to the job.

"Now, what about this psych exam?" I asked her. "Can you get me by it?"

"It should be relatively easy for someone with your supposed abilities," she mocked. "Still, we can do a little reinforcing before you leave here, with your help. I have a tech on call."

"That'll do," I told her. "But you're not going to do anything crazy like pick up any of the café staff, are you? They all have to be in on it, at least in another cell that supports mine. I'd just trail and track 'em, if possible. My own intention is to make myself invaluable enough to the organization that I'll be passed ever upward. If everybody's as amateurish as these people, you have no real problem, only an irritant. So what if they can play games with the system as long as they're still trapped in it? But if, at the top levels, there's somebody or some group really able to use what they've got, then I want to meet them."

She looked at me with those steely eyes. "Why?"

I grinned. "Because I want your job. Because, maybe, I'd like to be First Minister before I'm forty. Or, maybe, the guy who tells the First Minister what to do."

"Ambitious, aren't you?"

I shrugged. "I'm young."

CHAPTER SEVEN

Working Both Sides of the Street

The psych job was no big problem. In fact, the hardest thing about it was not betraying how much more I knew about the tech's machines than she did. Still, as someone allegedly under psych probes for over a year after the murder, I could be expected to have a certain amount of familiarity and expertise.

The routine psych exam was designed to catch problems before they developed into something that might cause real trouble for the Guild and the system. I did learn, by casual conversation while taking the exam, a bit of interesting additional information to file.

There was no psych school on Medusa; all psychs native to the Warden system were trained on Cerberus. It stood to reason, therefore, that this Opposition might also have Cerberan origins. I had no evidence, of course, but such a level of technological expertise combined with such an amateurish and naive set of people led to the inescapable conclusion that we—the Opposition, that is—were the arm of a widespread, Confederacy-backed underground whose main objective, at least on Medusa, was to get organized and remain in waiting until needed.

I got along well with the cell members, particularly once I disdained that silly robe, hood, and veil the rest of them used. Hell, they all knew who I was anyway, so why fool with that sort of stuff? To my disappointment, most of them were also in the Transport Guild—I wanted to broaden my base—although at least two were fairly high up. But they were such eager amateurs, that I felt I had to more or less lead them along and also maybe dangle some bait for the higher-ups. Therefore, at one meeting

I dropped a real bombshell. They were doing their usual debating-society stuff about the problems in breaking the system as opposed to crawling around in the cracks when I interrupted. "I think I'm pretty clear on how to destroy totally TMS's hold on Medusa." All of a sudden you could have heard a pin drop.

"So? What master plot has the superkid come up with now?" one of them finally asked.

"Let me tell you about the harrar," I began. "They're too big not to eat all the time, and too big and fat ever to catch anything. Yet there are plenty of harrar in the wild. You remember some of the old wives' tales about them?"

They nodded and shook their heads and mumbled and finally somebody said, "But nobody believes that crap."

"On a world that's been settled for this short a time, there's almost always a good reason for those tales," I pointed out. "And the harrar itself fits in perfectly. They can change shape. They can make themselves look like other, more familiar things and then just sit there until prey comes near. Maybe they even attract it. But they change shape all the same. On a more primitive basis, I think the tubros have a little of this ability as well. They have a tail that looks like their necks with a ball of fat on the end of it. Why? A neck with no head, or a ball of fat, isn't going to fool any predator worth its salt. I think they make that ball of fat look just like their pointy heads, when they have to. All of them change color to fit their background, as do almost all the animals on Medusa. Hell, even *we* do that, sort of."

"But that's animals," somebody noted. "What's that to do with us, even if it *is* true?"

"I think humans can do it, too. The fact is, the Warden cells that make up our bodies are basic living cells for plants and animals. They're not like normal human, plant, or animal cells, but they're more like each other than like normal cells. They protect us from cold and heat and even from starvation, within limits. Given air and water we can live anywhere and on most anything if we had to. Nature is really pretty consistent. Shape-changing is simply a practical survival characteristic the Wardens could develop."

"Then why can't we do it?" somebody wanted to know.

"Because we don't know how. I suspect that if we were

out in the wild the ability would come more or less naturally. But it *does* exist, even here. I've seen scars heal almost while I was watching them. I've seen three people I knew change sex so absolutely you'd swear they were born with that new sex. If we can accomplish something that total, we can surely make changes with any face and form."

"That may be," Sister 657 put in, "but nobody can control these things so it does no one any good."

"I think they *can* be controlled. I think the harrar and the tubros' tail tell us it's possible. With them it's probably instinctive, but the ability is there. It's only a matter of our finding out how to do it. I'm convinced the government knows. They went to a lot of trouble to suppress any idea that it's possible because they know it is. Their system is one based on visual and audio surveillance. Anybody who looked and sounded just like somebody else could use the card of whoever they appeared to be. Replace somebody—almost anybody roughly your size—and you can walk where he or she would walk and the monitors would never pick up the substitution. A lot of TMS's offices, for example, have no monitors themselves. The watchers don't like to be watched, and they need a few places off the record sometimes. A relatively small group of malleable people could walk into TMS as prisoners and wind up replacing everybody in top authority. A coordinated effort could collapse the system beyond easy repair."

"He makes it sound so easy," our other male member grumbled.

"No, it's not easy, and the plan is not without risk. Some people would die. A lot of homework would be necessary to keep detection away as long as possible. But our group has enough people placed in top levels to phony those records now—they're using the same principle I'm referring to, only in a more limited way. They understand that a totalitarian government is dependent on its technology for its controls and is secure only as long as that technology works and remains in their hands. They're going slightly nuts just because we beat the system, even though we haven't done anything threatening to them. Take away their system's confidence in knowing that the person on their recordings is really that person and you have rabid, absolute paranoia and fear on the part of the leadership. Shake it and it topples. It's more fragile than you've been brought up to think."

This set off a furious debate that was ended by Sister 657 with the comment, "All this might be true—if such body control is really possible. And that's a big if."

"I'm not so sure it is," I replied. "Look, we're pretty low down on the Opposition chart right now, but somebody up top is very bright and very well placed. If we can get this idea kicked far enough upstairs we might find out for sure. Can you arrange it?"

"I'll try," she assured me, "but I still think it's nothing but a fairy tale."

I had been on Medusa for more than six months when I finally got an answer. I'll say this for them—whoever was at the top was cautious in the extreme. The information, when it came, was both good and bad at the same time, and not something that could be used immediately.

Yes, all humans on Medusa were potentially malleable, but in order to accomplish a change, you first almost literally had to develop a sense of the Wardens and their connections, one to another. Once you had this sense—this ability to "talk" to your Wardens—you could, through hypnosis or psych machine, perform what was needed to be performed. The trouble was, nobody had ever found out how you accomplished it. Oh, it was possible, and had been done, but those who could do it could not explain how they did it, or even accurately describe the sensation. Nor had they been able to teach others. And unless you had that "sense of communication," as they called it, all the hypnos and psych machines in the world couldn't do a damned thing.

There was a general feeling that people who had the ability were born with it, at least as a latent ability that could not be learned. The government spent some time looking for those people, spiriting them away to a special compound far from anything and anybody else. They had hoped to breed the ability, but that plan had fallen flat. There *were* reports that many of the Wild Ones could do it, and often did, but whether this was voluntary or a response to the harsh conditions under which they lived was unknown.

Stimulus-response, that was the answer; but what stimulated this "sense" into action? Find the stimulus and you had the key—but Opposition sources had failed to find it and hardly believed in it, at least for the record. Still, if either certain social conditions or psychs could induce sex changes, then there *had* to be a way to induce the rest of it.

Certainly this same "sense" was responsible for the fabled powers of the leaders of Lilith, although there, too, the power was not for the masses and could not be acquired. You either had it or you didn't. That thought was depressing, since the same sort of thing might be the case here. Neither I nor anybody I knew might have that ability.

On Charon and Cerberus, though, everybody had it, at least to a degree. On Charon a person required training; on Cerberus the ability was involuntary, automatic, and universal. The lack of consistency between the three other worlds didn't help in finding a Medusan key.

Although I'd been warned about it, I can remember the shock at my first experience with the sex-change business. It wasn't some gradual thing—one person slowly changing —it was dramatic, taking place entirely in a matter of days. Medusan society was certainly the least sexist in any sense I could remember. Oh, certainly, there was complete sexual equality on the civilized worlds, but the two sexes still were physically different, hormonally different, and it was never really possible for one sex to understand the other totally. Neither sex had ever been the other. On Medusa you could be one or the other, either according to some odd formula the Wardens had or because you wanted to through psych sessions—and that was the key to my theory, the clincher. If something so drastic as sexual change could be induced, *any* change could be induced, if only you had the key.

This brought me to the Wild Ones. Nobody really seemed to know much about them except that they had a primitive hunter-gatherer tribal society. There were no romantic legends about them on Medusa; the very thought of living away from power and transportation and automated meals terrified even the bravest Medusan. That was irritating, but understandable. What was less understandable was why the Medusan government allowed Wild Ones at all. They served no apparent purpose, contributed nothing to the society—although, it's true, they also took nothing from it—and remained a totally uncontrolled, independent element who owned the wilderness portion of the world, and that meant the bulk of it. I knew from bitter experience that totalitarian minds like those of Ypsir and his associates would find the very existence of such bands intolerable. Their psychology simply wouldn't allow people to remain so free and unfettered for long. Of that I was absolutely certain, unless one of three conditions existed: (1) they performed a useful, valuable, or essential service to the government—highly unlikely; (2) they did not exist —even more unlikely; or, (3) no matter what Medusa could do, they couldn't catch them.

And now I had reliable reports from above somewhere that the Wild Ones were reputed shape-changers, that they were at least on equal terms with the harrar. So, logically, the third choice seemed the most probable. Medusa wanted them, but had been singularly unsuccessful in catching those primitive folk. That conclusion led, too, to the question of just how primitive they might be, but this was something I could only learn by going and seeing for myself. If they were indeed a bunch of tribal types munching roots and grunting, I'd be stuck with them and out of luck.

Right now working both sides of the street had its advantages for me, but that, too, couldn't last forever. Major Hocrow would keep me going on the leash only as long as I was feeding her information that was either useful or might lead to useful information. If too long a dry spell came along, or if she decided that was all I could get, I knew my future wasn't too bright no matter what her assertions were as to my ultimate destiny. She was a good agent, with just the right nose for trouble, and she smelled a rat in me.

On the other hand, no matter how disappointing a debating forum these so-called rebels were, they were scared enough of the Medusan government and TMS to kill at the first sign of a double cross. Since they were such nervous amateurs, it wouldn't take much to push at least a couple of them over the edge against me. The man in the middle is always living on borrowed time.

About the only bright spot was that both sides realized

I was not sentimental enough for them to use Ching against me. I was really fond of her. As hard as that was to admit, I also had to admit that I was really far more comfortable with her around, even if she was just *there*, doing something else quietly in the same room, than on the few occasions when I was alone. I liked to think that my feelings were more paternal than anything else. It was deadly for anyone in my line of work to ever form real attachments—and never more so than here and now. I was convinced I was above really needing other people except as tools or means to ends, but I did sort of realize that Ching needed me.

It would have been ridiculous and unfair to drag her to the café at irregular intervals while in Rochande, then knock her out for a period and try and cover. Not only was doing so impractical, the routine would soon become something she would do anything to avoid. Actually, it was Hocrow's tech who came up with the answer, with my help. Ching already knew I was up to something with TMS, and she trusted me. Therefore I was able to put her under the second time at Hocrow's and use the tech to reinforce the hypno. With a simple posthypnotic command I could make her either a totally loyal member of Medusan society or a totally committed Opposition member, pretty much going along with whatever I was playing at the time— only believing in it. Since we already knew their screening procedures, it was pretty easy to fake her past the Opposition's security checks.

In the meantime, the routine continued. Ching was bright enough to understand that my position, and thus, hers as well, was precarious at all times. I had to admit that I was not fond of that situation. I felt a little guilty at having thrust her into it, but, dammit, I hadn't *asked* for her.

Winter snows gave way, at last, to spring, and yet the situation dragged on, with me stuck at a stone wall. I *knew* my proposal for revolution was valid, and I was even more certain that those in the top levels of the Opposition not only agreed but had the means, somehow, to crack that needed stimulus. The only real question was why they didn't act. Certainly it wasn't out of fear of failure— what they had now was dead-ended and stagnating—but something else. If, in fact, I was correct about the off-planet origins of that leadership, it might mean that we were waiting for a concerted, multiplanet effort—but that wouldn't do any good here, I knew. These people simply didn't have adequate training, nor did we really know what sort of "soldiers" they would be if push came to shove.

And yet, I was curiously reluctant to move on my own. I was still trapped by the system as well, and I didn't like it at all. Sooner or later, I began to understand, I would have to break free, and take the chances beyond the simple ones I had taken to date. But somehow I was reluctant to do it. I had so little data. If only I knew more about the Wild Ones! I couldn't help but wonder if my counterparts on the other three worlds were feeling this frustrated. In a perverse sort of way I kind of hoped they were—I wouldn't like to be the only flop.

Not that I really gave a damn about the mission any more, though I was very slow to realize that. When I had awakened on that ship, even before planetfall, I had pretty much closed my mind to the dear old Confederacy and its causes and ways. It was odd how easy it was to slam the door on a lifetime—but then, *I* wasn't the one who slammed the door. They threw me out, then slammed it shut behind me.

Still, the primary objective of the mission and my own personal objective remained the same. I wanted the Medusan system overthrown, and I wouldn't have minded knocking off Talant Ypsir one bit. And yet, here I was, months in, stalled and half-beaten. Damn it all, I didn't even know where Ypsir was, and I had no means to get to him if I did.

What was happening to me down here? What was I changing into? In my quest for the key to physical metamorphosis, had I, somehow, had a mental metamorphosis that slipped right by unnoticed?

As had happened before, my next play was forced on me by factors beyond my control. It began with the summons to a particularly urgent meeting of the Opposition, one which all cell members were expected to attend. I was actually a little excited by the summons—maybe, just maybe, somebody had finally decided to move.

What I found in the maintenance room was not just my cell, but five separate cells, perhaps sixty people, all crowded into a place that could hardly hold one-third that number. Up front somebody had set up a screen and small recorder. A sense of extreme tension pervaded the air, yet few speculated or even said much to one another. The cells were uncomfortable being this packed together, and not just in the physical sense.

A tall woman from one of the other cells, all masked and robed as usual—even Ching was so disguised, although I still refused—looked around, took a count, then, satisfied, began by asking for quiet. The request was quickly granted by the uncomfortable crowd. Ching and I climbed up in the back on top of some crates so we could get out of the crush and still see at least the top part of the screen.

"We have been directed by our leadership board to gather you here and play this recording for you," the woman told us. "None of us have any more idea of what it contains than you do. Therefore, we will proceed to find out as quickly as possible. I am told that the recording card will destroy itself as it plays, so there can be no repeats." She punched the card into the recorder, and the screen flickered to life.

They could have saved themselves the trouble of a screen for all it was worth. It simply showed a man, masked and robed himself, sitting at a desk. It was impossible to tell anything about the scene, even the planet of origin, and it was obvious from the start that even the voice was distorted.

"Fellow comrades in opposition to the Lords of the Diamond," he began, "I bring you greetings. As some of you may have guessed, you are a part not only of a planet-wide organization but a systemwide group devoted to the overthrow of all Four Lords of the Diamond."

There were gasps and some rumbling in the crowd.

"All of you have your personal reasons for wishing to overthrow the Medusan system, reasons we well understand. Simply because you are a part of a larger plan, please do not for one moment think that your own hopes and objectives are not part of that plan," the man went on. "Events have a way of overtaking plans, however, and that has happened in this case. The Confederacy itself is taking an active hand against the Four Lords, and has some chance of success. It is time, therefore, to explain to you all a little of what this is about.

"An alien race, totally alien to anything we know, discovered humanity before humanity discovered it. That race is somehow bound up with our homeland, the Warden system itself, and they are very clever and have a very good understanding of the way people work. Instead of warring with the Confederacy, they contacted the Four Lords, who jointly accepted a contract to destroy human civilization outside of the Diamond."

A lot more whispering and rustling now, and I could hear some snatches that included the words "mad" and "insult" and the like. Clearly this cloistered group, few or none of whom had ever known anyplace except the Warden Diamond, either didn't believe the man or they couldn't care less about the aliens. This reaction was understandable, and, I found, exactly what the speaker had anticipated. Either he was a psych or he had some good ones prepare the talk.

"Now, I know this doesn't seem to apply to you, but the fact is, it does. The Four Lords have made this contract and they are in the process of carrying it out. Their means are irrelevant to you, since they are worked against non-Diamond people, but those means depended on secrecy to the very last minute. Now that secrecy is blown. The Confederacy knows. Knows, but not enough. They are left with two options. We are one. The Four Lords must go, and be replaced by more honest, Warden-oriented people who will work for the Diamond and not on some sort of mass revenge. But we are no tools of the Confederacy, I assure you. We do this for our own good."

Nice dramatic pause here, I thought.

"The second and only remaining option as to the overthrow of the Four Lords and the consequent flushing out of these aliens is simple. The Confederacy, if it can not achieve or see the first, will not hesitate to do on a mass scale what they fail to do on a simple scale. They propose to incinerate the four Warden Diamond worlds totally and kill every living person and thing upon them."

Another pause and much agitation and some really loud comments rose from the crowd. It sounded angry and upset.

"They have the power to do this. They have the means. And those aliens won't save us. If they could, they wouldn't have needed the Four Lords in the first place. Therefore, this organization of good, serious men and women of the Diamond, very different on each world but nonetheless there, was formed not to save the Confederacy, which means nothing to us, but to save our homes, our worlds, our very lives. The Four Lords will not back down. They are in this to the death, since anything less than the aliens' total victory will destroy them. And since we know very little about them ourselves, we have no reason to think that, even in the case of a now improbable alien and Four Lords victory, those aliens would then be friendly to us. We have no choice.

"However, each planet is different, and must be dealt with by different methods—and is best dealt with by the natives of those worlds. Therefore, the members of Medusa's Opposition must now sit back, reflect, and discuss the situation among themselves. Cells will be asked within no more than two weeks to propose plans for action. Those plans will be examined and coordinated by us, and then a single master plan will be developed. We will win. We must win. I leave you now to discuss the situation in your individual cells. With your help, Medusa, TMS, and the very idea of monitors that strangles the world will be vanquished within a year."

With that the recording stopped, and there was instant pandemonium that took the group leader some time to quiet down to a dull roar. Finally she got enough of a lull to yell, "Discussion will be in individual cell groups. Those with numbers beginning in four will file out first, then those with six, following your cell leaders. Those in my cell will remain here! Do it now!"

Everyone stood around for a few moments, then a small group of four started toward the exit, followed by the rest, still grumbling and talking. As for me, I was reasonably excited by this development, since it meant action in the foreseeable future. I could just imagine the furious debates that would ensue when we met in private from now on. But something still bothered me a little. Was it *really* true that they had no plan, or was this simply a test? And would the truth sell to these folks?

I saw Sister 657, and turned to Ching. "What do you think?"

She shrugged. "It's hard to believe."

"It's true," I told her. "I knew it before I ever got to Medusa."

She thought about that one for a moment. Finally she said, "But *is* it any of our business, really? I'm not sure I even know what he means by aliens, and as for the Confederacy, all Outside is just a fairy tale to us, anyway."

I expected more of this logic when we assembled in our cell meeting. A lot more. What could you expect from people who weren't even sure what wild animals lived on their own native world? What did the concept of "alien" mean to them, anyway? Cerberan or Charonese was as alien as they could probably think. The idea that somebody, somewhere, could or would give an order and be willing and able to blow up a world was incomprehensibly abstract. I suspected that the Opposition leader had his hands full. I could tell just from his accent that he was a transportee himself, probably from the civilized worlds. His fancy, wood-paneled office wasn't in the Medusan style, at least none I'd ever seen, leading to the inescapable conclusion that our leaders were Cerberan or Charonese, not Medusan. That would also be the ultimate conclusion of the group, I knew—and would cause even more intense anti-leadership feelings. For the first time these play rebels were being asked to do something, possibly to put their lives on the line, and they would do anything to avoid that.

Our group was going out, and I jumped down and helped Ching down as well. We turned and followed the others, bringing up the rear of the group. I moved only a few paces outside the door when I stopped and ducked back inside. Ching, startled, looked at me. "What's the matter?"

"TMS!" I shouted so that everybody could hear. "It's a trap!"

The monitors also heard my echoed warning, because there was the sudden sound of an amplified official voice. "This is TMS! Everyone inside that room will come out, one by one, hands on heads, starting exactly one minute from now! We will gas anyone left after the rest have emerged, so there is no reason to hold back. You are trapped, and there is no way out. You have fifty seconds!"

Ching looked at me, scared and confused. "What will we do?"

I peered back out the door and saw perhaps a dozen agents, lined up on both sides of the catwalk about ten meters on either side of the temporary bridge. I had never seen TMS monitors armed with anything more lethal than a night stick, but these held very familiar-looking laser weapons.

I turned back to Ching and lowered my voice. "Now, listen carefully. I'm going to try and bluff us out of here with Hocrow's name. At the very least that should get us taken to her." I turned and looked at the remaining Opposition members in the room. Most had their hoods off and defeat registered all over their faces and in their mannerisms. They were sheep who'd do what they were told, like good little children, now that they'd been caught.

"Thirty seconds!"

"Damn!" I swore. "No, that Hocrow thing won't work except as a diversion. She's got to be behind this, at least partly. That means I'm no longer useful to her. We'll get psyched with the sheep. We've got to escape."

"Twenty seconds!"

"Escape? *How?*" Ching's whole expression showed that the very concept was alien to her. On Medusa, you were raised from birth to believe that there was no escape.

"I'm going to get one of those guns, then go over the rail into the sewer. Follow me if you want, but it's gonna be rough."

"Ten seconds!"

"But—where can we go?"

"Only one place. It's that or the Goodtime Girls, love. Ready?"

She nodded.

"Come out *now!*"

I walked out, hands above my head, and Ching followed. The rest of the cell walked behind us, looking very dejected. I could now see the others who'd gone before us lined up on both sides, and I couldn't help but be disgusted at the sight. Not a single weapon was aimed at them; in fact, nobody was even looking at them. Yet there they stood, hands meekly over heads, waiting for the rest of the sheep. Well, by God, they had one rabid dog in this bunch. Still, I couldn't believe that these were the shock troops of a real rebellion. If they had any guts or weren't so completely conditioned by their society, they could have easily taken all those TMS agents and their weapons. *Escape? Where?* Rule one: first escape, then go where they aren't.

Thanks to the illuminated stripes on its top, you could see a pretty long ways up and down the pipe, and the dozen TMS agents were all I saw. Only two on each side held laser weapons, short rifles from the looks of them.

"Get over against the wall with your traitorous friends!" snapped the laser-armed woman closest to me.

"Hey! I'm with Major Hocrow—I'm her inside man!" I protested.

"Major Hocrow is under arrest, just like you," the monitor snapped back. "You'll meet her in traitor's hell!"

Oho! Well, that was interesting. At least it meant that Hocrow was either being done in by a subordinate who was walking into her job or she really was with the Opposition and was one of those who ran cover for us. I would never know which, but the comment removed any last doubts I had about what I was going to do. There was no reprieve, and, once out of here, no chance at all.

I walked on past the monitor with the nasty tone, who, I saw, was no longer even looking at us but idly holding the rifle while gazing at the people coming behind us. I was about the same size as the monitor, but I had several advantages, not the least of which was that I wasn't conditioned by Medusa and I knew how to use that fancy rifle.

I whirled, pushed, and knocked her head into the rail, then reached out and grabbed the rifle from her loose grip as she struck.

In one motion I ducked, came up with the rifle, using it to push Ching on past, then opened fire on the line of monitors across from me. The beam, set to kill, sliced through them all pretty neatly, leaving just one weapon and four unarmed monitors at my back.

Men and women screamed at the violence that was not and had never been a part of their lives. I grabbed the groggy monitor I'd pushed into the rail in a hammer grip and, using her as a shield, started firing at the others.

I still would have failed, though, if three of the sheep

still pressed against the wall hadn't made a split-second decision and rushed out. The officer holding the laser rifle on the far end was pushed into the muck, toppling nicely over the rail. The other three monitors, looking not just stunned but actually stricken, had eyes only for my rifle—and they stood still as stone.

"Thanks!" I called out to the three who'd come to my aid. "I couldn't have done it without you!" One of them waved, and I looked over at Ching. "You all right?"

"You—you *killed* them!"

"It's my job. I'll tell you about it sometime. Right now we have to get out of here—fast." I looked up and down at the Opposition members, some of whom still had their hands over their heads. I could sympathize, sort of. What they'd just seen was impossible, and that's why it'd worked. The monitors were simply too self-assured and too relaxed, too confident that the sheep would all be meek. They reacted very slowly, and, amateurishly, they had their rifles on narrow-beam kill, which allowed me to get that whole neat row with a single shot. Even the monitors were products of Medusa, conditioned to certain kinds of behavior and confident in their total mastery over the common herd.

I pushed my prisoner into the others and freed myself of any physical restrictions. The monitor rubbed her head and looked at me with a mixture of fear and confusion. "You better let us have that! There is no escape. Your entire organization is broken."

I smiled at her, which confused her all the more. "Okay, you Opposition members, listen up!" I yelled. "They're picking up our people all over the city, maybe all over the planet. You have only three choices. You can kill yourselves, go with the monitors, or come with me!"

"Come with you? Where?" somebody yelled back nervously.

"Outside! In the bush and the wild! It's the only place to run!"

That suggestion stopped them for a moment. I let them mull over the implications, but only for a short period. We had to move fast, before we were missed. This group of monitors was the usual bunch of egomaniacal incompetents, but TMS had much better than these, and it wouldn't take very long for their best to set out after us. I wanted to be long gone by then. "Anybody here know where the sewers dump outside the city and how to get there from here?"

"I know 'em pretty well," one of the three who'd pushed at the right moment called back. "I think I can get us out of here."

"Who's coming? I have to know *now!*"

It didn't surprise me that only the three who'd showed any guts wanted to come. Counting Ching, who was still looking pretty scared and confused herself, and me, that was five out of almost sixty. Some rebels!

"You three come up with me!" I called, then turned to Ching. "Coming?"

She was frightened and shocked, but she nodded affirmatively. "I go with you."

"Good girl!" I looked at the three. All were women, and one was familiar. "Well! Morphy! I *thought* you'd have the guts!"

Our demanding shift supervisor looked sheepish. "You knew?"

"Almost from the start. Introductions later, though." I flicked the rifle field to wide scan. "This won't hurt anybody," I said loud enough for all to hear, "just knock you out for a couple of minutes. I gotta say, though, that you deserve what you're going to get from TMS." I looked around. "Last chance." Nobody moved.

I fired first at the side with the monitors, then turned as the others on the other side screamed once more and started to panic. They all dropped in their tracks, although they were going to be a pain to crawl over on the catwalk.

I looked at them, feeling oddly confident and solid with the rifle in my hand. Four women and me. That could make the wild easier to take, that was for sure.

"C'mon, tribe!" I said, and we started picking our way through the unconscious bodies toward the clear area of the tunnel.

CHAPTER EIGHT

The Wild Ones

When we'd gotten pretty far from the fallen crowd, I stopped and turned to them. I had had the foresight to pick up the other rifle as we'd moved by the dead monitor on the end, as well as a power pack from the monitor's belt, but the charges were still limited and I was pretty sure I was the only one who knew how to fire the things.

"Okay—now things get messy," I told them. "They'll have squads all through this tunnel, and we're going to have to crawl in the muck below the catwalks and keep very still when they pass near so they go right on past. Understand?"

They nodded. I looked at the one who had said she knew the sewage system, a very attractive women perhaps in her early twenties. "You said you knew these sewers. Can we get near a train at the exit point?"

She looked startled. "I thought you said we were going out with the garbage."

"Argue later. But for the record, now that we've said that it's exactly where they'll look for us. Remember, they've got all sorts of scanners in these tunnels, too, and they'll all be looking for us. I've looked at their regular locations, though, which depend on the power cables, and they're all located above the catwalks. If we're quiet enough, and careful enough, they won't see us down in the muck below. They have fixed focal lengths, so anything below the catwalks is a blur. Let's move—you lead. Morphy, you know what I'm thinking?"

She nodded. "Let's try it."

"Okay. Follow the leader, no talking unless I tell you. Let's go, gang—over and into the muck." One by one they

116

complied, although not without some real hesitation. The stuff was really awful, thicker than I would have thought and close to waist-deep.

I couldn't resist thinking we were in deep shit, but it was the only oddball thought I allowed myself and it was too literally true to be funny. I had deliberately returned along the route we'd taken from the café, on the theory that those monitoring devices might still be out of commission, but I couldn't depend on it. This mission would be played by ear, and first we had to get to an exit point—a long, long way in the sewage.

The next several hours were nervous ones, although my hopes that the initial escape route was still blocked were borne out. Several times we stood right under squads of TMS herding Opposition members to exit points, and several more times we huddled in the stinking muck as small, very efficient armed patrols double-timed above us. We were all pretty well covered with the stuff and slipping and sliding as we moved, and it was clear we couldn't keep this up indefinitely.

So far we'd been extremely lucky. My escape was still something of a miracle, but it simply proved that when you have even one potential wolf you don't send sheep out to capture other sheep, even if the sheep you send are arrogant bastards. After the initial escape, we were protected by the flaw in their visual monitoring system and the very complexity of master sewage drains under a city of close to 350,000. There were probably a couple of thousand kilometers of drainage tunnels under the city, and TMS simply couldn't cover more than a fraction of that with its personnel. They had to wait for us to make a mistake, to betray our position, so they could concentrate their forces in that area.

I was proud of all four of my companions, who held together under some of the worst conditions I could think of, not only physically but mentally, knowing that just one little mistake would betray us to these overhead monitors. The monitors, I was sure, were all staffed by real live people as well as by the computers.

Finally, I had to ask the one who was supposed to know the tunnels if she really did. Frankly, none of us could take much more of this, and, sooner or later, we would certainly be found. "How much farther to the trains?"

"At the rate we're going, maybe an hour more," she whispered.

I didn't like the sound of that. "How long to any kind of exit near the city border?"

She thought a moment. "From the sector numbers at the last junction, maybe ten minutes to a drainage outlet. But there'll be an energy barrier there."

"I'll chance it. We can't take much more of this. Lead on."

She shrugged.

What seemed like an hour later we came close to the outlet. I could hear the thing rushing like a falls, and we were now waist high in sewage, which was developing a fairly strong current. There were no catwalks in the direction of the outlet, so there would be maybe thirty meters when we'd be fully exposed. There would certainly be a visual monitor up there, if only as a final check on animal entry should the energy barriers fail.

I tried to angle myself as best I could to see what the outlet looked like, but all I could see was the sewage dropping into some sort of sludge pool below and the unmistakable light purple of an energy barrier. "I wonder if that barrier is beyond the drop," I said aloud. "If it is, we might be able to go over the falls and then, beneath the surface, under the barrier. Do you know how much of a drop it is?"

She shook her head from side to side. "It varies. This plant is located in an old stone quarry. It might not be much of a drop but the holding pool could be fifty meters deep."

I gave a low whistle. "Well, that washes that idea, I guess. Let's go for the transport terminal after all."

At that moment, from just ahead of us there came the sound of many feet running in step, which then ceased abruptly. I heard a lot of shuffling around not too far down from us and saw the glare of spotlights on the sludge below. Obviously I'd blown it—the monitors here had to be a lot better than most.

"All right! We know you're down there!" a sharp woman's voice called. "Come out now, one at a time, or we'll come down and get you. And if we have to get into that slop we will not take you alive!"

I looked at my four companions. "What'll we *do?*" Ching asked, looking to me as if I had all the answers.

I sighed. "Nothing to do, really. Can you all swim?"

They nodded, which helped.

"Then take a deep breath, launch yourselves into this muck, and stay below it, letting the current take you over."

Morphy looked down uncomfortably at the muck. *"Under* it?"

"The whole way. It shouldn't be for long. Either that or they'll be here in a couple of minutes. We're already so stinking this won't make much of a difference." I took a deep breath, let it out, took another, let a little out, and ducked under, hugging onto my two rifles for dear life.

It was a miserable experience to top all other miserable experiences, particularly since I had to keep my eyes closed. All I could tell was that I was moving, with agonizing slowness; but aside from trying to stay below the surface without knowing if in fact I was doing that, I also couldn't be sure I was being carried with the current. I finally decided I'd hold out until I either fell, got knocked cold by the energy barrier, or had to come up for air, in which case I'd come up shooting.

It seemed as if I had been down for an eternity, when, oddly, the sludge seemed to thin and I felt less pressure to breathe. Then, suddenly, I broke the surface not from the top but in front of me, and I had to duck very quickly to pass just under the energy barrier. Then I was falling, and falling fast, still in the midst of a sludge river. I lost both rifles in the fall, which was at least twenty meters, then struck the main pool below, arms out to try and cushion what I sincerely believed would be a crippling or fatal impact.

I went into the pool effortlessly, and continued down for a bit with the momentum. I instinctively angled myself, treating the pool as common water, and arched back up again, breaking the surface.

There was no current in the pool, which was surrounded on three sides by sheer rock walls. Down at the far end was the structure of what had to be the automated treatment plant. It wasn't much—Medusa didn't really care what happened to the environment outside—but it operated in sunlight only, mixing the raw sewage with natural water and forcing it out into a river that led directly to the ocean. Just enough to keep the stuff from backing up and contaminating the natural water supply of the city.

The damlike structure wasn't very high, and I headed for its sloping white concrete wall. I reached it quickly, and crawled out onto it. Gasping for breath, I decided to make for the top of the thing, which was only about seven or eight meters above on the slanted surface. I would wait there as long as I could to see if anybody else made it through, but I knew that TMS would be out here as soon as that squad leader figured out what we'd done and radioed back to headquarters.

I was halfway up before I realized that I hadn't exactly swum that distance conventionally and even now was climbing the wall in a most unconventional manner. My arms, now a dark sludge-brown, were almost flipperlike! I realized that, somehow, I'd changed—and fast. There would be time for more self-examination later, I decided— but first I had to make the top or it was all for nothing.

I waited there nervously, but not for very long. My eyes quickly adjusted to the near darkness, and I soon saw two other shapes pop up and make for the wall, then a third.

When the first one got to the edge of the retaining pool and climbed out, I got something of a shock. It was a weird, inhuman sort of monster, all black and shiny, with an angular head, flippers, and a pair of strong, webbed hind legs. The creature began to crawl up toward me, wiggling up on its belly, and I almost recoiled in alarm until I suddenly realized that my own arms resembled those others. A second one made it and started the climb as the first one almost reached me, caught sight of me, and cried out in fear.

"Don't worry!" I called back. "It's just me! The Wardens changed us to live in that muck! Get up here—all of you! We'll change back soon enough if we get away from this!"

The others had similar reactions, but got talked up nonetheless.

I looked at them, and could see their skin begin to lose some of its shimmer and start to—well, *ooze*, as if our bodies were made of a puttylike substance that had a mind of its own. Strangely, I felt a little better about that—here was a stimulus with proof! If you placed yourself in an untenable environment, you changed. You changed into whatever would allow you to survive. This certainly explained the Wild Ones' ability to escape from TMS, and probably accounted for the shape-change legends as well. The Wild Ones used the ability to hide and to survive.

If I could just get my hands on a psych machine and convince somebody he was in a different sort of environment, it would work—but still not under real control. You would become an improvised monster, whatever your Wardens required for your survival.

But how did the Wardens understand just what you needed in that instant you needed it? And from where did they get the incredibly sophisticated knowledge of biology to accomplish the change so quickly?

We waited another five minutes, and I checked the roll. Ching had made it, although she was terribly confused and terrified by the shape change. Morphy had come through and one other, whose name I still didn't know. Our guide through the sewers, though, was not here.

We were becoming "human" again, and quickly, as the Wardens inside us sensed our changing environment. In fact, we were becoming our old selves, indicating that either the original pattern was always reverted to when the Wardens were "at rest" or that a strong sense of self-identity would reimpose it. The one thing that was not coming back was hair, I noted; and our skin remained that dark brown of the "monsters" we had briefly become.

It was fascinating to watch my own arms slowly flow, change, rearrange back into the more familiar patterns. When we were humanoid enough to have full upright muscle control, I took one last look for a fourth head in the pool. Nothing. "We have to get moving. I think I see a patrol over there on the far side."

Morphy looked at me, then back at the pool. "But we're still one short!"

"Can't be helped. Either she couldn't change or she got plugged or caught. Either way, we can't help her by getting caught or shot ourselves. Let's move!"

The one whose name I still didn't know looked puzzled and confused. "Where? Where do we go now?"

I sighed. "Somewhere else, of course. Follow me!" Then I was off along the top of the plant. Coming on some steps on the other side, I started down as laser tracers started illuminating the night. Once we hit the rather shallow river below, I just ran into it and waded across to the other side, not even checking to see if the others were following. I didn't have the time, and if they weren't there, I couldn't do anything about it anyway. I was heading for the forest located just on the other side of the river, and I wasn't going to stop for anything until I made the cover of those trees.

Suddenly I heard Morphy's voice yell, "Drop!" and I didn't wait to find out why. I dropped right into the water, which, by this time, was not deep enough to cover my body. After I was down, I raised my head a little and looked up, seeing what Morphy had seen. A small illuminated bubble with two TMS monitors in it was flying almost noiselessly down the river, shining a spotlight on the whole river course. I made a quick check to see that everybody was, indeed, down, then froze as the thing approached, passed right over us, and continued on. In this light, and with this shallow, rocky bed, we had to look like rocks to a copter going any speed at all. But I was pretty sure this wasn't something TMS did every day; we were being pursued.

When the lights disappeared, I stood up again and we all made it to the far bank and the cover of the trees. I finally allowed myself to let up a bit and collapsed on the ground. The others did the same, and it was a little while before any of us could talk.

Finally I said, "Well, the age of miracles has returned. We got away with it sure enough."

Morphy looked back at me with a grim expression, then at the other two. Except for our coloration and the total absence of any body hair, we all looked pretty much as we had, although the transformation or whatever it was had split our flimsy clothes as well. "Stark naked, in an unknown wilderness, hunted like wild animals, and without a hair to our name, and he thinks he's winning!"

"Not to mention starving to death," the strange woman put in.

I grinned. "I am. We are—will—win. We didn't go through all this to lose now. And if that tumble in the sludge didn't teach you that we are survival machines, I don't know what will. But I think we'll have to get as far from here as we can tonight. I don't think they'll hunt us very far or long—it just isn't worth it, even though we're all going to be pretty wanted by this group."

"After those others tell about what you did back there when we were first captured, I'd say they'll want *you* more than anybody," Morphy replied. "What you did to those monitors wasn't—*human*. I wonder if even you realize that you knocked over the armed monitor, grabbed her rifle, turned, killed four monitors, then whirled back to cover the others in something under five seconds?"

"Five sec—" I was struck speechless for a moment. No wonder the job had seemed so easy! Five seconds for the entire thing! In my original fine-tuned body, *maybe*, just maybe, I could have done it, but here and now . . . knowing what to do and making your body do it are two different things. Ask any fifty-year-old space pilot. And yet, the answer to it was obvious.

"I knew what to do," I told her, "and the Wardens supplied the rest. I was under such tremendous tension, picking my position and mentally preparing for the moves, that the Wardens must have made the necessary survival adjustment—the same principle that turned us into whatever it was we had turned into briefly back there. If you had the knowledge and the will it would've worked for you, too. So you see, we're not exactly helpless out here. We carry our protection with us. We were made for this planet —I almost said *designed* for it, and maybe that's right— and *this* is Medusa, not those comfortable, sealed prisons we call cities here."

"That was some . . . strange thing that happened to us, you can't say it wasn't," our mystery woman put in. "I never heard of anybody changing into anything else before, except maybe sex."

"That's true," I admitted, "but the system's designed against it. We're all kept in artificial, stable environments where that sort of thing just won't happen. Even so, I'm sure it has, maybe when somebody's gotten into an accident or was in danger of drowning or something. Transformations may occur every day. But if so, those people are rescued, hustled off to psychs, and put right. Even memories are sponged from the minds of people involved directly or of the people who observed it. And, by the way, I think we ought to know who you are. I'm Tarin Bul."

"Angi Patma, Construction Guild," she responded.

We made introductions all around. I was particularly concerned with the usually outgoing Ching, who now seemed quiet and sullen, still in shock. I walked over to her. "Come on—we're gonna be fine," I soothed.

She looked up at me. "I know."

I frowned. "What's wrong, hon? I was proud of you!"

She was silent for a moment. Finally she said, "You killed four people, Tarin. Killed. And you're not even a little sorry about it."

I sighed. "Listen, Ching—I had to do it. It was the only way. When someone is marching you off to your death, and happy to do it, he forfeits his own right to life. Those survivors—they're still going to get those fifty-five or so who remained. None of them are going to be left alive, at least not without destroyed minds. That is a worse crime in my book. Remember, these people were picked for TMS for the same reason everybody else on Medusa is picked for his job. They *like* bullying, scaring, and even killing people."

"Don't you?"

That stopped me for a moment. The fact was, I really did love my job, of course. But there *was* a difference. At least, I hoped there was. "I'm not interested in bullying or scaring anybody, except for that kind of person. People who like to hurt other people is who I hunt and get. That's not so bad, is it?"

She didn't seem sure, and the more I thought about it, neither was I. From birth I had been raised to believe in the Confederacy, in its perfection and its ideals. But, in that context, what *was* my job, anyway? The same as TMS here? To track down those who posed a threat to the Confederacy's system—or who abused or perverted it—and send them to psychs, or to the Warden Diamond, or, on rare occasions, to their deaths. True, most of the Confederacy was a far better system than Ypsir's Medusa, but the people here did in fact believe in that system, including those in TMS. In *their* minds they were no different from me. Did that make us different—or the same? Medusa was nothing if not a perversion—a distorted mirror image—of the Confederacy's system and dreams. That must have been why I felt so uncomfortable with it.

I rose to my feet. "Let's get walking. They'll have foot patrols through here anytime now, and we've already stayed too long. Let's make all the time at night we can. We can talk on the way."

They *did* send a few patrols and copters after us, and we saw or heard them from time to time, but they made no more than a minimum effort, which simply wasn't good enough. To their minds, being out in the wild was tantamount to being dead anyway, and nobody was really worth the kind of effort that would have been needed to track us down. Again it was Medusa's own system that allowed us our freedom, although what sort of freedom remained to be seen.

The biology texts hadn't revealed the half of Medusa's natural history, though. Not only were there hundreds, perhaps thousands, of different plants large and small, but the forests literally teemed with animal life. All of it was strange-looking on the surface, but at the same time very much like many other planets. Perhaps the theory that ecosystems developed under nearly identical conditions came out much the same way was true. Here, as elsewhere, trees were clearly trees and insects clearly bugs—and they served the same functions.

The first real concern wasn't eluding a ho-hum pursuit, but finding food. Coming into spring in the "tropical" regions meant that there were a number of berries and fruits around, but little looked ripe and all was unknown to me.

"How do we know what's safe and what's not?" Angi complained, hungry like the rest of us.

"I think it's simple," I told them all. "At least, it should be. If there's anything *really* lethal around it should produce some kind of warning that our Wardens will trigger. That berry, there, for example, smells really foul, and I wouldn't touch it. Even my initial indoctrination, though, said that we *could* eat almost anything, with the Wardens converting the substance into what we and they really need. I'd say, for now, we just pick something that at least seems practical to eat and eat it."

It took some time, though, and a lot of guts, before we decided to go through with a test. The leaves and unripe fruits tasted from bitter to lousy, but once we started eating we found it difficult to stop until we felt full. All of us suffered a bit from stomach aches and the runs that night but after a somewhat fitful sleep on the open ground we all awoke feeling much better. After that our Wardens adjusted even more to our new situation and provided the guidance we needed—much as I'd hoped. Some stuff that tasted lousy the first time tended to taste quite good after that, while other stuff just tasted worse and worse. With that neat sorting and classification system to go on, we had no more trouble, although I confess that Ching wasn't the only one who dreamed of good meat and fresh fruit.

Well, we wouldn't starve, so the next thing was to adapt our lifestyle to this new environment. Clothing proved unnecessary, as always, and after what we'd been through modesty was no longer a factor. Shelter from the cold rains and occasional ice-pellet storms was provided by the forests and, if necessary, we could rig portable lean-tos from branches and the broad leaves of a prevalent bush. In point of fact I had the survival training and the means to make permanent dwellings, if necessary, but I had no intention of founding a village at this point. We had three months before the first snows, with the best weather yet to come, to find the Wild Ones. That had to be our first priority.

Over several days I made a broad circle around Rochande and then headed toward the coast which that handy map in my head said was there. From that point, and using the sun for direction, I could determine our approximate location and chart where we were going.

The first few weeks were education weeks. We learned what we could eat, where it was most likely to grow, and what caused problems. I gave a small seminar in survival skills—building lean-tos, that sort of thing—and we also learned the habits of many of the animals. The tree-dwelling tubros were all around, but if you didn't bother them they wouldn't bother you. The vettas stayed mostly in the clearings and on the plains, so we tended to avoid such places. We had not met a harrar as yet, and I, for one, had no intention of doing so if I could help it.

Then there were the occasional thermal areas. The place wasn't full of them, but they were far more numerous than I originally would have guessed. Geyser holes, bubbling mudpots, and fumeroles turned up in the damnedest places and, occasionally, we even came across a hot thermal pool. Once you got used to the sulfurous stink, these pools were very handy for bathing. We even tried some experiments in wrapping all sorts of food in leaf bags and boiling them.

We also got to know one another better than I think any of us had ever known anyone before. I will say this for all three of them—they were inwardly tough. Though complaints were numerous they had by and large accepted their lot fatalistically and began to look upon this new life as some sort of great adventure. I wondered, though, if they would have fared so confidently or so well had I not been there to teach them a few tricks of the trade.

There was no more purpose in concealment, and I explained to them just who and what I was. In a sense the explanation seemed to reassure them, and the fact that I was a professional agent somehow seemed to soften Ching's initial revulsion at my killings. It became less of a radical change in me than a reversion to form, and she seemed better able to accept that.

We lapsed into a total familiarity so easily I often wondered if the Wardens had anything to do with it. Morphy became "just Bura," Ching was still Ching, and Angi's last name I just about forgot. As for me, I accepted everybody calling me by Ching's pet name for me—Tari—and we became just one big family.

The fifty-five who remained behind continued to weigh heavily on me, though, and I decided to find out why they stayed and these didn't.

Bura, it seemed, was a native but had once been much higher in the Guild. Years earlier she had married into a family group that included another exile to the Diamond, a rough-and-tumble man built like an ox who had a horrible temper with those outside his own family group but was kind and gentle at home. Still, she admired his independent spirit, his disdain for TMS and the system, and,

I suspect, she damn near worshiped him. One day he had one too many run-ins with TMS, of course, and he'd blown up and literally snapped a monitor in two. Most of the family, to save their own skins, were willing to testify against him as to his murderous instincts and to his inability to "assimilate" into Medusan society. Bura refused, for which she was transferred halfway around the world and demoted to a passenger-service shift supervisor with no hope of advancing any further. At that she'd gotten off lucky, but when the psych she was sent to by TMS for adjustment instead introduced her to the Opposition, she was more than ready and willing and quickly rose to cell leader—Sister 657, of course.

Angi had a less understandable background. Born and raised on Medusa, and never to her knowledge having had any contact with Diamond transportees, she nonetheless, was always somebody who didn't quite fit. As a kid she'd beaten the bus fares and done some minor shoplifting— for which she was never caught—and she'd qualified for training as a civil engineer. The subject fascinated her, but the restrictions, the lack of creativity, the sheer sameness imposed from above, had always gotten to her, so she'd never progressed very far. When you built just one way, and all of the tough problems had already been solved, it was a pretty dull profession. She'd been doing quality-control supervision for a massive repair of the bus system in a sector of Rochande—"real thrilling work," she called it without enthusiasm. Again it was a routine psych exam that introduced her to the Opposition, and she joined simply because it was another something different to do. She had been the one who had pushed the armed monitor over the rail—"strictly on impulse," she told us.

None knew the other courageous woman, the one who had led us out of the city only to be denied freedom and life herself, but all of us agreed that, no matter where— or whether—she was at the moment, she was and would always be a member of our family.

Family is exactly what we became in those early days of Medusa's spring. On a world whose culture was based upon the group marriage, there was no real jealousy or bad feelings between any of the women, and certainly not from me. In fact, this period of isolation, just the four of us living much as man's ancestors must have lived back on the ancient home world of man a million years ago, was in many respects the best time of my entire life. It was during this period that, I think, I turned my back once and for all on the Confederacy.

We made our way in zigzag fashion from coast to interior thermal areas and back again, developing a sense of where the thermal regions were. We headed north because Bura's long tenure on the trains had shown her that some Wild Ones definitely lived between Rochande and Gray Basin. She had caught glimpses of manlike shapes in the distance several times—in the direction of the coast. Occasionally we would find traces of habitation, signs of a temporary encampment, but there seemed no way at all to tell how warm or cold the trail.

Ultimately we never found them—they found us. Exactly how long we were alone in our wandering tribal existence I don't know, but summer was definitely upon us when, one day, stepping into a clearing, we suddenly found ourselves surrounded by several new people.

The group consisted of one man and six women, at least one of whom appeared quite pregnant. Like us, they were dark-skinned and hairless, a condition that looked quite natural and normal to us now. All wore skirts of some reddish or black hair and all bore homemade bows and spears. Obviously from their manner they'd been observing us for some time, but they said nothing and made no move toward us when they showed themselves. They just stood there, looking hard at our little group. We, of course, looked back.

Finally I shrugged, put up my hands palms out. "We're friends. We mean you no harm."

For a while they made no response, and gave no indication that they understood my words, and I grew nervous that there might be some sort of language gap. No telling what sort of culture people raised in this wild would develop. But, finally, one of the women asked, "What tribe do you come from? Where are your tribal marks?"

"No tribe," I responded, feeling relieved. "Or, say, rather, that we are our own tribe."

"Outcasts," one of the others hissed, in a tone that did not indicate approval.

"Not from a tribe," I said quickly. "We escaped from the cities."

They showed some surprise at that, the first real emotion I'd seen any of them display. I had never really dealt with a primitive group before, and I was winging it, hoping I wouldn't put my foot in my mouth. Those weapons looked pretty grim. One of the women whispered to the one who appeared to be their leader, "The demons live in those places. It is a demon trick."

The leader shrugged off the comment. "What do you wish here?"

"A tribe," I responded, trying to get as much into the mind-set as I could. "A place to belong, to learn the ways of the world and the ways of a great tribe of people."

That seemed to be the right response, because the leader nodded sagely to herself. She seemed to think it over, then made her decision—which, I noted, was final no matter what the others thought. "You will come with us. We are the People of the Rock. We will take you to our camp, where the Elders will decide."

"That sounds good to us," I told her, and, with that, they all turned and started back into the forest. I looked at the others, shrugged, and followed.

CHAPTER NINE

The Demons of the Mount

They had not mentioned that they were several days from this camp of theirs, and that didn't become apparent for some time. They allowed us to follow them, all right, but kept themselves apart, not talking to us any more than they had to and occasionally taking suspicious glances at us when they thought we weren't looking. It was clear that, while a leader's decision was absolute and to be obeyed, it didn't mean you had to agree with it.

They carried sacks of some kind of skin, in which were various supplies, bows, extra spear points, that sort of thing, but no food. That they foraged for, much as we had, although they had a dietary element that we'd lacked to this point. They hunted vettas and tubros, and did it expertly, considering the primitiveness of their equipment. They could stake out a place silently for an hour or more, seemingly not moving at all. But when a vetta, for example, came close they would rise around it in a circle, tossing spears and shooting arrows with precision and lightning speed, bringing the panicked animal down. Then they would disembowl it with a different, even nastier sort of spear. The vettas, too, were Warden creatures, and you had to kill them quickly or repairs would begin.

Once they were sure the animal was dead they would skewer it on a couple of spears and carry it between two of them, the poles expertly balanced on their shoulders, until they came to a thermal pool. There, experts wielded stone axes in butchering the animal into various small parts which were then wrapped in leaves and cooked in the thermal pools. As one who had, at one time or another, eaten natural meat on frontier worlds, it wasn't

131

more than a curiosity to me, but to my three wives it was a sickening experience. Butchering an animal is not pretty, and none of the three had ever seen it done before or even thought about it. I had to work pretty hard to prevent them from showing their disgust.

"You have to have real guts," I told them, "like you did back in the escape. If they offer any to us, take it and eat it. You don't have to like it, and you can be disgusted by it, but we need them."

"I don't know why we need anybody," Ching protested. "We were doing pretty good, I think, and we were *happy*."

"Vettas are happy until they're caught and killed," I retorted. "We're more than animals, Ching. We're human beings—and human beings have to grow and learn. That's why we need them."

We *were* offered some of the kill, after the rest had taken their pick of the best cuts, and I complimented them on their great skill as hunters—which also seemed to please them. I think they knew that my three city-dwelling companions were upset by the hunt and kill, and were vastly amused by their reactions as they tried to bite into the chunks of meat. Angi, whose motto seemed to be "I'll try anything once" was the most successful; Bura ate as little as she thought she could get away with and looked extremely uncomfortable; Ching finally forced a mouthful down, but she just couldn't conceal her disgust and refused to eat any more. I didn't press her; I thought throwing up would be in the worst of taste.

I was relieved to see that our tribal hosts were taking things so well, and I began to suspect that some of them, at least, were neither as naive nor as ignorant as they pretended to be.

They had a ceremony at the end of the meal that seemed to have solemn religious overtones. Dead vetta would not keep; only the skin was savable, and you had to strip off the meat and bone from it completely and "cure" the skin in the thermal pool. When the host died, the Wardens began to die as well, and decomposition was swift. I had found this the case with fruit and berries, although not with cut wood and leaves. It was almost as if the Wardens were determined to keep a very clean, almost antiseptic, wilderness, yet knew enough to leave behind those parts that were useful to man.

The ceremony itself was interesting and, as usual with such rites, incomprehensible to me. It involved praying and chanting over the remains, with the leader eventually casting what couldn't be saved into the thermal pool in the manner of an offering, or sacrifice. I wanted very much to know more about such ceremonies and beliefs, if only to keep from stepping on toes, but didn't dare ask right now. There was time enough for that later.

Two more days of travel to the northwest, which included some more hunting, lay the camp. On the way, we approached and actually crossed the tracks of our old train; it brought a twinge of nostalgia to Bura, at least, and certainly to Ching.

The camp was far more than that. Nestled up against the mountains, invisible from anywhere on the ground beyond, it was in every sense a small city. A large circle of stones, some placed by humans, some natural, forming an area more than a kilometer in diameter inside the "walls," guarded the camp from the ground and from the wind, although the roofless area inside was open to the elements. A small stone amphitheater was carved out of the rock floor in the center of the interior—with what my old training told me might be an altar at the bottom. This and a fire pit dominated the place, but there were many conical small dwellings made of skin and supported by strong but temporary wooden beams all over. The bulk of the population was not below in the common yard, but above, actually within the sheer rock wall behind, in what appeared to be dozens of caves. They were all over the wall, high and low, and there were no ladders—only small, well-worn hand- and footholds carved into the sides of the wall. Tribal members, however, scurried up and down that wall and in and out of the caves as if they were born to it.

At the base of the cliff, at ground level was a single cave, a bit larger than the others. Through obviously man-made channels, streams from the snow melt above flowed down in small matched waterfalls to holding pools on both sides of the camp. From there the water was either diverted

for use within the compound or allowed to overflow and
run off through outlets in the protective wall.

Angi, in particular, was impressed. "This is one hell of
a job of civil engineering, mostly done by hand."

"Remember, we're not dealing with a long time period
here," I reminded her and the others as well. "The two
Medusas were only really completely closed off to each
other forty or fifty years ago. It's entirely possible that
some of the original pioneers are still alive here.

It was, in fact, this dichotomy between the inevitable
pioneer resourcefulness and the primitive, religion-based
lifestyle of these people that bothered me the most.

We were told to wait near the amphitheater, and we
could only stand there and look around.

"How many people would you say live here?" I asked
our engineer.

She thought for a moment. "Hard to say. Depends on
how deep those caves are and what kind of chambers are
inside, although I doubt if they're too big. This is meta-
morphic rock, not sedimentary."

"Make a guess."

"A hundred. Maybe a hundred and fifty."

I nodded. "That's about my guess at the top end."

"It's so *small* for a town," Ching put in.

"Uh uh," I responded. "It's too *large*. How do you feed
a hundred and fifty people when you can't store food? If
those tents there were out on the plain, near the vettas, or
in the forest, maybe I could see it. A population this small
might be supported there. But we're half a day from any
grazing or edible forest land. There's something pretty fishy
going on here."

Various people, almost all women and all with those
tribal skirts, went here and there and up and down, always
giving us curious looks, but we were left pretty much alone
for quite a while. Finally somebody seemed to remember
us, and a pregnant woman—not the one with the hunting
party—emerged from one of the skin tents, and walked
over to us. "Come with me," she said. "The Elders will see
you now."

I gave a let-me-do-the-talking glance at the other three,
hoping that was a good idea, and, not surprisingly, the
woman led us over to the ground-level cave.

The first surprise were the torches, nicely aligned and lit along the walls of the cave. This was the first exposed fire we'd seen the Wild Ones use, and really the first real flame we'd seen in a long time.

The cave went back pretty far in the cliff, causing some mental revision of how extensive the interiors could be. More interesting, perhaps ten meters in there appeared an abrupt boundary in the cave wall. The first part of the cave was natural, but the rest of it beyond the boundary had been carved with modern tools, probably a laser cannon.

About a hundred and twenty meters in, the cave opened into a large rectangular chamber, perhaps fifteen by ten and with a five-meter ceiling. Only half of the room, however, was usable; about five meters into the room the floor suddenly stopped and we were looking at a fast-flowing river. Beyond the river, again another five meters, was a recess in the rock, carved by laser—you could tell by the neat squared-off corners. Inside the recess stood three large wooden chairs, with no sign of how anyone would get into or out of that recess. But get in they did—two very old women and an equally aged man sat there, looking at us. I think they were the oldest people I'd ever seen, but they were very much alert and looking at us.

So Elders was not a title of respect but a literal one.

All three were as hairless as everybody else, but their skin was a stretched and wrinkled light gray, like the surrounding rock. In the torchlight they looked eerily impressive.

I glanced around, but could see no sign of our guide—or anybody else. We were alone with the wizened Elders of the People of the Rock.

"What is your name, boy?" one of the women asked in a cracked, high-pitched voice.

"I am called Tari, and also Tarin Bul," I responded.

"But those are not your true names."

I was a little surprised, particularly since this was not a question but a statement of fact. "It is not," I admitted. "However, it is my name now and the only one by which I go."

"You are not a native." The words, again fact and not question, were uttered by the man, whose voice was scarcely different from the old woman's.

"No. I was sent here from the Confederacy."

"As a convict?"

At last! A real question! I had begun to worry. "Against my will, yes." That was true enough. No use telling them any more than I had to for now.

"These women are your family?" That was the third one. "They are."

There was a pause, then the man said, "You told the pilgrims you fled Rochande. Why?"

As concisely as I could, I told them about the Opposition, its betrayal, and our narrow escape. I went into no detail as to motives, just presented the bare facts, concluding with our long search in the wild for others. They sat impassively, but I could tell that their eyes were bright and alive with both intelligence and interest. When I finished I expected more questions on our lives, but that was apparently not of further interest.

"What did the pilgrims tell you this place was?" the first woman asked.

"They just said they were taking us to their tribal camp."

That response brought a chuckle from all three. "Camp. Very good," the second woman commented. "Well—what do you think of this camp?"

"I think it is not a camp or a tribal village," I answered.

"Indeed? Why not?"

"You can't possibly feed all who are here. And you called the hunting party pilgrims."

"Very good, very good," the old man approved. "You are correct. This is not a camp. It is more in the nature of a religious retreat. Does that disturb you?"

"No. As long as we're not to be sacrifices."

They seemed to like that reply; it started them chuckling again. Finally the first woman asked, "What do you expect of your life here in the wild? Why did you seek out those whom the city dwellers call Wild Ones?"

Well, they sure didn't try to pretend they were ignorant or naive. "Knowledge," I told them. "Much of this world is in bondage, and the people don't even all realize it. The city dwellers are becoming about as human as vettas, and not nearly as free. Or, like the tubros, they cling to their safe, secure havens where they don't have to think and only have to do what they are told to be provided with their basic needs."

"And this is wrong?"

"*We* think it is. This Lord of Medusa is evil. He has killed the spirit inside people that makes them human—and he enjoys it. Worse, he has gotten Medusa involved in a clandestine war against the Confederacy itself that might possibly destroy the entire planet."

"And you think you four can stop him?"

"I think we can try," I told them honestly. "I think I would rather try than do nothing."

They thought that one over. Finally the second woman asked me, "In this world picture of human, vettas, and tubros you paint—how do you paint yourselves?"

I smiled. "We escaped. Fifty-five went meekly to their mind-deaths. We are harrars, of course."

They all nodded and did not return the smile. The man said, "In our past we, too, dreamed of destroying that evil system and freeing Medusa for the people. We three were adults fifty-one years ago when the cities were enclosed and the early monitor systems installed. Only one of us—myself—was born here, and I was born before this place became a prison and a madhouse. Less than a thousand, including us, escaped planetwide in the pogrom that resulted in what you have today. But we were clever. Like you, we escaped with nothing at all."

I nodded, having figured as much. "But this place—it was built before the crackdown?"

"It was. Not all of it, of course—just this cave and the network in back of it. Call it an escape place, if you like. Records of its very existence were expunged from Medusa's files after the pogram was inevitable but before it took place. From here, with our hands and those of others, we carved the rest."

"It's very impressive," I told them, and meant it. "Running water, something of a sewage system, shelter—very impressive. But badly located to support any size population."

"Oh, we don't wish a large population," the first woman told us. "That would attract attention. It is neither our purpose nor intent to support anything more here than you see, particularly now. You see, at one time we had such

dreams as you have. But did you think that Talant Ypsir
created the system and initiated the pogrom? He did not.
He was still high and mighty back in the Outside at the
time it was initiated. He only refined it, made it even more
complete. He is the third Lord since it began and each
one has been worse than the one who came before. The
first two died by assassination—and the second one was a
true reformer who intended to reverse the changes and re-
concile Medusans with their land. He was, instead, seduced
by the same handy drug as his predecessor and successor—
absolute power. It is not enough to kill the Lord. It is not
enough to kill the Lord's Council. To accomplish what you
wish would require the failure of all technological support
of the cities, transport, and space. The population would
have to be forced *en masse* into the wild, whether they
wanted to go or not. And that is something that cannot be.
They have the arms and the means to see that it does not."

"And so, with this realization," the man picked up, "we
decided that we could only ignore them as they now ignore
us. Build a new and different culture suited to the land
outside their system."

"But their system will come for you one day," I pointed
out. "In the end, it will engulf you because it must."

"Perhaps. We think not. We hope not. But our way is
the only possible way."

"But it isn't!" I protested. "Your goal *can* be achieved.
The potential is here. How many—ah, Wild Ones are there
now?"

"We prefer Free Tribes," the first woman told me. "There
are between thirty and forty thousand worldwide. That is
an estimate, of course—our communication lines are primitive."

Thirty to forty thousand! What an army that would
make! If only . . . "Such a force could infiltrate and take
the major cities, cripple the industry and transportation
network, and destroy the balance of Medusan control."

"How? Ten thousand near-naked savages, most of whom
think even a flashlight is magic and who have never seen a
light switch or things made of steel and plastic?"

"I believe it can be done, with training. I believe it can
be done because I believe in the possibility of self-con-

trolled body malleability. That is what I am looking for here."

They remained silent—as if thinking about what I just said. They didn't seem very surprised one way or the other about my assertion of controlled malleability. Finally the first woman said, "Foolish one! Do you not think your idea has not been thought of before? From the start it was the only reasonable course. But at the beginning we were disorganized, scattered refugees, without the numbers or abilities. An entire generation was mercilessly hunted all over the planet, and it learned how to survive—but in the wild. The next generation was born here and had nothing but what seemed like fanciful tales of magic. The generation after that, the current one, feels no kinship whatever to the city dwellers—they are demons. Now we have the numbers, but not the will. We built the culture that keeps them alive and holds them together, but it is a primitive one. If we had ten thousand, perhaps even five thousand, people like you four, perhaps we could do it. But the gap between your cultures and your minds and theirs is too great."

I was not prepared to concede the point, but I was very interested in the implications of what she said. "Then controlled malleability is possible."

They didn't answer me; instead, the second woman asked, "Well, what are we to do with you, then? You will never fit into this culture. You will never accept it, and your efforts will bring the others down upon it. You cannot return to the cities. So for now, you will have to stay with us as our guests—but you will not disrupt the people or their customs or beliefs, understand? Until we decide what to do with you you are welcome to our hospitality. But we are perfectly willing, and capable, of terminating you as well. Do you understand?"

I nodded. "I think we do."

"Then, for now, this audience is finished." With that intonation a small boat appeared from the left inside the cave, showing just how you *did* get to the other side and in and out. The underground river, diverted through here, was apparently deep and navigable. The craft was basically a wooden rowboat, with a separate and overlarge tiller. Inside sat a tall, stately-looking woman. "Get in— all of you," she commanded.

I looked at the other three, then complied. There was no use in pressing anything with the Elders right now, and time was needed to find the information I sought.

Fortunately the current was with us in this direction, so the oars were secured and the pilot let the river take us with it. We left the cavern, then went around a fairly sharp bend, and came to another landing, but didn't stop there. We passed several more such landings, with tunnels leading off in both directions, before we reached the one the pilot wanted. She tied off the boat with a rope, then jumped out and helped us up onto the rocky floor. We were led back along a narrow cave that seemed mostly natural, but which opened into a fairly large chamber. By torchlight we could see it contained a thick floor of some strawlike material, a few crude handmade wooden chairs, a small writing desk but nothing to write with, and very little else. It did, however, have a crude water system; a streamlet issuing from a small rock fissure was channeled into and along a trough. The stream was pretty swift, and it exited through another small fissure at the other end of the room. Just before that exit point was a crude, hand-rubbed toilet top.

"The water is fresh and pure," our guide explained. "The current is swift enough so that waste products will be swiftly carried away. Food will be brought to you shortly, and regularly. Please stay here until the Elders decide what to do with you. Swimming in the river is not recommended, however. The river's eventual outlet is the larger waterfall in the courtyard, and the drop is more than forty meters into stone." With that, she turned and was gone.

Bura looked after her for a moment, then turned to me. "I gather we're prisoners, then?"

"Looks like it," I had to admit. "But these people know what I want to know. However, maybe they're right. Maybe we can't make our revolution. But I *still* want to know how to change my form to suit me at will. Whether we can build an army or not, that knowledge would sure increase *our* options."

Ching looked around and shook her head. "I knew we should have just stayed in the forest. They're gonna let us rot here until we're as old as they are."

I went over to her, hugged her, and gave her a small kiss. "No they won't. For one thing, they just don't know what to do with us right now. Give them some time. I don't think they want to be like TMS and the city people, and that's just what they'd be like if they killed us. Besides," I added with a wink, "if we got out of the Rochande sewers, what's this place?"

It quickly developed that Ching's fears were grossly misplaced. While we were, in fact, being held prisoner, our time was not to be wasted in some dank cell inside a mountain but in what proved to be quite an education for all of us. And the food was good—an odd sort of fishy-tasting mammal as a main course, but supplemented with good fresh fruit and the tastiest edible leaves. A very small portable power plant from the old days still worked; it was used for a small hydroponics setup entirely within the mountain that fed the staff. What else it might power I didn't know.

We were regularly visited by various people who knew an awful lot about Medusa and its history and ways; they brought with them bound hard copies of much computer data now denied the citizens of Medusa's cities, not to mention large, laboriously handwritten chronicles of the Wild Ones—sorry, the Free Tribes—and their customs.

The first Lord of Medusa to close off the society was a former naval admiral named Kasikian, who had led an abortive and hushed-up coup attempt at Military Systems Command. A lifelong career military man, and a strong disciplinarian, this civilized worlder, born and bred to command, had taken charge on Medusa. He had started out organizing the small freighter fleet, having been given the job by virtue of his vast experience. But he eventually drew to him a number of other military types, plus a lot of disaffected, and this time his *coup d'état* worked flawlessly. After a period of consolidation, Kasikian began reorganizing Medusan society along military lines, with strict ranks, grades, and chains of command. He was an efficient organizer no matter what his political ideas may have been; it was he who modernized and expanded the industries of Medusa, and he who built the space stations that now circled all four Warden worlds. Ironically, his effect was most dramatic on Cerberus, which was transformed from a primitive water world to an industrial giant that took what

Medusa produced and made it into whatever the Diamond needed.

But after two coup attempts against him, Kasikian became increasingly paranoid, and so was born of his fears and Cerberan computer skills the original monitor system. The society was even more rigidly structured and controlled in military fashion. As a final gesture, realizing he could never extend total control over the people unless they were consolidated in the key cities and kept there, he ordered the pogrom: those who would not commit themselves fully to his system and his government and come into the cities were to be ruthlessly exterminated.

The Elders had explained that less than a thousand survived the bloodbath that followed, most fleeing to a few key pre-prepared places such as the one we were now in, places that had been erased from the records and were, to all outward appearances, just new, small primitive enclaves. Still, Kasikian ordered those few escapees ruthlessly hunted down, no matter what the cost, and he became so obsessed with that mission that he was careless at home. A young officer who was an aide to one of the admiral's top associates managed to get him as he relaxed in his luxurious command quarters and kill him.

But this young officer, motivated by idealism and revulsion for bloodshed, became pretty bloody himself as he and his followers hunted down and executed all those in the top five grades of the admiral's government. By the time Tolakah, new Lord of the Diamond, felt secure, his hands were as bloody as the admiral's—and he not only grew as paranoid, but was soon seduced by his power. The other Lords, particularly Cerberus', used his paranoia and love of power for their own ends. They needed what Medusa put out, and the system there suited them just fine.

But the monitor system worried Tolakah. He and his own people had managed to get around it, so he knew how vulnerable it was. As a result, he was delighted to get Talant Ypsir, an expert in administration whose ideas on how societies should be organized closely paralleled the late Kasikian's. Using the computer talent on Cerberus, Ypsir plugged the holes and created a nearly ironclad society—but not for Tolakah's benefit. Tolakah, in fact, was personally beheaded by Ypsir while the administrative specialist was showing him the master computers in the orbiting space station that totally sealed the society. Complicity with the other Lords was probable; they distrusted the erratic Tolakah, and preferred someone who *knew* he was as corrupt as the others, and enjoyed it.

In the meantime, the last of the survivors of the pogrom managed to gather in the various secret places, and decided on an organization for their society in the wild. Dominant among them was Dr. Kura Hsiu, a cultural anthropologist by trade, who'd come to Medusa as a life study of the Warden organism's effect on society. She was particularly drawn by the idea of a society where people changed sex as routinely as they changed their clothes, and she considered the work worth the sacrifice. But not now—as a fugitive and exile in the wild. She realized that the remnants were no match for Medusa's power, but Ypsir seemed to be lapsing into a tolerance as long as they didn't bother or interfere wtih him. Medusa was too big a planet for it to be worth tracking down that small a group, which the last two Lords had both considered dispersed and neutralized.

Dr. Hsiu realized that the new generation would be born in the bush, and that they would be culturally far removed from their own children, and so she set about creating a society that would allow the Wild Ones to grow and develop as a native culture, free of all past cultural pollutants. In many ways, it was the greatest task, experiment, and opportunity for an anthropologist in history.

The greater family, or tribal system, seemed the only logical way to go. Groups would have to be large enough to support one another, yet small enough to move with the weather and the food and still not attract Ypsir's attention. A simple system, based primarily on age, was developed and taught—the younger would respect and follow the elder's lead, and eventually, if they lived long enough, they, too, would run things. Originally intended just to keep the first generation in guiding control as long as possible, the tradition became quickly institutionalized in the harsh land.

Since political unity beyond the tribal system was impossible, the only basic overlay that would unite the tribes in any way would be a religious one. So the few centers of refuge became holy shrines, and a system of simple belief based on many religions was established.

Early on, though, the religion had taken an odd turn. Instead of worshiping some anthropomorphic god, the religion turned inward, to planet worship, of all things. God lived not in the heavens but inside the earth itself, one god for each world. This seemed logical to the young ones, for did not the Elders say that the heavens were filled with stars and planets and that humans went between them? If God was not in space, then, where was she?

The original Elders went along with the theory because it worked; Dr. Hsiu herself noted that similar faiths in one form or another existed on all three of the other Warden worlds. Later Elders came to believe in it, and most, but not all, now did.

By the second generation in the wild, things had become pretty institutionalized. The Free Tribes everywhere prayed in the direction of the Mount of God, a particularly high peak in the frozen north said to be the backbone of God the Mother Medusa Herself. This explained both the ritualized prayers and the sacrifice of the animal remains back into the pool— a return to Mother Medusa.

The religious centers became retreats for study and meditation, as well as old-age homes for the most elderly, and also places where those who were pregnant came to give birth, if they could. This explained the pregnant woman with the hunting party, and as well why so many in the courtyard had been pregnant.

As to why the Mount of God was chosen, that particularly piqued my interest. It was said that a hunting party had stumbled upon it shortly after the pogrom was in full swing and the hunt was on, and had battled "fierce demons who seemed to besiege the mount but could not climb upon it; demons more horrible to behold than the human mind can comprehend." These "demons" got a number of the party, but the rest took refuge on the mountain where they had what can only be described as a classic religious experience. They claimed that somehow they had actually touched the mind of God, and as a result of that experience *they had found themselves able to change their shape, form, or gender at will.* This was apparently the beginning of the change toward planet-worship, and their experience was borne out by others who made the journey in their footsteps.

Here was God, then, in a tangible but not easily accessible form, under constant attack by terrible demons who wanted to destroy Her but could not climb the mountain to do so. The demons were terrible enough in taking a fearsome toll of the curious, the pilgrims, and all others; but the experience of anyone able to make it to the mountain and then back off again was the same—a sense that they had talked with God, and had acquired the power to control every damned cell in their bodies by sheer force of will.

I could certainly see why the revolution of malleables would be a real pain today for other than cultural reasons. Whatever those animals or creatures were that the accounts called demons, they were terrible and deadly—and very real. I felt sure of that. It would be tough getting enough people to that mountain, and back. Still, that mountain had *something,* some strange power that not only conferred this ability for life but also convinced a lot of hard-headed scientific materialists of the claptrap of this silly religion.

I knew then where I had to go next. Surprisingly, the Elders agreed.

"Yes, you must go," said the first woman, who I thought might well have been Dr. Hsiu. "You alone are the key to your family's salvation. Without your drive and relentless will the other three would settle down and accept this culture. They dream your dreams because they love you. If, then, you make the Great Pilgrimage, and survive the demon trial, you will come mind to mind with God and you will *know.* Then will your life picture and world picture be irrevocably changed, as ours was. And, if you must still dream your ambitions after that, you will at least find the power that you seek."

I smiled and nodded. "I think, though, that we should have more training in the use of the primitive weapons here first. I don't want anybody killed out of ignorance."

"We?"

"Why, yes. All four of us. We are together in this, one."

"No."

I looked puzzled and felt angry. "Why not? Give me one good reason for it!"

"I will give you two. Your wife Angi is four months with child. Your wife Bura is three months with child. They must remain here for the term."

"Well I'll be damned!" I said, genuinely surprised and shocked. "It never occurred to me. It really didn't." Even after all this time on Medusa, the idea of natural birth as opposed to scientifically controlled laboratory birth was simply not connected in my mind. "But why didn't they tell me?"

"They did not want you to know as long as you were bent on your killing mission. Pregnancy does not show as much on us as on normal humans at this stage, nor does it produce any of the negative symptoms that normal human first-trimester gestation does." She paused for a moment. "They were going to tell you and I stopped them. But now you know, and now you must make your decision. Go to the Mount of Gods, or remain to raise your children with those who love you."

My mind was racing at all this, and I felt a little angry and betrayed that they hadn't told me straight off—but, then, they had been behaving a little odd lately and I'd simply passed it off.

"What about Ching?" I asked. "If the other two are pregnant, then she sure should be. We've been together a lot longer."

"As far as we can tell, no, but on Medusa a pregnancy usually has to be fairly well along before we know for certain. We believe she is determined to go where you go, do what you do, no matter what; being with child would prevent that. On Medusa, a solid mind-set *not* to get pregnant is sufficient to leave it that way."

I thought it all out, trying to decide if the new situation really made a difference. It did, dammit, but I also had my own responsibilities to consider beyond the family. What good would it do to remain and have lots of kids and then look up one day to see a Confederacy world destroyer bearing down on Medusa, wiping out all of us and our futures? If anything, I thought, this made it even *more* urgent that I find the means to get to Talant Ypsir.

Or was I just kidding myself?

"How long will it take to get to the mountain?" I asked her.

"Seven weeks—and it is in the north and east."

Fourteen weeks round trip. It was possible, anyway, to get there and back in the period before Angi was due. "Weapons?"

"Do you know how to use the sword?"

I almost laughed out loud. Considering Tarin Bul's background, the question was a joke. But I wasn't really Tarin Bul. "I've fenced for sport," I told her, "but not with swords."

"That's the best I can do. We have no pistols or rifles. The swords are hand-made, melted down and remolded from some useless metal artifacts we found here."

"I can handle it," I assured her. I was pretty sure I could handle any weapon, and I'd have weeks to get used to it. "And Ching?"

"Are you sure she will go with you?"

"*You* are," I pointed out.

She chuckled. "Yes, I am. She may choose what she wishes or feels comfortable with. You will go with a small group of sincere pilgrims, including a doubter or two going to see for themselves, and these will include experienced spear and bow masters."

"These . . . demons. What are they like?"

"They are almost impossible to describe. But to reach the Mount you must cross an ever-frozen inlet of the ocean. There is no other way that is practical. They live there, in the waters under the ice, and can break through and grab you and drag you down as you cross. Their tentacles are tenacious, and their great mouths are on top of their heads. They are terrifying, and deadly, but remember this—hurt them and they will retreat. They do not like being hurt. But it is difficult to hurt them through their armor."

I frowned. "They have shells?"

"No. Armor. They wear some sort of hard protective suit that is impervious to our weapons. Aim for the tentacles, eyes, and mouth. It is the only way."

Armor? On a creature living in the frozen sea? Or a tough suit that would act like armor, perhaps . . .

Now I knew for certain that my choice was made. I would have to go. Unless I was completely and utterly wrong, the challenge was irresistible.

I was going to meet our damned, elusive aliens—and find out just what the hell they were doing up there that started a religion.

CHAPTER TEN

The Goddess Medusa

"What're *you* mad about?" Bura wanted to know. "You're the one who's leaving."

"Well, at least I expected you to try and talk me out of it," I retorted.

Angi looked me right in the eyes. "Would it matter? Would you not go if we cried and pleaded?"

I sighed. "Probably not. I *have* to go."

"And we understand that," Bura said. "We don't like it, but we know you well enough by now. There's something inside you, something eating away, that just isn't going to go away. It's just . . ." Her voice trailed off and she turned away.

I reached out and put my hand on her shoulder. "I know. The children to come. You can't believe how rotten I feel leaving you now—but, with luck, I'll be back in fourteen weeks. If it was much longer I'd wait until after, you know that."

"You probably would," Angi agreed, "and you'd slowly go nuts. You know it and we know it. So—go. But . . . come back to us, Tari."

I admit I was starting to feel a little teary myself, and I hugged and kissed them both, and they hugged and kissed Ching. I turned to my original pair-mate. "I still wish you wouldn't come. They need you here. Particularly if—"

"I go where you go," she said once again. "I'm not going to sit here and not know."

"All right, then," I sighed, "let's get going."

We walked out to the courtyard, where the rest of the party was gathering. With Ching and myself it was a group of fourteen, led by an experienced northerner named

149

Hono. Like the others, she'd been born in the wild; the Free Tribes tended to keep to one name if doing so didn't lead to confusion. We had been practicing with the group for several days, and I had to admit that Ching seemed to have a better handle on spear and bow than I did. Yet using my increased muscle power and some of my fencing steps and moves, I could wield the sword very effectively in close quarters. It was a close quarters weapon only, though, and I sorely missed those two laser rifles at the bottom of the slag pit.

There was one more round of emotional good-byes, and attempts on all parts to pretend that things were really just fine and normal, but both Ching and I were glad when we left the compound and our people behind. It wasn't a question of out of sight out of mind, but, rather, a strong feeling inside me that if I didn't get out of there soon I would be unable to leave. Having found a closeness and an emotional bond I had never before even conceived of, I was now turning my back on it and going back to work for a system in which I no longer had any faith. I liked to tell myself, and Ching, that we were doing this for ourselves and for the planet's protection and not for any outside force or government. But there was still both the love of challenge which was part of my personality and the uneasy sense that three more of me—one each on Charon, Lilith, and Cerberus—were leading different lives with similar objectives. It would be intolerable for me to fail if any one of them were to succeed. I wished I knew more about them and their fates.

At least we didn't have to walk all the way. Four sleds pulled by tame vettas awaited, large enough to carry us and our weapons, tools, and portable shelters. The vettas raised their odd-looking heads and snapped their wide, flat bills at us as we approched, but that was just their form of recognition.

The sleds proved efficient, though neither comfortable nor fast, since we were traveling long ways over grass and rocks and the vettas, restrained in their harness, could use their power but not their speed and grace. The trip was bumpy as hell, but it beat walking and carrying the stuff.

Ching remained pretty tense and quiet—clearly she disapproved of the trip, of leaving the others, and of most everything concerning my objectives. She wanted to sit back, meld into one or another of the Free Tribes, and just live out her life. The war, the aliens, the Four Lords themselves seemed at best distant, at worst unreal or incomprehensible to her. But she did understand that she had a family and, away from TMS and the guilds and modern Medusan society in general, was enjoying a sense of personal freedom she had never known before. The primitiveness of her new life style really didn't bother her. The sense of oppression—a sense she'd been born and raised with—had lifted from her, giving her what she wanted; Bura, Angi, and I gave her what she needed.

And yet, here she was.

The Elders had spoken of a cultural gap between the Free Tribes and me that might never be bridged; here, too, I felt, was another gap that remained despite all our closeness and intimacy. Ching could never understand why I had to go; I could never understand why she had to follow —but I could no more stand in the way of what she had to do than I could allow her and the others to stand in my way. In that sense, as the days passed out in the bush and the air grew colder with the northern journey, we did more or less affect a practical sort of thaw. We did not understand each other, and we knew it; but we respected each other, and, for that time and place, that would have to be enough.

We fell in with a small hunting group backed by the trip leader, Hono, and also including Quarl, Sitzter, and Tyne. Neither Ching nor I were very good or effective hunters, needless to say, and I doubt if Ching could bring herself to kill for food—although she had grown used to the idea enough to be able to eat an animal when it was no longer recognizable as what it was—so we were dependent on our little group for our nourishment. The four hunters were easy, likable, and outgoing people with a feel for life, but, as the Elders had warned, they were of and from a different world, space, and time from me. Medusa had made the stone age not only possible but somewhat antiseptic—and how very easily humans had reverted to that primitive state.

Ching was aware of the gap between us and them as I was. They plied us both with honest questions about our former lives and worlds, but they accepted only little bits of it. The trains they saw from time to time, and because they understood natural magnetism in its basic form they could stretch their minds at least to accept the idea that great magnets could pull trains from point to point. Of course that wasn't the way the trains worked or used magnetism, but it didn't really matter. Of monitors, psychs, computers, and long-range communications, though, they had no real understanding or grasp, and they accepted stories of such things with a grain of salt. As to how and why large numbers of people would willingly seal themselves in cities and never hunt or explore or live in the bush—that was really beyond them.

I began to understand the problem the Elders had posed for me, as much as I hated to admit it. Although intelligent and resourceful, these people were in many ways like small children on the frontier. You could make one *look* like a city dweller, but he would find it impossible to cope with the simple, everyday things of modern technological living. By the time he learned, assuming he wasn't run over by a bus first, he'd have long since exposed himself to the authorities.

By the end of our journey, I was more than willing to give up my dream of an army of malleables infiltrating and destroying the Medusan cities. It just wasn't going to work. I wasn't going to overthrow the system by that means, and perhaps not at all—that task would have to be left to others. Certainly there were others, I had to remind myself. Krega had never said I'd be the only agent, and it would be foolish for them to have put all their eggs in my lone basket. Somebody had trained and equipped the Opposition; so even if its members were now ineffectual, the leadership was more than competent. They would try again, and again, until they came up with the right combination. At least, I had to hope so. This planet was too well organized and the system too tight for it to be so easily overthrown by just one man.

But that did not diminish the other objectives. Whatever we were going toward was very much connected to all that had happened before, to all the reasons I was here to begin with, and, most certainly, it was connected to the ultimate fate of me and my family—and of Medusa itself. This knowledge simply had to be acquired, no matter what the cost.

We were in sight of the mountains when we had to abandon the sleds and really get to work ourselves. That mountain view was deceptive. Three days of hard, dangerous walking remained, the last day over pack ice. The last hunt had been tough, and still we had left little to toss back to Mother Medusa. From here on in, any food we might find would be sheer luck.

The barren wasteland before us was frightening enough. Up here, in the far north, glaciation was omnipresent—the whole thing was a massive ice sheet—with jagged ice ridges piled up making anything except foot travel impossible, and foot travel itself difficult. The air was crisp and clear, but there was a steady wind blowing small, localized ice-crystal storms all over.

Our period of danger from the "demons" would start now, since under all this stuff was a jagged and irregular coastline that you simply couldn't tell from the frozen ocean. The last day we would be almost literally walking on water, which posed real dangers, since underneath all this ice the ocean was being whipped into a frenzy by thermal currents. The ice right above them might be thin enough to cause a human to fall through. The wonder was that anybody had ever found and crossed this desolate, frozen horror in the first place.

We used hand-made snowshoes provided back at the citadel and strapped our feet into boots made from the skin and hair of tubros and quite literally woven into the snowshoes themselves. Yet, amazing as it might seem, the windy cold that probably approached minus 60° C. was only slightly annoying. What sort of internal changes had been wrought inside us by the Wardens to keep us and them alive I couldn't guess, although I noticed our appetites had greatly increased as it grew colder and we had all built up noticeable amounts of fat all over our bodies. It seemed amazing that we could survive such cold, but I realized that on many worlds other animals, including a large number of mammals, survived conditions at least this extreme and even thrived in them. I doubted if any of us would ever thrive in such a place as this, but we endured.

The Mount of God was not difficult to find in this ex-

panse. Its glacier-covered slopes rose up as a white mono-
lith before us, dwarfing surrounding mountains that were
pretty high themselves. Just looking at it was to experience
a strong sense of awe and wonder. It was easy to see how
the mountain came to be known as Medusa's backbone.
Weathering and glaciation had worn and shaped the top so
that it did sort of resemble the backbone of some great
four-legged beast.

Our Wardens had to work overtime to keep us warm and
comfortable, and to protect our eyes and other exposed
areas. Two weeks earlier, all of us, male and female, had
begun sprouting hair all over our bodies including on our
faces—and now that hair and our skin was turning to
milky white against the white landscape. The most interesting and occasionally irritating change was that our eyelids
grew quickly transparent. So soon we walked across the
ice with our eyes shut against the wind and ice crystals
and still saw perfectly well.

It was hell, however, to try and sleep that way no matter
how dark it became. Not that any sleep was really comfortable on that icy landscape, or very long. It was just
something else in the way of hardships to get used to, and
I was doubly impressed with the dedication of those who
made this pilgrimage out of faith or to confront and allay
their doubts, instead of out of foolish curiosity, as I was
doing.

On that last, cold trek, it took only a few hours for our
first casualty. One of the group simply walked over an area
that looked for all the world like the rest of the frozen
landscape, and it gave way beneath her, swallowing her
instantly. By the time we reached the spot and were argu-
ing over whether or not we could do anything the water
had already started to refreeze.

We lost two more just getting to the final inlet before
the mountain itself, a second to another hidden soft spot in
the ice, a third to a crevasse that suddenly opened up as
two ice packs shifted subtly, then closed in again, crushing
the woman to death.

Now we were nine for the final stretch, and I could only
shake my head and look back at the horrible landscape we
had already traversed. "And, just think, we have to cross
that stretch again to get back."

Almost as I said those words the ice gave way beneath my feet and I felt myself falling, as if through a trapdoor. I screamed out and raised my hands, but I was in over my head before I felt strong hands grip mine and hold me, attempt to pull me up, and not quite make it. I knew in that instant that I'd had it—I was going to drown—but almost as I reconciled myself to that fate I felt myself being lifted back up out of the hole and onto the ice.

I wasn't very lucid for a while there, but I remember seeing a stricken and anxious-looking Ching—and also Quarl and Sitzter—fussing over me. I drifted in a fog as my body fought the one enemy the Wardens could not overcome so easily—shock. It was some time before I came out of it. It was dark, and I was in a *wapti*—one of the portable skin tents—covered by fur and skin. A serious-looking Hono entered and glanced at me, then smiled when she saw I was awake. "Welcome back."

I coughed. "Thanks. How long was I out?"

"A couple of hours. You've been rambling something fierce, but I think you are self-repairing nicely now. You should be all right by morning, I think, if you made it this far."

"I'll make it," I assured her. "I'm not going to spend one more day on this stuff than I have to."

She nodded and seemed satisfied, then pointed near me. I turned my head and saw Ching, out cold and snoring slightly, alongside me. "She was the one who saved you," Hono told me. "I never saw anybody move so fast whose own life wasn't at stake. She was on you, grabbed hold of your arms, and held you while yelling at us until we could reach you. She used up a lot of strength, but she actually got your head above water herself."

I looked over at her, sleeping so soundly, and felt an emotional tide rising within me. "And I tried so hard to talk her out of coming."

"She loves you very much. I think she would give her life to save yours. In fact, I know she would. You have something very rare and valuable and important, Tari. Cherish it."

I should have been happy, proud, overjoyed at something like that. Why then did I feel so much like a heel?

This is it, I told myself, and meant it this time. Having

come this far we'll go the rest of the way, and back again, but this is it. Sorry, you bastards, my job stops with this one. No more. When we leave here we will return to the citadel, bear and raise those babies and make more, and carve out a new life for *all* of us. They had let me go because they loved me. Ching had come along because she loved me. And me, good old selfish me, had I given them anything other than mere sperm in return? For the first time, really, I took a good, hard, objective look at myself and I didn't like what I saw. It took something like this to make me realize my egomania, my selfish drives, my all-consuming love affair with myself. But I wasn't above love—I needed it. I needed them. And love, I now understood, wasn't just something you received as a matter of right, but something you gave in equal measure.

I was no longer the most important person in my life. Three others were now paramount, and I swore that I would never forget that again. And, with that sincere vow, I managed, finally, to drift back into a fitful and uncomfortable sleep.

The next day dawned ugly. Gray clouds had moved in with relatively warmer air and there was the possibility of snow. Hono didn't like it any more than the rest of us, but she was pragmatic about things.

"We have two choices," she told us in a small group meeting that dawn. "Either we stay here another day or we press on to the Mountain. What do you say?"

Tyne, who usually said little, really decided for us. "That's hard weather coming, perhaps a front of some kind. It's been known to storm for days, even weeks, up here, once conditions are right. If that's so, our chances are better on the solid mountain than staying here—no matter how lousy things may seem."

"Then we go," Hono declared. "Anyone want to do otherwise?" She looked around, but nobody else responded. Frankly, by this time we just wanted to get this thing over with. Even some of the most faithful could be heard muttering that morning that sacred places should be easier to get to.

As for me, Ching sensed the change inside me. I think I was successful in convincing her it wasn't any back-from-the-dead conversion but a genuine reassessment. My thoughts on the sacred mountain, however, were still all business. Hard to reach, yes, and terribly dangerous—a fluke that anybody on this planet ever found it. A perfect place for an alien base, perhaps an entire hidden alien outpost or city.

We started out under thickening clouds and were soon encrusted with ice particles, although the snow remained aloft for the moment. The last crossing was relatively smooth compared to the previous two days' worth, but considering the landforms, its smoothness said that the ice was relatively thin, the water beneath warmer, and thus, far more dangerous.

Still, it was midday and the first snowflakes had begun to fall before anything happened.

It looked for all the world like another one of those damned holes, and we might have just put it down to that, except this time it happened right in front of me and I had a clear view.

What pulled Yorder down through the ice was not any natural soft spot, but something below. One moment she was walking there, then she *stopped* and turned to look back at me—and something, I couldn't tell what, broke through right beneath her and just sucked her down with tremendous force.

The others came running, but there was nothing any of us could do. Nonetheless, I brought out my primitive bronze sword and crouched, looking around. "They're under the ice!" I called. "Let's keep moving! Don't stop for anything or they'll break through and grab us! Those suckers are *fast!*"

They sure were—I had no sooner pulled myself up and started on when the ice exploded around us in the building wind and snowstorm. The eight of us fixed our weapons and assumed a protective formation while continuing to move.

"They're striking at random!" Hono shouted. "Tari's right—move! And don't stop for anything unless you can kill it!"

We made our way across the ice as the enemy started playing a psychological game with us. Using the now swirling snow as a cover, they would pop up and break the ice at random points all around us, again and again, ahead and behind and on all sides, occasionally even showing large, dark shapes looming in the whiteness for brief periods.

They don't like to be hurt. . . .

They *were* really playing games with us, and I think we all knew it. A patrol, most likely, just a small roving guard detachment; they were bored, and now they had something to play with.

Several times the dark masses would hold on the surface long enough for one of our three remaining archers to get off a shot or two, but hitting anything under these conditions was nearly impossible.

Of course, game or not, these wretched conditions certainly didn't help the "demon" patrol, either. I doubted whether they could see any better in this crap than we could, and if they had any kind of tracking devices below us they either didn't work on us or were too scrambled by the weather conditions to allow any accurate mark. They were also, obviously, forbidden to use modern arms— almost certainly because such a report would eventually get back to others in the Free Tribes and blow their demonic cover.

Still, I wanted to see one. No wonder all our surveillance and all our monitoring hadn't detected them—and no wonder they required a life zone very close to human requirements yet were physically unable to move among us without bulky suits. Air-breathing, water-dwelling mammals! How I'd like to see one!

I got my wish as the ice erupted just ahead of me and one overconfident creature pushed up halfway through the surface with a roar. It was so close I made a slash at it with the sword, and struck the tip of a waving tentacle. The air was suddenly filled with a terrible high-pitched scream of agony that echoed across the ice as it dropped back into the water with blinding speed. And I almost regretted getting my wish.

The pear-shaped head was ringed with extremely long tentacles, perhaps three meters or more, covered with thousands of tiny little suckers. Below the tentacles were two huge heart-shaped pads of some wet, glistening material that must have been eyes. Where the head met the body, there were at least two visible pairs of stalklike arms or legs or whatever that terminated in scissorlike claws from elbow to end. The skin itself looked almost like a thing separately alive, a mottled, sickly yellow and purple that seemed to me to be constantly in motion, although, I told myself, that could just be water draining from it. The creature certainly earned its demon reputation—it was the most grotesque living horror I'd ever seen. Whatever evolution had produced such creatures had been brutal indeed, and if they weren't killing machines nothing in nature ever was.

Although I saw only a bit of the upper torso, there was no question that the old Elder had been right—the torso, at least, was covered by a metallic-looking suit of some kind, which resembled a chitinous exoskeleton. But I'd never seen an exoskeleton with a metal ring at the top and obvious vacuum connectors around it.

I didn't stop to question the thing, or shout my impressions to anybody else, but all of a sudden I knew I was glad of the side I was on. I had seen no sign of a mouth or nose, but the roaring when they broke through indicated to me that they had a lot of their equipment elsewhere.

Their mouths are on top. . . .

After I'd struck a glancing blow to the one, though, they stopped playing their game. Obviously they were not going to take any more risks now that their self-confidence was shaken a bit. That scream may have been just a normal yelp of pain to them, but if it translated at all into human terms, the emotion in it was unmistakable. They sure didn't like to be hurt.

The attacks became more cautious and intermittent now, and, therefore, easier to fend off. At the same time the snow seemed to slack off for a moment, and we saw how close we were to the first outcrop of the mountain itself. With a shout we broke and ran for it, taking our chances, but running a cautious, zigzag pattern that gave the creatures less opportunity to preplan an opening. More than that, the ice was becoming thicker now as it packed up against the rock wall of the mountainside, and that made following us even more difficult. I wondered if the things could move on land at all, but finally decided that they must be able to do so.

When the last of us reached the solidity of the mountain

itself, even though its ice-encrusted side was not distinguishable from the pack ice, we all dropped in sheer exhaustion from the tension of the run. "Safe!" Ching sighed.

A sudden buzzing sound, impossibly loud and ugly, came from the direction of the ice. Wearily, Hono and I crawled up to see what was making it.

"Archers!" Hono screamed. "They're coming for us!"

All the tension flooded back as the archers jumped up and moved forward. There was still snow falling, but it was light, and we had about a kilometer's visibility. Out there, on the ice, we could see four of the creatures rise from the ice and into the air, where they grouped, suspended as neatly as a neg-grav car or copter.

Ching joined us, saw them, and gasped. "Are they using some kind of flying belt or what?"

I shook my head in wonder. "I don't think so, honey. The bastards have wings!"

She frowned. "Where are the tentacles? Those huge things . . . ?"

Hono pointed. "They're still there—see? But they retract, somehow, into the head, making a short ring of horns. Demon's horns!"

"They're well out of range of my bow," Quarl said in frustration. "Are they coming on, or not?"

"I'm not sure," Hono responded, "but this is getting on my nerves. I wish they'd do *something*."

"They are," I said softly. "They're showing us what they can do, more or less. I don't think they *are* coming—I think they're just giving us a demonstration that they'll still be there when we come back."

Hono shook her head in wonder. "What creatures can these be that are so insane? Part creature of the sea, part insect that flies and crawls, and is that thing hanging down a tentacle or some sort of tail?"

"They're all of it, and probably more," I responded. "They're living, breathing, thinking creatures that look as if they were put together by a committee, but put together for every environment, every weather or climactic condition, every land form or sea type. Given the kinds of air and temperatures within our broad range, I think they could live on any world I've ever seen. They sure scare the hell right out of me."

"Those are no demons," Hono said flatly, surprising me. "I don't know what they are, but they are no demons."

I nodded. "You're right on that. They're a smart, tricky, clever race from out there in the stars somewhere."

Ching looked at me in mixed shock and surprise. "Then *those* are the aliens we were told of?"

"Some of them, anyway. I suspect these are bred for just this kind of job. Manufactured to survive up here and kill anybody who comes along. If *we* can genetically breed what we need, there's no reason they can't go one step further."

"But then they should have the city weapons, or worse," Sitzter noted. "If they have such things, why do they not just sit back where they are and blast us off of here?"

I was wondering that myself. It didn't make sense for them to expose themselves like this and yet have no backup of their own equivalent of laser pistols and whatever, which would make short work of us. "Maybe—I know this sounds crazy, but just maybe it isn't *allowed* around here," I suggested. "It looks like they don't like to come on the mountain for some reason, either, so I think we're safe for now —until we start back, anyway." I turned and looked at the imposing Mount of God, most of it hidden in cloud. "Shall we see what's so special about this mountain, then?"

Hono grinned. "As long as we are in the area, why not?"

We climbed up and away from the aliens, and soon the buzzing faded then stopped altogether. What they were going to do I had no idea, but I had new respect for those Free Tribesmen who'd made it here and back. No wonder most of them became highly respected priests and shamans of their tribes.

Once anybody reached the sacred mountain the instructions became pretty vague—just climb away from the flats a bit, everybody had said, then spend one night there, and that would be it.

We had lost just about everything except those weapons we retained and the hair skirts and snowshoe boots we wore, and which we now had to discard to climb. It took less than two hours before we came on an area that was small, reasonably flat, and had, surprisingly, some exposed rock, rock that looked far darker and mineral-rich than the usual stuff found on Medusa. But it provided a sheltered area, with something of a rock overhang—if we trusted the ice on top to stay put—and seemed as good a place as any to camp out. The wind and snow were whipping themselves up anyway, and there didn't seem much point in further exploration during the few remaining hours of daylight. We did, however, look around the small redoubt and found some signs that we were far from the first to ever reach it or spend the night there. In some of the exposed rock, for example, were carved designs, petroglyphs of some sort, although most of them were pretty obscure and it was impossible to take any meaning from them.

Ching examined the drawings with fascination. "What do you think they used to carve them? The lines are so deep and smooth it almost looks as if they were carved by some weapon or machine."

I nodded, but hadn't a clue.

The petroglyphs were useful for an hour's diversion, but that was about it. The wind was up, the snow blowing all around us, and it was growing dark. We eight survivors gathered around mostly for comfort rather than conversation.

"You know, I've been thinking about these aliens," Ching commented, snuggling up to me.

"Who hasn't?"

"No, I mean those retractable tentacles on their heads. Remind you of anything?"

For a moment I didn't know what she was talking about, then, suddenly, it hit me. Medusa. The symbol of the planet and its government, taken from some ancient human religion. The woman with live snakes for hair. "Yeah, I see what you mean," I told her. "But if I remember right, you were supposed to turn to stone if you looked at Medusa. They finally killed her by making her look at her own face in a mirror or something."

And that, oddly, was very appropriate to me, in a perverse sort of way. Medusa, the planet, had been my mirror; it had reflected all that was wrong or corrupt in me and all that was wrong or corrupt in my society. How odd that such an effect would happen here, on a world filled with those kicked out of my old society and their offspring. I couldn't help but wonder if the whole Warden system didn't have that effect. This was a bad world indeed, an evil world, far worse than the banal sameness of the civilized worlds, yet it served, it served. . . .

Sitting there, holding Ching close to me and reflecting on all of life as one was supposed to on a holy mountain, I drifted off into sleep. It was a deep, almost hypnotic sleep, partially a result of the release of tension from the day's horrors, but it was not dreamless. In fact, it was filled with images, stray thoughts, and odd sensations that made no sense.

I dreamed that I was in the presence of something great, something that was very, very young yet eons old—an alien force that was neither friendly nor unfriendly, neither monstrous nor beautiful, but strangely detached and indifferent to all around it.

There was a great energy and vitality to it, and a tremendous sense of self-importance. It was a believer in gods, for it was a god and a true one, as its very existence proved—for did not all else in the universe, both matter and energy, exist to serve, feed, and nurture it? It was worshiped, yes, by lessers with some small grain of intelligence, yet had no sense of obligation or caring for those who worshiped it. It was worshiped because it was a god, and gods were so far above mortal beings that worship was simply the natural way of things. All who did not recognize this and worship and serve would die, of course, as it never died; but the inevitability of their death was not so much a threat as a matter-of-fact statement of belief. Ultimatums were for lessers and were, in fact, not really understood by it, nor were threats or any other petty human emotions. These things would be because that was the natural order, the way things *were*.

I had no sense of the thing's shape or form, and calling what I perceived thoughts was not really correct. Rather, these attitudes were simply radiated from its mind into mine, and translated there—inadequately—into terms I could grasp.

Beyond that initial perception, the impressions were beyond any hope of translation by my mind; here were concepts too alien, too complex, too fast for me to grab hold of, let alone understand. Only the vastness of its intellect, and that curious feeling of ancient newness pervaded my consciousness. I had the feeling of falling, falling into the mind of the thing itself, and there was a danger of being engulfed, swallowed by that which was totally incomprehensible. My mind shut it out, refused to allow the tremendous onrush of sensory input so alien to humanity that it could not even be correlated. In a sense, I had the feeling that the thing was aware of me, yet mostly indifferent to my existence. Or—maybe not. I felt a gentle nudge, a mental shift from it that swept me away from its tremendous, unfathomable presence, and I found myself shrinking, shrinking into nothingness, into a microbial world. No, I was not merely swept there—I was *relegated* to it by imperious decree.

And, slowly, I became aware once more of my body, but not in the normal way. It was as if, suddenly, a new sense was opened to me, allowing me somehow to see, hear, feel every single part of my body.

I heard the Warden colonies within me sing to one another, and while the sound was incomprehensible the sensation was pleasing and powerful. The Wardens, I realized, were in constant communication, cell to cell, throughout my entire body, yet they were not, in any normal sense, alive. Information was flowing in their song, though, information flowing into my body and into the Wardens from some source I could not trace.

I knew I was still dreaming, yet, strangely, I felt wide awake, my mind never clearer or more sensitive. Somehow, I knew, I could interrupt and tap that flow, even if I could not understand it. And, in this new way of seeing, I realized, for the first time, just how unhuman I had become. Each cell an individual, each cell infinitely programmable, operating as a whole but not limited to it. The information for almost any order was there, the information for any transformation of any cell, group of cells, or the entire organism in fact, and while I could not understand the source of that information or the language the Wardens used to govern the cells and cellular interaction, I could speak to them, mentally, and they would respond.

When I awoke it was dawn. Things looked the same. Everything and everybody looked the same, and yet . . . Awake, fully conscious, I could still see, still sense the Wardens inside of me. Something very strange had in fact happened in the night I'd spent on the mountain—I had become my dream. Not the dream of the god-thing, but the dream of a new and formless creature, whose collective *consciousness* totally owned and controlled his body and every cell in it. The last link not only with the Confederacy but with any sort of humanity as I knew or understood it had been cut.

In a real sense, I was as alien as those terrors on the ice.

CHAPTER ELEVEN

Saints Are Not Gods

The reaction to all this varied a bit with the other seven on the mountaintop, but it was clear that we had all been profoundly changed by the experience. The few who were willing to come out of the clouds and compare notes, such as Hono, Ching, and myself, found that our primary encounters with the *presence,* whatever it was, were quite different and highly subjective, though the discovery of our own bodies and the Wardens within was almost exactly the same.

"But what was it?" Ching wanted to know. "I mean— is it really a god?"

"Most of the others have no doubts whatsoever," I noted, also gesturing a little for some caution. I didn't want to start any fights over theology at this point, and lowered my voice to a whisper. "I think, somehow, we were in contact with the alien mind. Or *an* alien mind, or something. I think their power plant and base is under here somewhere, and somehow, maybe through the Warden organism, we connected."

"But the thoughts and pictures were so *strange.* . . ."

I nodded. "That's why we call 'em aliens. We were somehow inside a mind so different from ours, with so little in common, that we could hear each other, maybe be aware of each other, but make no real common connection. If you were born unable to see and then, for a short period, saw a picture of a forest from the air with no explanation of what it was, that would be akin to what we experienced."

"And how we—feel—now?"

"Somehow that connection sensitized us to the Wardens. When we contacted that other mind, it was through the

166

Wardens, somehow. And when we broke contact with it, our brains had been taught how to keep in contact with those in our own bodies. Honey, we haven't changed a bit. *Everybody* on Medusa is like this. But we're some of the very few aware of the fact."

"Hey! Tari! Look at me!" Hono's voice called, and we all turned and gasped at what we saw. It wasn't Hono at all, but a beautiful, stately goddess, the epitome of grace and beauty and strength—an angel. "I just pictured this in my mind and told my body what that picture was—and I had it!"

Just like that, I thought wonderingly. As simple as that.

We spent the rest of the morning experimenting and found that there was little we couldn't do if we willed it. Hair came and went, sex changed and changed again in a matter of minutes, in a curious process that seemed much like stop-motion photography. What you willed you could become, and the others could watch it happen. It was, in a sense, a new art form. Even mass seemed unimportant; the Wardens not only obeyed commands, but seemed able to reduce size if needed or create more cells out of energy. To be sure, it was easier to create the new mass than to get rid of it, since getting rid of it turned out to be extremely painful, but to some it was worth the price.

Since making such changes demanded a tremendous knowledge of biology, biophysics, biochemistry, you name it—knowledge all of us lacked—it became obvious that the Wardens translated the mental visions into reality by drawing on a vast body of knowledge beyond us. Where? I wondered. Some vast, high-speed computer someplace was feeding the things. It had to be.

Was the computer in fact what we had somehow connected with the night before? An alien computer, whose programming would also be so alien and so complex it would appear to us as a godlike superbeing? It was a good theory, anyway, and a computer had to be located someplace. That, in turn, would mean that the Warden organism was not a natural thing at all, but something artificial, something introduced into the environment of the four worlds. And who but those ugly bastards out there on the ice could have done that?

So they were here, below the waters, perhaps by choice,

when the first exploiter teams arrived. They hadn't discovered the place—they had been here all along. Did that mean, then, that *they* could do this as well as we—or better? The combined powers of all four worlds, perhaps—shape-changing, body-switching, the power to create and destroy by sheer force of will . . .

But if that were true, then why the robots? Why deal with the Four Lords at all, for that matter—let alone allow them to run their clandestine war against the Confederacy? And why that dangerous game of cat-and-mouse on the ice?

The clearer things became, the muddier they became. I was fascinated by the problem and hoped to spend a lot of time on it, but only in an intellectual capacity. I was still sincere about my vow, and this was my retirement mission —although it had a wonderful payoff.

"We have talked with God, and She has made us Her angels!" Quarl whooped with pride and glee, and that seemed to be the general consensus. Only the more pragmatic Hono, a doubter to begin with and with a somewhat wider intellectual horizon than the rest, was anywhere near restrained. Yet even she was exultant with the new power, which was as good or greater than promised.

"It has occurred to me that the Elders have been here and have received this gift," she remarked to me. "Ugly old crones, aren't they?"

I grasped her meaning at once, for the same thought had also occurred to me. Although this ability might fade with age or lack of regular workouts, the fact was that it was almost impossible to accept those Elders' appearances as more than theatrical façades at this point. The others, too, understood the implications, and I was glad to pounce on them.

"Think about what that means," I warned them. "This power is to be used when necessary, and only for good, not to frighten or amuse yourself or others. You have great power, but you also have a sacred trust now. This isn't something that can be passed on or taught. We all earned it. Now we must return to use it wisely."

That statement sobered them a bit, as I hoped. I was anxious to leave before too much of the day was gone. New power or no, I didn't want to cross that stretch at night with our horror-show friends out there waiting for us, and I really didn't care to spend another night on this mountain. Once the connection had been established it would be easier the next time, and a few of us were far enough into madness now that no added exposure was needed.

Hono picked up her spear. "We walk down, then."

I thought a moment. "No. Maybe we don't. Let me try a little experiment here. Be brave, and don't be *too* surprised if it doesn't work." I looked at Ching, winked, then concentrated, drawing on my long practice of mind control and autohypnosis.

At once I began to change. I knew it, could see it, feel it, even as I willed it, and I knew that the message was adequate even as the process started.

The others, Ching included, watched in amazement at the transformation as my hunch paid off. Somewhere in that Warden computer there were the blueprints for a very large creature that flew.

"What is it?" several cried in alarm.

"How the hell do I know?" I croaked back. "But it has talons to pick up and rend prey, and it *flies*. Draw upon yourselves, become this thing as I did, and have a little faith. Then we'll *fly* back over that cold waste!"

That very thought—of flying strongly for a day or less rather than three days of dangerous walking—was enough. Now, for the first time, I could see in the others the creature I had willed up from some unknown source. Great, black man-sized birds, with oddly human eyes and curious, twisted beaks and taloned, powerful feet that could grab and rend if need be.

"Now what?" somebody called out.

"Let the Wardens do the work!" I called back. "We want to fly, so we will fly!" Awkwardly I walked out of the protected rock shelter and into a pretty strong wind. The drop was not sheer, but the ice-covered ground did fall away fairly fast. If this didn't work, I was going to be a bug spot down there someplace, that was for sure. And yet, I had to be first. Mind control and autohypnosis would provide the relaxation and confidence I knew I'd need, control the others sorely lacked. But if I took off, if I flew, faith would no longer be necessary, and would be replaced in them by will.

I concentrated for a moment, then looked out again and could *see* the air as clearly divided layers and swirls. Not as something solid—I could still see *through* it—but rather as differences in *textures,* a softness here, a bright clarity rushing through there. "Take off with a strong leap into the wind!" I told them, then summoned up my courage and leaped, spreading my great wings as I did so.

I plunged down at an angle, barely skimming the tops of the slope, and only my mental control kept me from panicking and crashing. Down, down, and then I let loose the last of the tenseness and—as I'd told them—allowed the Wardens, replacing the bird's instinct, to take over. I bottomed out the drop and glided upward at an equal angle, up into empty, cloud-filled skies! *I flew!*

Ching, to her credit, got over her amazement quickly and followed my lead as I watched from above with nervous eyes. Oddly, she had an easier time of it than I had. Perhaps, I thought, there's more to faith than I'd thought. Then, one by one, the rest launched themselves, and I circled nervously and waited for them.

Once in the air, most were exultant, like little children, doing loops and swirls and having a grand time. I finally had to move to herd them in, reminding them, "We have a long way to go—don't waste your energy. You're not immortal, just powerful!"

"And strong," Hono shouted back. "We are truly blessed!" But she accepted my lead as we formed up close together and headed back out toward the ice.

I hadn't taken the low ceiling into consideration. We were still certainly within easy sight of the ground, as I didn't want to risk bodies as large and relatively cumbersome as ours controlled by novices in any real storm.

Since those creatures on the ice could see us if they were looking for us, or had some simple radar scan, I wanted to get up some speed to put as much distance as possible between them and us. The air currents helped a great deal; though we had a little trouble with firm control, there were levels where we could just rest on the currents and let them carry us, with a minimum expenditure of effort.

"There're our demons!" Hono snarled, looking down and to the west. "Looks to be the same four. I don't think they see us."

"Let's keep it that way," I responded. "We don't have the time or the experience to tangle with them."

"They killed four of us!" Sitzter protested angrily. "And who knows how many others? We are powerful, strong, and blessed by Mother Medusa! We should avenge our sisters!"

"No!" I shouted. "Dammit, if *we* can do this the odds are *they* can, too!" But my warning was too late. The madness that power brings and the religious fervor that had been kindled on the mountain was just too much for them, and, after all, they were hunters. First Sitzter, then Hono, and finally the others peeled off and made for the four large, dark forms below.

I picked up my speed and made a dangerous turn, trying to cut them off and steer them away. "This is madness!" I cried, but they were beyond talking now—and the aliens below had now spotted us.

Hono had taken the lead, as befitted her role as master hunter and group leader, and dove on the four dark forms. The aliens suddenly shot up into the air and dispersed, then hovered in an obviously preplanned diamond formation that allowed each to come to the aid of the others. I had a pretty strong feeling that these were pros who had been through situations like this many times before. I didn't like it at all. A strange idea popped into my head that these four, out here like this, were bait in a subtle trap as well as a discouragement to any mass movement to the sacred mountain.

Hono approached the lead alien, whose pressure suit, complete with some sort of backpack, was now clearly visible. The alien didn't let her get very close. The creatures looked really strange now, with just fifty centimeters of each of their ten tentacles showing. Those tentacles were three meters long and apparently independent of one another. Hono was coming at the hovering alien at great speed, but the alien never wavered, never even moved, until the great bird was almost upon it. Then, suddenly, the creature zipped a few carefully measured meters to one side, enough for Hono to miss and also to render her unable to break her forward momentum. Tentacles shot out not only from the target creature but from the next closest, and they hit home. Hono whirled in midair and great feathers flew off in all directions. Clearly she was totally off balance and she plunged like a stone to the ground.

Quarl and Sitzter flew right behind her, and the other three behind them. Suddenly the sky was a mass of feathers, screams, and flying tentacles extended to full length, skillfully and independently wielded with expert skill.

I pulled up, seeing Ching following behind me, and tried to create a diversion for the others. It worked to an extent, pulling one alien's attention off the furiously attacking great birds and allowing a gap in their tight tentacle-tip-to-tentacle-tip formation. But instead of using the opportunity to escape, Tyne and Sitzter went after the exposed alien. Tyne grabbed hold of a snaking tentacle with her talons and, while it wasn't really clear who had whom, she managed to yank the alien off balance and whip it to one side. The alien let out one of those piercing screams, and fun time was over.

A dozen more suddenly shot up through the ice, and these bore small handlebar-shaped devices held between two forward tentacles. Energy shot from the nub of the "bars," the newcomers being totally uncaring whether they hit their own or us.

That was enough. Tyne was down with her alien, and Sitzter and two others soon after. I decided there was nothing I could do and swooped up and away, toward the cloud bank overhead. Suddenly I heard Ching scream, "Tari! Watch out!" I immediately dropped, rolled, and sped off in another direction, but not before I saw Ching take the beam that had been meant for me and drop like the others to the sea floor. Then I suddenly made a complete upturn as a handy current came by and shot like a rocket up into the clouds.

I remained there for some time, trying to decide what to do next. Certainly the game had been over ever since Tyne had grabbed that one alien soldier, and they suddenly brought up their reinforcements with their equivalent of hand weapons. The indiscriminate way the gunners had used their weapons could indicate a callous disregard for individual lives, but somehow I didn't think so. The beam seemed very wide field, and if it were a death weapon it would be better suited to large battles or simply to clean away all comers across the ice from fixed positions. No, it was almost certainly a stun weapon, which meant they were even now cleaning up on the ice below, checking unconscious bodies, both theirs and ours, for signs of life.

That they were killers was clear from their earlier actions, but I didn't believe they were indiscriminate killers. Otherwise why give the prey what could only be seen as a sporting chance, provided that prey didn't threaten the lives of one or more of them?

I knew I had to have one more look, perhaps several more, and I came out of the clouds cautiously, ever on the alert to duck back into them. A dozen or so aliens were on the ice below, as I expected, setting bodies out in a row and examining them. Three alien bodies were visible, along with our own people, who were, I noted, rapidly reverting to their human forms. They didn't see me, and I didn't drop down too close, getting back up into the cloud cover again and circling around.

I counted six half-bird, half-human bodies down there, which meant at least one other besides me had gotten away —but I had no real way of telling who. I was pretty certain, though, that Ching had been hit, and that was my main concern. I liked Hono and most of the others, but they had brought this upon themselves despite my best efforts and were in any event impossible to save. The only hope I had was that, after a while, perhaps near darkness, the aliens would relax enough so that I might try a dive-snatch-and-grab operation on Ching. I had no idea if she or any of the others were dead or alive, but I had to assume that they survived until evidence proved otherwise. My only practical question was how long I could maintain this form and this energy level.

Quick dips in and out of the clouds revealed to me that some, at least, were alive. They moved occasionally, and were quickly slapped down by fast tentacles or pushed back by one of the four scissorlike appendages growing from the trunk.

If one were alive that raised my hopes that all might be. With the great self-repair abilities we all had, almost any survival was as good as not being injured at all.

The aliens were very professional and very methodical about the whole thing, but they were, I thought, pretty casual with people who could change into something else, perhaps even into aliens. That would be what *I* would do if it were me down there. But over the next hour or two, the most any of the captives, now totally restored to human form, did was sit up. These weren't like my fifty-five sheep back in the sewers, so it stood to reason that if they didn't change and try and fight their way out they couldn't. If the Warden organism was, as I suspected, an extension of some alien computer, then obviously the connection between the computer and the captives had either been switched off or turned way down. The real question was what the aliens were waiting for. If they were just going to kill the captives, they could have done that long before and been gone to wherever they were most comfortable. But if they meant to take the crew prisoners, for some sort of questioning, they showed no inclination either to bring up transport or move them to safer and more secure quarters. They seemed, in fact, to be waiting for something. As sentinels they were also pros, their weapons and stations positioned so I could make out Ching in the group below. But I had no prayer of reaching her and getting back out without being shot myself.

Still, I waited, just out of their sight, I hoped just out of their reach, unwilling to abandon Ching unless I was certain there was no chance I could help her. If she was the price of all this discovery, I told myself sincerely, then the price was too high.

Finally, what they were waiting for arrived, and it was not at all what I expected. A large transport copter, specially outfitted for extreme-cold-weather use, came rushing out of the south, green and red running lights blinking and two large headlights slanting down on the ice itself. With growing apprehension, I watched the vehicle approach. Then I saw TMS markings on its side. It set down near the group, hovering just a few centimeters above the surface that could not have supported its dead weight. Carefully, one at a time, four TMS monitors climbed out onto the ice, laser pistols in hand. They gave harldly a glance or nod at the alien sentries, but went straight to the prisoners who, one by one, were taken to the copter and rudely pushed inside.

Although the copter was large enough to hold all that weight, it would certainly have a far slower return than it did coming out from wherever it was. I hoped that I could either follow it or get a good idea of its destination before my energy gave out. The copter rose slowly from the alien camp, hovered at about forty meters, and, staying below the thick clouds, started off. I followed as cautiously as I could, but it quickly became clear that I could never really keep up or even catch them. At one point just before they applied full power, I managed to get close enough to read the base city's name around the TMS shield on both doors.

Centrum.

I had never been to Centrum, nor met anyone who had, but I had heard the stories about it. The map in my head showed that it was far to the south, almost on the equator itself, and on the west coast—a distance of more than ten thousand kilometers. It was ridiculous even to *think* that the copter had come from there—it would have taken days at its average speed—but Gray Basin was close indeed, by air, perhaps three hundred and fifty or four hundred kilometers south, or about two hours' copter time with a full load.

Wearily, I turned and headed for Gray Basin, heading first due south so I could pick up some map landmarks. It would take me considerably longer than two hours to make the city, even with cooperative air currents and good weather, neither of which was a certainty. I still had no idea how much longer I could last.

A shape joined me in the darkness. I was already bone-tired and totally depressed, just going on sheer automatics, or I would have noticed it before it came close. When it did level out next to me, I was too weary even to take evasive measures, but, fortunately, it wasn't necessary.

"Tari?"

"That you, Quarl?"

"Yeah. Uh—dammit, I'm sorry, Tari."

"We're all sorry. I'm sorry, you're sorry, the rest of 'em are *really* sorry, it doesn't make any difference. What is, is, Quarl. We go on from there."

"We'll never catch them, you know."

I sighed. "I know. But I think I know where they're going, and that'll have to do. At least it's a city I know backward and forward, so I may be able to slip in and out of it without much trouble."

"You mean *we*. I'm going, too. They're my friends, too, Tari."

"No, Quarl. It wouldn't work. They'd pick you up in a second no matter what your powers. It's a whole different world in there, a world that's built to keep everybody in, to see what everybody's doing all the time. I know that world, and I know how it works. You don't. They'd have you in ten minutes."

"Then I will make them pay dearly for those ten minutes!" she spat, "but I am going in."

"I'd kill you first, Quarl, if I could, for the sake of the others."

"Huh?"

"They wouldn't kill you. They'd knock you out, knock you down like they did the others back there on the ice. Then they'd take you to a place that is truly hell, where men can steal your mind and soul and learn everything you know."

"I can not be tortured so easily!"

I sighed. How do you explain a psych complex to a stone-age woman? "There's no torture. No pain at all. You just can't know what they can do. And when they get you, they'll find out that I'm there and then they'll get me. It's no good, Quarl. I have to do this alone."

"You sound strange. Tari. Not like a brave one going after his own, but more like one who has lost all hope."

"No, I haven't gone that far, Quarl, but you're right. First of all, I'm tired. I'm on my last energy reserves, and the dawn and the landmarks tell me that I've got at least two more hours to go. And, yes, I would rather go home."

"But you go anyway. You do not seem surprised."

"I'm not. Somehow, I knew that it would eventually end, that it would come down to this, a final chase, a final hunt. Just when I found what I really wanted and was ready to give it all up." I chuckled dryly to myself. "It just wasn't meant to be, Quarl. I could *see* happiness, hold it in my hands, but I could not realize that I had what I wanted most in the world until it was no longer there."

"Among my people, the Kuzmas, there is a strong belief in fate and destiny for all people," Quarl told me. "Each of us is born to that destiny, but knows not what it is. So I can understand your feelings, my friend from the stars. But perhaps you will win, hey? Anything worth your life's devotion is worth risking death for."

Perhaps she was right, I thought. Those fifty-five back in the sewers—play revolutionaries, children daring the fire and kidding themselves—came down to their moment of truth. But the cause was proven not worth their miserable lives, even though they would suffer horribly. No risk, no gain.

But I *had* apparently impressed Quarl enough that she endangered the whole mission. "What do you wish me to do, Tari?" she asked.

"Go back to the citadel. Tell them what happened. Tell them that the demons are not demons but beings from the stars who work with the city people and have great weapons. Warn them of that. And tell them exactly what happened to all of us as far as you know it. Leave nothing out, make nothing look better or worse than it is. See Angi and Bura. Tell them—tell them that I love them both very much, and that if there is any way to do so I will return to them. See that they and my children are cared for."

"Until you return."

"Yes," I responded in a litanous monotone, "until I return."

Quarl saw me almost to Gray Basin, then flew off to the south and west. I saw the city in the distance, looking ugly in the late summer when no snow or ice covered it, leaving only that brutal gray roof and the stacks peering from it. It stretched out as far as the eye could see, and I hated every square meter of it.

Still, I settled down directly on that roof and found a place that didn't look *too* uncomfortable. I let myself relax for the first time, allowing my skin, bones, every cell of my body, to revert to my old form. I was too damned tired to do anything, but I forced myself to sit and think for a moment.

The copter was from Centrum, yet it was undeniably headed here. Why? Why a Centrum copter, anyway—and what was it doing this far north? Medusan government business, most likely—unless they had a Centrum copter near all major cities to differentiate national from local authorities.

And if that was the case, then all of the prisoners would be in the hands of the central government, not the local TMS office. They would probably be shifted to Centrum for disposition. That made sense. They knew a lot about a lot of things, including the sacred mountain, the malleability trick and its possibilities. They also had experience with the aliens at close hand. These wouldn't be things that Ypsir's people would like a regional psych office or the usual TMS monitors to come across. Too many might get ideas of their own, and there'd be somebody around who would be from Outside as well, somebody who would equate those demons with alien creatures and draw some interesting conclusions. No, the prisoners would be taken directly to party headquarters at Centrum, a bastion of protection, and handled by people who already knew the terrible secrets these prisoners could spill.

How would they get them there? The train was out—too long and too public. And air traffic seemed limited to local practical vehicles like the copters, which would be too slow. That brought Gray Basin back into focus, for it had one thing several other cities and towns of relatively equal importance and distance did not have.

It had a spaceport.

I stood up wearily. I was just barely atop the city, and when I entered it, I would have to do so from below. The access points from the roof were among the most heavily monitored places of all, and I knew it. Still, I wasn't so far gone that I couldn't use the vantage point to some advantage. I climbed up a ladder atop a large and dormant stack and looked out in the direction of the spaceport. I could just barely see it, off in the distance: a small cluster of warehouses and a tiny terminal in an ovoid pattern around the landing pad that was otherwise in the middle of nothingness.

There definitely was no ship in.

How long I had I didn't know, but I realized it would be better to lose them through sleeping than to lose them by rushing in as tired as I was. Ironically, I was going from the stone age back to my most nasty and sophisticated technological self for this mission, and, even then, I'd be taking risk after unacceptable risk. I had to rest and renew myself, so I went back and lay down as the sun rose high over the sealed city beneath and was soon asleep.

I hated going in yet again. I hated risking all, with the odds so totally stacked against me, knowing that even if I got away with anything myself the odds of saving Ching were very slim indeed.

But damn my filthy hide, I just couldn't resist the challenge.

CHAPTER TWELVE

Into the Lion's Den

I didn't sleep nearly as long as I needed, but it was a good, solid sleep and just what I needed to restore my confidence and get my brain working again.

Entering the city wasn't much of a problem, but once in, I wasn't at all sure what I could do. The only thing certain was that my theory of breaking the system by transformation was about to get a real test. The trouble was, I would have to be slow and careful to have any reasonable chance, and I just didn't have the time for that.

Having served in the city in Transportation proved invaluable. Of course, to enter I simply waited for a train to come up and stop, then I walked in with the train when they turned off the energy barriers to admit it. Once inside the entry tunnel, though, I was in the yards for the trains and had to make my way carefully to the passenger section. Having worked the station, I knew where the monitor cameras were located and where the inevitable "dead" zones were, although they were hardly conveniently located for my purposes. At this point, naked and hairless, I was an easy mark for a monitor and a sure flag, so getting into position without being observed was time-consuming.

I was counting on the Rochande passenger train, my old workhorse, to come in late. There were inevitably a number of TMS personnel on board, not for patrol but either coming back from some training mission or arriving after assignment to Gray Basin. It would still be a ticklish operation, requiring a lot of luck, but overall I'd had more than my share of that lately and had to trust that I'd get a bit more.

There was a spot between the passenger platform and

the automatic baggage-handling section that was part of
the freight operation which did not overlap two cameras.
By a zigzag route I managed to make it across the yards
and take a position behind a moving stair that was at the
far end of the passenger section. For the first time it hit me
that I would have to kill a few people if I went ahead with
this; although I wouldn't feel too badly about TMS or government personnel, an innocent or two would also be necessary. I didn't really like doing that, but could only remember again the fifty-five who wouldn't try to escape and who
were, in many ways, typical not only of the people here but
of the whole system I was fighting.

I had a pretty clear plan, based on my observations and
experiences during my life here. It is in the nature of my
business, and of my mind, to file just about everything
away, even when it serves no apparent purpose. You never
know when you'll have to use one trivial or not-so-trivial
item or another.

The initial move would be ticklish. There was a clock
overhanging the passenger-discharge section that said I had
to remain there, undiscovered, for at least two hours. To
make my move too early might blow the whole scheme.
Several station personnel passed very near me at various
times, but thanks to my new Warden sense and my own
self-control I was able to remain hidden in the shadows. At
least, no alarms went off.

Finally, it was only ten minutes before the train was due,
and I was starting to get nervous. None of the station people had passed in almost half an hour, and I needed one,
my first innocent victim, any time now. The train was actually within earshot, stopped for the barriers, before I got
my chance. A grade-four passenger-service agent walked
from the baggage office up toward the platform. As she
passed, I moved fast and silent from my shadowy place.

The deed was done in a couple of seconds. I had created
a sharp, serrated ridge of cartilege on my arm and reinforced the muscle. I decapitated her rather cleanly, then
had a nervous moment as the head started rolling out almost into camera range. I grabbed it, but it was messy and
unpleasant.

I had timed the maneuver perfectly and applied just the
right amount of force. Decapitation sounds terrible, and it

is; but considering the Warden's amazing powers you had to strike an immediate, certain death blow or you'd have it. The other advantage was that the shock caused the body's Wardens to snap into futile action to seal the wound, so surprisingly little bleeding occurred.

I made no attempt to duplicate her features more than roughly; I hadn't seen them long enough in presentable condition to do so. Still, I managed it, displacing some of my extra mass into height to manage to fit, however uncomfortably, into the clothes which were, mercifully, close enough to the color of Medusan blood to mask the stains somewhat. The girl's sandals, however, would never fit without a lot of work, and I didn't even try. None of this disguise really had to last for very long.

I had an uneasy moment when it looked as if two others were going to walk back by my hiding place with its grisly contents, but, fortunately, at that moment the train rounded the bend and slid into its slip. Everybody snapped to professional attention.

My luck had held up to this point, but now I'd need more. I waited until the train was completely in and docked, then watched the doors slide open and the passengers begin to emerge. When I spotted two TMS uniforms with duffels I went into my act, fully aware that the others would also see, but counting on the usual mob inclination on Medusa to let TMS handle things whenever there was a question of responsibility. I pulled the trunk of the woman's body out a bit, so an arm and leg were showing, then stepped out myself and cried, hysterically, *"Monitors!* Come here! Please hurry!"

Nobody calls a cop on Medusa unless there's terrible trouble. I saw the two young faces, a man and a woman, glance over at me, look puzzled for a minute, then follow my arm that pointed to the exposed limbs. They dropped their duffels and trotted over to me.

"What's the matter?" the woman asked, sounding more concerned than nasty.

"T-there's a body there!" I stuttered, sounding scared to death. Both of them looked shocked, then turned and knelt down as I angled myself so that the moving stair shielded me from the platform. By then most of the people had gone up and we had no curious gawkers, but there was certain to be a couple of curious train people pretty quickly.

The two monitors were pushovers. I managed to chop them both cold before they realized what had happened, then killed them a bit more cleanly but no less efficiently. I had to move damned fast—their bags were still on the platform, and the camera would at least have seen that.

I quickly got rid of the transport clothing and pulled off the man's monitor uniform. I was working against time and just barely got it right. Fortunately, the man was not too far off my size, so I was able to adjust myself for a reasonable, if slightly uncomfortable, fit. It only had to *look* presentable.

I took the risk of rolling the bodies out and under the train when a quick peek showed, incredibly, nobody looking in my direction or even, it seemed, aware that anything was going on. Then I walked back out onto the platform, picked up a bag, turned, and called back loudly, "Okay, I'll meet you in the main terminal!" Hoisting the bag on my shoulder, I then took the moving stairs myself.

The main terminal was, of course, still pretty busy, and that helped a lot. I needed another switch, one not so easily traced, and quickly, but no opportunity presented itself. I walked into the lavatory, looked through the bag, found some evidence that this private was a new transfer to Gray Basin, and decided to take a chance, at least for the moment. The train wouldn't be turning around until it was cleaned and serviced, about two or three hours. If they didn't look for that passenger agent too hard, I might have some time before the bodies were discovered. Such callous murder was so totally alien to this society they would search everywhere for the missing agent before looking for a body. The other recruit was almost certainly new herself and unlikely to be missed immediately, either. If, and it was a big if, the computer hadn't flagged the two of them dropping their bags and running out of view. But who could know?

Using the private's card, I took the bus to TMS headquarters. I needed another TMS body because, again, I bore only a vague resemblance to the dead monitor. Luckily, I knew Gray Basin's TMS building pretty well, including, thanks to the probably late Major Hocrow, many of its own dead areas.

I got off a couple of blocks before reaching headquarters and managed to toss the bag into a trash receptacle before walking boldly down to the building. If only the people knew how many dead zones there were in any major city there'd be hell to pay, I thought with some amusement. The alley with the trash bin had a camera, but it was mounted high on a wall and easily seen. So by just keeping the trash bin between me and it I couldn't be seen. They still might send somebody to check the trash, of course, but by then I'd be somebody else—I hoped.

I entered by the garage rather than the front door, my uniform being sufficient to get no more than nods from a few monitors.

There was a single camera mounted on a slowly rotating and wide-open mount in the center of the car-maintenance garage. A piece of cake. I just walked along until I found a monitor checking a car for something, struck up a mild conversation, then, when the camera and mark were easily in the right positions, chopped him. This time I had had a few minutes to study the intended victim's features and the luxury of a less messy kill, so I had no trouble in duplicating her features. She was a fairly large woman and things fit pretty well, and, under the car, I was able to change quickly and efficiently into her uniform.

I found the replication trick a cinch, at least as far as I knew. Just concentrate on the victim, match his or her Warden configuration to yours, and let your Wardens emulate the pattern. It was kind of weird to feel hair grow out rapidly on my head, and to watch flesh act as if it were something independently alive and fluid; but the actual change was *so* damned easy, now that I had a few minutes.

When I climbed out from under the car I was the private, to all onlookers, anyway, and again I timed the camera just right to stash the body in the car's trunk. With any luck, it might be a couple of days before the body was found, and I didn't need that long.

Satisfied, I took out "my" card, called the elevator, and rode up to the desk and central processing area I knew so well. This was always a busy area, and the risk I ran here had mostly to do with meeting some friend of the person I was supposed to be. I couldn't hold that kind of pose for a moment against somebody who knew the original well.

The important thing, though, was to look and act as if you belong and you're working on somebody's instructions. Usually that's enough to get by in public areas, where people just don't expect this sort of thing. I went in back to the small compartments, each with its own terminal, that TMS monitors used when filing reports. I picked an empty one, flicked on the terminal, and started.

While I expected no trouble in breaking the simple computer codes generally used, I was surprised to find that these terminals needed no codes at all. You just stuck in your card, which certified that you were a legitimate TMS monitor, and that was enough when the computer monitor checked appearance against file. No fingerprints, no retinal check, just a simple method for a society that took far too much for granted.

I punched up KOR—CHING—LU and then sat back and waited for the data to come up on the screen. I scrolled quickly through the basics to the last entry, which was what I wanted:

ARRESTED 1416 OFFICERS CENTRUM 17–9–51. PROCESSED GB TMS 0355 18–9–51, JUDG UD, SUBJ. REF. CENTRUM DISTRICT, REL. CENTRUM CUST. 0922 18–9, DEPT. 41 1V GB 1705. CASE CLOSED. REF. #37–6589234.

It wasn't hard to figure out what had happened. Ching had been brought here in the early morning, processed, judged guilty and sentenced to UD—Ultimate Demotion—then turned over to Centrum officially. She was to leave at 1705—in less than an hour. The computer didn't say how, but it had to be via the shuttle. I punched the reference number given and got a similar readout:

HONO, W–O UNCLASS., ARRESTED 1416 OFFICERS CENTRUM 17–9–51. The rest of the listing was identical to Ching's, except, of course, that the end reference referenced Ching's case. So they were both going out on the shuttle. Well, maybe I should, too.

Bluff and bravado will only get you so far, but it does wonders in a tightly regimented society. I walked out the front door without any problem and headed for the bus to the central terminal. I wasn't about to risk trying for a TMS car—the motor pool authorizations would be pretty tightly watched. Then I stopped, cursed myself, walked around to the garage, and found the car with the body still hidden inside. This, of course, *had* to be *her* car, and that would make things easy—if the damned thing worked.

It did, and I was soon out of the garage and heading toward a city gate, a dead body under the back seat and a really irritating squeal coming from somewhere in front that had obviously been the reason for the service.

I reached the road gate to the space terminal with no problem, but had to get out, present my card to the monitoring machine, and tell it that I was going out to the terminal with some special paperwork that some other monitor had forgotten. It was a routine enough thing, and I had no trouble getting the barriers lowered quickly.

The shuttle was already in, and I made it with almost twenty minutes to spare. I hadn't been back here since arriving on Medusa, but the place hadn't changed much. It was small and cramped and not very impressive, since passengers were infrequent. I saw only a couple, both official-looking, sitting around now. No sign of Ching or Hono, though, let alone of the arresting officers. For the first time I began to fear that I'd blown it.

My confusion must have been all too apparent, for one of the government employees waiting to board, a white-haired man of middle age, stood up and came over to me. "Something the matter, young woman?"

I was a little startled for a moment, since I'd forgotten I was playing a woman at this point. Actually, this was the first conversation I had had with anyone since assuming this identity, and the change had almost slipped my mind.

"Yes, sir. I have some papers that never got cleared for a couple of prisoners supposed to go out to Centrum, and now I don't see 'em." The voice sounded funny, but more or less female, which was all that mattered on a world like this.

He frowned. "Let me see them."

I was ready. I had made hard copies of several forms with the dispositions of Ching's and Hono's cases for just such an eventuality. They wouldn't fool a monitor, but they'd get by a bureaucrat, I hoped.

He looked them over, smiled, then handed them back.

"Well, it's easy to see why. They departed on the eighteenth —that was yesterday."

I was thunderstruck, and for a moment my self-control failed. I hadn't slept a few hours, I'd slept almost a day and a half on that city roof!

I must have looked really crushed—as I was—because the government man said, "You're going to have some problems, huh?"

I nodded, thinking as fast as I could. "Yes, sir. I'm pretty new here, and while I just was told by my boss to get these things down here, when I come back with them and they see the wrong date it won't be my sergeant who gets the blame. Discipline's pretty rough up here, too."

He seemed genuinely touched. "Give me your card."

"Sir?"

"I said, give me your card. Let me see what I can do."

I was afraid he was going to call me in and try and square a nonexistent mission with an unknown superior, but I had no choice. I did, however, eye the exit. I was outside the city here, and all I really needed was some running room. Unfortunately, I was also in the most heavily monitored type of buildings on Medusa—since it was exposed to the outside—and one connected to live evaluators with automatic rifles all over the place. If I made a run for the door now they'd hit the alarm; if I stood here, I was probably trapped. The only thing I could think of was to let this scene run its course and take a last-gasp chance at a panic escape when the right time came.

The man was back from a small office in a couple of minutes and he was smiling as he handed back my card. "I think we can arrange for you to complete your mission, Monitor. I'll square things with your superior, since you're not due back on duty until 0800 tomorrow anyway." He winked. "Nobody will ever know, huh?"

I was thunderstruck. "Then you'll take the papers with you to Centrum and see that they're delivered?"

"Oh, my, no. I'm not going to Centrum, unfortunately. But there's plenty of room on the shuttle, and I've logged you as my guest as far as Centrum, with a return on the morning flight. The trip is still going to cost you some money you probably don't have—Centrum's not cheap— but you'll get there and back and be able to deposit your

papers with no one the wiser at your end, since I've cleared
it on my personal assurance."

I could hardly believe this. "You mean you want me to
come with you?"

He nodded. "And better hurry. We're about to board.
Well? How about it?"

I considered his offer. Out there was freedom. The shuttle
meant new dangers, and I was probably too late to do much
anyway, even if I could find them. Still, I'd come this far,
and this seemed the only sensible thing to do under the circumstances, so I nodded. "All right, sir—and thanks."

Of course, the question I had weighed was not that hard
to answer. Nobody, and I mean *nobody,* has this kind of
luck. When too many things keep going right, you just have
to know you're being had. I don't know whose bodies
they'd found, or where my slip had come, but somebody
had gotten a lot of laughs at seeing me do my routine,
knowing all the while that I was a day late and didn't realize it.

Obviously escape was out. They'd never let me make the
door, and it would be a very uncomfortable ride. It seemed
to me that going along with things would at least bring me
close to Ching and Hono, even if very dangerously, and I
was still not without resources.

The shuttle was the same comfortable craft I remembered, only now there were only the two government
bureaucats and myself aboard. The takeoff was smooth and
effortless, although not without the press of many gravities
into the soft foam seats and the unsettling but thrilling feeling when the boost was cut off.

"Dunecal, next stop, five minutes," the speaker said
crisply. "Remain in your seats and strapped in at all times."
That surprised me, since I'd assumed we were going directly to Centrum, where my welcoming committee would be
waiting. But, sure enough, we descended smoothly and
were soon in Dunecal, main city of the central continent,
and my benefactor's destination. He wished me well, and
departed, acting for all the world as if he had no idea who
or what I really was—and he may not have known, I reflected.

"Loading passengers now," the speaker announced. "Centrum next stop."

I thought about jumping ship at this point, but there seemed no purpose to it. I was hooked and was being reeled in slowly for the amusement of whatever sportsman was on the other end.

Three passengers boarded at Dunecal, a man and woman in government black and another young woman whose looks were so startlingly different I almost had to stare.

Women on Medusa were no beauties. Oh, once you got used to them they were fine, but all were chunky, and had a masculine muscularity about them. There was, after all, a chance that anybody could flip from one sex to the other and so the average person was a bit of both, really. I had frankly almost forgotten the difference between normal human and Medusan females until this young woman came on.

She was certainly Medusan—her casual clothes would not have been sufficient protection for anybody else—but, then again, she wasn't. Her olive skin looked far softer than the tough hide we all took for granted. She was built as few women I'd met were built and had mastered all the right sexy moves. She also had a sweet, sexy smile on her very pretty face and her hair was longer than normal and light brown—the first of such a color I'd ever seen on Medusa, and one I'd rarely seen anywhere else, for that matter.

"Take that seat and strap in, Tix," the man instructed.

She smiled. "Oh, yes, my lord," she said in a childish-sounding yet sexy voice, and did as instructed. I noticed she never stopped smiling and just about never took her eyes off him. The other two strapped themselves in and the man noticed me staring at the young woman.

"Never seen a Goodtime Girl before, huh?" he called out conversationally.

I shook my head. "No, sir. I'm from Gray Basin, and we don't see any there."

"I daresay," he answered with pride. "You just arrest 'em and send 'em to us and we make 'em." He chuckled at that.

I responded with a smile I didn't feel. There was something creepy about Tix, something *unnatural*.

I'd heard mentions of Goodtime Girls, of course. Everybody had. Entertainers, consorts, concubines, and a little of everything else, it was said—mostly for the entertainment and gratification of the bigwigs. But nobody *I* had ever talked to had actually seen one, or really knew anything about them except that theirs was a different kind of job. I always wondered why, on a planet ninety-percent female, there weren't Goodtime Boys.

The man proved chatty. Either he, too, was ignorant of who I was or he was putting on a mighty fine act. I gave him my cover story, with the truth when explaining what I was doing on the shuttle. He seemed to accept it.

Goodtime Girls, it seemed, weren't employees, they were slaves. Oh, he didn't call Tix that, but it was clear that all the euphemisms were stand-ins for the word "slave." They had been convicted of crimes against the state and sentenced to Ultimate Demotion. Most UDs, as he called them, were sent off to the mines of Momrath's moons, but a few were selected and turned into Goodtime Girls by expert psychs in the government's Criminal Division. "Some of 'em are real artists," he told me proudly. "You wouldn't believe what Tix looked like before they worked on her."

"There are no Goodtime Boys?" I couldn't resist asking.

He shook his head from side to side. "Nope. Something in the process having to do with our little buggers the Wardens. When they remove the psyche or whatever it is they take out, the subject's invariably locked in as female." He gave a leer in Tix's direction, and she nearly shivered with delight. "Not that I mind that a bit."

I had to repress the urge to shiver. In all the barbaric acts of mankind, the worst was certainly abject slavery, and probably the worst of the worst was to create willing, natural slaves with a psych guide and a pysch machine. The system seemed terribly perverted, somehow, as well as downright crazy. Why have slaves on a world where robots were happily employed? The only possible answer was instant ego-gratification for the kind of mentality that worshiped only power. This guy had been "given" Tix by the government for doing such wonderful work and reaching a government grade level that warranted a Goodtime Girl. He took her with him as a highly visible status symbol, and because he got his jollies having a personal slave to order

about. It was the ultimate reflection of the sickness of this
society, I thought sadly. What kind of a place was it that
was run by people who had psych-created fawning slaves
the way influential people in other societies owned great
gems or great works of art?

I repressed a sudden urge to kill the fellow and his companion right then and there, and maybe the Goodtime Girl,
too, although, in more than one sense, she was already
dead.

About twenty minutes after takeoff the speaker came on.
"Please remain strapped in your seats. We are about to
dock."

The man and woman both frowned, and she turned to
him. "That's odd. I didn't feel any deceleration."

He nodded. "I wonder if something's wrong?"

There were no windows, so there was no way of knowing, but I tensed up. Here we go, I thought, and got myself
mentally ready for any move that could be made.

I felt a shudder and vibration, then three quick deceleration bursts, and we slid neatly into the dock. There was a
hissing, and then the rear door slid open. The man unbuckled himself and walked over to the door, looking out,
still puzzled. "This isn't Centrum," he said, confused. "I
think this is the space station."

I unbuckled myself, sighed, stood up and walked back to
the door. "Just go back to your seat," I told him, "and relax. I think this is my stop."

CHAPTER THIRTEEN

A Victim of Philosophy

The lock was of the modern, standardized type, with the shuttle docked in space against a long tubular entryway into the space station itself. I knew that all four planets had such stations, and that the Four Lords made good use of them. The master computer for Medusa was here, for example, but I was unprepared for the enormity of the place. It had good artificial gravity, perhaps a bit lighter than I'd become used to. From the entry tube you could look out through a transparent strip and see the gigantic structure stretching away from you on all sides. It was more than a mere space station; it was more like a small floating city several kilometers across, large enough to be self-sufficient in those things that would support a sizable population.

At the end of the long walk up the entry tube I came upon a second airlock chamber, which I entered without hesitation. If they'd meant to kill me they could have done so far more easily and less messily elsewhere. This second lock was pretty much an insurance measure against premature leak and emergencies, but it also served as a neat security cell. Up top was the ever-present monitor, almost certainly with a real person on the other end, and a series of small and unfamiliar-looking projections that could have been either decontamination or weapons.

The first door closed behind me, but the second did not open right away. Suddenly those projections flooded the chamber with a pale blue force field that had a rather odd effect on me. The sensation must have been similar to that of being suddenly struck deaf or blind or both, yet I could see and hear perfectly well. What I no longer could do was sense or contact the Wardens within my own body. They had cut off communications, somehow, and, in so doing, had reverted me to my original form. I could see and feel it happening, with no powers except my own brain.

The ray cut off quickly, and the outer door opened. I found it very difficult to move, though, as if heavy weights had suddenly been placed all over me. I wasn't quite sure what they were doing, but I guessed that they, not I, were now sending to the Wardens in my body somehow, and they were telling them to produce this sensation. It was quite effective. I could still move and act normally, but any quick or sustained actions would be beyond me. I had walked into the trap, and now they had me good. I had a vague thought that I should have made a run for it back at Gray Basin, no matter what the risks, but it was a little late for that now.

A strong-faced Medusan woman in government black waited for me in the reception lounge, along with a monitor sergeant armed with some sort of small, light sidearm. It was certainly no laser weapon, and I guessed it to be some sort of stun gun, which made perfect sense in this situation. You could shoot hostages as well as the hostage-takers with no fear of permanent injury to either, and you were unlikely to burn accidental holes in the space-station wall.

"I am Sugah Fallon," the woman announced, "director of this installation. You are, I would guess, the one called Tarin Bul, although I expect that that's not your real name, either."

"It will do," I told her wearily. "I see you know a lot more about the Warden organism than even I expected."

She smiled. "Research into the possibilities is never-ending, Bul. You would be amazed at the things we can do these days. Come. It must be days since you ate, so we'll attend to that first." With my every move physically restricted, I had little choice but to follow her. Besides I *was* starved, I had to admit.

The food was good, and it was fresh. "We grow it all ourselves," Fallon told me with some pride. "In fact, we support a staff here of over two thousand permanent party personnel plus half again as many on transient business. It is from here that the entire monitoring system is guided.

All the records are here, and all are centrally coordinated and beamed by satellite to every city on the planet. Our laboratories and technical specialists are drawn from all four Diamonds worlds, and are the best in their fields."

I really *was* impressed. "I'd like to see the whole thing sometime," I said dryly.

"Oh, perhaps you might, but we will show you only a few departments today, I think. You'll be fascinated by what we're doing in those areas, I think."

"Alien psychology?"

She laughed. "No, sorry, that's off limits. You understand we have to be somewhat circumspect with you since we know that you carry some sort of broadcaster inside your head. Until that goes I'm afraid your movements will be rather limited here."

"How do you know about that?" I asked, not bothering to deny it. This wasn't a fishing expedition—they knew a whole hell of a lot.

"We know a bit from some of your compatriots. You may be interested to know that the agent sent to Lilith *did* manage to kill Marek Kreegan, although in a rather oblique way, and that Aeolia Matuze of Charon is also dead, partly thanks to your man there. On Cerberus, though, your man failed, and did a most interesting thing—he joined our side without even making a real attempt at Laroo."

That *was* news, most of it welcome. Two out of four wasn't bad at all, everything considered. Her comment further indicated that none of the other three had revealed that they were, in fact, the same person as myself. I wondered about the turncoat on Cerberus, though—was his conversion sincere, or some sort of ongoing ruse? The fact that he was alive and apparently influential indicated to me that he couldn't be counted out.

"I suppose it's too late for me to defect," I said half-seriously.

"I'm afraid so. Defections under duress are *so* undependable. It really was nothing personal, either, that you failed. You accomplished a tremendous amount that we would have thought impossible, and you've caused a major reassessment of our entire monitoring system. In fact, if you hadn't attacked the Altavar on your way out, you would still be free and a tremendous threat to us. Even so, you could have escaped. You have a weak spot, a sentimental streak, that your compatriots seem to lack. It's what's done you in."

I shrugged. "I owed it to them to see what I could do. Besides, if I couldn't pull it off, I was neutralized anyway, with no hope of ever really doing anything beyond living with the Wild Ones. Call it the testing of a theory—and the theory proved wrong. I simply underestimated the system. Just out of curiosity, though, I'd like to know when you got on to me."

"We knew you were in Gray Basin when we sent somebody to check on the missing monitor at the station," she told me. "However, we really didn't have any idea of who you were until you punched Ching Lu Kor into the computer. Since the monitor you were pretending to be didn't have knowledge of, interest in, or anything to do with that case, it raised a flag here. From that point on, of course, we had you. We were pretty certain it *was* you, since few others would have the combination of nerve and timing to pull off such a thing even that far." She paused, then added, "You should have kept switching identities every hour or so."

I nodded, then added, "I could still have gotten away if I hadn't misjudged how long I'd slept. That was my key mistake and I admit it. One little mistake in a long string of successes, but that's all you get in this business."

"That's why the system always wins. We can make a hundred mistakes, but you can make only one."

"Tell that to those two you said are dead."

The comment didn't faze her. "Their systems were quite different from ours. Technology doesn't even work on Lilith, and it's easily negated by a strong mind on Charon. They will have to develop systems better suited to their own homes as we have evolved this one."

"I'm not very impressed with this one," I told her. "It's a dull, stupefying world of sheep you've created down there, people without drive, ambition, or guts. And for the elite on top, human slaves kept as status pets—like something out of the Dark Ages of man."

She didn't take offense. Her reply, in fact, was indirect and at first I didn't see where she was going. "Tell me one thing that's puzzzled me, Tarin Bul or whatever your name is. Just one thing. I know you've been conditioned so that we can't get any information from you by force, but I *would* like to know the answer to one question."

"Perhaps. What is it?"

"Why?"

"Why what?" I was very confused.

"Are you really as blindly naive as you say you are, or is there a real reason why you continued doggedly on your mission once you were here?"

"I told you I found your system repugnant."

"Do you really? And what are the civilized worlds if not an enormous collection of sheep, bred to be happy, bred to do their specific jobs without complaint, and also without ambition or imagination. They look prettier, that's all—but they don't have to survive the hard climate of Medusa. What you see down there is simply a local adaptation, a reflection of the civilized worlds themselves. And do you know why? Because most people *are* sheep and are perfectly content to be led if they are guaranteed security, a home, job, protection, and a full belly. In the whole history of humankind, whenever people demanded democracy and total independence and got it, they were willing and eager to trade their precious freedom for security—every time. Every time. To the strong-willed, the people who knew what to do and had the guts to do it. The people who prize personal power above all else."

"We don't have cameras in people's bathrooms," I responded lamely.

"Because you don't *need* cameras in the bathroom. You've had centuries of the best biotechnology around to breed out all thoughts of deviant activity, and a barrier not of energy but of tens of thousands of light-years of space to keep out social contamination. The few who slip by, people like you, are sent here. That's why so many of them wind up in charge, and why the system here is a reflection of the civilized worlds. We grew up there, too, Bul, so it's the system we know and understand best. We're the people most fit to rule, not by our own say-so, but the Confederacy's. That's why we got sent here."

I opened my mouth to reply, but nothing came out.

There had to be a flaw in the logic somewhere, but I could find none. However, accepting her thesis didn't make things any more pleasant. "If I admit the point, then all I can say is that the system itself is corrupt, bankrupt, and wrong, whether it's here or in the Confederacy."

"Then you *are* naive. Both Medusa and the Confederacy have given the masses exactly what all the social reformers have clamored for all these years—peace, plenty, economic and social equality, *security.* All other alternatives that are not variations of the plan have resulted in mass privation. You saw nothing wrong with the Confederacy while you were there because you were a part of the power structure, not one of the sheep. You chafed here because we tried to make you a sheep. But if you'd come in as a government official, perhaps a monitor officer, you'd have felt right at home."

"I doubt that now," I told her. "I have lost my faith."

"Then, perhaps, that's why you really did what you did. Think about it. You could have been home free, yet you persisted. You could have turned back at several points, yet you came on against hopeless odds. That isn't the act of a trained Confederacy assassin, even a disillusioned one. You came willingly because you know what I say is true. You cannot accept the system in any form, yet you accept the fact that it is the best one. For one like you, living as a savage in a dead-end existence would eventually drive you crazy, yet you could not embrace the system. You didn't really came after us to rescue anyone, Bul. You came here to surrender, and you did. There is no place in this world for one like you, and you know it."

I didn't want to believe that what she said was true, and I would not admit her conclusions no matter what. I had no desire for suicide, no need to purge myself. She had it only partly right, I realized, and I would not give her the satisfaction of admitting even that to her. I could *not* exist on Medusa; there *was* no place on it for one like me. I came either to destroy the system or die trying.

Or was I just kidding myself?

"What happens to me now?" I asked her.

"Well, first I think we should give you something of an education. I think, perhaps, we should first take you to your friends. It should be interesting to see your reactions to our rather unique art form."

We stood on a walk overlooking a vast expanse of plant growth. In many ways it was reminiscent of a resort complex back in the civilized worlds, with white sandy beaches, small pools of clear water fed by artfully constructed artificial waterfalls, and a safe but beautiful flower-filled planned jungle.

"The First Minister's personal pleasure garden," Fallon told me. "A place to totally relax and get away from it all."

I squinted and looked down. "There are people down there."

She nodded. "The garden is staffed by several dozen Goodtime Girls," she told me. "They are there to fulfill his every wish, indulge his every whim, as well as keep the place in perfect condition."

"At least in the Confederacy we don't turn people into robotized slaves," I noted acidly. That was one clear difference.

"Oh, no, you don't," Fallon admitted. "However, you killed four people in cold blood just to get this far, and who knows how many others over your career? The Confederacy takes the so-called criminals people like you catch and either totally wipes their minds and rebuilds childlike, menial personalities, or they totally remake your psyche into their own image if they can. In extremely violent cases, they simply kill the people. They send only the best to the Warden Diamond, but only because they have done something unusual or creative—or are highly connected politically, which is the most important factor in being sent here, since someday those determining the criminal's fates may be caught doing something naughty and sent down themselves. The difference between the Council and the Congress and the so-called criminals like Talant Ypsir and Aeolia Matuze, two former government members, is only that Ypsir and Matuze made some enemies and so were prosecuted. They're no different from any other Confederacy rulers. The personality goes with the job."

"But—slaves out of some thirteen-year-old boy's wet dreams?"

"They serve a purpose. All are criminals by *our*

standards. Their guilt is not in doubt in the least. The strongest and cleverest we send to the moons of Momrath —*our* Warden Diamond, you might say. The rest, the ones who cannot be trusted to continue at all, we either kill or change. We change them. We make them useful. In many ways we're more humane than the Confederacy. Come."

We walked back into the main station complex and past a door that read PSYCH SECTION, AUTHORIZED PERSONNEL ONLY. I knew what the next stop was. My faithful armed guard, who had not so much uttered a word or changed her dour expression, followed.

"Originally the idea was just to change the mind-set into something useful," Fallon continued, seemingly enjoying the grand tour she was giving me. "We have, after all, a lot more menial jobs than the civilized worlds. But we discovered that when we did a wipe on a Medusan, a funny thing happened. The body, whether male or female, reverted to a primal female form as well." We stopped in front of a door, which opened for us. We entered an observation room for a psych machine. "Recognize the subject in the chair?" she asked me.

I looked hard. Connected as she was to all sorts of tubes, sensors, and the like, it was at first difficult to get a good look at the woman "on the couch," as psychs liked to call it. Still, I recognized the general facial features and form quite well. "Ching," I sighed.

She nodded. "We're almost to the state we call 'at rest' in our process here. You can see that the skin is abnormally soft and pliant, there is no hair or any blemish or unusual feature. The basic form is female but not unusually so."

I nodded, feeling sick again. So this was what this business was all about. They were going to take great pleasure in making me watch, and I knew they could force me whether I wanted to or not.

"It's actually rather unfortunate that all Medusans reach this base female pliancy. It would be useful to have some Goodtime Boys. But don't think that all Goodtime Girls are mere sex objects. I'm afraid many of our top male administrators prefer to use them that way, as does the First Minister, but there can be a number of different types. My two, for example, are like very muscular young boys, very cute. Female, of course, but you'd hardly know.

It's the new art form I was talking about. The artists are our top psychs, who can actually feed information through the psych machines to the Wardens within a body, once all mental resistance is eliminated. Goodtime Girls to order, according to preference. All still smart, able to learn all sorts of things as instructed, and all totally and completely devoted to their owners."

"Who is . . . she being made up for?" I asked, my previous meal turning sour in my stomach as I watched.

"Haval Kunser. He is my counterpart on the planet itself, you might say. He runs the administrative side of the government. Both of us are equals, just below the First Minister, who sets the policies we carry out. Of course, Hav probably won't keep her. He'll give her to somebody as a reward or something. We even export a few to the other Diamond worlds. Ah! I see the psych is ready. Now watch."

"I don't want to see any more," I snapped.

"What you want is of no concern," she responded coolly. "I can freeze you in place and make you, so shut up. Whining doesn't become a Confederacy assassin."

And, of course, she was right. How different, really, was this from the young woman I'd killed on the train platform? The only real difference was that I hadn't *known* that woman. Maybe Fallon *was* right, after a fashion, I told myself. The more I looked at myself coldly and dispassionately, the less I liked what I saw.

The process was fascinating to watch, in a macabre sort of way. The same fluidity I had used to become a bird and a bunch of people was now being used on Ching's body, but not by her. She was effectively dead, I knew, although I couldn't accept that fact emotionally yet. How many deaths *had* I caused in just this operation? Krega had said twenty or thirty minds were destroyed for nothing just getting one "take" in the Merton Process that had put a recording of my mind into Tarin Bul's body.

Ching had always been short, slightly built, like many Medusan women, but now she was—well changing before my eyes. She did not grow in height but weight was redistributed to the hips and bust, and her whole body was becoming sleekly redesigned. The head was modified far less, although her slightly too large ears were trimmed back and her face was softened and slightly rounded at the mouth and chin. When they were done, I could still recognize Ching on the table, but probably nobody else could have.

Hair was added, but only on the head, and it grew with astonishing, almost comical speed—a light reddish brown in color, which surprised me. I had to admit I was fascinated even though revolted. "Hair color can be changed?"

"And eyes. Actually, anything can be almost anything. That is the beauty of it."

In a few more minutes Ching was physically complete. I could see the shadowy form of the psych punching in and controlling and mixing small recording modules. The last step—the mental buildup. Finally she was detached from the machine and all its connectors and left there in what looked like normal sleep. The lights came up, and I saw her stir.

"Now, you remember her," Fallon said, "and you saw it all. Now observe her as she awakens there."

It didn't take long. The woman I'd known as Ching stirred, smiled, then opened her eyes, smiled wider, sat up, stretched, and looked wonderingly around the psych lab as if she'd never seen it before and had no idea what it was, which was probably the case.

Fallon flipped an intercom switch. "Girl?"

She looked up in happy anticipation. "Yes, mistress?"

"What are you called, girl?"

"I am called Cheer, mistress. Please let me serve you."

"Go through the rear door. There you will find a wardrobe. Pick out whatever clothing you feel is proper for you, use whatever cosmetics and jewelry you like, and brush your hair. Then go through the *next* door and stand and wait there until I come."

"As you command, mistress. I live to serve." And, with that, smile still on her face, she jumped down and walked out of the psych chamber and into the other room.

Fallon turned to me. "Well? What do you think?"

"Very impressive, but if this is to soften me up to spill all or something, it won't work. I'm not *that* impressed."

"You should be. She was, I understand, quite a fighter under the psych probes. We got very little information out of her on her life with or without you. However, she couldn't avoid giving us information and impressions on you, since you were the reason for her resistance. Come. Let's go into the other room."

We walked down the corridor to a rather bare office that didn't seem as if it were being used for much of anything, and waited. All I wanted now was to get this over with and get down to my ultimate fate. All this was leading somewhere, I knew. I wanted to know where.

In short order Ching appeared and then smiled and bowed low. "How do I please you, mistress?"

Fallon looked her over. She was a truly tiny and curvaceous beauty now, that was for sure; her moves were sexy and provocative. Her voice had a throaty tone that seemed at once sensuous and childish. Hell, I'd once been a thirteen-year-old boy myself.

She had chosen some small golden earrings, a matching necklace, and a silvery clinging slit dress, and she had expertly and discreetly applied some lip rouge and eye makeup, and painted her newly created long fingernails to match the lips.

Fallon turned to me with a slight grin. "Well? How does she please you?"

"She looks . . . stunning," I managed.

"Want to see her do tricks?"

"No, I—"

"Cheer—get down on all fours and lick the man's feet."

I started to protest, but "Cheer" joyfully and immediately complied. The exercise was disgusting, somehow unclean, and I stood there only because I had to.

"That's enough, girl. Get back up."

"Yes, mistress." In a moment she was back up and looking expectantly at Fallon.

"Now, go out this door. There you will meet a man dressed like me. He will be your master and will tell you what else to do. Now—go."

"At once, mistress." She was gone.

"Definitely a giveaway," Fallon commented, mostly to herself. "The kind who provides company for visiting dignitaries and the like and does dances on tables." She looked over at me. "Useful to others, though. She's frozen, just like that, for just about her whole life. No external aging, no physical changes that aren't internal adjustments to climate or weather conditions, no attitudinal changes. If she got lost or separated down there, she'd plead with people to return her to her master. She'll give pleasure, and only in serving her master will she find pleasure. Now, isn't that better than the mines or death or a permanent job as a janitor someplace?"

"I'm not convinced," I told her. "I don't think I'll ever be convinced."

"Probably not," Fallon agreed cheerfully, "but it's the way of the world. Come—we have one more interim stop."

Again we walked out into the corridor and went down to yet another office, this one obviously used and cluttered with all sorts of stuff. Fallon rooted through a desk drawer and finally came up with what looked like, and was, an artist's sketch pad. She flipped over a few sheets, and I could see that there were, indeed, drawings in pencil and ink on them. Finally she found the one she wanted, held it up, and handed the pad to me. I looked at the image.

"What do you think?" she asked.

The drawing, a very good drawing by a very skilled artist, was of a stunningly beautiful woman, perhaps the most stunning vision of womanhood I'd ever seen. Rendered in colored pencils, the drawing showed a dark-skinned beauty with long mixed blond and light brown hair, two very large and sexy dark green eyes, set in perhaps the most sensual face I could imagine. The body was large, lean, sexy, and sleek, but the sexual organs were very exaggerated. The artist had drawn multiple views, including one of the figure crouching, animal-like, like some perfect primal savage, wearing some sort of spotted animal skin. It was an incredible vision, a bestial sex machine. Even though it was only a cartoon in colored pencils, I felt the intent in the artist's skilled strokes and could only whistle.

Fallon nodded. "I'm glad you approve. This has been the First Minister's special project for some time, although he's been waiting for just the right time to translate it into reality."

"Ypsir drew these? He's quite talented, no pun intended."

"Yes, he is—in quite a number of ways. And, yes, he drew that, in addition to working with our best artist psych for better than half a year to create the mental and emotional sets. The hormonal is obvious. The primal savage, the perfect and uncorrupted natural woman, he calls her. I wish sometimes I'd been built like that."

"You'd have a terrible backache," I noted.

She shrugged. "She's far more than a mere Goodtime Girl. He calls her Ass, by the way. His strong male libido is as firm as your own, I might note. She'll be his constant companion, his mark of perfection, you might say. He owns many great works of art stolen from the finest museums in the Confederacy, but he intends her as his prize possession. Everyone will drool with envy, but she will be totally and absolutely committed to and devoted to him. A tamed wild animal, you might say, totally passive, yet with the wild streak that will make her all the more exotic, and with a bit of a twist. Like a good devoted tamed thing of the wild, she will do whatever is necessary to protect him. Here is a multipurpose, totally sensuous creature that is also a work of art."

I nodded. I understood Ypsir pretty well after this; he was certainly the most slimy soul I could ever remember coming across. "I see," I said.

"I don't think you do," Fallon responded. "I think you don't fully appreciate the First Minister's sense of justice. Not just anyone would do for Ass, of course. He likes to be reminded constantly that he is in total control, so she is to be a symbol of his superior position, his superior system, and his basic invulnerability to the Confederacy and its schemes. Ass, you see, is not for her ample posterior, but rather, short for assassin."

"No!" I screamed, and tried to lunge at her. The monitor behind just put me out with a single brief and localized shot.

I was strapped to the psych machine, feeling pure fear for the first time in my life. Not anxiety, not concern, but real fear. I did not fear death—never had—but this was something else. I always feared going under a psych for a total wipe; there was always the chance that something of me might yet remain, might *know*, and that was the ultimate horror to me.

Fallon and two techs completed the attachments of my

numb body to the "couch," and she stepped back. "This will be most interesting," she said, enjoying my discomfort. "You have not only a unique destiny and vision but Jorgash, the psych back there and our top psych on all Medusa, will be renowned as a brilliant artist and technician for the results."

"Bastards," I tried to snarl, but very little came out.

"You can see the First Minister's point of view," she went on. "Not only will he have his dream, but he will know that his dream was once one of the Confederacy's top assassins, one devoted to killing him at all costs. You will be a constant reminder and reassurance to him of the impotence of the Confederacy here, and, in a real mark of irony, you will be his most devoted slave and bodyguard. He has ordered the entire changing process visually recorded, by the way, so he can if he wishes prove to anyone—including your precious Security—that you were, indeed, their big-shot assassin. Talant Ypsir will be here tomorrow, by the way, on his way to a Four Lords conference called on the satellite of Lilith. I spoke to him just now, and he wants me to set up video recording in a studio room, so he can put you through *all* your paces before he leaves. And you'll get your wish, really. Not only will you reach the Lord of Medusa, you will meet the others as well. He surely won't be able to resist showing you off to them, perhaps even bringing you into the meeting on a gold leash like the pet you'll be."

Damn her! She was enjoying every minute of this!

"Good-bye, Tarin Bul or whatever your name *really* is. I'm sure you realize that all this is going to your control as well, and so do we. Therefore, the first thing to be done is locate that little organic transmitter in you and excise it. But maybe we'll send your control a copy of Talant's recording session. Wouldn't that be true justice?" And, with that, she walked out and the door hissed behind her.

I could not move, literally. All I could do was die a little each second as I heard the master psych turning on various devices.

Suddenly I felt another presence in my head. It was the start of the psych process, of course, but merely the preliminary test of my blocks and defenses, set up by the best psychs in the Confederacy. I could not be broken, nor could they—my mind, however, could be destroyed just like anyone's else's, perhaps with a lot more effort. In fact, my immunity to psychs in general was now the root of my greatest fear. What if they didn't get it all? What if there was one tiny corner that was still me, unable to act or do anything yet *there* . . . ?

I heard a recording cube slip into place in the dark. It begins, I thought, and steeled myself.

But it wasn't the beginning. Instead a thin, reedy man's voice began feeding directly into my brain. "Listen, agent," he said, "I am Jorgash, the psych in this project. Like all other Medusan psychs, I was trained at an institute on Cerberus, the only such institute for psychs in the Diamond. It is run by a master. Neither he nor we have any taste for the Four Lords, for Talant Ypsir, for this incredible alien alliance that might well destroy us all, or for the rest of it. We did not train to be torturers, but healers. Long ago we established our control over many of the top-level bureaucrats of Medusa, since Ypsir insists they all undergo psych loyalty reinforcement to him. We gained control of Laroo on Cerberus in that way, with the help of your comrade there. But that is out for Ypsir himself; he won't come near a psych machine. Since he was once in an accident with Fallon and Kunser and at their mercy—and they saved him—those are the only two others he trusts implicitly. They won't undergo psych, either, for any reason.

"It would be relatively simple to kill Ypsir, but that would do no good. Unless Ypsir, Fallon, and Kunser are all killed—and in a relatively short time—the elimination of one will simply elevate another. Fallon, in particular, is adept enough at the couch to create others outside our influence, as could Kunser. They make it their business to know. They do not trust *any* psych, but neither do they suspect that almost all of us are involved. But before any can move toward an effective takeover of the entire system, we will need all three dead close together. Accomplishing this will be difficult—*may* be impossible. The three are rarely together, with Fallon and Kunser meeting only twice over the past three years and only once with Ypsir present. I say this so as not to encourage you unduly."

I felt some hope rise in spite of myself. Was this just

a trick of a master psych or was this for real? I had no way of knowing.

"I cannot save you," Jorgash continued. "I could not save your friends. But their minds didn't have your strength or your core identity, built up and reinforced by master psychs. If I did not execute this program almost exactly as Ypsir tailored it, if any of the original you remained even on the subconscious level, it would show. It would show physically; you couldn't help it, and that is exactly what a cautious Ypsir will be looking for. What I propose to do I frankly admit I have never done before, and understand only in theory. If my master teacher were here he could do it easily; he created the process long ago, for other purposes and for other times.

"What I propose to do is to push whatever of your core identity I can into a specific recess so remote from consciousness that it might as well not be there. It won't be measurable in any way, and, in addition, all communication between the matrixed area and the rest of your brain will be cut. It is a delicate operation—the difference between obliterating this core and storing it thus is a measurement best expressed as a forty-place decimal point. Even I won't know if I hit it right or not, nor exactly what was saved—if anything. But what I am trying to save is your total hatred and contempt for the Medusan system and particularly for those people who would do this sort of thing to human beings. If your hatred is strong enough, if your thirst for revenge is strong enough, it *might* just survive, although so buried, and cut off that even you will not know it is there. In theory, if this part of you remains, a single stimulus could be used to trigger it, reconnect it to your psyche. The stimulus I will give you and reinforce is a situation in which *all three* principals are in your presence simultaneously. If I succeed, your blind hatred will rush out and you will then kill all three or die in the attempt.

"Now, this is a long shot. One of the three may die, in which case you may find youself in the presence of the other two and not have your rage triggered. Or all three might never be together in your presence, in which case, again, it will not trigger. But all three *have* been together and may well be again, particularly under war conditions.

It may be a week, a month, a year, ten years. We can't know. But we can hope, and that is the chance I must take."

A chance *he* must take!

"What you will be after you kill them, assuming you do and survive, I cannot say. Most likely the action will bring about a total release, after which you will again and always be what Ypsir has made you. You might become a wild beast. But you might have rational potential, depending on how much of you survives. Regardless, so thorough will the physical transformation and freeze be that you will physically, hormonally, and emotionally become what I intend to make of you. That I promise, although it is no comfort. Under a really good psych you might be restored intellectually, although, of course, as a new and different person with no past memories. I can do no less and still convince Ypsir and his test battery. Again, this may all fail—even my teacher succeeded only with fewer than ten percent of his subjects—but I *can* offer you, and your control, the hope that that beautiful creature by Ypsir's side is in fact a ticking bomb that if triggered, could create such a power vacuum on Medusa that those under our control would assume power. I must proceed now, and I am sorry, but I hope this is some comfort. I have already spotted the absolutely ingenious organic transmitter in your brain, so I know your control has this information, too. Now only he and I will know. Time is short and the process long and arduous. Forgive me, Bul, or whatever your name is. Good-bye."

Searing pain inside my head . . . Feel like I'm going to implode . . . Oh, God! I—

TRANSMISSION TERMINATED. TRANSMITTER DESTROYED.

Epilogue

═══════

1

He came out of it slowly, and shivered a bit as he lifted the probes from his head.

"That was most unpleasant," the computer said.

He chuckled. "Well, God bless Dumonia, bless his devious hide. We might get something yet."

"You seem remarkably fit for one who just underwent a wrenching defeat, faced his worst fear, and stared at mental savagery. Better, in fact, than you came out of the last three. I fear for your sanity."

"You needn't," he assured the computer. "It doesn't matter, anyway. I have to argue with you, though, on the failure. We've finally met our aliens, gotten their names, and confirmed some of my wildest and least certain deductions."

"Then you have solved the enigma?"

"I *think* so. Morah's comments still worry me. I still have that gaping feeling, not that I'm wrong, but that I've missed something. That was confirmed by Ypsir's own attitudes just now."

"But we never saw Ypsir."

"We didn't have to. But he's a slick old greasy bastard, an old Confederacy politician, remember, and here he was about to make a recording that he intended to flaunt to the Confederacy. That's confidence. You don't flaunt something like that if you expect to get into a losing war soon. Yet he knows the relative strength and power of the Confederacy military. He is depraved, vicious, and almost inhuman, but he's not stupid. Even with two of the Four

Lords gone and the scheme blown wide open—they knew about us, note—he still expects to win. Why? Unless our fundamental assumption about these aliens, these Altavar, are wrong."

"You think there will be a war, then?"

"I'm almost positive. Actually, it's pretty odd, but the best chance of avoiding war was the man who doesn't fit, Marek Kreegan. I wish now he had lived instead of this slime ball Ypsir."

"I do not understand. He was a traitor."

"He remains the one who doesn't fit. Look at the Four Lords. One is a classic gangster, a master hoodlum, and the other two were former politicians so corrupt they crawled. And then there's Kreegan. What the hell was he really doing there? And how did he come to be accepted as an equal Lord by the other three? Remember, we just learned that the other Lords actually deposed Ypsir's predecessor because they found him too much the reformer and not really corrupt enough to share in the running of their criminal empire. Everybody keeps going back to Kreegan, too—the only man who wasn't shown corrupt, and who they all seemed to depend upon even though they had no reason to. Not only did he not come from the criminal class—he was self-exiled, remember—but Lilith has the least to offer the hidden war. Yet there he is, at the forefront, the leader."

"He did not seem admirable to me."

He chuckled. "Maybe not, but he sure reminded me of me, and vice versa. I look at Kreegan and I see a man on a mission, a very long and complex mission, not a corrupt criminal."

"There is no record he was on a mission."

"Not for us. Well, maybe for us—but not officially. I think Kreegan, somewhere, on some other mission, stumbled on the aliens. I don't know how, and I doubt if we ever will, but he found out what was going on years before we knew. Decades, perhaps, since there's some evidence those aliens have been here all along."

"Would it not have been more effective to report this information?" the computer asked.

"Report it? With what? He probably had no physical evidence. The Confederacy only believed it when they couldn't avoid the truth, and even now they tread softly and slowly through the Warden Diamond rather than hitting hard and fast when the evidence that this is the heart of the conspiracy is right at hand. They would have declared Kreegan insane and destroyed him or sent him to the Diamond anyway. And so he played his role to the hilt, worked hard for twenty years—*twenty years!*—and finally became Lord of Lilith so he could take control of events. I think we killed the greatest Confederacy agent in human history before his plans came out."

"You think he was setting the aliens up for the kill, then?"

"Oh, no. If anything, I think he was totally committed to his covert war against the Confederacy, using those damned robots. He preferred a weakened, shaky, off-balance Confederacy to an actual war. That's just what he was trying to do, in fact. I'd bet on it. And that fits in with Ypsir and Morah. I think these Altavar are stronger than we dreamed. I think Kreegan assessed them as the probable victors in an all-out war, with huge masses of humanity killed. Sure! It fits! He had to choose between a covert war that would dismember the Confederacy or an all-out interstellar conflict he felt we could not win."

"Are you going to include that in your report?"

"No. They wouldn't believe it, anyway, and if they did they wouldn't understand. It makes no difference in any event, except that explanation lays to rest a few of my remaining questions. He's gone, and only Morah, who is good but really hasn't the skills of a Kreegan, is holding things off right now. Somewhere along the line, Morah and Kreegan met, and Morah, the brilliant master criminal, developed a Kreegan-style sense of what had to be done. He came around to Kreegan's point of view. He is doing what he can, but he knows he isn't up to the job. Damn!" He sat deep in thought for a moment. Finally he said, "Call Morah. Tell him to keep that meeting in session, that I'll get back to him as soon as I have consulted with my superiors."

"That is easily done. Has it occurred to you that they all are together in a highly vulnerable and exposed space station around Lilith at this time? Just one well-placed shot . . ."

"And then we would have to deal blind with the Altavar, and I'm not even sure we *can*. Besides, with what will you shoot them down?"

"This picket ship has more than enough armament for such a simple task."

He chuckled. "So man can triumph over computer after all. How the hell do you suppose Altavar have gotten in and out of system, not to mention those robots? Where would be the first place you'd try out and test those robots to see if they really could fool everybody?"

"Oh. You mean that this ship is under their control and in their hands. That is a most unpleasant thought."

"Bet on it. If you need any further confirmation, just remember that I sat down in a com chair up there, punched in Morah's name and planet, and got a connection in seconds. No hunting around, no guesswork. The comm people knew who he was and exactly where he was at that point."

"I could detonate this module, at least protecting our information."

"I certainly hope not. Right now I'm the only one from the Confederacy that Morah or any of the others will trust at all. They know me, in one form or another. I'm right there with them. I'm Cal Tremon, Park Lacoch, and Qwin Zhang, but uncontaminated by Wardens. I'm the only man they're going to believe, because I'm the only one they have expert evaluation of." He laughed. "I don't think you're going to get to kill me anyway, old friend."

"It is not my intention to do so unless the mission is compromised."

"Maybe, maybe you just don't know it. But it's irrelevant." He got up from the chair and moved back to the desk area, pulling down a pen and a pad of paper. He always used pen and paper for his notes rather than a terminal. You never knew who or what was listening in on a terminal, but if you ate your notes you knew exactly where they were and in what form. Old habits were hard to break now.

He was at it for some time, until, finally, slips of paper, cards, and scribbled notations were scattered all over the place. Finally he picked them up, looking them over, put them in an odd pile, smiled, then nodded. He reached up and pulled down the special comcode set.

"Open Security Channel R," he instructed the computer. "Tightbeam, scramble, top security code. Let's let them in on the fun."

It took several minutes to establish communications through the various secret links over such vast distances, but because these signals traveled in the same oblique interdimensional way as the spaceships, communication was virtually instantaneous at this high-priority level. Once the phone was answered at the other end, that is, and all the information was matched to decode what was going in.

"Go ahead, Warden Control," came a very slightly distorted voice from the speaker. "This is Papa speaking."

"Hello, Krega! You sound tired."

"I was sound asleep when your call came in, and I'm taking a couple of pills now to wake up. I assume this is some other special request you want—like the Cerberan thing?"

"No. This is my report. I have the strong feeling that something important is still missing, but I have no way of finding out what it is. Instead, I have assembled everything that I do know and all that my deductions lead to. I think I have enough information to allow us to act and I think time might be of the essence now. There is a war council going on in the Diamond right now, and I think our time's about run out."

"All hell's breaking loose throughout the civilized worlds," Commander Krega told him. "That sleep you got me out of was the first I'd tried in four days. It's chaos! Supply ships routed wrongly, causing factories on a dozen worlds to shut down for lack of raw material, causing dozens more to have to ration food and other vital materials because the ships didn't arrive. Even some naval units have opened fire on one another! The number of those damned robots—and the scale of the operation—is massive, Control! Massive! There must be thousands of them, all at different, usually routine posts along the lines of communications, shipping, you name it. Our Confederacy holds together by total interdependence. You know that."

He nodded and couldn't suppress a slight smile. So Morah had put Kreegan's war into operation unilaterally, as well as mobilizing the vast political and criminal organizations the Four Lords controlled. "How are you holding out?" he asked, almost hoping for a really bad answer.

"We're coping—but barely!" Krega told him. "We were prepared for this kind of thing, considering what we already knew, but the scale is beyond anything we imagined —and it's devilishly clever. The people they took over are very minor, routine links in complex chains, but they're at just the right point to make a minor mistake on a shipping order, or routing order, or even battle order. And so damn minor the mistakes are hell to track down. They didn't go for the admiral, instead they went for a minor clerk who types up or sends out the admiral's orders. We can hold now, but there are already food riots in many places and I doubt if we can stopgap this for long. You're right about the time business. If you can't give us an out, we've got no choice but to take out the whole Warden Diamond—now."

"I'm not sure you can, Papa," he said bluntly. "We missed it on these aliens. Evidence shows they're every bit as strong or even stronger than we are. Hold on to your hat. You aren't gonna believe all this."

"Well, get going, then. But I'm not sure I go along with that military-strength idea. Logic argues against it."

He smiled wanly. Why are aliens evil to a psychotic murderer? That question bothered the Charonese, who didn't answer it. He could.

Evil is when a race casually contemplates genocide against another not because another race is a threat but because it is inconvenient.

He was about to begin his report when something occurred to him. "Papa? Tell me one thing I don't know. Our other prime operative down there, this Dr. Dumonia. Who the hell *is* he, really?"

"Him? Former Chief, Psychiatric Section, Confederacy Criminal Division. Not under that name, of course. He devised a lot of the techniques we still use on agents like you."

"And he retired to *Cerberus?*"

"Why not? He's in a volatile profession, Control. All a psych ever sees are really sick minds. They finally just get fed up and can't do it any more, or they crack themselves. He was a little of both. Well, we couldn't kill him, after his invaluable services, and we couldn't use a psych machine on *him*—he's so good with one of those things he's invulnerable to them. So we gave him a complete cover identity and he picked Cerberus, where he could establish a mild private practice and work when he felt like it on either criminal or normal people with problems. He's pretty sour and disillusioned about the Confederacy, but he's not fond of the Four Lords, either. This alien thing really got to him, so he came out of retirement and set up an organization for us."

"I'm glad he stayed on *our* side."

Krega laughed now. "He'd better. He's got a few little organic devices similar to that transmitter we used with your people inside him, including a couple of a new design that he doesn't know about. If he ever became a threat a remote signal from a flyby would splatter him from Cerberus halfway to the Confederacy."

There was no real answer to that. After a moment of dead air, Control reshuffled his notes. "Ready to report."

"Standing by to record. On my mark . . . Go!"

2

A great deal of the information in this report is deduction, not direct observation. However, I must point out firmly that every deduction made here is not only logical in the context of the Diamond and our known situation, each and every deduction holds true for all four worlds. I feel that the information presented as fact herein is true and correct and borne out by remote personal observation. Let's begin by addressing the broad points of the extraordinarily complex and subtle puzzle that is the Warden Diamond itself.

Point 1: No matter what, it is obvious that the four Diamond worlds are not natural. Each of the four worlds was certainly within the known "life zone" before being transformed into its present state, but mere location in the life zone is not sufficient to guarantee any conditions remotely survivable. This obvious terraforming process of all four would have been easily confirmed had normal scientific thoroughness been applied to the Diamond worlds, but since the appearance of the Warden organism, with its bizarre effects and by-products, such an examination was not possible in the early years and would be subverted by the locals at the present stage of development. Still, from sheer deduction it is obvious that the worlds were extensively terraformed, and I will offer but a few of the abounding examples to prove my point. For example, there is no evidence that any of the planets are the products of natural evolution. While there are different examples of the dominant life form on each world, there are no clear primal orders—each class of plant and animal is unique and in place.

Despite the fact that any naturally evolving life on the four worlds would have to have a common origin—the plants, for example, are too close to one another and to ones familiar to us—the dominant type of animal life on each is without serious competition and without any sign that the other three forms existed except in minor phyla. Thus, the cold-blooded reptile dominates on the warmest planet, the insect is virtually alone on the lushest, as is the water-breather on the world that is mostly sea, and the large mammal on the coldest planet is the dominant form on both land and sea. In other words, despite a certain common origin, four different kinds of life dominate four different worlds with the other forms either eliminated or reduced to minor and static roles. Frankly, the whole thing smells more like some sort of experiment than any chance occurrence—which form is best for what, perhaps. To accept current biology on all four worlds is beyond my credulity range.

Point 2: All of the flora and fauna on all four worlds logically match with our carbon-based life system, and all are integrated in biologically expected and balanced ways, except for the omnipresent Warden organism, which is unique unto itself. Here is a totally different kind of life that has no microbial relatives yet is static enough that its properties and behavior on each world is uniform and predictable. Such an organism might be expected to mutate with lightning speed—after all, this is the common theory applied to the three worlds other than Lilith, that *we* spread the organism and it instantly mutated to meet the differing conditions. So I am asked to accept an organism that mutates instantly and perfectly to other planets, yet shows not the slightest sign of mutation or deviation on any of the four themselves. I find this biologically inconceivable. Therefore, I am forced to the conclusion that the Warden organism is an artificially created form of life superimposed on all four worlds by a common intelligence.

The Warden organism is far too simple a creature to do more than cause an illness or two, yet it is integral to all four worlds and symbiotically matched to them. On Lilith the Warden organism obviously serves as a sort of planetary manager, keeping the ecosystem stable and static; this is what led to the prevailing view of a single source. I submit that evidence exists in ample amounts that the organism is equally the planetary manager of the other three worlds, and that a little hard research will show this to be so. We drew our original conclusions about the Warden organism because of its widely variable effects on humans and human perception and ability. But the Warden organism was not created and does not exist with humans in mind at all—it is there to keep the ecosystems of the four worlds within certain stable tolerances—in effect, to eliminate as many variables as possible.

Charon and Medusa further demonstrate that the Warden organism, while chemically rather simple, has the ability to act collectively and to draw upon a vast amount of complex knowledge. This is less obvious on Cerberus and Lilith, but I can cite examples there as well, and I need only note how fast it is able to regenerate damaged and lost tissue in humans on all four worlds. But how is it able to draw upon and use such knowledge?

At first I was drawn to the hypothesis of a collective intelligence for the organism—that is, each colony represented a cell or collection of cells in communication with other colonies, or cells, making up a single and physically discorporeal entity. I find no evidence to support this supposition, though, and much to support the conclusion that this is not true. People of Charon travel to Medusa, and vice versa, with no ill effects, although, surely, the distance between planets would be more than enough to sever their Wardens from any such planetary consciousness. On Lilith, for example, people can directly perceive the lines of communication between Warden colonies, yet they can perceive nothing of this while on other Warden worlds. Nor, in fact, could I conceive of such organisms even collectively storing and analyzing so many quadrillion-plus data bits just to do some fairly complex regenerations.

But when I thought of the Wardens not in terms of cells but rather in terms of neural transmitters and receivers, the system made far more sense. Consider the nerve endings in your index finger. They serve only one function really—they transmit information to the brain. Burn them and the irritation reaches the brain, and the brain then transmits back through the same network corrective measures to repair the burn. Warden colonies, then, are the neural transmitters and receivers of information, remote sensors to a central brain source. Such a brain must in fact be a tremendously versatile computer of near infinite capacity. This theory then fits in with everything else.

Everything all four worlds say about the Warden organisms on each also belies an external power source, as has been hypothesized as the reason for the so-called "Warden Limit" after which the Wardens run amok and destroy their hosts. The Wardens have been shown to be able to draw whatever they needed from the host for normal operation. On those rare occasions when more was demanded of them than the host could provide, they have shown a limited ability to make energy-to-matter and matter-to-energy conversions, although they are clearly not specifically designed to do so and, when demanded, this causes pain, discomfort, or danger to the host. Such an organism, unless far too much was demanded of it, would hardly self-destruct for the reasons supposed.

However, when you realize that the Warden organism is, in fact, too simple an organism to do *anything* for itself, being merely a transmitter and receiver, what the limit implies is the limit of its ability to transmit and receive information from its computer.

It is equally obvious that four different frequencies, perhaps four entirely separate transmitters, are in operation. This is why a Cerberan, for example, appears "Wardendead" to a Charonese, who sees the Warden network in everything and everyone on his own world. But where are the brain's transmitters and receivers—the Wardens' base station, as it were? I suspect that there is a central computer outside the Diamond zone itself, perhaps on or beyond Momrath, although that gas giant with its rings and thousands of moons would be the most logical and logically placed location. This would transmit, in turn, to central areas, or subcomputers, on each of the four worlds, which would in turn directly govern those worlds. The two-tiered system would be extravagant, but it is one way of explaining why there is a fixed quarter of a light-year distance for travel from all four Diamond worlds, yet Cerberans can travel to Charon, for example, cut from their own planetary net but not from the central computer.

On Medusa there is a "sacred mountain," and, remaining there overnight, one is subjected to nightmarish alien dreams and sensations only to awaken the next day with a far greater control of the Wardens in his own body. This mountain, I am convinced, is over the central processor for Medusa's Wardens. Medusans are already plugged into their Warden network, but here, so close to maximum signal, their Wardens are far more excited than elsewhere. The experience is somewhat akin to, I believe, what communications scientists call "front-end overload," in which a signal too powerful for the electronics of a transceiver will produce a blasting but unintelligible signal. However, the human brain, which has some control over its Wardens, reacts to this overload much as protective circuits would in electronics—it recoils and damps the overload down. The tremendously high level of excitation the overload produced in the Wardens, however, makes the host far more aware of them and their energy flow.

I am convinced that such points exist on the other three planets. I note, for example, that on all four worlds there are curiously similar religions based on planet worship, of a god who resides inside the world and is the source of all power for that world. If we were able to transport the entirety of Lilith's population to its central processing facility, I am convinced that everyone would share the powers now limited to a few. The few who do, in fact, are mostly transportees to the planet who are likely to be more conscious of the energy flow than those born with it in place. I shudder to think, however, of what such an overload would do to a Cerberan—madness, perhaps, or constant, uncontrollable body-changing, or perhaps the merging of minds into a single mass entity.

Point 3: We are faced, then, with an incredibly advanced civilization technologically, far beyond anything we can imagine, a civilization that can terraform four worlds, and stabilize and maintain them with a single clever device (the Wardens), yet does not apparently use them for anything. Although these aliens, who are apparently called the Altavar, maintain a token force near the Medusan processing center, and probably near the others as well, I do not believe they inhabit any of the four worlds in any numbers. One of my counterparts theorized them as air-breathing water mammals, but I find it difficult to see how such a civilization could have developed such a high degree of technological advancement if limited to water. Indeed, the few Altavar that I saw, via my remote, appeared equally at home in air and sea, and probably would also be on land. These, of course, were bred to the conditions in which they had to live and work, and are most certainly not representative of the Altavar masses in form of capabilities. Perhaps they are a token force, not guards or soldiers but on-site mechanics or engineers for the processor who simply relieve their boredom with random attacks on any who venture close.

Now, since they went to all this trouble but do not at this time inhabit the four worlds in the broad understanding of that term, it remains to be determined why the project was undertaken at all. Certainly it has all the earmarks of a carefully established scientific experiment, but if this is so, they made no attempt to remove an inconstant variable when introduced—humans—even though they could have easily done so, and in a manner convincing enough that we wouldn't have bothered with further settlement.

Since they do not use the worlds now, they either had use of them in the past, in which case they couldn't care less about humans being there now, or they have a use for them in the *future*, in which case they would care a great deal about our being there. Since they obviously do not care about present use, but are still very much around and involved in an action against the Confederacy, their use of the Diamond is obviously in the future.

It bothered me from the start that the aliens, who alleged-ly could not take our form or infiltrate directly, could still immediately know all about our civilization and go just to the Four Lords, the only people likely to be on their side against us. Obviously, therefore, they came specifically to the Diamond, or were called there by the small permanent party when we landed on the places, and *then* discovered us. So we have a small cadre of aliens in place when we suddenly show up, which greatly surprised them. One can imagine the problem the small base parties faced. It would take some time to report our arrival and have experts from wherever good little Altavar come from get here. Mean-while, of course, the Warden organism was invading and trying to cope with this new element and threatening to destroy or transform the first exploiter teams. If I were in charge of such a base, I would play for time, and the best way to play for time would be to do what I could—and fast—to hold a representative segment of this new race for study while discouraging further approach and settlement. They did this by simply adding human beings to the pro-gram of their central computer, making the Warden, in effect, an alien disease that had terrible effects not only on "alien" life forms but also on "alien" machinery. It was a clever and resourceful ploy, and we fell for it hook, line, and sinker.

The Altavar, obviously, were pleased with the arrange-ment and pleased that it had so obviously worked, and felt no need to go further at this time. I suspect, though, that they were as surprised as we were at the odd and peculiar by-products the Wardens produced in human beings. I don't think that those by-products, those bizarre powers, were programmed in, for their best interest would be in leaving us trapped but still ourselves, both for study and for control. It's simply possible that the bioelectrical system that powers the human body operates within the same sort of range as the Warden transmitters, or fairly close. This would explain why some people have more powers than others, and some have little or none, on three of the worlds, anyway. You might say both our brains and nervous systems and their quasi-organic machines work on the same wavelengths.

A side thought is somewhat illuminating and a little disturbing. In effect, the Warden invasion of human bodies made the humans on the Diamond creatures of the master computer just as the plants and animals and probably anything and everything else are. Everything from simple biology and biophysics all the way to the content of those human minds was sent to that computer. This information would give them all they needed in the way of human nature, human politics, human beliefs, and human history as well. This is how they learned so much about us without having to pay us a visit.

This means, too, that they knew about our agents as soon as they were "assimilated" into the Warden computer system. Knew about our entire plot, in fact. So either they never made use of this information, which is possible, or they really find the Four Lords and their operation irrelevant to them. They certainly did nothing to tell the Four Lords of our plans, nor to inform them of any of our operations. They did nothing to warn or save Kreegan or Matuze, and they did nothing to warn Laroo or to keep him from coming under our control and influence. In point of fact, they must have known about Laroo's treachery to them, but made no effort even to block the information on their damned robots from coming to us for analysis. They supply the robot masters to Cerberus, yet don't really care if we know about it or even find a way to subvert the process. I find all this enlightening, and disturbing. It implies that they feel they have sufficient defenses to be invulnerable to attack on *their* interests—as opposed to those of the Four Lords and the people of the Diamond—and also that this entire sabotage war and its robot campaign are not something initiated by them but entirely conceived of and run by the Four Lords.

But if they can defend easily, why allow this odd and diabolically clever campaign against us in the first place, one that would almost certainly attract attention to themselves when it was put into operation or prematurely revealed, as happened?

The only possible answer is that several years ago the Altavar decided that they had at this time to make use of the Warden Diamond, and that we would get in the way. They decided, I believe, to attack the Confederacy in an all-out and brutal campaign of genocide but were talked out of it, or at least convinced to defer it, by Marek Kreegan. The evidence for this is all over my alter-ego experiences and can be examined at leisure, but that evidence is inescapable. Kreegan, then, is a rather odd sort of hero. Fearing racial extermination and wholesale destruction of planetary populations in a defensive war against a foe technologically superior to us and unknown to us in the ways that count—including the location of their worlds and fleet—he sold them on a different sort of campaign, one that would strike at the very heart of the political and economic union of the worlds of the Confederacy, causing us to turn inward, to be unable to retain our unity, which is our only strength. It would cost countless lives, of course, and push much of humanity back into harsh barbarism, but we would survive. The other Lords bought the plan for revenge, and because it held out the promise of escape, to leave the Warden Diamond and be the ones to pick up the shattered pieces of the Confederacy. The Altavar bought it simply because it accomplished the same purpose as all-out war but much more cheaply. It is also clear that they didn't have much faith in the plan's success, but were willing to give the Four Lords just enough time and material support to try it just in case.

Point 4: The aliens have decided we must be taken out, yet they have perfect confidence that they can lick us in any such war. Why, then, are we a threat to them at all? We don't know where to hit them back, nor do we know enough about them to pose anything like the threat to their civilization that they are to ours. Therefore, we *can* interfere in some way that will cause them real trouble. As of now, the only point at which our two civilizations intersect is the Diamond. Obviously, they fear we can destroy it, or badly louse it up, and this must be of central importance to them. Saving the Diamond is their one priority here, the reason they were willing to buy Kreegan's plot at all. So what *is* the Warden Diamond to them that they want it so badly? To go to these lengths it must be something of great racial importance to them, a matter of life and death.

The Altavar can breathe the same air we do. They are almost certainly made up of carbon chains in a way that will be unusual, but still very understandable to our biologists. Therefore, it's fairly easy to find their same racial least common denominators—they must be the same as ours. These three LCDs are food, shelter, and reproduction.

I think we can dismiss food out of hand. The amount of protein and other food products that these four worlds could produce is insignificant in the light of an interstellar civilization's needs. Besides, if they can work energy-to-matter conversions, they'll never starve.

Shelter is an obvious possibility. These four worlds were deliberately terraformed and stabilized, so they obviously were intended to be settled. But a population that could be settled on four normal-sized planets is pretty small and hardly worth interstellar war to protect. Considering the number of terraformable planets humanity has found just in its galactic quadrant, total war over the colonization rights to four worlds we couldn't use anyway because of the Warden organism just doesn't make any sort of logical sense.

That leaves reproduction. Defense of their young would make the behavior and attitudes they've exhibited so far totally comprehensible. Assuming their total alienness— evidence indicates that their thinking would be very strange to us, as you might expect—we might extend that to their biology as well. There is no reason to believe that their reproductive method is anything like our own. If we accept the Diamond as a breeding center, though, we must assume they reproduce very seldom or very, very slowly. If so, they are almost certainly extremely long-lived, and, by inference, this would indicate that the number of their eggs, or whatever, is enormous to require four worlds. The Warden organism, then, might be a protective device, keeping conditions for the eggs optimal while also defending them against basic threats. Its defensive capabilities may be very great, and the eggs must be deep inside the planets themselves. I suspect that the fact that there is geothermal activity only on the frigid world of Medusa is evidence that only there is some sort of temperature regulation necessary. They need it warm.

Point 5: Assuming this reproductive function, a number of very interesting possibilities arise. While protecting their young is the *only* solution that logic admits, then the Diamond worlds are there not only as needed protection for the eggs but also to serve as carefully controlled biomes for the young to settle. It's a fascinating concept—colonizing worlds by first terraforming them, then planting the eggs which, when they hatch, will become the perfectly adapted indigenous population of those worlds, complete with the Warden computer links to teach them all they need to know. I admit, however, to be missing a key element here, since all this implies that space travel and terraforming and computers are essential to their reproduction. It is patently absurd to think of such a race, since how did it get born or evolve in the first place?

Of course, if we just accept the idea that their civilization is far older than ours, this problem partly resolves itself. After all, human beings now reproduce in technologically perfect genetic engineering laboratories throughout the civilized worlds. A race just coming upon the civilized worlds and ignorant of our history and of observing the "natural" way on a frontier world or the Diamond might well have the same puzzle the Altavar present to me here. They would wonder how we ever reproduced before we had the technology the bioengineering labs implies. Much the same must be at work here. This is not how they evolved or how nature intended them to breed, but it is the way they choose to do it now—because, for them, it's better, easier, more efficient, or whatever. Take your choice.

Summary: The aliens created the Diamond worlds as incubators and new homes for their young. They are slow-breeding and long-lived, and thus this must represent a whole new generation for a large mass of Altavar. They can not retreat or back down without abandoning their young, and while I doubt that the Diamond is the *only* breeding ground for them, it is of sufficiently large size and scope that anything interfering with the hatching and development of the young would be tantamount to genocide in their minds.

When humans showed up, the aliens used their mechanism—the Warden organism—and their planetary computers to understand, evaluate, and assess our entire civilization. As long as the hatching, or whatever it is, was sufficiently far off, they had plenty of time in which to do so. But we obliged them by sending our greatest criminal minds and political and social deviants to the Diamond, and their attitudes shaped the human societies that grew on all four worlds. As a result, their picture of us is rather negatively slanted, to say the least. The hatch time approached—although it may still be a decade or even longer away—and they had to decide what to do. Whether for science, or study, or just out of scientific mercy, they contacted the Four Lords with a view to saving the Diamond population. But it was then also communicated to the Lords that the rest of humanity was simply too great a threat and would have to be wiped out.

Kreegan, upon becoming Lord of Lilith, came up with and proposed his own scheme to the Altavar, who were willing to let him try it but neither expected it to work nor concerned themselves with the fates of the Four Lords. But because the Four Lords made a mistake, the Altavar now feel backed against a wall. To their minds, delaying much longer will risk genocide of *their* young, and if it's them or us, they'll naturally choose us. They know our military strengths and weaknesses, our weaponry, our military mind, and everything else an enemy dreams of knowing. Apparently none of that worries them. They are confident that they can crush us, and I believe they will attempt to do so by preemptive strike, after the Four Lords campaign has wreaked as much damage and disruption as it can. I think we are no more than weeks, and perhaps only days, away from a total war that may result in the near elimination of human—or perhaps both—civilizations.

Conclusions and Recommendations: I think they not only can beat us, but I suspect they have fought at least one such war before. They are too supremely confident. However, we as a race would survive. We are too numerous and located on too many worlds over too much space to be wiped out totally. Pushed back into barbarism, the collapse of interstellar civilization and the death of at least a third of humanity would be the least I would expect in such a conflict, but we would survive. Our only recourse would be that we could, obviously, destroy the Diamond with a concerted, possibly suicidal all-out revenge attack

—the thing they fear most, and so do I. Such an attack would enrage them and rob them of their next generation; it would be our last blow, but much of their force would remain intact.

I may be totally wrong, and they may think in so alien a manner that they will not react in a way I can predict, but I feel I must point out how *we* would react under such circumstances and urge that we act as if they're more like us emotionally than unlike us. If the situation were reversed: if humans beat the hell out of the Altavar but, in the process, the Altavar managed to destroy every human being's ability to create children by any means, thereby ending the race in slow agony, *we* would then seek out Altavar wherever they were, in their ships, on their worlds, and once they were beaten and defenseless, we would then systematically wipe them out to the last one. In other words, destroying the Diamond might well result in total human genocide.

Obviously I'm telling you that we can not win in this situation. If you refuse to face that fact, refuse to accept my report and its conclusions, then I believe both races could die. The impossible, the unthinkable, *will* happen. When man first went into space and colonized other worlds, a great pressure was lifted from the collective psyche. The human race would not be totally destroyed by itself in war, at least not easily. And when, finally, we grew so large and so expansive and merged into the single system that the Confederacy represents, we thought we had put any possibility of racial destruction behind us. People could die, even whole suns could explode and take their worlds and populations with them, but humanity would survive.

If this chain is now started, it will be impossible to stop. We have finally come face to face with the horror once again, and we have only ugly choices.

The Four Lords are now meeting in Council and are waiting for my call. The only hope we have is to do everything right, and, therefore, it is essential that you follow all of my recommendations immediately and without fail.

(1) No matter how this sabotage campaign is going, it is essential that only reports of complete disarray and disaster

reach this picket ship, which is totally infiltrated with the robots. At all times from this point the Four Lords and the Altavar must be convinced that Kreegan's war is *winning,* that his plan is working perfectly. If the Altavar receive the slightest hint that it is not, they will probably launch a massive preemptive strike on us.

(2) Negotiations must be opened immediately. I will be the go-between, because, having three surviving alter egos down there, I will be one they will trust. However, we must be linked directly to the Confederacy Inner Council, who must all be on call to appear on visual transmission. It must be clear that they are dealing with someone—me— who speaks for the Council and that I have the force sufficient to make my agreements binding on the Confederacy.

(3) As much of the fleet as can be depended upon not to be needed for emergency actions against the current war campaign must be rushed to the Diamond on full alert. Only with the threat of immediate destruction of the Diamond will we have any leverage at all. Put your best military minds in that fleet and get it here—fast, and on full war alert. You can expect ship-to-ship attack if negotiations fail or if they decide to test us.

(4) No matter what you think of the Four Lords and their organizations, they are not stupid and they will not be lulled into any false agreements. They know that their own worlds are on the line, which will keep them honest, but as agents of the Altavar they also know our real position, which isn't great. They have also, obviously, been promised safe evacuation in the event of an attack by us, so they are only concerned about their populations, not their own hides. I must warn the Council that the demands the Altavar will make will be stiff and severe. We must negotiate and be prepared to give up a great deal, perhaps much that we hold dear. But we must find a solution that will result in the Altavar feeling safe and secure—and we must mean it and guarantee it with our actions, not just words. They know us too well to accept our promises or a treaty.

This is Warden Control, awaiting your decision and instructions.

3

"Well? What do you think?"

"It is the only logical solution given the data," the computer replied. "You should have been a computer."

"High praise. Well, they got it now. How do you think they'll take it?"

"They will refuse to accept your conclusions, of course, but they will play along with you and the Four Lords for now. Did you expect anything else?"

He shrugged. "I don't know. I doubt it. Given what you know, can you compute the current probabilities of all-out war?"

"Too many variables. But I would say you have a ten-percent chance of pulling something out of this."

He sighed. "Ten percent. I guess that'll have to do. Wake me when they call back." He paused a moment. "Well, it doesn't look like *you* will be ordered to kill me, anyway."

The computer did not reply.

It took them almost five hours to reach some kind of consensus, which, considering the complexity of the Confederacy and its bureaucracy, was almost miraculous time.

"We can arrange for a complete visual hookup," Krega told him, "but we'll have to do an open broadcast. I suppose that doesn't matter, since they *should* be able to see and hear your communication with Base."

He nodded. "They will insist on a remote location. I will try and stall to give the fleet as much time to position itself as I can, but I must have one secure line and this is the only one I'm reasonably sure about. The computer tells me that I can transmit back to this module from anywhere within the Warden system and that it will do the rest. The Council stays on the public and visual band; you stay on this one, and if I have to get word to the Council I will tell you and you will personally tell the Council."

"Agreed. Uh—if you go down there you're going to be stuck along with the rest, you know."

"I'm not worried by the prospect. However, I don't believe that it's necessarily true, either. I think they now have their Warden organism under pretty complete control. No matter, though. This is a time of ugly choices, and given the choice of being blown to hell in a war or having to live on a Diamond world, my choice is pretty well made. Commander, no matter what, I'm convinced that, after this, all that we know will never be the same again."

He switched off, then turned to the other side. "Get me Morah on the Lilith satellite."

It took only a couple of minutes to fetch the dark, eerie Chief of Security. "We had about given you up," Morah told him.

"These things take time. Your moves against the Confederacy are having major disastrous effects and they're worried, but they want to talk." Briefly he outlined his proposal for himself as negotiator with the Council following by direct link, site to be selected.

Morah thought the proposition over. "This is not simply a trick to bring up the fleet?"

"We don't have to. A major task force has been lying only a couple of days off the Diamond for weeks, waiting for any hard evidence from me so they could act. They're going to come in reasonably close no matter what, but I think the Council will keep its word as long as we keep talking. It seems to me that delay now is in the best interests of the Altavar as well, since we are already in position while they can use the extra time to position their own forces."

Morah seemed to consider the idea, then nodded absently. "All right, then. But any move by the task force to attack positions on the Diamond will terminate everything right then and there. You understand?"

"I understand. You name the place and time."

"Boojum is the seventh moon of Momrath. We have an all-purpose communications center there, with sufficient room and comfortable facilities. Can you reach it by 1600 standard time tomorrow?"

He nodded. "I'll be there, along with the comm codes needed to plug us all in. However, I want certain people present from the Diamond as well."

"Oh? Who?"

"First, I want a senior Altavar empowered to deal for its

people. The Council insists on it. Second, I'm not clear on the political situation on the Diamond itself right now. Who will represent Charon?"

"I will, as temporary, or acting Lord," Morah replied. "Kobe will represent Lilith, and the two surviving Lords the other two."

"I'll have to have a psych named Dumonia from Cerberus there."

"Indeed? Why? Who is he?"

"One of my wild cards. Dumonia is Lord of Cerberus but neither you nor Laroo realize it. Laroo is nothing more than an unnecessary puppet at this point." He enjoyed the total sense of shock and surprise Morah conveyed. *Score one,* he thought with satisfaction. Now Morah could not be so absolutely certain of anything. "I also would like, if possible, Park Lacoch from Charon, Cal Tremon from Lilith, and Qwin Zhang from Cerberus present."

Morah found that amusing. "Indeed? And which side do they represent?"

"Good faith," he responded. "You were going to bring Lacoch anyway, so why not have them all? Who better to evaluate my own sincerity and behavior?"

"Done, then."

"I notice you aren't surprised that I want nobody from Medusa except Ypsir."

Morah cleared his throat and seemed a bit embarrassed. "We are all well aware of what happened on Medusa. I'm afraid Ypsir hasn't stopped crowing about it yet. A most brilliant and ruthless but totally unpleasant man, the sort of man that turned us against the Confederacy in the old days." He frowned thoughtfully. "Um—it will be unavoidable that you and Ypsir and his—pet—will meet. I can assume no personal vendetta as long as we are negotiating?"

"Until we are finished with this business, yes. The stakes here are much too high to allow myself the luxury of personal revenge right now."

Morah looked back into the screen with those piercing, inhuman eyes. "I have the strange feeling that you are not telling me all."

He grinned. "Tell me, if you don't mind—where did you pick up those interesting eyes."

Morah paused for a moment, then said softly, "I went to the Mount once too often."

It was arranged that he would go by picket boat to Momrath. The boat would be completely automated except for him, and would return automatically without him and be totally sterilized. Later, he was assured, if he could leave the Diamond at all, he would be picked up.

Curiously, he found himself reluctant to leave what, only the day before, he had regarded as his tomb.

"We will be in continuous touch," the computer assured him.

He nodded absently, checking again his small travel kit.

"Um, if you don't mind, would you answer one question for me?" the computer asked. "I have been wondering about it."

"Go ahead. I thought you knew everything."

"How did you know that a battle fleet lay only two days off the Diamond? *I* knew, of course, but that information was deliberately kept from you. Did you deduce it."

"Oh, no," he responded breezily, "I hadn't a clue. I was bluffing."

"Oh."

And with that, he left the cabin with no trouble and traveled down many decks in the picket ship to the patrolboat bay. The boat was no luxury yacht, but it was extremely fast and had the ability to "skip" in and out of real space in short bursts of only a fraction of a second. Unlike the lazy freighters that took many days to traverse the distance, he would make his assigned rendezvous in just twenty-five hours.

He felt a curious sense of detachment from the proceedings after this point. The final phase, and, in a sense, the final scam, was on its way, working itself out to conclusion. One misstep and not only he but everything and everyone might go up, and he knew it. The fact that he'd failed on Medusa and had succeeded only by flukes on Lilith and Charon bothered him a bit. This whole mission had shaken his self-confidence a bit, although, he had to admit, he had never tackled so ambitious a project before. Indeed, no human being in living memory had ever shouldered such responsibility.

Something still bothered him about his deductions and conclusions, and he knew what it was. His solution of the maze in the Diamond was too pat, his aliens assumed to be too predictably like humans in their thinking. It was all too damned pat. Life was never pat.

He slept on the problem, and awoke nine hours later with a vague idea of what was wrong. It was the animals and plants, he realized. Familiar forms, bisexual and asexual. Since they obviously weren't created for human viewing, they must reflect the general lines of thinking of the Altavar, who would draw on their own background and experience. No matter how bizarre the Altavar looked, how different their evolutionary roots from those of man, they must have evolved in roughly similar environments. They were highly consistent in their makeups of the worlds, yet here was a basic inconsistency. His view of them did not conform to the kinds of worlds they built.

The screens picked up the vistas he passed, and recorded them for later viewing. He amused himself by punching up all four Diamond worlds, now in anything but a diamond configuration, and blowing up the images as best he could. None of them really showed much in the way of surface features at this distance, but he found himself oddly transported to each as he looked at its disk. So odd, so unusual, so exotic . . . So deadly.

If they're really homes for Altavar young, why the hell did they tolerate human populations in the millions on them?

Questions with no easy or clear answers like that one disturbed him. For most of his life, the Confederacy had been his rock, and he had believed in it. He, himself, had caught some of the very people down there on those four worlds, sending them to what he believed to be a hellish prison. He still wasn't very impressed with the Four Lords and their minions or with the systems they had developed; but, he knew, he felt no real difference when looking at the Diamond or at the Confederacy. He felt like a confirmed atheist in the midst of a vast and grandiose cathedral, able to appreciate the skill and art that went into its construction but feeling pretty sure it wasn't worth the effort.

In many ways he identified almost completely with Marek Kreegan, who must have had similar thoughts upon coming to the Diamond, and, most likely, even before. That priestly role was more than mere disguise, it was a subtle and humorous tweaking of the man's nose at Man's odd and distorted attempt at building institutions that served him. How many thousands, or tens of thousands, of years had Mankind been trying to build the right institutions? How many had slaved in faith at that building, and how many, even now, deluded themselves as they always had that, *this time,* they'd gotten it right?

Once upon a time sixty percent of the people didn't believe in their system. Only twelve percent thought there might be something better than the system they hated, something worth bothering to fight about. Loss of faith equaled loss of hope, then, in that large a segment of the population, and it didn't, in historical retrospect, seem out of line. People tended to extremes, and hope was a very mild extreme when faith became impossible, while despair was easy and all the way down the other end of the scale.

He pounded his fist on the console hard enough to hurt his hand. "Tarin Bul" had given in to despair, yet had died with slight hope. Qwin Zhang had risked everything on hope, and won. Park Lacoch had refused to be seduced by a good and happy life when he knew that others he did not even know depended on his actions. Cal Tremon had been used and abused by practically everyone for their own purposes, yet he had never surrendered.

Four people, four distinct individuals, who were, in every sense of the word, sides of himself. He hoped, he *thought,* he had learned something valuable, something the Confederacy had never meant to teach him. Now it was his turn.

The great orb that was Momrath filled the screens early on in the trip, and he watched it grow closer with eerie fascination. Ringed gas giants were always the most beautiful of places, and, in more than once sense, the most forbidding as well. At last two moons of the great planet were large or larger than any of the Diamond worlds, yet he went not to them but to small and frozen Boojum. Well, Momrath had been the one place he hadn't visited, in a sense, as yet, and it seemed appropriate that it be *his* world.

He settled back to await the landing, still deep in reflection.

Task Force Delta was composed of four "war stations," each surrounded and protected by a formidable battle group. Clustered around the barbell-shaped station that was the nerve center and computer control for its awesome firepower were hundreds of "modules," each complete in and of itself. Most were unmanned; war these days was very much a remote-controlled affair, with battle group leaders merely choosing from a list of tactics, giving their battle group computers the objectives, and letting everything else run itself. Not a single one of the modules was intended for defense; the battle group provided that. Yet among all the clusters, there were weapons that could take out selected cities on remote worlds, could level a mountain range or even disintegrate all carbon-based life forms within a proscribed radius while doing no other damage. Other modules could ignite atmospheres with sufficient combustible gasses in them, while still others could literally split planets in two.

One such station could wipe out an entire solar system, leaving nothing but debris, gasses, and assorted space junk to orbit the sun, or could, in fact, even explode that sun. There were only six such stations in operation throughout the vast Confederacy, and four of them were concentrated here in the task force, the largest ever assembled.

The protective battle group was composed of fifty defensive ships, called cruisers after ancient seagoing vessels none could remember at this stage, built along the same lines as the war stations. But their modules consisted of hundreds of scouts, probes, and fighters, again almost all needing no human hand or brain, capable of taking continuous streams of orders from their base cruisers or, in the event the cruiser was destroyed, from any cruiser or the war station itself. Nothing else was needed; the combined firepower and mobility of a cruiser was equal to an entire planetary attack force, complete with human and robot troops that could land on and occupy a cleared stretch of land and hold it until relieved provided the cruiser's modules continued their air and space cover. As well, the human marines inside their battle machines could be so effective that a squad might be able to take and destroy a medium-sized city, even if the city were defended with laser weapons, immune to the lethal energy rain their supporting fighters could unleash.

In theory the task force was as close to invulnerable as could be imagined, combined with the punch of an irresistible force. The only trouble was, its powers, weapons, programming, and tactics had never been tested under real battle conditions. For several centuries the Confederacy military had been amost exclusively devoted to policing itself.

A forward cruiser, still more than a light-year off the Diamond, launched four probe modules, one to each of the four Warden worlds. They sped off, skipping in and out of subspacial modes, in a near-random approach to the system, their next direction determined only after they came out for that brief moment and saw where they were. With no humans or other living organisms aboard to worry about, they made the trip in less than an hour.

Stern-faced men and women born and bred to the art of war sat in the center of the battle group, watching the four probes track on a great battle screen showing the entire probable sector of engagement, while subsidiary screens scrolled data slow enough for the human observers to see, although the data was far behind the reality being fed back to the master battle computer.

In precision drill, the four small steely blue-black modules arrived off each of their four target worlds simultaneously and quickly closed on their targets. Their armament consisted entirely of defensive screens and scramblers for potential adversaries; they were the forerunners, the testers of defenses and the data-bearers to the command and control center far off but closing.

"Measuring abnormal large energy flow between the four worlds," a comtech reported to the battle room. "Our probes also report scanning on an unusual band, origin each of the four targets."

"Very well," the admiral responded. "Close to minimum safety zone on each world. All photo recorders on. Commence evasive action on scans."

As soon as the order was given it was done. The admiral

wanted to know how well his hardware could be tracked after it was first discovered.

It could track very well indeed, it seemed, and the odd sensors kept pace effortlessly with the variations in course and speed; even shields and jamming techniques had no effect.

They approached within twelve hundred kilometers of the respective planetary surfaces, not too far above the orbits of the space stations of the Four Lords.

All data ceased on all boards simultaneously. Startled comtechs and observers leaped to their consoles and ran every kind of data check they could, to no avail. There seemed no question that, on all four worlds simultaneously, something had fired and totally destroyed the probes.

They ran back the last few seconds frame by frame, looking for what happened, but could see nothing and had to call upon the computers for help. Ultimately the computers could simulate what could not be seen. It had been an electrical beam, a jagged pencil line of force looking more like natural lightning than something fired from any kind of known weapon, reaching up and out from an unknown point below the upper atmospheric layers of each world and striking each probe, destroying it instantly. Only a single burst had been used in each case, the burst lasting mere milliseconds yet packing enough punch to destroy the heavily armored probes completely.

Commander, Special Task Force, sighed and shook his head. "Well, we know that we'll have a fight when we go in," he said with professional objectivity.

Five seconds after the probes were destroyed, all Confederacy satellites around the Warden Diamond were taken out, leaving only one channel of outside communication unjammed.

4

He had to admit that while the rock wasn't much it offered a really fine view. The great multicolored orb of Momrath filled the sky of Boojum, and the small probe boat settled into a cradle dock on the bumpy and drab surface. The setting made it seem as if the moon and ship were about to be swallowed by a sea of yellows, blues, and magentas.

He donned a spacesuit and depressurized the cabin, waiting for the lights to tell him he could open the hatch. The cradle dock was built for the blocky, rectangular freighters rather than for the small passenger craft he had used, so there was really no way to mate boat to airlock. He noted two of the Warden shuttlecraft parked in the rear of the bay, but was surprised not to see any ship of unfamiliar design. Either the Altavar hadn't arrived as yet, or it utilized a different and less obvious mode of transportation.

As soon as he was at the hangar-level airlock, a small tug emerged from a recess in the far wall and eased up to his ship, grabbing hold with a dual tractor beam and then easing it into an out-of-the-way parking space. He hoped he'd remembered to tell them that the thing would automatically take back off on command of the picket ship in an hour or two, then shrugged off the thought. What good was taking over an enemy ship like the picket ship if your spies were incompetents? He shouldn't be expected to do *everything*.

The light turned green and he opened the hatch, stepped inside the chamber, closed and hit reseal behind him, and waited for the light on the inner door to open. He was reminded a bit of that dual airlock in Ypsir's space palace. Sure enough, there was even a camera here, and some of those odd projections.

He barely had time to reflect on the implications when he was bathed in an energy field from those same projections, just as his counterpart had been back on Medusa. It was over quickly and caused him no unpleasantness; in fact, he felt no sensation out of the ordinary at all. He couldn't help wondering what all that was about, then. An automatic precaution? If it were some kind of decontamination, it would have been better served if they'd waited until he took off the spacesuit.

The inner lock's guide light turned green, and he opened it and walked into a fairly large locker room. He quickly removed his suit, then opened his small travel bag and donned rubber-soled boots, work pants, and a casual shirt. He checked the small transceiver's power, then left it in the case along with a change of clothes and his toiletries,

then picked up the bag and walked out of the locker room
and down a small utilitarian hall to an elevator. He felt a
bit light but not uncomfortably so; they were using a
gravity field inside the place.

The elevator was of the sealed type, so he had only the
indicator lights to show how far he was being taken. Not
too far, as it turned out. While there appeared to be at
least eight levels to the place, he went down only to the
third one before a door rolled back.

Yatek Morah, wearing a shining black outfit complete
with a rather effective crimson-lined cape, stood there to
greet him.

He had been used to thinking of Morah as a large man,
but, he found, they were both about the same size. The
eyes hadn't changed much, though, and were still hard to
look at.

He stepped out of the elevator and did not offer his hand.
Instead he stood there, looking at Morah. "So."

"Welcome to Boojum, sir," Morah responded, sounding
fairly friendly. "Odd name, isn't it? The outer planets and
moons were named for some follow-up scout's favorite
fairy stories, I think. Rather obscure." He paused a moment. "Speaking of obscure—just what do we call you?"

He shrugged. "Call me Mr. Carroll. That'll do, and it's
certainly appropriate both to history and to our current
situation."

"Good enough," the Security Chief responded, apparently not aware of the irony in name or tone. "Follow me and
I'll give you the grand tour. It's not much, I'm afraid—this
is a mining colony, after all, not a luxury spa. Oh, you
might be relieved to know that that shower bath we gave
you has an interesting effect. The Warden organisms, which
are thicker than dirt on this rockpile, will totally ignore you.
That should relieve your mind."

He couldn't help smiling at that. "As easy as that. Well,
I'll be damned." He followed the man in black down the
corridor.

Morah first showed him his room, a small cubicle less
than a third the size of his module on the picket ship, but
it would do. He thought about retaining his bag, then decided not to and tossed it on the bed. "Better let your people know not to touch that bag without me around," he

warned Morah. "A few things in there can be very unpleasant if you don't know exactly how to talk to them."

"Although this is nominally Ypsir's territory, I am in
complete command here," the security chief assured him.
"You are currently under what might best be expressed as
diplomatic immunity. None of your things, or your person,
will be touched; whoever touches them will answer to me."

He accepted that, and they proceeded. "The Lords are
staying along here, in rooms similar to yours," Morah told
him. "The others are sharing a dorm normally used by
mine security personnel. I'm afraid there's been a lot of
grumbling as to the accommodations, but only Ypsir has a
livable place here."

"It'll do," he assured the other man. "I've been in worse."

A small central area between the single rooms and the
dorm had been set up with a large conference table and
comfortable chairs. "This is our meeting hall," Morah told
him, "and, I'm afraid, also our dining hall, although the
food comes from Ypsir's personal kitchen and is quite
good."

The three people assembled in the room when they entered all turned to look at the newcomers. One of them
looked so shocked he appeared to be having a heart attack.
"You!" he gasped.

He smiled. "Hello, Zhang. I see nobody warned you."
He turned to the other two. "Doctor, I am most happy to
see you here, and I'd like to thank you for all your help."
Dumonia bowed and shrugged. The third man he didn't
recognize at all. He was a tall, thin, white-haired man of
indeterminate age. About the only thing that could be told
about him was that he was certainly a Medusan. "And you
are?"

"Haval Kunser, Chief Administrator of Medusa," the
man responded smoothly, putting out his hand.

He took it and shook it warmly, replying, "It's *very*
good to meet you. I know you only by reputation."

He turned back to Zhang, who looked only slightly less
stricken. "Are you going to drop dead or shoot me or relax and have a drink?" he asked his Cerberan counterpart.

"Well, what do you expect?" Qwin Zhang responded tart-
ly. "I'm still not over the other two yet."

His eyebrows went up. "They're here, then?"

"Everyone is here," Morah told him. "We can proceed after dinner if you like."

"The Altavar?"

"Two levels down. Not only do they prefer it down there, but I'm afraid they stink like a three-day-old corpse. Our body odor is similarly offensive to them, so you can understand the separation considering the cramped quarters. I'll certainly take you down and introduce you if you want to verify that they're here, but I think otherwise we should let them sit in by remote, for, ah, mutual comfort. Don't answer until you've smelled them."

He chuckled. "All right, I have no objection to the remote, although I *am* going to have to verify their physical presence. I'm afraid that some in the Council simply don't believe in them."

"Understandable. Through that door there, and we'll meet the others." They walked into a large room that looked more like a barracks than anything else, in which several people were sitting and talking or reading or writing. All heads turned as they entered, followed by Zhang and Dumonia, and he saw immediately that Zhang's reaction was not going to be unique. Tremon, for one, was so startled he stood up and banged his head on an upper bunk.

"Tremon and Lacoch you know," Morah said pleasantly, "and the others are either associates of theirs or aides of the Four Lords like Kunser. Communications, coordination, and a subsidiary meeting room with visual facilities have been set up on the level below us. It's all ready, Mr. Carroll."

Tremon and Lacoch both shook their heads at that. "Mr. *Who?*" Lacoch muttered, but did not press the matter. He looked over at two others near them and smiled and bowed slightly. "Darva and Dylan. Charmed." The two women stared back at him in puzzlement. He looked over at Tremon. "No Ti?"

Tremon looked a little stunned. "So it *did* work!"

"Better than you could ever know," he responded softly, then turned to Morah. "I'll give your techs the codes to open everything to the Council so they can make the proper checks and set up a time. I'm not sure how many on the Council we managed to get together but it'll be a working majority. Then I'd like to meet privately with my three former operatives, if that's possible, and separately with you, Doctor. Then I'll go down with you to meet the Altavar, Morah, and we can get started."

Morah looked a little uncomfortable. "Um, I believe all that can be arranged, but I would recommend eating before going down to meet the Altavar. Lord Ypsir has invited you to dine with him in his private suite above us." He paused a moment. "Nothing says you have to accept, you know."

He thought about it. "Does he know the full extent of who and what I am?"

"No. I thought it would be . . . judicious not to tell him. And although he has this whole place wired up, my own people are controlling everything there."

"I thank you for that. In that case, I'll accept his invitation. Oh, don't worry. I'll be a good boy."

Morah thought a moment, then nodded. "Very well. I will so inform him. It is now—let's see, 1720. Give me the comcode and I will see to the checks with my people, and also arrange for you not to be disturbed in the meeting room until . . . shall we say, 1900? We'll set your dinner date for then. After, or in the early morning, you can meet the Altavar. Shall we set negotiations to begin at, oh, ten hundred tomorrow morning? That will also give the Council plenty of time, and my men can hook up the Altavar and Council visuals. How does that sound?"

He nodded. "Excellent." He turned to his counterparts. "You three want to come outside with me? I think we have some talking to do. Of course the ladies can come, too, if you wish."

He stood there looking at them as they studied him. Tremon was still a big, muscular brute of a man, just as he remembered him, and Lacoch still had a somewhat reptilian cast to him, including a tail. Zhang was in the body of a young civilized worlder, and looked much like he did himself, although he was certainly physically older and felt ancient. He found it interesting that neither of the two with their ladies there had included them in on this reunion, although it saved making explanations.

"I assume we're being totally bugged, so I won't say anything I don't want Morah to know," he began. "I want to start by stating flatly that I was with you all the way on your worlds. I know you very well, and you know me."

They were fascinated that, after all the different events that had happened to them, they found it difficult not to begin speaking at the same time, and one quite often could complete another's statements.

Still, he let them get their resentment out, and, perhaps, their pride as well. Zhang pretty much said why he didn't want Dylan in the room when he stated, "Hell, you were there, sort of, all the time. Every time we made love, you did it, too. That's not an easy thing to face, or to explain to her."

"Then don't," he suggested. "Let's get this straight. We are *all* individuals. I am Mr. Carroll, for reasons only you three probably understand. You're Tremon, and you're Lacoch, and you're Zhang. I think the easiest way to explain it to others is to explain it in more natural terms."

They all nodded and said, as one, "Quadruplets."

"Why not? It's closer to the truth now, anyway. Have you all been briefed on the situation?"

They nodded, but he found they were still a bit sketchy and he filled in the details. It was surprising, once they got down to business, how quickly the anger and hurt and resentment vanished and they worked almost as a team. Finally, though, Lacoch asked the loaded question. "Where's our man on Medusa?"

He sighed. "Three hits, one miss. Not a bad record."

"Dead, then?"

He nodded. "Yes, dead. But his information was the clincher. Damn it, though, I'll always feel guilty about that. After I got the report from you, Lacoch, on Charon, I had it pretty well down. If I had gone directly to Medusa at that time, instead of delaying as I did, he'd still be alive. It was that close."

Tremon whistled. "You know, I think all of us hated your guts up until today. I know I did." The others nodded understandingly. "But, with you here, in the middle of this shit, I think we got off lucky. Not the Medusan, of course, but the three of us, anyway. We're the individuals, and we're the free ones living our own lives. You got nothing, nobody, not even the Confederacy in a pinch, and you got all the crosses."

"And yet you've really changed," Lacoch put in, again getting nods. "We all sense it. Sure, *we* changed, but you were with all three of us and you still got the load. The big load. That's what this is all about, isn't it?"

He grinned. "In a way, yes. If we never had this meeting, never had this talk, none of us would be really free of the others and you know it. Now you—all of you—are free and only I am not. If this all works out, I think the four of us will do very well indeed as . . . brothers. If not—well, who knows what will happen to any of us?"

They accepted that in silence for a moment. Finally Tremon said, "The Council will never bargain in good faith. You know that."

He sighed. "Not yet they won't. Not without the shedding of blood on both sides. I'm going to do my best, though, tomorrow, to put it together. We'll see. At least you of all people understand my motives and loyalties."

"I think we do," they all said softly. The meeting broke up a little after that, and Dumonia was summoned to the conference room. The little man with the needless glasses and nervous ticks didn't try to conceal his position of strength from him, but he *was* curious.

"You are really the original of all of them?"

He nodded. "If original is the right word. And I experienced all that they experienced, Doctor, but without any little memory tricks. You might tell me, though, how the hell you managed to erase yourself from Zhang's mind. I thought any tinkering like that was damned near impossible with my—his—mind."

Dumonia smiled. "And who do you think created many of those techniques in the first place?"

He sighed. "I wish you'd been on Ypsir's satellite a couple of days ago. I assume that you're behind the Opposition projects there?"

He nodded. "But what happened that you wished for me?"

Briefly, he told Dumonia and asked, "What's your long-term prognosis?"

"Well, Jorgash is among the best I ever taught, if that's

any consolation, and your kind of mind is best for that procedure, but—and it is a big but—he would have to guess on your mental blocks and patterns where I would know. In any event, I would counsel you to think of Bul as dead, for dead he certainly is. I realize your guilt but I also know this Ypsir. He knows that you were Control for Bul, and that's why you've been invited to dinner tonight. You should understand him, too, to an extent, and realize that if you *had* been in time to intercede, he would have accidentally on purpose done it anyway. The only real human being in Ypsir's mental universe is himself. Everyone else is either a tool or an enemy authority. To the enemy authority—and to himself—he must continually prove that he is better, stronger, superior. You are the tool of that authority, the Confederacy, and, therefore, you represent it. If I were you I would not go to dinner tonight."

"Why? You think he means me harm?"

"He is not so foolish. But if you cannot accept the fact that this Tarin Bul is dead, as dead as if he had been shot through the heart, and that this new person is exactly that, a new and different person you do not know and have never met, he will torture you horribly. You must put aside your guilt, for it is misplaced. There is nothing you could have done to stop this. *Nothing.* You would only have hastened it. In the case of Bul, you must abandon hope with that guilt. Otherwise, cancel and eat here with us."

He nodded. "I'll handle it. But what should my reaction be?"

"You are not yourself here!" the psych snapped. "You are not even the Confederacy! You are all of mankind, and all of the Diamond as well! You've been elected, without your consent, to a post that makes you more nonhuman than these Altavar things! You must be above all human concerns, all personal concerns, for the duration of this conference! If not, you are lost."

He nodded and smiled wanly. "Then you know at least as much as I do about this."

"I know what Laroo knows, and that is quite a lot. I assume that you are here because you know, too. If you don't, then God help us all."

He sighed. "Well, I don't pretend to have all the an-

swers, or, maybe, any answers at all, Doctor, but you've
convinced me I have to go to dinner tonight."

"Eh?"

"If I can't handle Talant Ypsir's mad egomania, how the
hell can I handle tomorrow?"

5

After the cramped quarters below, he was surprised at the
size of Ypsir's apartment. Surely the man hardly ever
visited Boojum, and so this place spoke volumes about the
man's mind. Ypsir must have a place like this on every
damned one of these moons, he assumed.

He entered a main hall and turned into a room at the
sound of conversation. They were there, all of them, the
old and the new, and he recognized the ones on sight that
he had not yet met. The tall, distinguished man with the
snow white hair was Duke Kobé, new Lord of Lilith. The
tall, muscular, handsome man was Laroo, in his robot
body totally indistinguishable at this point from a normal
human one. Morah was there, too, temporarily representing
Charon. He made a mental note to ask him sometime what
happened to his pretty little killer. And over there, laughing and joking, a distinguished-looking civilized worlder
with incongruous flaming red hair and mustache, his eyes
mischievous-looking and flanked by "laugh lines," dressed
in deep black and gold. He just had to be Talant Ypsir.

Scampering around were four scantily clad young women
of inordinate beauty and sexual endowments, supplying
hors d'oeuvres, replenishing glasses, lighting Kobé's Lil-
ithian cigars, all with a smile and an adoring expression.
Goodtime Girls, happily plying their trade. Idly he wondered if they were always here, waiting for that incredibly
rare occasion when their master might show up, or whether
they were part of his traveling party.

Ypsir spotted him, grinned a politician's grin, and made
his way over to him, hand out. "Well, well! So you're the
man's who's going to save the universe!" His manner was
joking, not sarcastic-sounding, and he recognized the man's
public *persona* in an instant. The eternal baby-kissing hypo-
critical politician, the crook who knows full well he's go

everything in the bag. He snapped his finger and a Good-time Girl was immediately at hand, eagerly awaiting a command. "Get Mr.—Carroll, I believe?—a *homau* and a tray of those little sausage things with the cheese inside."

The girl was quick to obey and was soon back with both. He sipped the sweet drink and took a small sausage on a toothpick and tasted it. The drink was a bit sweet for him—he recognized it as some blend of Charonese fruits and alcohol—but the appetizer was quite good.

Ypsir engaged him in small talk for some time, and he found it remarkably easy to do. His indignation and out-right hatred were still there, of course, but under complete control. He doubted if he'd ever met someone so internally corrupt and evil, but he'd tracked down and caught a bunch of very unpleasant types in the past, and quite often he'd had a meal with them and been forced to endure their bizarre lifestyles and values.

All the men in the room except himself were in that class, he realized. Laroo had been the criminal boss of a dozen worlds; Morah had run the criminal brotherhood's scientific branch, which included projects that would probably make the Goodtime Girls seem tame. Kobé had in his youth been a master of the robot and computerized alarm systems, personally looting more works of art by great masters from impregnable fortresses—or so they were thought to be—than any other single human being. And yet, oddly, he felt almost a kinship with those three, whose careers were based upon disdain for the very values he now disdained, and who, beyond that, were at least sane enough to live in the real universe.

Of them all, only Talant Ypsir hoped he would fail to stop the impending war. Dumonia had been most specific about that point. Ypsir saw the destruction of the Confederacy, and perhaps the whole non-Warden branch of humanity, as something very much to be desired. He was assured of survival with his harem, and that was all that mattered to him. He did not consider the Altavar any threat, because they did not interfere with him or threaten what he considered important. In fact, to Talant Ypsir the entire alien race was just another tool against his enemies.

Ypsir held up a finger and grinned broadly, ever the jovial, friendly politician, only his incredibly cold eyes betraying anything of his inner self. "Wait here! I want to show you my most precious possession!" And, with that, he ducked from the room.

He heard the others whispering admiringly of what they knew was coming. But when Talant Ypsir re-entered, in spectacular fashion, he was aware that the eyes of the other Lords—Morah's inhuman, burning orbs in particular—were all upon him and not on the newcomer to the room. To Ypsir, this was fun torture; to the others, it was very much a test of his own self-control and resolve. If he blew it now, there would *be* no tomorrow morning.

She was almost inhuman in her wild, exotic, sensuous beauty, far beyond the sketches he'd seen in Fallon's office. Despite all his knowledge and feelings, he was almost overcome by wanton desire, by pure lust, and that, he realized later, was the key.

You must think of her as someone you do not know and have never met.

It was easier to do than he'd believed.

She entered on all fours, playfully tugging at a golden leash held by Ypsir, whose face showed absolute ecstasy and triumph. Ypsir was having a doubly fine time, not only tweaking this outsider's nose and, by so doing, the Confederacy's, but also showing off to the other Lords, his political equals, with an air of *I have her and you never can or will.*

Ypsir and the girl halted just inside the entrance door, and she rolled over and then partly propped herself up on one arm, legs crossed, and looked up at them with those enormous green eyes, at once sexy and, somehow, wild as well.

She was, he thought lustfully in spite of himself, the ten best pornographic performances ever given all rolled up into one. She was quite literally *designed* to create instant envy and lust, and he could only stare at her. She looked straight into his face and there was no glimmer of any recognition at all, but there was a vibrancy, a fire in those eyes that was not in any of the Goodtime Girls.

Ypsir looked down at her with pride. "Tell the nice men your name," he urged softly, as if talking to a trained animal or a child.

"I'm Ass," she purred. "I'm a *baaad* Ass."

"And why are you named Ass?"

" 'Cause Ass was 'sassin. Ass try to kill Master."

He was under control now, perfectly so, and glanced out of the corner of his eye at the others. They were still looking only at him.

"And what happened when you tried?"

"Master too smart. Master too wise for Ass. Master *so* generous. Master no kill Ass. Master no hurt Ass. Master make Ass *love* him. Master take ugly, evil 'sassin, make into Ass, to love Master."

Despite the depravity of the scene, this was becoming interesting, he thought. If they retold her that much, how much *did* she know of her former self? Not enough to recognize him, certainly. This was different from what he expected, yet it was consistent. *Ypsir wanted her to know.*

"Do you remember who, you were?"

She looked slightly confused by that one. "Ass not 'member old self. Ass no want to 'member."

"Are you happy now, Ass?"

"Oh, yes!"

"Would you want to be anybody else—anybody or anything in the whole wide universe?"

"No, no, no, no, no. Ass loves being Ass. Feels *so* good."

Ypsir looked up straight at him. "Your former agent."

"Very creative," he responded dryly, sipping at his drink. "And very lovely. Maybe we missed a bet, Lord Ypsir. Maybe we should have made *you* into a gorgeous beauty like that instead of sending you to Medusa. That's what *you* would have done with you."

Ypsir's face clouded, and he literally shook with emotion, his inner self coming out in the twisting of his face, in his expression, in his every mannerism. It was a frightening, totally evil visage, a demonic creature that could no longer hide behind the mask of the cheery politician for very long.

He was about to add more, but felt Morah's arm touch his and thought better of it. He'd done his job, and that was all that mattered, but he took a strong pleasure in twisting Talant Ypsir's vision of beauty back upon him by applying the Medusan's standards to himself.

Ypsir took a minute or so to regain control, and slowly that terrible demon faded and the cheery politician was back with only a nasty leer remaining. He knew now, though, that he was in complete control, and his self-confidence, which had been badly wavering, flowed back into him in a grand surge. He also now knew that, while he still couldn't believe in a god, he would always afterward believe in the existence of pure evil.

The rest of the evening was strained, but he found the right balance that not only Morah but the other Lords could approve. Not that Ypsir didn't try, parading Ass, making her do pretty disgusting and degrading things, and pushing him as far as the Medusan could push using her, but to no avail. Ypsir fought his war with grand and ugly gestures; he fought back with sarcasm and flip comments, and totally frustrated the great Lord of Medusa. It was a very rare evening, really, he told himself, equally unpleasant and rewarding.

Morah got him out of there as soon as dessert was finished, though. Ypsir would be boiling, horrible mad for hours after. Still, the Charonese was more than impressed by his behavior, and seemed to regard him even more as an equal now than before.

"He will kill you if and when he can," Morah warned him. "Ypsir is not used to losing face so badly. Only the presence of the other Lords restrained him tonight, for his object is not ours."

He nodded. "Shall we meet the Altavar now? I don't care how foul they smell—they almost have to be a breath of fresh air compared to the company we've been keeping this night."

"Come with me," Yatek Morah said.

The smell *was* pervasive and pretty much as Morah had warned. On a full stomach it almost made him gag, and he restrained the impulse to do so only with the greatest difficulty and discomfort.

The Altavar were not quite what he expected. They bore a general kinship to the demons of the ice, but only a kinship, in the same sense that Ass was generically related to Commander Krega.

The first thing that struck him was the sheer alienness of the special quarters for the three Altavar. The lighting was subdued, the furniture odd and blocky and totally unfamiliar in form or function, and there was an odd, figure-eight shaped pool of water to one side. He knew the creatures were watching him with interest, but he couldn't really tell how. The retractable tentacles and odd, heart-shaped pads on their "heads" were familiar, but their bodies trailed into a large, nearly formless mass that seemed constantly in motion. They did not walk, but oozed as they moved, leaving a slender trail of slime behind them. Obviously none of these creatures could fly, or move very fast at all.

The one nearest to him and Morah moved to a small device and extended a flowing stalklike appendage until it reached the box and actually seemed to enter it through a small compartment on the side. A speaker crackled.

"So this is the one who caused so much trouble, Morah." The voice, totally electronically synthesized, sounded eerie as the dank enclosure added reverb to its already inhuman tones.

Morah bowed slightly, although whether or not the gesture had any meaning to the creatures couldn't be known. "He wished to meet you prior to the talks."

"Why?"

The question seemed addressed to either one of them, and so he answered. "Partly curiosity. Partly to add to my knowledge. And partly because protocol demanded it."

"Ah, yes, protocol," the alien replied. "It seems important to your people." It paused a moment. "You hold yourself well. In many ways you remind us of the one called Kreegan."

"We were from the same place and in the same profession originally," he told the Altavar. "I suspect we thought more alike than either of us would have admitted. You respected Kreegan, I know. I hope that I may earn a measure of that respect tomorrow."

"You and he wished to save your people. This is a normal and natural thing to us, and we weakened out of our compassion. We hope sincerely that we did not err on that basis, for the cost will be far greater to you and infinitely greater to us if we did. It was our original intent, you know, to eliminate a number of your worlds in a carefully measured pattern so that your technological capabilities would be broken for at least three centuries. This would have allowed us the necessary time to complete this phase of our task."

He was appalled at this revelation, and the casual way in which it was delivered, appalled as Marek Kreegan must have been many years ago when, assuming his rank as Lord of Lilith, he had first met this or some similar Altavar. Say there were nine hundred human worlds, seven hundred of them the civilized worlds. Three billion per civilized world, and an average of a half-billion for the others, would be— The Altavar was talking about eliminating over one *trillion*, three hundred and twenty *billion* people! And now, the creature had said, the risk was far greater than that!

He drew in his breath and swallowed hard. "Let me get this straight. You wished to eliminate over a trillion of us so that we could not interfere with your activities for three centuries?"

"It has worked in the past," the Altavar said calmly. "The last time we did not do it with a civilization it cost us dearly in time, lives, and materiel, and your own civilization is easily ten times the largest we have encountered before."

So calm, so natural and normal, so clearly confirming much of his thesis about the Altavar and their motives.

"We hope that this time we may reason with your leaders, and avoid all war, but this may not be possible," the creature continued. "We have studied your people well, and we understand you."

"Do you, really? I wonder." All he could see was not a terrible, gruesome alien form and stench, only an entire race of Talant Ypsirs, shorn of any need to be cheery, political, or human in any sense. The Medusans called them demons with no real understanding of how right they were.

"We know your concern," the Altavar told him. "Once, you see, our race was much like yours. We grew from a single world not unlike your own, although, obviously, evolution took a different path. We breathe the same sort of air, we drink and are made up of the same water. Our cells would be understandable to your biologists. Only the most warlike, competitive races survive to expand, so do not think us any different from you there, either. We, too,

had our empire of several hundred worlds. And when faced
with threat, we, too, fought. Because our history is so much
like your own, we know full well what your Confederacy
will do, how it will behave. But we are far older than your
kind. Our objectives have changed, our purpose is firm and
sure, our entire race committed to a single set of goals and
objectives, while yours exists only to exist and to no real
purpose. We desire none of your worlds. We desire none
of your territory, nor your people.

"But your people will never believe that, for they know
no higher purpose. They will not accept, or countenance,
our great task, nor understand it. This is sad, for if there
was any way to avoid the spilling of blood we would do
so. That, we think, is why we were willing to allow Kreegan his chance. That and the fact that we had the luxury
of time. We still have some time, but we fear his plan has
achieved instead this current situation. Tomorrow we will
begin to resolve it."

He nodded. "Yes. Tomorrow. Thank you for speaking
to me." He looked at Morah, who nodded, turned, and
walked out without another word. He followed, remember-
ing that the Altavar didn't stand on protocol.

It took a little while of breathing good air before his
stomach would settle down enough to have any sort of
conversation. Morah waited patiently for him to recover.

"Well, did you find any surprises in your pet theories?"

He thought a moment. "Yes and no. It depends on just
how well that thing translates. I heard the right words, but
words can mean different things to different people."

"Tell me," the security chief said, "just out of curiosity—
and if you can without giving away your own position.
Just why do you think that the Altavar are so obsessed
with the Diamond?"

"Huh? I assumed it had something to do with reproduction, but if I heard that thing correctly it may not. What
did I miss?"

Morah thought his answer over carefully. "Then my
guess was correct. You are a good agent, Carroll, and you
have the most brilliant deductive mind I have ever encountered, Kreegan included. Do not feel badly. You labor
under a handicap impossible to overcome."

"I knew I missed something—but you still haven't told me what yet."

"I think not. Not at this time. If anything, the true answer would make even the slender hope of settlement impossible. Reproduction is a good theory, and you should stick with it. The Council will understand it, perhaps accept it, and it will do as a basis for negotiations. The true answer, however, they will never accept, for they share your fatal flaw—and mine, too, for I had to be shown to believe."

He looked at Morah, frowning. "Then at least tell me the flaw."

"These are aliens, Mr. Carroll. They are, as the old one said, far closer to us than their hideous appearance and smelly hides admit, but they are alien all the same. They were shaped by a history that went vastly different from ours, and they reacted in a way, I suspect, that we could not. It should be obvious that their values, their institutions, their way of looking at things is very different from our own and would require a mind-wrenching adjustment to understand."

"Do *you* understand it?"

"Sometimes I think I do, but I cannot really say so truthfully. I know what they are doing, and why they are doing it, but that is not the same thing as understanding it. I think it is time we both turn in, Mr. Carroll. Tomorrow, we settle it, and, in a sense, I fear that the hopes of Kreegan and, in fact, myself, will be dashed. I know those people too well, those high and mighty Confederacy leaders. You see Talant Ypsir and see a monster. I look at the Council and the Congress and the planetary leaders and I see a great gathering of Talant Ypsirs, and would-be Talant Ypsirs if they thought they could get away with it. That is the true reason they established the Warden Diamond; you have only to recognize it yourself. They wanted a place of security, refuge, and escape in case *they* were caught. The Four Lords of the Diamond are not truly any different from the Nine Hundred Lords of the Confederacy, who are merely greater hypocrites." He turned to go, and the agent reached out and softly took hold of his arm for a moment.

"Morah—I have to know. Just whose side are you on?

What is your ultimate game? You hate the Confederacy, but you have the same contempt for the Four Lords and the Diamond systems. You hoped that Kreegan could save humanity, yet you work for the aliens. What is your game?"

The chief of security sighed. "Once I had a game, Mr. Carroll. I don't any longer. I am trapped in a near-endless madhouse of a universe I did not make and cannot control or truly influence. From our viewpoint the Altavar are incredibly wise and totally insane, but insanity itself is a matter of degree. I am certainly insane by the standards of the Confederacy. Think of me as you would yourself. Neither of us asked to be here, nor did we fight for the responsibility that has been dropped upon us. Both of us do what we must because we are here, not because we are even the best people to be here. And, being totally insane ourselves, while we do not wish the ruin, carnage, and senseless violence that impends, we will both, wearily and without joy, work like hell to pick up the pieces."

"That's a pretty shitty universe you live in."

Morah grinned. "I wouldn't bring this up tomorrow, but, for the record, the Altavar have three sexes. One contributes sperm, one egg, into a third who bears the young. And given a near-perfect medical knowledge, they live about three times as long as we do." And with that, Yatek Morah went off to bed.

6

The conference was an awkward affair, but it was the best that could be done on short notice. He wondered from the start why such a minor moon, ill-suited for this sort of thing, should have been chosen, but suspected it might have been to accommodate the Altavar.

The technicians had rigged a screen at each end of the "conference room" and a similar setup, but not two-way, for the aides and assistants and others in the dorm next door. Inside the room sat the four current Lords of the Diamond dressed in their best, or most dramatic, as well as Dumonia and "Mr. Carroll," the last two facing the rest despite the fact that Laroo was really Dumonia's surrogate. Morah, it seemed, didn't fully believe his statements on Dumonia's power and neither recognized it nor told the others. Dumonia, for his part, was happy to be there as a representative of the Confederacy, although he found that concept highly amusing.

To the Lord's right, on the screen, was an Altavar, possibly the same one he'd spoken to the night before. To their left the screen showed two men and a woman, all civilized worlders, dressed in formal robes of office. These were the senior ranking members of the Council, the rest of whom watched on a larger screen in an adjoining room back in the Confederacy.

He surveyed the Four Lords and shuffled his note cards nervously. Several times he tried to catch Ypsir's eye, but while the Medusan kept taking sidelong glances at him he otherwise would not acknowledge the agent's existence.

When both sides' comtechs certified all was ready, Morah began the meeting, as he represented not only Charon but also, to some extent, the Altavar themselves.

"These proceedings are open at ten hundred Base Mean Time. I am Yatek Morah, acting Lord of Charon. To my right is Talant Ypsir, Lord of Medusa, then Wagant Laroo, Lord of Cerberus, and, finally, Duke Hamano Kobé, Lord of Lilith. We speak with full authority for the populations of the Warden Diamond. Across from me sit Mr. Lewis Carroll, authorized agent of the Confederacy, and Antonini Dumonia, the Confederacy's resident agent on the Warden Diamond." Morah kept a straight face but Dumonia almost broke up. "Representing the Party Council are Senators Klon Luge, Morakar O'Higgins, and Surenda Quapiere. Representing the Altavar Managerial Project staff and with full authority to represent all Altavar involved in this spacial sector is Hadakim Soog. The name is an attempt to represent the actual name in our speech, and is used simply because the Altavar translating devices will recognize those syllables and transliterate them into Altavar and vice versa. There being no neutral parties present, I will assume the chairmanship for the time being, if there is no objection."

Nobody spoke or moved.

"Very well, then," Morah continued, "we will proceed. Mr. Carroll, will you please state your position?"

He smiled and nodded. "There is no use going into all the circumstances that brought us to this point. If we didn't all know them, and if it wasn't now a matter of record at all governments concerned, we wouldn't be here. It is the Confederacy's position that there is nothing here to fight about, put as simply and bluntly as possible. As far as we can determine, the interest of the Altavar is entirely in the Warden system, as are the interests of the Four Lords of the Diamond. The Confederacy is a very large group not in conflict with the Altavar or any other territory, and, therefore, believes that this matter may be settled simply. We are prepared to cede and concede to the Altavar sovereignty of the Warden solar system for a distance of twenty light-years from its sun, and we are further prepared to guarantee that no people or vessels not now belonging to those in residence in the system will encroach upon this zone, nor will Altavar access or egress from the system be in any way impeded even if it cuts through regions under Confederacy sovereignty. The four worlds known as the Warden Diamond, and their posssessions and colonies, will be given free, unconditional, unilateral independence and may work out whatever arrangement they like with the Altavar. If the Altavar are sincere in stating that they have no interest in Confederacy space beyond the Warden system, this should be sufficient. Any violations, of course, would constitute an immediate act of war, but the vastness of the surrounding zone would provide ample warning."

He looked around to see how this was being taken—he had hashed it out on the security band well into the night with the Council and Krega—but saw no emotion whatever on the intent listeners. Well, not quite all—Ypsir was cleaning his nails with a small pen knife.

"In exchange for this," he continued, "the Confederacy expects an immediate and total cessation of hostilities now underway against it by the Four Lords of the Diamond with the acquiescence of the Altavar, withdrawal of all such agents to the Warden Diamond, and a formal agreement that any future territorial or interest conflicts between the Confederation and the Altavar be settled by arbitration with both sides renouncing the use of force against the other. We feel this is more than fair."

Morah waited a moment to see if he was finished, then

saw his nod that he was. "Very well, then," the Charonese said, "do you have anything to add, Doctor?"

Dumonia shook his head negatively.

"All right. I sense some objections among the Four Lords, but I will defer them at this time, and ask the Council to confirm this offer."

"We do," Luge's voice came to them after a momentary delay caused not by interstellar communications but by the lag from the subspace relay they were using on the picket ship. "In fact, the offer was approved twenty-one to four by the full Council and thus is binding upon us if accepted."

Morah nodded and turned to the impassive Altavar. "Manager Soog, are you prepared at this time to answer the offer?"

"We are," the eerie synthesized voice responded. "We would very much like to accept the offer, which answers our basic needs and our objections to the current arrangement. However, we feel we cannot do so. The history of the human race argues against you, Confederacy. It is a most consistent record, no matter the technological or social levels. From the very beginnings of your history you have shown yourselves to be totally intolerant of those who are different. The record is a clear record of repression. Treaties are signed and sworn to and systematically violated at the first opportunity. You persecuted your own for a mild difference in skin color or bone structure, or because some worshiped a different god, or even the same god by different names. Treaties between nations held only so long as both nations felt so strong that they could destroy the other. Not once do we see social or political agreements made and held by mutual respect, only by mutual fear— and then with all the efforts of both sides devoted to destroying even that balance.

"You took these attitudes with you into space," the creature went on, "and continued them for a while, until the years and the practicalities of distance and the advance of technology merged you racially and culturally. Still, the fact of this merger only caused redirection of this trait. Fully a dozen nonhuman races were discovered in your outward expansion. None equaled your power or emulated your culture. Five you utterly destroyed simply because you could not understand them. The other seven you conquered ruthlessly, and imposed your culture and your system upon them by force. With two of those you first concluded treaties of peace and friendship and the exchange of ambassadors and technical skills, because they were spacefaring races. But as soon as you decided that they could be no threat to you, you ruthlessly rushed in upon them and crushed them, ignoring your treaties. Understand that we do not necessarily condemn this trait, nor condone it, for it is natural to an expanding spacefaring culture and we have seen it before. We were even guilty of it ourselves, once. But you see where this leaves us in the current situation.

"Your treaties are worthless, until you know our strength and power, knowledge those treaties buy you because they buy you whatever time is needed. Sovereignty so easily given away may be more easily taken back. Nor can your military and government leaders rest easy as long as we are hidden behind a shield of their ignorance. Unless we show you all, you will try all the more by any means to learn and thus interfere. If we *did* show you, either you would determine us too weak and thus rush in to crush us, or we would be too strong, in which case you would spare no effort to catch up, then surpass us technologically and militarily. Your proposal, then, simply buys you the time you need to gain advantage, or it puts off the war, allowing you to build up and improve your forces. It offers us nothing of substance, and we must reject it."

The three Councillors looked extremely distressed and uncomfortable at this assessment, and Dumonia leaned over and whispered to the agent, "Take 'em off the hook, son. They're outclassed."

He nodded. "Then do the Altavar have a counterproposal to avoid war?"

The creature did not hesitate. "We see only one possible guarantee of our own security and safety. The Confederacy will turn over to us control of all spacecraft of whatever size or type capable of interstellar travel, and will build no more. All interstellar travel and communications between human worlds and all forces capable of harming us will be entirely under our control and supervision for a period of three hundred and fifty years from the date of commencement of the agreement. We will guarantee to maintain all existing passenger and freight routes and establish whatever added schedules are needed for the maintenance of the economy and the well-being of the people. We will not interfere in the internal political affairs of the Confederacy in any way. Expansion or the possession or control of any spacial weapons for the interdicted period will not be permitted."

The Councillors gasped, and all Four Lords smiled knowingly. "But—that would leave the entire human race totally and completely at the mercy of a race and culture of which we know nothing, having to trust all your promises at face value!" Senator Luge exclaimed. "Surely you can't be serious!"

"You proposed to cut loose unilaterally fifty million plus people who are Confederacy citizens under law and put them under these people, you know," Talant Ypsir snapped. "If it's good enough for us, it should be good enough for you!"

Morah let the outburst pass, and the Councillors ignored it. "These are negotiations in progress," he reminded them all. "Let us keep our decorum. Manager Soog?"

"Can the Senator or his advisors suggest any other way we can guarantee our security?" the alien asked.

"Our word is—" the Senator started, but the alien cut him off.

"Your word is valueless. Even you know this. Even as these proceedings begin, a vast and powerful war fleet is within range of the Warden system. On the very eve of negotiations it launched four military probes of advanced design against us. We know what your word is worth, Senator."

There was consternation and frantic whispering on the Council's side. Finally Luge seemed to calm everyone down and turned back to the camera. "May we have a recess to discuss a counteroffer?"

Morah looked around. "Is there any objection? No? For how long, then, Senator?"

"One—uh, sorry, two hours."

"Agents? Manager? Lords? No objection?"

"Let them have their meeting," Laroo snarled. "It'll probably be hilarious."

"Very well, then. This meeting is in recess for two hours and will reconvene at twelve thirty standard."

Both screens winked out, and everybody seemed to relax. Both Ypsir and Laroo seemed extremely pleased by the way things had gone; Kobé was as impassive as Morah, who looked over at the two opposite him and asked, "Well? Do you think it's still possible to reach any sort of agreement?"

"I doubt it. Not until we've gone through the bloody motions. How about it, Morah? Will they understand a show of force and resistance, or will they simply go all-out?"

"They understand the game, if that's what you mean. How they will play is anybody's guess and is certainly beyond my ability to predict. However, they have gone along with it this far, and that is an achievement."

The agent rose from the table. "I have to call my people."

He gave it to them straight, but they didn't really believe him. Not all of it. He was surprised at the start that they had accepted most of his report as gospel—certainly the computer had backed him up, and their own analysis of the same data seemed to have reinforced it. What they could not accept was the concept that the Altavar were in any sense militarily superior to the Confederacy. In weaponry, yes, but not in total weapons systems or firepower.

"But what kind of a solution can you have?" he asked, frustrated. "Nothing less than their offer will give them the security they want, and we can't possibly accept it."

"We think we were more than fair in our initial offer," Luge replied, "and it is still the only offer we can live with. Ypsir certainly has a nerve suggesting we can't turn over the Diamond to the Altavar—by their own admission now they are in a state of open rebellion. But these squishy, tentacled things give me the creeps. We all wish we had something other than the Diamond to hold over them, but we don't. We don't know their power or their forces. In one respect, old squirmy had us pegged. Power and fear of power is the only thing that really counts in situations like this. I know you think they can beat us, but we can't see any way that's possible. The only way to get us the information we need, and to learn the true situation once and for all, the Council feels, is a demonstration attack."

He sighed. "I thought as much, but I'm against it. I don't know what it is, but I have this crazy feeling that the Altavar, and Morah, are laughing at us."

"Bluff. They have no place to even hide a fleet, and even if the Diamond is extremely well defended, as we think, they are entirely on the defensive there. Any fleet of theirs capable of menacing the Diamond would be weeks, perhaps months away. Since the Diamond is all-important to them, we must put it in jeopardy. This will force their fleet, if in fact they have one, out into the open to counter us, or it will reveal their bluff. Either way, we'll know what we're facing."

"But if you attack the Diamond you lose the only card we have," he pointed out.

"Not the Diamond. Not entirely. Just one. One of the four worlds. A demonstration of power—for both sides. If they can keep us from doing it, then we'll know something. If they cannot, they risk losing the other three, one at a time, unless they agree to our original terms. This way we destroy a quarter of their eggs or whatever, but leave them three quarters. Unless they choose not to call us, in which case the bluff is revealed and we are in complete control. We still feel that if they could have destroyed us, they would have done so at the outset. The fact that they are talking at all indicates our original hypothesis is correct."

He shook his head sadly. "I was afraid it would come to this, but I hoped not. You will have to give the ultimatum yourself—I simply cannot bring myself to do it." He hesitated a moment. "You intend to target Medusa, is that correct?"

Luge looked slightly surprised, then nodded. "Yes. It has the smallest population, is the system's industrial base, and is also, in fact, the only world where hard evidence of an Altavar colony exists. Eliminate Medusa and you eliminate the technological base of the Diamond. None of the others could support the needed factories."

"I'll need details," he said softly.

"What you suggest will cost you far more than it will cost us," the Altavar told the Council. "Perhaps it was destined to be this way. But there will be no limited, demonstration wars. If a Diamond world is destroyed, then we will take appropriate action to bring this matter to a conclusion."

"You ask us to take your word for your honesty and trustworthiness with nothing whatever to support it," the agent interjected, trying to avoid what he was beginning to believe could not be avoided. "You say that our racial histories are not as different as they are similar. You surely must appreciate, then, that a civilization with over nine hundred worlds cannot totally capitulate on the word, the promise, the threat of one opponent whose entire race and history are a blank to us."

"We know," Soog responded, and there seemed genuine sadness and regret in that electronic voice. "We have known that all along. That is why generally we simply make an all-out comprehensive attack. It is far less costly to our side, yet comes down to the same thing."

"But if you felt this way all along, why didn't you do it here?" Luge responded sharply, thinking he had scored a point.

"If you were faced with this prospect, and there was but a five-percent chance this could all be avoided, would you not try?" the Altavar asked him. "We saw that one chance, and allowed ourselves to be convinced of it. It was a mistake, and many more will die because of that mistake, yet we are not sorry we made it. To have *not* taken the opportunity would have always left the question begging—did we wipe out so many countless intelligent beings for nothing?"

"I'm sorry," Senator Luge said, not sounding very sorry at all, "but we simply cannot accept your unsupported threats. If you can stop us from destroying one of the worlds, then do so. If you can not, then you better call all this off and accept our terms before we do."

Morah, sounding very nervous, broke into the proceedings. "How long before you strike? The Altavar must have time to deliberate this matter and take it up in full."

The Council could understand that. They would have had the same problems, and the Altavar probably had greater distances to figure in, and, perhaps, a slower communications system. "Beginning at 2400 this night, we will allow exactly seven standard days for deliberation," Luge told them. "Then we will either have a settlement, or we will commence offensive operations—unless the Altavar can come up with a counteroffer we can accept in the meantime. This channel will be kept open, and our agent will remain on the scene, in case anything must get through to us."

"Seven days!" Morah thundered, rising to his feet. "But we can not possibly evacuate a world in seven days! Using the entire Warden fleet, with pressurized freight containers, we couldn't hope to evacuate a tenth of the population of the smallest world!"

Luge nodded. "This is a demonstration, not an intentional bloodbath. We have many grievances against the Four Lords, but have no wish to destroy the innocent. We are operating on contingency plans made up when the task force was dispatched, and thus, we have provided for some of this. Sixteen transports, capable of moving twenty thousand people each, with drives capable of making interplanetary trips in one to two hours, are available. If you move only the people, at the most rapid rate, you ought to be able to make four trips a day even with loading and unloading. All ships are automated and computer-driven, but will be commanded by anyone you designate to obey voice orders. The ships will be on station in orbit off Medusa within hours—if the Altavar defenses don't shoot them down. If you start as soon as they arrive, and mobilize the rest of the Diamond fleet, and cram them in as best you can, you *can* evacuate the planet. Or you can settle this now."

Talant Ypsir was up and screaming as he heard the target. "You can't! You bastards! You swine! You hellish spawn of animals! That is *my* world you are talking about! *Mine!* Not the Altavar! It is *mine* and *I will not let you rob me of it!*" The combined effect of his inner nature and the Medusan peculiarities of the Warden organism started to change his appearance. He became, in that instant, something terrible, horrible, loathsome to behold, a monstrous, ever-changing vision of evil itself. The creature turned to the agent who sat, impassive, across the table, while next to him Dumonia watched the change with horrid fascination. "*You!*" Ypsir screamed, pointing a rotting, crawling finger at the agent. *"You put them up to this!* I will *kill* you, *kill* you, *kill*—" He made to launch himself across the table.

Yatek Morah turned in the same instant, a laser pistol in his hand, and pointed it at Ypsir. "Oh, shut up, Talant," he sighed wearily, and pulled the trigger. Ypsir collapsed instantly into unconsciousness and slid beneath the table. They all looked down at the crumpled heap and saw it slowly changing back to the familiar face they knew, the expression alone soon becoming the only measure of the hate that was inside him.

Kunser entered the room from the back dorm in an instant, but they all saw immediately that he was not threatening. "Let me get a couple of people in here and get him back upstairs," he pleaded. "We have a lot of work to do."

Morah nodded and holstered the weapon. "We will move everyone we can to the southern continent of Charon at the start," he told the Medusan assistant. "If time becomes short, we'll start putting them down wherever we can on Lilith. Cerberus simply can't handle any such loads. Tell Ypsir when he wakes up that he can settle scores in eight days. If he does anything else than exactly what this meeting decides, or in any way makes trouble before that point, he will meet the fate of his predecessor instantly. Remind him that we do not need to know where he is or what he is doing, that the Altavar can and will simply order his Wardens to consume him if *any* of the rest of us say so. Is that clear?"

Everyone else in the room was just getting over their stunned and shocked feelings at the proceedings when Ypsir was finally carried out and away. Even Luge remained frozen on the screen, horrified and shocked by his first direct look at what the Warden organism could do.

Only Morah remained completely in control. "These proceedings are now in indefinite recess. All parties agree that commencing seven days from 2400 this night a state of war will exist between the Altavar on the one hand and the Confederacy on the other."

Luge seemed to snap out of it. "Any move against us prior to that point will result in even more dire consequences," he warned. "We are allowing this period not only in hopes of a diplomatic solution but also out of common decency and mercy. If any attempt is made during this period, or is perceived by us to be made, we will abandon our plans and instead all modules will be directed by the task force with the intent of inducing the sun to nova."

The others on both sides looked particularly shocked by the threat, but the Altavar seemed to take it in stride. "That would be most interesting," it noted coldly. "However, it would cause quite a lot more problems than we are currently prepared to handle. We will, therefore, uphold the waiting period. But make no mistake on this, Senators. Neither you nor the Confederacy will survive many hours after you know just what you have done."

The agent who called himself Mr. Carroll frowned and looked nervously at the Altavar on the screen. What an odd way to put it, he couldn't help thinking. What a *very* odd way to put it. . . .

<h1 style="text-align:center">7</h1>

Talant Ypsir spent most of his time brooding on his palatial orbiting satellite, but he did not interfere with the evacuation nor prevent his aides and infrastructure from doing what had to be done. For himself, though, he spent almost all of his time in his pleasure garden accompanied only by Ass, emerging only briefly to make certain that the station itself would be moved from orbit by tug.

The transports, too, were built on the modular concept, so it was relatively easy for the great ships to break into small compartments and move down to various collection points on the surface. These were troop transports, designed to hold half of what they were being asked to hold; but in a war without troops they could be spared by the Confederacy, which was, according to Commander Krega, still confident that the Altavar bluff would break at the last minute.

The Medusan population proved unusually easy to move. Virtually all of them had been born and raised to obey the orders of the monitors and their superiors, so while they grumbled and complained a lot they did pretty much as they were told. There was some panic in the big cities, among groups who simply would not believe that there was a threat. Others suddenly lost faith when their well-ordered society was proven incapable of protecting them, but these were quickly quelled by monitors with efficient brutality. It was also simply stated that those who did not want to go could remain—but their lives would probably be abnormally short.

Mr. Carroll was particularly concerned about the colonies of Wild Ones. They were too spread out for all of them to be contacted easily, and most disbelieved the news if they heard it and fled into the wild. Finally, he commandeered a shuttle craft and went down to a particular settlement he knew well.

The shuttle landed not in a cradle but on a flat, something it really wasn't designed to do but could because the possibility of an emergency landing always existed. The door opened and he emerged, the only one aboard, dressed in a protective orange spacesuit with the helmet removed. Still, he wore goggles and a small respirator as he walked up to the rock cliff with the twin waterfalls, aware for the first time of just how hard this land really was on one not redesigned as a Medusan.

The courtyard was deserted, as he'd expected, but he didn't hesitate a moment, walking up to the one ground-level cave and inside as far back as he could. The torches were still lit, which told him that people were in fact still here somewhere. He cursed himself for not bringing some additional light source. The last time he'd been here he'd been riding along in a Medusan body and hadn't realized just how damned dark and dangerous the path was.

As he'd hoped, the three elders waited for him across the underground river, eying him without suspicion or fear. He stopped and faced them.

The old woman on the right spoke. "So you have come back after all."

The comment startled him. "You know who I am?"

"Your body is Warden-dead, yet your spirit shines through," the other woman told him. "Your walk, your manner, your turn of speech is the same."

"Then you know why I have come."

"We know," the first woman responded. "We will not

stop anyone from leaving anywhere on this world, but we will not go."

"They're going to do it," he warned. "They're really going to do it. The kind of heat and thermal radiation they will use will melt the very crust of this planet. I know you understand what that means. No Warden power is going to save you, and the way the Altavar are acting, they can't save you, either."

"We know, and yet to go would be to call our lives and beliefs that we have held for so many years a lie," the man put in. "When they do as you say, we trust in the God of Medusa to save us, or take us, as is Her will. But no matter what happens there, they will unleash upon themselves a power greater than the pitiful Confederacy can conceive, and She will be angry. We place our faith in Her."

He sighed. "If you want to be martyrs, I can't stop you. But you have fifty thousand people across this world, and they are your responsibility, too. They can survive, if we know where they are, and if we can get to them some word that we can be trusted."

"It is impossible to notify them all in the time remaining," the first woman pointed out, "but surely more than half have knowledge of what is to come. Some will go, and none will be stopped from going. It is the same here."

"You have explained to the pilgrims here that they are likely to die in two days?"

"We put it to them just that way,"the man assured him. "We told them that physical death was almost a certainty. Only a very few said that they would like to go, and most of them have not changed their minds."

"There are two here, though, who should go. I think even you must realize *that*."

A few moments later one of the small boats came, bearing two occupants he knew well. They stared at him in frightened bewilderment. He helped them out of the boat, and was immediately aware that both were obviously pregnant, Bura Morphy exceedingly so. Both Bura and Angi just gaped at him. Finally Bura said, "They told us Tari had returned. Who are you?"

"Tari is dead. You know that," he responded sadly. "I am his—father, in a sense—and his brother."

Angi gasped, realizing before Bura the implications of

that. During the weeks in the wilderness, Tarin Bul had told them of his origin. "You are the man who . . ." It was all she could manage.

He nodded. "I am. You can't possibly understand this now, but you must believe me. I was with you in the sewers under Rochande, and with you in the wilderness. I was with you when you came to the citadel, and with Tarin Bul until the moment of his death. I am not Tarin Bul, but he is with me. I have come to get you."

"They say they're going to blow up the planet. Is that true?" Bura asked him.

"That's true."

"And nothing can stop it?"

"I tried—Lord, how I tried! But we have an enormous group of men and women who are in the strange position of being totally confident of their power and scared to death at one and the same time. We are trying to save those we can. You carry what future there is for Tarin Bul inside you. Don't kill him completely. Come with me."

They looked nervous and uncertain. Bura's hand took Angi's and squeezed it tightly. "A pack of mad harrar couldn't keep us here one more minute if we have a way to get off."

He grinned. "Fine," he said, and turned back to the elders. "You may not want to leave, but may I address the others here? Give them one last immediate chance?"

"You have our permission," the first woman said. "Go to the courtyard, and we will send them to you."

His speech was impassioned, eloquent, convincing, and mostly futile. Out of perhaps two hundred, only seventeen —all, it turned out, refugees and escapees from the cities— took his offer of escape. He could tell that others, perhaps many others, wanted to go, but were being held back not so much by physical means as by an odd sort of peer pressure. The phenomenon was new to him, and frightened him a little, but he could do no more.

Not a single one of them had ever been on a spacecraft before, and he had some trouble making the adjustments in restraints and in calming nerves before he could take off. Fifteen of the seventeen were female, all of whom were at least seven months pregnant. The citadel, he knew, was a place where tribes within a weeks' journey came when it was time for women to bear their young.

Once over their initial fears, they seemed to enjoy the ride. As time grew shorter and shorter, though, and the evacuation fell more and more behind schedule, he knew that the shuttle would be needed desperately elsewhere. He headed for the Cerberan space station, calling ahead to Dumonia's people to take on his passengers for now. Ypsir's Medusan station was already beyond the plane of the Cerberan orbit on its way in-stream by tug, but even if it had been available he wouldn't have used it. He knew full well what would happen if it were known to Talant Ypsir, as it would be, that two wives of Tarin Bul, pregnant with his children, were within the Lord of Medusa's station—all that really remained of Ypsir's formerly absolute power.

He was surprised to find Dumonia personally waiting for him when he arrived, and after he got the refugees as settled as possible they had a short time to talk. Dumonia had an easy and relaxed style and the perfect manner, and their talk was pretty wide-ranging, considering the time limit the agent had for turnaround. Dumonia saw the human angle.

"You know," he said, "that this thing can only end in one of two ways now. Either there will be no more Diamond, or no more Confederacy."

"Mr. Carroll" nodded. "I'm well aware of that. If there's no more Confederacy we're still alive, but in a hell of a fix with no more imports and the Altavar no longer in hiding. On the other hand, if there's no more Diamond we've just done a lot of work for nothing."

Dumonia grinned. "I think not. You must understand that the Confederacy is ripe for collapse. It won't take an awful lot to bring that about. Making so many worlds so interdependent has left them far too vulnerable. I'm sure that's what Kreegan had in mind when he dreamed up this human-replacement business. Unfortunately for all of us, such action was not enough, and if it hadn't been a desperation scheme it would have been obvious from the start. As fragile and corrupt as the system is, it is still firm enough to keep together a massive population spread out over impossible distances. In its own way the Confederacy was quite amazing, eclipsing any empire in humanity's past. But it *needs* collapsing—all empires do, after they have peaked, or humanity grows stale and dies."

The agent nodded. "I've come to pretty much the same conclusion myself. It seems horrible, though, that so many will have to die."

"It's always been the case. Back in the very old days when we were only on one planet with simple weapons, occasional wars—even with bows, arrows, and spears—spurred progress. But it is no different, really, if your population dies by the sword or by a fusion bomb, or laser blast, or any other of our modern ways. Still, we finally reached the point on that old world where we couldn't afford big wars any more without wiping ourselves out. So we replaced them with small, limited wars, until even these became too sophisticated for any sort of control. Space took much of the pressure off—colonization did that. But political needs and technology unified us, made a human empire of more than nine hundred worlds possible—and kept us in place for a few centuries. Now it falls under the new barbarians."

"The Altavar strike me as inhuman, and really frightening, but not as barbarians. I wish I understood them better. I'm not even sure I understand their actions now. Why not strike—if they can? Or if they can defend Medusa, why allow all this?"

"I don't know," the psych told him. "The Four Lords really don't know, either—except Morah, I think. I doubt if Kreegan knew, although perhaps he did. They, too, bought a bill of goods. The Altavar convinced them that they were no threat to the Diamond, perhaps simply by demonstrating that they'd been here all the time. The Four Lords were attracted to a war by remote control, one with no seeming risk and a lot of rewards, including escape, since the Altavar demonstrated to them early on that they could control the Warden organism. Even those robots are totally operated by a variation of the same little creature, each responsive to its own self-contained programming so it can come and go as it pleases. You know, the Confederacy managed to bypass and even reprogram Laroo and others since, yet they really don't know how the damned things work. Thanks to Merton and her colleagues we knew where the computer-control center was and figured a different but effective input-output system for it, but we still did it by counterprogramming, feeding self-canceling instructions. We couldn't build one if we tried, nor create our own total-control mechanism."

He nodded. "You joined our side—for which I'm eternally grateful, by the way—because you feared the aliens. Now what do you think?"

Dumonia shrugged. "Who knows? In science, one takes what *is*, not what one would like things to be. In the end, perhaps because of the actions of both of us, we've come down to war anyway. If the aliens lose, so do we—end of problem. If the aliens win, then we must deal with them and with our own future. Obviously, I am cheering for the aliens even though I don't trust them one little tentacle-tip. You must understand, for a man who has devoted his entire life to learning what he can—and that's precious little, I assure you—of the workings of the human mind and personality, to be suddenly faced at my age with the necessity of learning the workings of a wholly different complex creature, was and is a bit intimidating."

"But if we survive—and have to go it alone—we must look forward. Suppose the Altavar really do let us alone on the three remaining worlds. What then?"

"I began my little operation out of a sense of personal survival," the psych replied, "but it later expanded, as you know. Ultimately, I hoped for a better, more free and open society on all the Diamond worlds. Turn them lose, with these strange powers, and see what could be built. It's more than enough challenge for an old man, don't you think?"

He nodded and grinned. "And for a younger one, too, I think. But what about the Medusans? I wonder if the destruction of Medusa might not also destroy their own potential and actual power. And, if not, whether or not they'll breed true to Medusa or to Charon or wherever else their children are born."

"We'll have to wait and see on that. However, I suspect that the computer for them is the same as the one for us. Probably one of those huge moons of Momrath, broadcasting and receiving on all four frequencies no matter what. In that case, they will retain their potential and breed true. Charon will become a biracial society, which will bear close watching. Eventually we must learn the Warden secrets and go out again from here, of course, but each of the three worlds can handle many times their present population. You could put half a billion or more on Cerberus yet, and perhaps three billion or more on each of the other two. The survivors will have several generations to solve the problems, and with far less ignorance than we've all had up to now. Show some bright minds that a thing is possible and sooner or later they'll drive themselves mad until they learn how to do it. That's what makes us humans something pretty special."

It was almost time to leave, but he had one more question. "What about Ypsir's girl? What if we could get her away from him—or if she freed herself?"

He sighed. "Jorgash is an expert on the Medusan variants. He tells me flatly that the process absolutely locks in the physiological design so that it cannot be changed at all. I suspect the computer treats them as trees or animals or such—things that must be kept stable. Remember, that's what the Wardens are actually for. Now, assuming your computer would let us, we could take that Tarin Bul recording you used for your report and feed it back into her, but consider the consequences. That body, those revised genetics, that hormonal makeup would, I think, drive you nuts. Still, she was made out of Tarin Bul's body, and the intellectual capacity is still very much there. The challenge is, at the moment, quite academic, but I'm fascinated by what *could* be done. Someone with her looks, moves, and drives and your superior intellect might potentially be running all our lives in a couple of years. It's something to think about."

"I think about it a lot," he told the psych master, "but I'll think about it more if I'm still alive and kicking three days from now. I have to go."

As he stood up to leave, Dumonia put a hand on his shoulder and added, in a concerned tone, "Watch out for Ypsir, boy. He was always *for* the war, remember—so bad is his hatred of the Confederacy—and now that war's come, but at a price he never expected to pay. He'll never forgive the Altavar for that, but he's very smart and knows it might be a long time before he can get revenge there. Thus, all of his hatred, all of his frustration, almost certainly will be taken out on you and your brothers here. Right now he's probably spending all his time thinking of how to get his revenge on you. Not by killing you—that's not his style and would give him only brief satisfaction. It will be something horrible, and far worse than we can imagine."

He nodded and shook the little psych's hand warmly. "I know that and I'll remember. If we're still around."

"Yes," Dumonia repeated grimly, "if we're still around. Empires never go quietly."

He was back on Boojum on the night before the deadline expired, as instructed by both the Confederacy and Morah. He opened his secure channel to Krega, a channel so secure that the field enveloping him would not allow any recording device, or even someone standing right next to him, to understand a word either way.

"There has been no reconsideration?" he asked, hoping against hope. "They're still behind in evacuation, and there are between fifty and a hundred thousand people we just can't get off under any circumstances."

"There has been no reconsideration on this end," Krega told him. "In fact, it's been difficult just to restrain some of our people, particularly the military, to this limited engagement. However, it's going to be awfully bloody. We have monitored some traffic not on our control system at various random points around the civilized worlds. They duck in and out of light before we can get to them, but some of them are pretty big. They haven't budged on your side?"

"Not a bit. I talked to Morah and to the Altavar and they're both firm—you might say even *eager*, on Morah's part. However, that unauthorized traffic gives me bad feelings. There's been no sign of any fleet massing here—I still haven't seen an Altavar ship, not even one to take off the party on Medusa. I don't think they're going to take on the task force head-to-head."

"We have a computer projection on their potential, even assuming a tenth of our firepower, and it's scary," Krega admitted. "Security and Military Systems Command have used the week to shift to remote backup positions. Unless this is more bluff, we think they have dispersed rather than

massed their forces for hit-and-run. If we had ten war
stations we could destroy hundreds of planets. We have to
hit them in one spot—yours, I'm sorry to say, but it's the
only one we have. They can hit us wherever we're not.
Come in, destroy a weakly defended planet someplace, then
get out fast. Choose another equally vulnerable. We can't
guard them all. We'd need eighteen hundred cruisers to do
a strong defense of all the worlds and we have less than
three hundred. Sounded like a lot when we built them."

And that was that. "They're willing to accept the possibility of a protracted bloodbath of those proportions?"

Krega chuckled dryly. "Son, maybe you're still naive.
The Council, the Congress, all the top people are in the
best, most well-protected rear areas. They'll die of old age
before *they're* in jeopardy. Face facts—they've got to win
no matter *what* the cost."

No matter what the cost . . . Yes, he reflected sourly, that
was the bottom line. Fallon had been right. Korman had
been right. They'd *all* been right. The Warden Diamond
wasn't the opposite of the Confederacy, nor were the Four
Lords of the Diamond the opposites of the Council. No,
they were merely reflections of the Confederacy, allowing
for local conditions. That was it—the break was now
complete, total, and irrevocable.

"Good-bye, Papa," he said, meaning it.

"Good-bye, Control," Krega responded and broke the
contact.

He threw the security transceiver as hard as he could at
the nearest wall. It bounced off and clattered and rolled
back to his feet.

The task force was already alerted. There was only an
hour to go.

8

Morah turned and nodded to him as he entered the cramped
meeting room. "Welcome, Mr. Carroll," he said calmly,
sounding in a good mood. "Have a seat. Some of my staff
are here and we thought we would make use of the transmission facilities and these screens to watch what happens
now. Unfortunately, Altavar ships are simply not built for

such as us, and the command center itself bears little resemblance to anything we could make use of. I have arranged to couple in our own devices to theirs so that we can, shall we say, watch the show."

Morah's manner irritated him. He could not really figure out the man, who moved so rapidly from tired philosopher to master agent to an almost Ypsir-like disregard for suffering and destruction. Still, until this was resolved, he was more or less along for the ride and would have to make the best of it.

A half-dozen others were seated around the table, some with small terminals, others with primitive pads and paper, but all looked more interested than worried by what might well take place. Most, but not all, were Charonese. Medusans were conspicuously absent, though.

One screen displayed the familiar computer plot showing the tactical disposition of the task force, the Diamond worlds, and representations of moving traffic and satellites. The plot extended to Momrath, but not beyond.

The task force had split into three sections. Two battle groups with their attendant cruiser protection had moved well away from the main force and were station keeping at right angles to the task force and the sun. The main battle group, with two war stations, was rapidly beginning to close on the target, its obvious move designed to draw out an enemy fleet and to draw and test interplanetary defenses, since all operations could have been carried out from any distance within a light-year of the target.

He frowned. "From the looks of it the Altavar are putting up no resistance at all," he noted aloud.

Morah sat back in his chair and watched the screen. "There will be no resistance to the objective except from fixed planetary defenses, which will become increasingly costly to the task force the more they close," he told the agent. "However, the subsidiary battle groups will be engaged at the proper time."

"Then there *are* forces in the area! Where?"

"You'll see them when the time comes, Mr. Carroll. Be patient. We are about to bear witness to a sight no humans and few living Altavar have ever seen. We have remote cameras stationed in-system and will be able to see things firsthand on the other screen. All of this, of course, is contingent on the Confederacy task force doing exactly what it said it would. If they try to double-cross us with a mass attack on all four worlds or any one other than Medusa, or if they come at us here, the script may change drastically. I *do* expect some attempt at the moons here, but as long as the main attack is centered on Medusa I believe we are in no danger."

As the standard clock hit 2400, there was a sharp, anticipatory taking in of breath by all concerned, but nothing happened immediately. The task force continued to close, now well within the orbit of Orpheus, the farthest out planet in the Warden system.

At 2403 the task force slowed, then came to a complete stop between Orpheus and Oedipus, next in of the planets, as shown in the total system insert, and the cruisers deployed in protective formations around the two main war stations. Suddenly buzzers sounded, and they could see a great number of tiny pinpricks of white light emerge from the war stations in a steady stream that lasted several seconds, then halted. The field, resembling an onrushing meteor storm, was on the big in-system board in a matter of seconds.

Streamers of blue light appeared in great numbers, lashing out from the moons of Momrath at the onrushing storm of modules. About a third of the modules broke from the main stream and headed toward the source of the fire, but the defenders were taking a tremendous toll. "The fools clustered them too closely together," Morah sneered.

And it was true. Bright flashes occurred all through the field and its breakaway segment, followed by tiny white lights winking out all over the place. The blue streams were moving so fast the eye could hardly follow them, but they were well directed and found their targets.

"Second wave away and dispersing!" an aide at a terminal called, and eyes went back to the insert. The new modular attack appeared to be about the same in number as the first, but it spread into an extremely wide field that was almost impossible for the boards to track properly. They were now coming in from all directions.

"That's more like it," Yatek Morah mumbled to himself.

He could only look at Morah and the others in wonder. Quite rightly, some of those modules were aimed directly at them, yet they didn't seem the least bit concerned. He sighed and gave himself a fatalistic shrug. Either they were safe, or they were not—but, in either case, as much as he'd like to be out there in a ship under his control, he was stuck.

"Open camera screens," Morah ordered, and on the rear screen a series of views appeared. One was a long shot from a position far enough from Medusa to show it only as a greenish-white disk, the view polarized enough so that the night side of the planet showed dully but completely as well. Then there were six smaller views, some from orbit around Medusa, others apparently on the planet's surface. One showed a city that might have been Rochande but also might have been any one of a dozen others, while another showed a long shot of the sacred mountain in the far north, a location he recognized well.

"The defensive shields are holding just fine," Morah commented to nobody in particular. "However, we can't possibly get all the probes if we're to save Momrath's bases as well as give cover to the other three planets." He turned toward the camera viewscreens and pointed. "There! See the sky near that plains view?"

They all looked, and could see clear streaks in the otherwise blemishless dark blue sky, streaks leaving a reddish-white trail. Now there were more and more of them, almost filling the skies as the attack modules separated after entering the atmosphere and split into a hundred equally deadly weapons each.

Massive explosions showed on each view, with huge domes of crackling energy ballooned up and out. One of the cameras was knocked out, but was quickly replaced by another. Obviously there were enough located all over the planet for them to get at least one good surface view.

The full disk view showed thousands of tiny bursts of light all over the globe, as if it were covered with windows and now suddenly had internal light, each window representing a lethal energy weapon of enormous destructive potential.

He glanced over at the situations board and saw, to his surprise, new formations in a new color, yellow, approaching the system from all directions in a coordinated circle. There was no way to tell their size or design from the board

codes, but there were a *hell* of a lot of them, at least a
number equal to the total task force. "The Altavar are
closing for attack," he said to the others, all of whom were
watching the merciless bombardment of Medusa.

Morah took a glance back at the board. "Yes. They
made it very easy on us, giving us the week. It allowed us
to plot their probable attack pattern and to position our
own forces so that they could emerge from hyperspace at
precisely predetermined points. They will engage only the
two smaller reserve task forces, however; the main body's
job is to restrict the main enemy force to its original target."

"But with a force like that they could have defended the
whole damned system!" he almost yelled in fury. "They're
deliberately throwing Medusa away!" *Why? Why? What
have I missed?*

The Altavar fleet split into three sections, two of which
moved to create a ball-shaped attack formation around
each of the reserve task forces, the main body moving
steadily on toward a position near Momrath.

From their movements, it appeared that the Altavar had
ships that were smaller than the Confederacy's cruisers,
perhaps much smaller, but with far greater speed and ma-
neuverability at sublight speeds. They moved so quickly
and precisely into their ball-shaped attack pattern and began closing in what seemed like one motion that the bigger
Confederacy ships had no chance to get out of the way or
disperse. Instead the cruisers positioned themselves in a
classical defense and began counterattacking the Altavar
formation immediately. The fury and totality of the engagement was such that the board became a riot of colors,
both white and yellow, and it quit making any attempt at
showing the actual action.

In a sense it seemed an almost romantic vision of war,
the ship-to-ship battle of long ago, but he knew it was not.
The board itself showed a vast distance, and those ships
probably never would see one another, except on boards
like this one that were far more detailed and localized.
Nor, probably, were very many lives at stake. This was not
really man-to-man or even ship-to-ship, it was computer
versus computer, technology versus technology, and it was
some time before it was clear who was going to win. The
Altavar's smaller, speedier, easier-to-turn and harder-to-hit

ships, supported by computers whose programs were based
not on problem theories but actual combat, had the edge,
assuming the forces were basically equal in strength.

The main task force between Orpheus and Oedipus re-
grouped, studying the side conflicts and learning from them,
but made no move to press inward or engage the main Altavar force, which was clearly now not headed for a direct
engagement but rather was establishing a large and formidable defensive perimeter inside the Diamond itself. The
task force threw a number of lethal modules at the defenders, but they were easily neutralized. The main concen-
tration continued to be upon Medusa for the moment.

But with both reserve battle groups now showing bright
yellow circles blinking on and off, meaning that the Altavar
had broken the back of that force, the main task-force
commander was not about to continue a methodical demonstration of increasing power against a largely deserted
planet. He opted to put an end to Medusa and then, if need
be, engage the main task force before the victorious remnants of the two main Altavar groups that were mopping
up their battles could regroup and join the defenders.

The agent felt a great deal of admiration for the task
force commander, whoever he or she was, for having the
good sense and guts not to split up that force and aid the
reserves, thereby weakening their own double group to
Altavar attack. That admiral understood full well that the
alien main group was there to defend the other three
planets and, possibly, Momrath, and could not afford to
leave those targets open to close and join battle with the
Confederacy task force. As soon as Medusa was taken care
of, then the task force would have to close on the now defending Altavar.

Only two cameras on the surface of Medusa were still
working, and one was up in the north, where energy weapons were melting the glacial ice with ease. For the first time
in a long while, perhaps since shortly after the surface was
created, there was open ocean on most of the planet, and
much of it was boiling.

"Salvo seven. This should be it!" somebody called, and
at that moment the last surface cameras went.

*He could see them at the citadel, those proud and fool-
ish Wild Ones, praying to their god as the searing heat and*

energy hit them. At least it had been quick. At least that . . .

And now simultaneously deployed special warheads went off simultaneously around the entire globe of Medusa, their heat so intense the very atmosphere was inflamed, and the crust began to melt. Great sheets of steam rose from the oceans and the ice, and the world turned slowly from bright white to a dull crimson as the magma underlying the Medusan surface was freed and fed by the material at the top.

It was a gruesome sight that yet so fascinated him that he couldn't take his eyes off it.

"Any moment now . . ." Morah said expectantly, then: "There! It's begun!"

He stared hard at the image, now blood red, and for a moment saw nothing he hadn't expected to see. Abruptly, he frowned and rubbed his eyes, as the image seemed to lose its consistency and become fuzzy and distorted. Medusa seemed no longer to be a disk at all, but some sort of stretchy blob of reddish-brown goo going off in all directions. And it seemed to be growing abnormally larger, until it was twice the size it had been, and he could only scratch his chin and mutter, "Now, what the hell?"

The glob seemed to flow in a single direction, then separate into two distinct masses, one of which clearly again was a planetary body of Medusa's size. The other mass, however, of almost equal size, congealed and writhed and twisted—and *moved.* Moved outward, gaining speed as it did so, *moving toward the Confederation task force* that immediately began throwing everything it had at the onrushing mass.

The Altavar fleet, in a wide, inverted V, moved in behind it, matching speed and direction.

"Close-up!" Morah snapped. "I want a close-up on the Coldah!"

His staff did what they could, and found at least one view from somewhere out-system that showed the mass of the writhing, terrible planet-sized thing that had emerged from the bombarded planet.

It was a monstrous, ever-changing shape, mostly energy but with some matter, taking no clearly defined substance for more than a second before changing into something else, like a mad ball of lightning gone completely berserk.

And yet it was not berserk—its course and speed were deliberate, and it continued to close on the fleet, ignoring all that was being thrown at it, absorbing module after module that could destroy a planet.

It was on the fleet before any counteraction could be taken, just wading in, shooting off tens of thousands of tendrils of fire and flame into the hearts of the ships, exploding whatever ordnance they still carried. Both war stations went up in blazes that matched Medusa itself, but much of the outer task force, beyond immediate reach of the Coldah's tentacles, began to fan out and those were now engaged by Altavar ships from the edges of the great fleet's wedge.

The agent angrily pounded his fist on the table. "Of course! Of course!" he muttered to himself. "Why the hell didn't *I* think of that? Not one species—two! That wasn't the damned Altavar computer I sensed on Medusa, it was the mind of this other thing!"

Morah couldn't take his eyes off the pictures, but nodded. "Yes, two. The Altavar serve and protect the Coldah."

"This—this Coldah. What the hell *is* it? What's it made of? How can the damned thing even exist?"

"We don't know. The Altavar, who have been studying it for thousands of years, don't know, either. They're not many in number, these Coldah, so we have no idea how numerous they might be or even if they are native to this galaxy or even this universe. They roam solitarily throughout the vastness of space until they come upon a world of the size and type and position they need for whatever it is they do. Long ago, thousands of years ago, when the Altavar were an expanding empire like the Confederacy, one came into an Altavar system and made one of their worlds its home. They are energy, they are matter, they are whatever they choose to be whenever they choose to be. In settling into that Altavar world, they killed three billion inhabitants. Naturally, that started a long and dirty war."

He nodded, seeing the possibilities.

"Of course," the security chief went on, "they attacked that first Coldah much as we just did, and with similar results. They made the thing irritable. It went right through their forces to another inhabited world and did the same thing. They continued to fight it, to chase it, to harass it as much as possible while trying to learn as much about it as they could. It became an obsession with the Altavar, as, of course, it would with us. But while the Coldah don't like company they *can* communicate with one another over great distances, and after a few centuries more of them showed up in the Altavar systems. Eventually the Coldah learned to anticipate the Altavar attacks and take measures ahead of time. The Altavar losses were gigantic, and they finally had to stop their continual, useless war and take stock, learn a bit more, then try again. Every time they failed. For thousands of years they failed. They learned a lot, though. When the Coldah inhabited a planet, it added little or no mass, apparently remaining in an energy state, and it sent out colonies of organisms to create within it a disguise of sorts—a perfect, natural disguise."

"The Warden organism," he breathed.

"The concept is not unknown in nature. As to why they always prefer our kinds of planets, and remake them into our kinds of planets, nobody really knows. They are the classic alien—so different from anything we know, any form of life we know, any life origins we can understand, that they are totally incomprehensible to us. Your man on Medusa once made a fringe contact with this one. Do you remember it?"

He nodded. "I thought it was the computer."

"What was your impression?"

He thought a moment. "It was aware of me, but didn't have much of an opinion about it. I got the impression of a sense of utter superiority out of the thing, and I had the feeling it noted me, then flicked me aside as we would a fly."

"I have been—far deeper—in contact over the years," Morah told him, "and I find it an impossible, frustrating task. I'm not even certain that what we get into our minds really correlates with the real Coldah. There is an undeniable sense of power—and why not? They have it, that's for sure. Beyond that—who knows? They are certainly aware we exist, and they are even aware of who their friends are, but that's about it. Perhaps, one day, we *will* know, but I somehow doubt it. All we can do is study them and learn what we can. They're impossible creatures, but whatever they do they seem to obey the laws just as we do. They just might know a few more laws than we do."

The viewscreens were blank now, except for the long-shot view of Medusa, still molten hot yet cooling even now, swaddling itself in an incredibly thick and violent layer of clouds. He turned to the plot board, which showed no white dots or forms whatsoever and yellow forms only in the mop-up battle operations. It was over. The greatest task force ever assembled by man had been met, and bested, partly by a better assembled force that had an easier time on the defense, and partly by a creature they could neither understand nor believe in even as it was killing them.

"Where's this thing going now?" he asked Morah.

The security chief shrugged. "Wherever it wants. Probably to another of our planets, to burrow in once again. They go from system to system until they find a planet within our life zone around a stable sun, then they burrow in and remake the surface out of matter and energy. It's never the same twice, but always something familiar to us, even the atmosphere. It'll stay there a thousand years unless disturbed, as this one was, then rise again, move on, find the next planet, and start it all again. You know, when they leave on their own they do virtually no damage to the planetary systems their little symbiotic riders create? They just leave 'em. I think a number of mysteries about how so many worlds have formed within our life tolerances may be answered by the Coldah. As random as they are, most of the planets they use are not initially inhabitable, but they leave them that way. Once they leave their little symbiotes don't destruct, as they do when in residence and taken away, but just sort of fade out. Normal evolution follows." He chuckled. "You know, it's even just possible that our own race, and the Altavar, grew up over the millions of years because of Coldah lifestyles. It's a fascinating concept."

"But the Altavar—they fought these things. And now they seem almost to protect them."

"That's true," Morah agreed, telling one of his aides in an aside to get them all strong drinks, "but in the thousands of years they fought and studied the Coldah, a funny thing happened. Somewhere along the line they got tired of it, just got sick of futile head-knocking, and sort of mentally surrendered to the big bastards. To the Altavar, the Coldah became their whole life, and in a probably gradual switch they came not only to accept the existence of these creatures but to actually work *with* them. Don't ask me to explain it—it's certainly religious, or mystic, in a way, and those are unexplainable even when we're talking about *our* faiths, yet they are coldly and scientifically devoted to the great project, as they call it. They protect the Coldah from outside interference whenever possible, and they try with their fleets to nudge the Coldah into worlds that need some work. Don't ask me how that's possible, but the Coldah, once the Altavar started helping rather than fighting, seemed to go along with it."

He nodded. "But not here."

"Well, it was impossible, for one thing. When the Coldah originally came to the Warden system we were still stuck knee-deep on old Mother Earth. These four worlds were pretty piss-poor rock piles with nasty atmospheres and surface pressures, just perfect. And when a particularly big, fat, Coldah arrived, it did something the Altavar, with all their experience, had never seen before. It reproduced by fission. It made triplets, in fact, and the one old and three new ones entered into the four Diamond worlds. Shortly after, they released, or made and released, or whatever, their little beasties, and they went to work on the world, making it over. Lilith, with the original mama Coldah, had the most rigid system imposed on it. Then the Altavar moved in. In the years they have studied, fought, then served the Coldah, they learned a lot. They can make their own Wardens, and they can give orders to these synthesized versions, too. Within limits, they can even play games with the Coldah versions, and they did here. Looking at the climates, they elevated one species on each to dominance."

"I figured that much out. Reptiles on the warmest world, insects on the lushest, water breathers on the wettest, and mammals on the coldest."

"Right. Part of their own grand project, really. Since the Coldah *can* leave, although not arrive, with a minimum of fuss—it's sort of like a big mist rising, they tell me—leaving the worlds to natural laws, they've been trying to influence their direction. It's a very long-term concept, naturally, but they are really trying to learn what factors and conditions produce intelligence one place and not another. It's pretty complex. Of course, our arrival screwed up the project here."

"And because, somehow, the electrochemical wavelengths on which the human brain operates were just slightly off the wavelengths used by the Coldah to command the Warden organisms, we developed these wild talents." He paused for a moment, then added, "I assume the Altavar are nowhere near those wavelengths?"

Morah chuckled. "No. Oh, they can tune in, as it were, mechanically, but not biologically."

He whistled low and grabbed a drink as it arrived, drinking a bit more in one gulp than he should. He needed it. Finally he said, "Then *we* became the project."

"Yes. *We* became the project. But in order to control it, and to minimize interference between ourselves and the Coldah, the Confederacy was in the way. The Coldah are headed, generally, in our direction—or back to it, I don't know which. The idea of *our* race, who can, as it were, tune in on at least one Coldah band, threatened the Altavar, their lifestyle, their system of beliefs. I think they were actually afraid that, if we followed the same pattern as they did, we could eventually establish contact, even *rapport*, with the Coldah. Maybe we can, although I think they may simply be too alien ever to understand or communicate with on more than a basic level."

He smiled wanly and shook his head in wonder. "Then, to the Altavar, *we* were the demons. *They* were scared of us stealing their gods. If the results weren't so tragic they'd be almost funny, you know that?" He thought a moment. "But if we were that much of a threat to them, the snake that could steal their Eden, why not just wipe out everybody but the project people—the Diamond?"

"They intended to do just that, as the old Altavar told us. But they are an enormous, mostly mobile population, spread out over half a galaxy, wherever there are Coldah. They faced an empire of vast proportions and unknown capabilities. They had to know how we thought, what our tactics were like, how we'd fight, all the rest. They had time. It's still three hundred years until the scheduled hatching, or breakout, or whatever it is the Coldah do. It was over four hundred when we first arrived here. They spent fifty years or more just getting to know us through the Wardens, watching us work, and realizing just how different our relationship to the Wardens was from theirs, and only then did they really send for their fleet, which must be assembled from incredible distances and then can only be spared in small pieces. It was easier for them to establish factories on worlds beyond the Confederacy, even Warden worlds themselves, and build the force they needed, along with using the Wardens to breed the Altavar necessary for the fight. By the time they had their fleet and their military ready, Kreegan was Lord of Lilith."

"And he stumbled on the whole truth?"

"Much as I did. On each world there was one point, one weakness, that was the Coldah's window to the outside. Don't ask me how it works or why, I don't know. But there was one point, usually in an inaccessible and nasty place on the globe, where this happened. On Lilith it's very near the north pole. On Charon it's a small island off the southern continent. I don't know how Kreegan happened on the north pole, but considering that the descendants of the original exploiter team had set up a planet-worship religion on Lilith they must have put him on to it. The signal strength, as it were, at each of those points is so strong it bleeds over directly onto ours, exciting our own Wardens and our brain's awareness and control."

"No wonder, then, Kreegan became Lord."

Morah nodded. "Local Altavar, bred for the conditions and for unobtrusiveness, try to discourage anyone from getting too close without blowing their cover, often masquerading as wild animals themselves. They mostly staff monitoring and control devices to keep tabs on the Coldah, whose signals increase consistently until they leave. By that monitor they can predict the Coldah's eventual behavior and be ready for it."

He thought a moment. "Then the ice demons weren't the only ones. There were those nasty beasties in the Charonese desert with tentacles, too, if I remember."

"Oh, the narils. Actually, they're not Altavar, but Altavar pets, in a way. An attempt to breed an animal with their own biochemical structure that was sensitive to the Warden frequencies. It worked only slightly, though. Some got into the wild and adapted themselves to the desert, that's all. The Cerberan bork is another botched attempt only that time their result scared them so much they haven't tried it again."

"I still don't understand why they'd go for Kreegan's plan, though."

"Oh, that's simple. They still weren't quite ready to tackle us yet. They were pretty sure he couldn't succeed, but he hit it off with them for some reason, and they agreed to go along simply because, no matter what, it would give them the strategic and military information they craved. If it worked, so much the better. But they couldn't stand for us in any event, a race with a powerful empire that also could reach, and even make use of, the Coldah and their symbiotes without a lot of mechanical aids."

"So what will they do to the Confederacy now—and to us?"

Morah sighed. "They will use small but deadly forces to hit weakly defended planets throughout the Confederacy. Eventually the remnants of this fleet not concerned with the Medusan Coldah's new habitat and settlement will join in scattered action. They will collapse the empire back into planetbound barbarism, but on hundreds of worlds. The Confederacy itself will continue to hold fanatically, all the while contracting to a defensible size and base, but they will be effectively neutralized for a long time. What they will eventually do, or become, you and I will never know, my friend. We'll be long dead."

"And the Diamond?"

"The Altavar computers can stabilize the Medusan variety for a while, perhaps rebuilding Medusa or, more likely, just letting it go. We will settle the Medusans on Lilith and Charon, and progressively we'll switch the programming on them over from Medusa to whatever new world they settle upon, if not with the current generation, then with their children. The Altavar will be around, but remain as unobtrusive as possible, for the next three centuries. Then, one after another, the Coldah will emerge in natural fashion, and, theoretically, our Warden powers will die out and we'll be just plain folks again. Or maybe we won't. Whether or not the Medusan young become Charonese or Lilithians or remain their own kind even with the Coldah gone and with subtle suggestion from the Altavar master computers will tell us a lot. If they *do* continue to breed true, then the Coldah's leaving will have no effect. If we, in those three centuries, can learn how to keep those Wardens alive, or replace them with synthetic equivalents as the Altavar now could do if they wanted, we Warden Diamond races could emerge as true, spacefaring, *Homo excelsius.* The Altavar can make their Wardens do whatever they want by mechanical processes. *We* can do it with sheer willpower, and remake ourselves if we like."

He nodded slowly. "And you were a biologist."

"I *am* a biologist. Sooner or later, working with the Altavar, I will know enough, or my staff will, aided by the computers of Cerberus, now free to expand their potential. We must build up our industry again quickly, and that is the first and vital task. We have the work force with the necessary skills in the Medusans, but we must rebuild the factories, out here first, then in space. The technological brains are all over the Diamond, and now the lid on technological development the Confederacy imposed is gone."

"You're certain the Altavar won't interfere?"

"So long as they perceive no threat from us, they will not. This is long-term planning, Mr. Carroll. It will take years to rebuild the industry and expand reasonable production. We have three centuries to do it all and learn what we have to learn. At the end of that time, if we have fathomed the full secrets of the Warden organism, we will sit here on our three remaining worlds in relative savagery and wave good-bye to the Coldah and the Altavar. Then we will go out ourselves, and see what of humanity survives and rebuild our civilization in strength, not ignorance. It is a challenge not only for us who will start this work but for our children and grandchildren who will complete it. And if we do our job right, they'll do it without the mistakes of the past rising again to stupefy human civilization. A race that can, by force of will, become any creature it needs to, destroy mountains with a finger and a push of will, and change bodies, sex, or whatever it is at any time will be a new type of creature, or creatures."

Yatek Morah leaned back, drained his drink, then pulled out and lit a Charonese cigar. Then he added, "Next time, we *will* be the demons—or the gods. And what about you,

Mr. Carroll? Where do you fit in to this unique new future?"

He leaned back comfortably and put his feet up on the table. "I think I have some unique qualifications in your grand scheme, Morah. I think I'm going to fit in fine around here, all four of me. But first a little unfinished business, if you'll do me a little favor."

"We'll see. Now that *you* know it all, I still have a nagging feeling that there's something you haven't been telling me."

"Oh, it's nothing important," he assured the Security Chief, "except to me."

9

He had spent a little time on Cerberus with Qwin and Dylan, who had been more than willing to take in Bura and Angi and delighted to add two children of a "close relative" to the family. Both Medusan children were finally delivered and looked like normal, healthy Cerberan children, although Dylan complained somewhat enviously over the easy and relatively painless way in which Medusans gave birth. At least children conceived on Medusa bred true to form despite the loss of the Coldah, although the Altavar were, of course, still feeding supplementary data the Medusan Wardens needed to everyone through the Snark computer network.

The Altavar, without asking, did in fact randomly cut a number of Medusans off from the computer, and were somewhat distressed to find that, while the subjects' Wardens became inert, they did not die off at all. Clearly there was something different about the human-Warden relationship, or something brand new was developing in the system, some new and unique variation of human life. For now he depended on Morah and his staff to keep the Altavar from getting *too* distressed at that.

The huge picket ship had been brought in-system, to an orbit between Medusa and Momrath, and was now being converted into a massive space factory as quickly as could be accomplished, while new industries, with some grudging

Altavar support, were rising on the natural moons of Momrath itself.

Dumonia had also been grudging as he assumed the public title and office of Lord of Cerberus, but it was now necessary. Working with much of Morah's team, however, he tended to delegate much of the actual running to Qwin Zhang.

Park and Darva had taken a little, short vacation to a small island off the southwest coast of the southern Charonese continent on the suggestion of Mr. Carroll. With a little training and work with Dumonia-trained psychs, they would certainly soon be fully in position to assume control of Charon, something that Morah very much desired for them. As he'd told Park before, the security chief had higher goals than being Lord himself, and, in fact, running the place only got in his way.

Cal Tremon, too, got a sudden yen to get away for a while and do some exploring, first. He might, he was saying, go all the way to Lilith's north pole. Then, perhaps, with an extended vacation back in the tropics talking with the scientific enclave there, he'd be ready for what he wanted to do next.

After keeping himself busy in this way, Mr. Carroll set course once again for Charon, against all advice. Talant Ypsir was still there, still very much alive, and still pretty vicious, all the more so because his people were learning a new life, one without omnipresent cameras and microphones and computer controls. Such things were needed elsewhere in the industrial rebuilding, and nothing new in that line would be produced for years.

It was with a sense of *déjà vu*, then, that Carroll eased his shuttle into the dock of Ypsir's still vast and impressive space station, now in orbit around Charon. He had not really left it since the war, allowing his less bitter alter ego, Haval Kunser, to organize things below.

The airlock signaled clear, and he walked into the tube and up to the second lock, getting into the small chamber and standing ready. There was the usual energy spray, but it didn't bother him this time. He'd already checked with the Altavar and found that, in fact, his body was as infested with Wardens—Altavar-created and artificial and with a neutral program—as anybody else. Ypsir's ray could do nothing to deaden or neutralize the already inert.

Two security monitors met him on the other side, more out of curiosity than anything else.

"Name?" one snapped.

"Lewis Carroll."

"What is your purpose here?"

"I wish to pay a call on First Minister Ypsir," he told them. "I represent the Four Lords in Council and we have need of your fancy computer here."

They looked uncertain, and he knew how much the mighty had fallen by their reaction. He decided to go easy on them. "Call Fallon. She'll know what to do," he suggested.

They nodded and seemed appreciative of the buck-passing suggestion. He sat and waited calmly for fifteen minutes or so until she came. She had never met him before, but he knew her, and she had heard more than enough about him from Ypsir. "Well! You're either a very big fool or you really have nerve, coming here," she told him.

He grinned, and it unsettled her a bit. At that moment an alarm rang, and a speaker broke in to state, "Administrator Kunser docking at Gate Three."

Fallon frowned. "Damn! What does *he* want up here now, of all times?"

"Why don't we go see?" he suggested. "In fact, I called him to come up. I'm representing the Four Lords in Council, with three votes already taken, and I'm here to arrange things with the fourth. Why don't we go collect him and we can all save time and see the First Minister at once."

She frowned. "Okay, but I still think you're nuts."

Kunser was as puzzled as Fallon, but right now, dependent on the goodwill of the other Lords, he was in no position to disobey an official request. He was surprised to see Carroll, though, although somewhat pleased. The agent could almost read his mind. *Morah's getting rid of his only threat this way.* But both he and Fallon were civil to the agent, and that was for the best. Both seemed interested in what would happen when Carroll met Ypsir, though.

To everyone's surprise, Ypsir, in a spacious office, was all smiles and cordiality, the politician supreme. In a corner, on satin pillows, reclined the stunning Ass.

"Well, now, what's all this about a vote and my computer?", the First Minister wanted to know.

"They need it. Its capacity is probably the largest in the Diamond, and it's doing nothing but running this station right now," he told them. "The fact is, this station can be maintained on a much smaller and more basic model Cerberus can and will supply. There are few manufactured goods right now, and we need them desperately. The picket ship is being quickly outfitted, but it's going to need your computer to control the industry we're putting into her. Nothing else will do the job, and we can't make any more major computers until we have the picket running."

"They had their nerve, voting without me," Ypsir complained.

He shrugged. "We tried. You didn't answer the call. That's why Morah sent me here."

Ypsir smiled. *One of the reasons*, he thought, in accord with his two assistants, but he said, "Well, I don't like it but I'm hardly in a position to object at this point. One hopes that the Cerberan techs can do it without having to shut down this station."

"I'm sure they can."

"Have you met Ass?" Ypsir asked suddenly.

He smiled and nodded. "Yes, I have. In more ways than one, First Minister. You see, using the Metron Process, *I* was Tarin Bul."

Talant Ypsir's face broke into a wide grin that became a real belly laugh. "Oh, my, but that's perfect! That's wonderful!" he chortled.

"The matter of the computer is not the only reason I'm here," Carroll added. "I've decided that I need a better position than errand boy for the Four Lords."

Ypsir, savoring the irony, hardly heard him. Instead he turned to Ass and said, "Did you hear that, my pretty? *You* were once *him!*"

Showing puzzlement and confusion, she looked up at the agent, but said nothing.

"Ass?" the agent called to her. "Do you know who these people are? This is Haval Kunser, and *this* is Shugah Fallon, and *that* is Talant Ypsir."

Her eyes grew even larger, and her mouth dropped a bit, and then she frowned, shook her head, and looked up again.

"I decided I'd either be dead or the Lord of Medusans," Carroll told her, but she wasn't really listening to him.

Talant Ypsir's head was torn from his body before the bodies of Fallon and Kunser had hit the floor.

About the Author

JACK L. CHALKER was born in Norfolk, Virginia, on December 17, 1944, but was raised and has spent most of his life in Baltimore, Maryland. He learned to read almost from the moment of entering school, and by working odd jobs amassed a large book collection by the time he was in junior high school, a collection now too large for containment in his quarters. Science fiction, history, and geography all fascinated him early on, interests that continue.

Chalker joined the Washington Science Fiction Association in 1958 and began publishing an amateur SF journal, *Mirage,* in 1960. After high school he decided to be a trial lawyer, but money problems and the lack of a firm caused him to switch to teaching. He holds bachelor degrees in history and English, and an M.L.A. from the Johns Hopkins University. He taught history and geography in the Baltimore public schools between 1966 and 1978, and now makes his living as a freelance writer. Additionally, out of the amateur journals he founded a publishing house, The Mirage Press, Ltd., devoted to nonfiction and bibliographic works on science fiction and fantasy. This company has produced more than twenty books in the last nine years. His hobbies include esoteric audio, travel, working on science-fiction convention committees, and guest lecturing on SF to institutions such as the Smithsonian. He is an active conservationist and National Parks supporter, and he has an intensive love of ferryboats, with the avowed goal of riding every ferry in the world. In fact, in 1978 he was married to Eva Whitley on an ancient ferryboat in mid-river. They live in the Catoctin Mountain region of western Maryland with their son David.

Dear Reader,

Your opinions are very important to us so please take a few moments to tell us your thoughts. It will help us give you more enjoyable DEL REY Books in the future.

1. Where did you obtain this book?

Bookstore	☒1	Department Store ☐4	Airport	☐7	**5**
Supermarket	☐2	Drug Store ☐5	From A Friend ☐8		
Variety/Discount Store ☐3		Newsstand ☐6	Other_____		
			(Write In)		

2. On an overall basis, how would you rate this book?

Excellent ☐1   Very Good ☐2   Good ☒3   Fair ☐4   Poor ☐5   **6**

3. What is the main reason that you purchased this book?

Author ☒1   It Was Recommended To Me ☐3   **7**
Like The Cover ☐2   Other_____
                        (Write In)

4. In the same subject category as this book, who are your two favorite authors?

ISAAC ASIMOV **8** **9**

ANDRE NORTON **10** **11**

5. Which of the following categories of paperback books have you purchased in the past 3 months?

Adventure/		Biography ☐4	Horror/		Science		
Suspense	☐12-1	Classics ☒5	Terror ☐8		Fiction	☒x	
Bestselling		Fantasy ☒6	Mystery ☐9		Self-Help	☐y	
Fiction	☐2	Historical	Romance ☐0		War	☐13-0	
Bestselling		Romance ☐7			Westerns	☒2	
Non-Fiction ☐3							

6. What magazines do you subscribe to, or read regularly, that is, 3 out of every 4 issues?

Newsweek **14** **15**

NATIONAL Geographic **16** **17**

7. Are you: Male ☐1   Female ☒2   **18**

8. Please indicate your age group.

Under 18	☐1	25-34	☒3	60 or older ☐5		**19**
18-24	☐2	35-49	☐4			

9. What is the highest level of education that you have completed?

Post Graduate Degree ☐1	College Graduate ☐3	Some High		**20**	
Some Post Graduate	1-3 Years College ☒4	Fiction			
Schooling ☐2	High School	School			
	Graduate ☐5	or Less ☐6			

(Optional)

If you would like to learn about future publications and participate in future surveys, please fill in your name and address.

NAME_____

ADDRESS_____

CITY_____ STATE_____ ZIP_____ **21**

Please mail to: Ballantine Books
DEL REY Research, Dept.
516 Fifth Avenue — Suite 608
New York, N.Y. 10036

F-2